A Novel

Joel Thomas Hynes

HARPER
PERENNIAL

This book is dedicated to the myth of the friendly Newfoundlander.

Published by Harper Perennial, an imprint of HarperCollins Publishers Ltd

First edition

HarperCollins books may be purchased for educational, business, or sales promotional use through our Special Markets Department.

HarperCollins Publishers Ltd
2 Bloor Street East, 20th Floor
Toronto, Ontario, Canada
M4W 1A8

www.harpercollins.ca

Library and Archives Canada Cataloguing in Publication information is available upon request.

ISBN 978-1-44344-783-6

Printed and bound in the United States

LSC/H 9 8 7 6 5 4 3 2 1

Also by Joel Thomas Hynes

FICTION

Right Away Monday
Down to the Dirt
Say Nothing Saw Wood

NON-FICTION

Straight Razor Days
God Help Thee: A Manifesto

DRAMA

Incinerator Road
Broken Accidents
The Devil You Don't Know (co-written with Sherry White)

SCREENPLAYS

Cast No Shadow (adapted from *Say Nothing Saw Wood*)

1

What's going on Johnny?

Come on, whatcha doing? How are ya? Poor Johnny. Touchy Johnny. In this mindset. How you are? Imagine. How's our John-John doing? How's he makin out, comin along, doing for himself? How's he keepin? Fuck. Slung halfways out the window for a haul, cause that's what this piss-arsed place is come to. Imagine that, tumbling out onto the street for the sake of a stale Number 7 cause where he might pollute his own room. Where he sleeps alone. Poor old Johnny. The vinyl sill busted and gouging into his ribcage. Oh yeah, Johnny could very well settle out on the front step, but that means back and forth the stairs every time and then sat out there, watchin the street . . . the temptation is too much now aint it? Might get foolish. Might wander off.

Buddy from next door takes his garbage out for tomorrow morning.

How together he is, how on top of it all he must be, hey Johnny? Then he sees a splotch of birdshit on his rig and dont he go over and polish it off with his sleeve! Rather have diseased pigeon shit on the clothes he's wearing than on the rig he drives. Pigeon shit. That's what's in his head too. All their heads. Dont bother askin Johnny what's going on around him. Who's screwing who. What the fuck is going on. Carry on little mouse, carry on.

Good night, buddy goes. Good night.

He makes for his door then.

What? What? Johnny shouts down. What did you just say to me? What?

He looks up at Johnny then. Looks right at old John-John, that's what he does. Looks right fucken at me. You cant fathom the gall.

Excuse me, buddy goes, what?

Right grand about it. Like first he's tryna be all macho-cool and casual about it, the *man*, taking out the garbage. But soon as he's called on it, soon as he's brought to task, he's rattled to the core and so instinct kicks in and he figures he might as well pretend he's better and better off and better for it by tossing in some kinda upper-crust turn of phrase. But our John-John's on it, dont even bother.

Excuse me, buddy goes.

His hand is on the knob and Johnny can tell buddy thinks he knows a thing or two about the likes of fellas like Johnny, hanging out his window with the splintered vinyl gouging into his liver, lookin like he's waiting for the fire department to come rescue him. But Johnny dont need no rescuing tonight, no not tonight. He can think of a few that do. But not Johnny, not tonight. But buddy might, yes, he might need a rescuing. Buddy might need the jaws of life to separate him from the sidewalk before all the *good nights* are said and done this night.

Excuse me?

You heard me, I said what? What did you just say to me?

I said good night.

Why, Johnny goes, what for? What's my night got to do with yours?

I said good night, buddy goes, I was being friendly. We're neighbours.

Well now Johnny, fancy that. Being friendly. Friendly neighbours. What's the score little man? Dont know do ya? Ask him Johnny. Betcha he dont know. Playing the role, that's all. Role-playing. Dress rehearsal, all of it.

You wait right there, Johnny goes, you wait right there.

What? Why?

Cause I'm coming down. I wants to have a little chat with you.

No thanks, he goes, no thanks.

And then buddy's away off into his house and the door latches behind him right quick. Hear how quick he latched that door? All scruffy rough and tumble with the birdshit on his sleeve and the hefty black boots with a dollar's worth of steel peeking through the right toe. He looks the part alright, he looks the part. But is he? That's always the grey zone. That's always the part you have to crack open. Is he the part or simply tryna *look* the part? Man or mouse? Mouse or man? Johnny slings the butt end at the back of buddy's rig and it hits it dead-on the back window and a shower of sparks floats to the ground and one settles into a puddle of grease or oil and stays glowing for a bit and Johnny's hoping, hoping, praying that something catches fire and blows everything to goddamn smithereens. That lovely rig up in flames, the bonnet landing up near Tulk's somewhere, bumper all aflame and rocketing in through the windshield of the car behind and then *that* bastard catching and blowing to bits, burning shrapnel flying into the shanty houses, a scorching fender right in on the kitchen table, right smack flame-smashing mad in the middle of the late-night decaf tea-party chatter and then the widespread panic with the howlin scramble for children and computers and photo albums and dogs and hamsters and these fucken little tarpaper shacks all leant one into the other burning and tumbling right down over the hill into the harbour. And Johnny knows, better than any man out there, Johnny *knows* that harbour's gonna catch what with five hundred years of toxic venomous scum and poisonous chemical slop gurgling and spluttering, seething a hundred fathoms deep. You knows there's something flammable about all that, something explosive. Burn burn burn. Right to the ground, right to the bottom of the harbour. Burn the works. And Johnny with it. Yeah. Cause they can batter to fuck this time around if they thinks Johnny's going kickin flaming doors in again and crawling around lookin to save grizzled old farts who could very well drop dead tomorrow anyhow. Fucken *Charlie*, Christ.

* * *

Johnny hears buddy mumbling something down there.

Through the walls. Cause that's the way, that's the way they got us all jammed in. So we can all hear each other belching and farting through the goddamn walls. Tarpaper shacks with big bloated price tags, all slapped together and clung to the side of the cliff like gulls huddling, cluster-fucked. Waiting. You wouldnt even wanna know the state of this dive Johnny's set up in. One of old Quinn's spots and the welfare pays Quinn a fortune to let it rot and crumble around the likes of Johnny, fellas like that. The bad guys.

Mumble mumble down there. Some sorta big talk to his wife or his girlfriend. An oath, a curse. Talkin about Johnny, gotta be. Big talk, nothing he'd say to Johnny's face. Role-playing. Shag this. Johnny's down the stairs and out the front hall to the door. He dont even bother to put the sneakers on cause he's not gonna be using his feet. You gotta be able to dance, dance, dance whenever the mood takes you. That's the rule, that's the law. Johnny gives the knuckles a good scrape across the panelling in the porch before he opens the door. Sting and burn, bleed, come on bleed. Clench and release, clench and release. Buddy started it didnt he? Good night, he says. Johnny's night. Good. Johnny raps on buddy's door. It's a new door with a big patterned window to let the light in. Must be nice, letting all that light in. Must be nice to have it all lined up, new doors, taking the garbage out.

Someone passes up the street behind Johnny. It's one of Shiner's girls. Lookin no worse for the wear, gotta say. Gotta say. She looks to be jonesing for a little soul food, no question. But she got that sturdy scuff about herself, that kinda dont-fuck-with-me baygirl stride. Sneakers and jeans. Busy busy. There'll always be money in love, like the fella says. Lotsa burdens needing a lift, egos stroked, arses spanked. Imagine that, paying someone to smack your arse! Johnny's . . . fucken . . . old Pius, he woulda made himself a fortune in his day.

In his day.

Johnny dont know the girl's name, but he says to her anyhow:

Hey little Susie, hey.

She stops for a second and swivels her head. Heavy drip at the tip of her nose. She must be hurting, yeah, making a beeline for Shiner's gear. He says to her:

Tell Shiner I needs him to drop down, tell him it's Johnny. Can you do that for me?

Susie nods and mumbles, totters on up the hill. She's hurtin now, she's feelin it.

Quite the package. Somebody's daughter. Christ knows what kinda wars she's come through before she landed in Shiner's lap.

Johnny's back to the garbage man's door and raps again, hard this time. Just a nudge, you know, one little bump and you knows the glass is going in onto the porch floor. If that's the way shit goes down.

Cold sting on the knuckles.

Hey Johnny, is that your phone going off now, up the stairs?

Listen.

Is it?

Just your luck, first time you stepped out tonight.

Fucken phone.

Buddy's missus comes to the window. No comment from Johnny, but still and all it must be nice. Must be a fine life for some. They got these red lights on in there, nice hanging lamp with a red bulb that looks all cozy and slutty seductive all the one time. Must be nice. Atmosphere. She goes for the handle and then sees it's not someone she knows and then sorta raises her eyebrows at Johnny.

That's your phone going off Johnny, listen . . . Fuck.

I needs to talk to your fella, Johnny goes.

She looks our John-John up and down and he knows full bloody well that if she could get away with it, the right time and circumstances, she'd fly at him and they wouldnt stop till they were spent, spent and spent. Sweaty and sticky and chowing down on fish and chips in their bathrobes. You can see it in her eyes. She wants to. But money and heat bills and garbage days and cozy red lights and pigeons shitting on the paint job, all that mundane slop bogs down the instinct, wraps around you like that bubbly plastic stuff that comes with important packages and it incubates you, shields you, suffocates your drive. It softens you.

Is your fella in?

Johnny sorta half smiles, tryna make it sound friendly, *neighbourly*. But she's a wise one, this one, she's a wise one. She knows not to open the door to strangers. Nice arse on her though, wouldnt have to pay Johnny to have a smack at it. She swings round on her heels and shouts out to her *man*:

I figured I'd let you get it.

She figured that, didnt she. Cause she's the one running the show, calling the shots. Dont ask, dont bother. Buddy pulls back the curtain then, and here's Johnny. Nothing to it. Good night.

What? he goes.

Come on out, Johnny says, come on out for a chat.

About what, he goes.

And he sounds heftier now, with the door there between it all, the security of that crisp new window. What's the score, little guy? Ask him Johnny. Betcha he dont fucken know. One smack, one little tap and Johnny's right through that window with his hand around your face. And then curled up for a movie on that swanky red chesterfield underneath the cozy slutty red light with *your* missus. Johnny's missus.

Come on out for a chat.

He stares at Johnny then and he knows, he *knows* that Johnny's the last standin Newfoundland wolf and he's the lost little lamb about to be led astray. Johnny's the hatchet and buddy's a little junk of year-old spruce en route to the split box behind the stove. Johnny's the big hungry tomcat lookin for a bouncy meal. And he's the scared little mouse. And one more step, a turn of that knob, and there's the slaughter and the feast. Come on, little fella, step out onto the chopping block. But he knows. He knows. You can tell. Even through the glass. That's all that's between Johnny and your days, little mouse. A sheet of glass. A door. A wall. A rig with a splotch of birdshit. Garbage days. Good night.

No, buddy says, no thanks.

Ahhh Johnny, you gotta laugh. A mouse in a man's boots. No thanks? Fair enough then. He dont even wanna have a chat. Christ Johnny, neighbours who wont even have a friendly chat with you? Very well. Wait it out will we?

Very well, Johnny goes. I'll see you around, neighbour.

Alright, buddy says, then sorta shakes his head like he's seen it all now. Seen it all, seen it all. And he disappears behind the curtain and the little red light in the porch goes out.

Johnny's back up the stairs again with the heart racing cause he can still feel the echo of the phone when he gets back to the room. Johnny was gone, what, not twenty seconds and off it goes. Christ. Sure enough then, the moment his foot hits the grungy old carpet inside his door it starts ringing again. It's like they knows. It's like someone must be calling up as soon as you steps out onto the street. Cause that's too much of a fluke if you asks our John-John. Someone must be watchin, of course they are. Of course they are. Come on Johnny, where are ya? Dont even think about it. Smack dab in the middle of the Hood. Eyes everywhere. Watchin. Prolly gettin paid for it. It rang in as soon as you stepped out and then again as soon as youre back. Might as well be on the bracelet for fuck sakes. No. None for Johnny thanks, that bracelet business. Shiner was on that one time. Big red itch scabbed around his ankle, he said, and the smell off it. Wander out of range for more than thirty seconds or so and this little electronic box kicks in and sends a signal to the phone line and then the phone calls the station on you. And if you smashes up the box, same thing. Something, that is. Boxes in the corner. Even the phone is watching, waiting for the very minute you fucks up. The very minute. Ratbags all around.

Johnny's phone is still ringing.

Ring ring. *Fuck off phone.* He lets it go for another bit. Then he's gotta answer or there'll be lots more trouble than he needs tonight, this good night.

Hello, Johnny goes.

Johnny this is Constable Hepditch, checking in, just calling down, you know.

I'm good man, thanks.

How's our Johnny tonight?

Best kind.

Away from the phone for a bit Johnny?

I never stirred.

Out patrolling for a lady in distress?

I was reading a book on the bed there.

Reading? Jesus. What book?

What odds is that?

Just making conversation Johnny, no need to get lippy.

I'm not, I'm just sayin what difference does it . . .

Exactly, what book were you reading Johnny?

White Fang, alright?

I thought that was a kids' book, isnt it? Jack London? Yes, I musta read that when I was ten years old Johnny.

Listen . . .

You werent out on the street or nothing just now Johnny?

No. What? I said I never stirred.

Well you mighta thought to pick up the phone when it rang.

I was on the toilet if you needs to know, alright?

Me and the lads were talking about you earlier Johnny, saying how lucky, just how fantastically lucky it was for that old couple in the fire that you happened by when you did.

This is Hepditch. Jealous. Knows he'd never have the fucken guts to face the flames like Johnny did. No commendations coming to Hepditch any time soon. No write-ups about him in the paper. No one talkin him up, callin *him* a hero. And it's not like Johnny is thinkin of himself that way, like he's a hero. That's just . . . it's not like that. He just went and done it, what needed to be done. It's not like something youre gonna stop and think about. Not really. I just went on in and done it. Never put much thought into it really. You go on and do it, you know? That's all Johnny's gonna say on the matter. The old couple's daughter tracked me down a couple of weeks afterwards, after the big blaze. She was all teary-eyed and slobbering when she saw the state of me fingers with the ragged bandages. That was on account of that fucken budgie bird, the cage when I grabbed it, tore the skin right off me hands. I'm out on the street and the old couple are safe and sound and the missus starts pointin up at the house shoutin for someone named Charlie. Next thing, fool he is, Johnny's gone back inside with a coat over his head and bawlin out for *Charlie! Charlie!?!* Only by chance I spots this framed picture of a budgie bird on a shelf in the hallway and here's the very name, *Charlie,* dancing across the bottom of the frame.

Stupid cartoon letters.

Fucken budgie bird?

Anyhow, the old couple's daughter cryin and that, on my doorstep, well I spose I musta been a sight, no eyebrows and the lids of me eyes all red and raw, me head nothing only stubble. But that's whatcha gets, those kinds of results, running into a burning building. No bother. She's there with the snots and hiccups and I'm tryna, I dont know, settle her down, cause she's standin there on my ratty doorstep and there's folks gawking all up and down Lime Street and you knows bloody well they're gonna think we're in a big racket, me and this missus. So I'm tryna settle her down and when she finally composes herself she looks at me and says thanks and asks me if I was afraid or not, when I done what I done. And it crossed me mind, there and then to . . . I dont know . . . out with it. But. Well she drove a long ways. And the way she was lookin at me. Her chin quivering like that. So I said all that same old stuff you always hears, on the news and that, same stuff everybody says, how I only done what anybody woulda done, how I spose I never thought about being afraid, never stopped to think about it at the time. I saw what was going on and thought to meself, well, this is where I am right now in the world, that's all. I happened by at the right time. And thinkin back anyhow, I was going through a kind of meltdown phase. Everybody was. And this wasnt even a week before all that shit went down with my girl . . . with Madonna. Fuck. The two of us were well into it all again. All the madness that goes along with it. Shit was not good. I was slipping back, slipping back into the old ways I spose. Next thing I knows I'm tangled up in this blazing house fire. Riskin me life to save a fucken budgie bird. What odds, I said, maybe this is a better way to go.

They always told me I was gonna burn anyhow.

Hepditch drones on, but if there's one thing Johnny is good at, it's tuning out all that bullshit the fuzz gets on with. Nothing coming out of his mouth that Johnny's even remotely concerned about. Fucken Hepditch.

Johnny is momentarily elated to find a little baggie on the floor next to the bed. No idea, no idea where it came from. Not gonna question it. He wets a finger and dips it down into the corner dregs of the bag. The tip of his finger comes out pinkish white with good healthy crumbs that he rubs onto his tongue and down the back of his throat cause he would not put anything up his nose in this town, not these days. He fancies he feels a fresh wave of clout and power before he can even close his mouth around his fingertip.

Listen to me Hep . . .

No you listen *Johnny*, you listen to me. It doesnt matter, you know as well as I, it doesnt matter if youre on the toilet or reading one of your little books or if youre asleep or balls-deep in your boyfriend, if you hear that phone ringing after 10 pm . . .

What?

. . . If you hear that phone ringing after 10 pm and you dont answer it, then we'll have to assume youre out on the prowl and we'll be down over that hill so fast you wont know what hit you. And you know well enough where you'll be heading off to then.

Saucy prick.

Listen, Johnny goes, this is the third time tonight now you fellas called down, and I was in, sure, long before curfew tonight. What's all the hassle about tonight?

This bit about it being the third call, this bit's not true. But Johnny figures where it's after twelve the shifts must have changed hands by now and unless Hepditch, fucken twat, is going sniffin around for the truth and then makin a big deal of it when he finds out that Johnny is lying, and sendin the old brigade down the hill to sort him out even though here he is where he's supposed to be . . . well it's all a gamble when youre talkin to this crowd. But maybe it's an easy thing for the lads to check on, who knows. Flip through a clipboard, something simple. Who knows. Roll the dice, Johnny. They knows pretty much every word they're told is lies, but they have to pretend some of it is the truth every once in a while, to keep from cracking up.

Hepditch goes quiet on the line for a bit.

Maybe he's in a bigshot mood. But I can hear the rattle in his chest. Johnny gets a glimpse of his own reflection in the edge of a picture frame on the wall. Pulsing purple worms busting outta his forehead. Come on Johnny, fuck sakes. The picture in the frame is of some chunky tattooed circus gal from way back when, standin next to a zebra, of all things. That was already on the wall, the picture, when I took the room. Mike Quinn's idea of decor, fine upstanding landlord that he is.

Hepditch lets out the big long sigh and goes:

Alright Johnny. We'll let it go. Youre in now. But dont think we wont be down over that hill in a heartbeat. You dont wanna spend the rest of it down by the lake do you?

Johnny's quiet then. He's not gonna give him nothing, not gonna make him feel like he's grateful. Johnny's the one who conned him. Fuck you Hep, yeah I was out on the street tryna start a racket, lookin for action. Whatcha gonna do about it? Twat. And if he wasnt a fucken twat he wouldnt be stuck in the station on the night shift answering phones. He'd be out catching the bad guys.

Alright Johnny?

Best kind.

Johnny hangs up then. Pig fucken shit. Pigeons. Fuck sakes.

Pacing then.

Scratching.

Sweats.

Six steps across and nine down. Six by nine. Nine by six. The cot in the corner. A fucken *cot.* Madonna down there in her cushy queen bed. *My* bed. Johnny only lugged the fucken thing on his back all the way from Hamilton Avenue. Swiped two sets of sheets and pillowcases in the mall and even got one of them fancy blanket cover thingys. Christ. Now he's tossin and turnin every night on a rusted old squeaky folding *cot* with not enough room for two cats to fuck on. This is . . . this is . . . What the fuck is going on Johnny, what's happening? Where're ya going? No smoking. Christ. Had the TV for a while, but hadda turn it in last week. Twenty bucks. What can you do? No batteries for the radio and the plug is ruined on it cause Johnny hadda use it for something else that no one needs to know nothing about. Not even a pen and paper, cant even write a letter to old Stevie in the Big House on the mainland. Long time since. Guitar turned in too. Seventy-five bucks! How long did that last?

At least though, if I was down by the lake, banged up down in the Palace, down in HMP, there might be TV with the full cable out in the hallway, at least. Might be. And there'd be no fucker tellin Johnny what he could or couldnt watch neither. Or how loud. Roam around a bit. Down the hallway. Off to the weights. Library even. *White* fucken *Fang*! Not like Johnny never read it seven times, the only book to his name. That was here in the room too. Fucken Hepditch. Yeah, all your meals fixed, right outta the Queen's kitchen, right outta Her Majesty's back pantry, that's what they feeds ya down there. Jesus. Not to say Johnny'd rather be banged up, but just to say it's not far off, this situation he's in now. Here's what it is—in the house from 10 pm and not allowed out until 7 the next morning. Sounds pretty cut and dry? Sounds like a simple set-up, no? But you never know when they're gonna call down, see, that's the problem. There's no pattern to it. And you knows bloody well there's some nosey old-timer, say McFlabberguts, across the street now, who sees every move anybody makes and calls the cops or the city or the fucken cable company whenever the notion strikes. And if Johnny dont answer the phone then the cavalry comes roaring down the hill. And if the Boys in Black shows up they means business and it's a one-way trip to the clink for Johnny, no questions asked. Toss a little breach of undertaking into the mix with the rest of the charges and away we go. And he cant smoke here in the house. Quinn dont want no one smoking, he's got alarms all over the place. Think he'd want the nicotine to mask the stench of the rot and mould. They says it's an insurance thing now, with boarding houses. But maybe it's that Quinn's an evil fuck. And there's some beast in the room opposite Johnny's that can be heard grunting his way through all manner of self-abuse every other night and it's a wonder he got either scrap of flesh left on his lad atall. So what's the difference, after 10 pm at least, what's the difference between this and the clink? None. Fuck all. Except I spose you got no screws shining their lights on you every hour on the hour to make sure youre breathing, that youre not after kneeling onto your towel, not after turning yourself into another media shitstorm.

But here, listen to this—it takes a good ten hours across the Island, right? Say Johnny had a run lined up and he left the house at 7 am. Say he left on a day he never had to sign in. Well he'd be across the Island and boarding the boat by the time they figured he was gone. Come curfew time and Johnny's halfways between North Sydney and Port aux Basques sipping a few cold ones and chatting up a couple of travelling hippie dolls. But youd have to make your move, you couldnt hesitate. He who hesitates is fucked. Cause if you didnt make the boat that very evening then they'd be watchin it, they'd be watchin for you. One chance. Then off to the mainland. What's-his-face is shacked up with some missus in Dartmouth, told Johnny his door is always open. There's places to go. Johnny knows a few bodies up around New Brunswick who can get him sorted out with a few new name cards and maybe a cash job. Stay away from anyone from home, that's all you have to do. No sense being on the run from Newfoundland and then going up away and falling in with a bunch of em. Youre askin for it then. No, carry on smart about it all, right across the country. Vanish onto the streets of Vancouver, get a nice pad, off to work in the morning, keeping the head down, get a missus on the go. Go to that beach on the weekends. That beach Madonna was always on about, what was the name of it? Some bible name, I cant remember. Fuck her and her beach. Bake in the sun. Never look back. Wait it out.

Federal, that's what Johnny's lookin at anyhow. Three to five they says. That's Dorchester. That's the jungle. And for what? What for? That's what Johnny wants to know. What do they got? Nothing. They got fuck all on Johnny. One of the good guys, that's Johnny, even got that commendation ceremony thing coming up next month. So, fuck man. What have they got? I mean yes, Johnny might be a bit hardcore, meaning that if you fucks with him he'll take you down and fucken down. But not without good reason. Not just for kicks. There's a difference.

She walked right into the teapot. She did. She picked up Johnny's guitar and was going smashing it. His guitar, you know. Fuck. She swung it at him. And he picks up the teapot then, her grandmother's teapot that she carted with her all the way from BC. Made like he was gonna smash it. Figured no jeezly way she'd call him on that. But Christ, she takes a run at Johnny then and cracks her face right off the teapot and bashes it in bits all over the floor. Big gash on her head. That's. What. Happened.

That's the true story of Johnny's latest plunge. Hard to grasp, but there you have it. Cause, come on, Johnny knows you dont hit a woman, that's something he's smart about. Not with a teapot. So, right, poor shocked Johnny with his fingers still bandaged and blazing itchy, he runs to the sink for a cloth, and dont she start in squelching and blaring. He grabs ahold to her shoulders and tries to get her over to the sink, right, cause of the blood. Man oh man, the blood. She keeps fighting him, tryna make it seem like he's restraining her or something, but that's not the way it went down, not atall. She starts in screamin for help. There's blood everywhere, all over Johnny's shirt, thick and greasy like oil all over the floor, and she's so loud and high-pitched with the blood running down her face, and then there's someone pounding on the front door and she gets away and makes a run for the doorway all howlin and sobbin and Johnny standin there covered in her blood with teapot shrapnel all over the counter and the floor and they even found some afterwards in his hair. And there at the door, there's that old bag McFlabberguts from up on the hill, who lives right directly across from Johnny's new digs now. She keeps the shop up the road and because she gobbles back the raw bologna by the ten-pound stick day in, day out, well she thinks she can tell it all at a glance, what's going on. And away the two of em goes, scrambling to get clear of the blood-soaked madman with the telltale scarlet cloth, standing in the cloud of steam rising from the sink and the stink of blood and baked rock in the air. Johnny runs to the door and sees the two of em jostling up the hill like the Russians were coming, and Madonna moanin and cryin and attracting all kinds of attention. But listen to this part, just listen, she looks back at Johnny and gives a smile. She smiles that smile. Really. Through the dust and the blood, as the song goes, she looked back and *smiled* at young John-John. She did. Like to say *Youre so fucked now Johnny boy*. One of those looks that can fucken haunt you to your dying day. *You are going down.* What a laugh, what a fucken laugh-riot, really, how they can snare you with the lips and the eyes and the sweet talk, the nice hairspray smells, ya know. Catch yourself wondering what in the fuck is she doing with the likes of me anyhow? Is she stunned? Is she off the head? Voices tellin her what to do? Did she get a bang on the skull? Is she recently escaped out of some institution? You catches yourself thinkin, man, she's got that smile, and that thing with her hair, that kinda shine, that glow about herself. She could go anywhere, with anyone, walk into any room and point at any man there and walk off with him. So what the fuck is she doing with Johnny, with me? Ahh, but then they lays something like this in your lap. Running face first into a fucken teapot. And you finds out she was just attracted to her own kind—wasters like Johnny. You finds out that she really is off the head, only she's likely ten times worse than she's letting on.

Poor Johnny.

Poor Johnny, pour him a fucken stiff one.

She'll carry on though, find her way back to the top, get all her papers in order, her life all squared away with some fucker, some dope-slinger type more than likely. Fuck. Maybe not. Maybe she'll head back to school or something, find some work somewhere. Fuck.

Johnny went in then and changed up.

Washed away as much of the blood as he could get at.

You gotta think fast. Changed his shirt and put on a loose pair of jeans and lined the waistband with tobacco and a pack of papers and even a wrap of gear he tucked into the hem of the pocket and got out a needle and thread and stitched it in place. Not an easy task, threading a needle under them circumstances. That was at the other place, Johnny and Madonna's place. They even had a fucken sewing kit.

Then he sat and waited and sure enough, not ten minutes but there was four cars outside the door. Four cop cars now. All for Johnny. He didnt put up much of a fuss. That was not consistent, one of those times he faltered, we'll say. Oh yeah, he tried tellin em his side of the story, but it didnt matter a fuck. And yes, yes, there he was with blood under the fingernails and chips of antique porcelain sprinkled across his scalp.

Plus, dont know why, dont know why, but Johnny had the handle of the teapot in his hand when the fuzz showed up. Musta picked it up from the floor and was gawkin at it when they got there. That was stunned. Priceless. Very reckless Johnny. Some might say fucken *idiotic*.

She walked into it, he said. She walked head first into the teapot.

How they all laughed at that, and Johnny almost joined in himself cause we all knows how retarded it sounds. Burnt right out. Christ. She walked into a teapot. Blood everywhere. This was only a few days after that story came out in the paper with that interview with the old couple from the fire, about Johnny being some sorta hero. So you knows now, the pigs, they had their fun making a big spectacle dragging Johnny off.

And now the bloody curfew, the abstinence, signing in, waiting for court. Not allowed even so much as a glance in Madonna's direction, not even if she was to show up tonight and beg Johnny for it, then he's the one busted. That's Johnny for ya. That's his lot. Waiting to go on down the line. Real time. Highly likely too, he's told. Told. Nothing definite, but it's a strong possibility. That'll be the third or fourth time now, gettin locked up. You dont wanna know, you dont want to know. But this time it's the jungle. This time is prison. Not jail. Prison. This time it's eyes to the floor and keep your fucken mouth shut or have it carved off you while youre taking a piss or having your breakfast or flicking through the channels. Wont be no reprieve, no special treatment just cause of who your old man is, that all ended when Stevie got sent down for a life bit. So, keep your mouth shut or it's a pencil in the throat. The bottom of a Pepsi can ground into your eye. Good old chair across the skull. Q-tip jabbed in through your eardrum. The hem of a blanket noosed round your throat from behind. TV adapter stuffed into a sock and welted into your kidneys. Handle of a toothbrush ground down to a needlepoint and drove into your guts. Fucken swarmed by . . . but hold on now, wait Johnny, hold up. Come on. Dont go gettin all twisted up about it. What have they got? What have they got on ya Johnny? Nothing. Sweet fuck all.

She walked into a teapot.

That's the truth and that's all they got.

Anyhow, have to wait and see if she even makes an appearance in court. Knowing Madonna. The states she likes to get herself in these days. Cant exactly see her up with the sun. Yeah, Johnny's got his doubts. And whose doubts are they? All Johnny's. No one else's. At least he's got that. But see now if she *does* show, wont that be a circus? And she will too, you just watch. She'll be there with her hair all done and the makeup, lookin right fresh-faced and innocent, fancy skirt, high heels. And what the fuck is Johnny gonna wear? It'll be all about the contrast, wont it? But watch when she dont show up. Cause she might not, knowing her. And that's Johnny off with it then. That's you off Johnny. Off and gone. Right to the boat. Right across the country.

Johnny picks up the little baggie again and pops it into his mouth and sucks on it, sucking on it. Like he would *her*, if she made an appearance tonight. He would suck and suck and he would not let up. Bygones. Yes, we'll be off to court the week, but for tonight, just for tonight, it's all away in the past. He'd lay her down there on the cot and forgive and forget all night long.

And that's alright Johnny, nothing to be ashamed of.

Wait now, there's Pigeonshit, the mouse man, the garbage lad next door again.

He's tapping something onto the wall. Tap tap tap. Putting stuff up, pictures, art. Decor. Atmosphere. Dont tell Johnny, dont bother. Here he's got seven smokes left. Seven rancid Number 7s. That'll do. That'll do. Where's Shiner, the prick? Where's Shiner at? Musta slipped her mind, little Susie. Johnny leans out the window again to see what he can see. There goes old one-lung Tom around the block again, trying, tryna wind himself down into the arms of some version of a sleep. But not since the wife died, no, not since the wife went. Johnny sparks up another smoke and jumped-up fuck if the little mouse man next door aint out leant up against his rig with the boots all laced up and the hood over his head. Standin there. Leaning.

You wait right there, Johnny goes.

Buddy dont answer.

Hey!

He looks up at Johnny.

Wait right there, Johnny tells him, I'll come down for a chat, hang on.

I dont even know you man, I was just saying hello earlier, I dont . . .

Dont play the role now, little fella, dont play the role, come on now.

Pretty bad, he goes, I cant put my trash out, cant come out in front of my own home without . . .

Without what? Someone wanting to have a chat with you? You must be right popular are ya?

Trash, he calls it. Hear that Johnny? *Trash*.

Johnny offers up a civilized wink to let buddy know it's all just a bit of fun, a bit of arsing around. But is it?

Listen buddy, lookit here, it'd take me not two seconds to get into your house if I wanted to. Two fucken seconds.

That stirs buddy up some, he dont like to hear that sorta talk.

I have a little two-year-old in there, he goes, asleep.

Oh man, fuck that pisses Johnny off, fellas hiding behind youngsters like that.

You wait right there now buddy, we're gonna have a chat.

About what? You dont even know me.

I know! You could be a fucken slimy little rat for all I knows. A slimy little rat.

Alright b'y, he goes, alright, whatever you says.

That's right, it's whatever I fucken says. Now we're gettin somewhere see, gettin places, it's whatever I says. So if I says I'm coming down and I'm gonna smash you there's not much you can do about it is there?

Buddy goes for his door then.

Shag this, he says, I'm off in out of it.

Listen I'm only messin with you, you knows that. But seriously though are you a man or a mouse?

He stammers, something I cant make out, something down under his breath. He dont like being asked that, not with his missus in there listening. Johnny is gettin right under his skin.

Ahh man, I'm only arsing around, I'm just muckin about, dont mind me. Just asking a simple question, that's all. Are you a man or a mouse?

Buddy spits on the sidewalk and ducks back into his house out of it then and, hey, you cant tell can you Johnny, you cant tell if that's the smell of the harbour on the wind or if the little mouse man just sullied up his drawers.

Now, come on Johnny. Come on. Youre alright. Yeah you fucks with people but it's all a bit of fun. Sensitive bastards. If they cant handle it fuck em. Johnny's the best kind. One of the good guys. Goddamn *hero*, aint ya? Got a lot on his mind. Johnny got a lot on his mind. I do. Come on. Where the fuck is Shiner? This is the shits. This is not lookin up, not at all. Not at all. It's coming down, that's what it's doing. Coming down Johnny, and it's gettin late.

Johnny leans right out the window again, stretches as far down the hill as he can see. There's a party down in one of the units at the bottom. Down around Madonna's. The old homestead. Sounds like a blast and a half and you knows, you knows there's gear knocking about. Run flat out Johnny, go on, smash your way in and grab something. Who the fuck is gonna stop you, who's gonna stand in your way? Cause you dont know Johnny if you dont think he'll smash smash smash through any fucker foolish enough to stand up. Go on Johnny. You could pull that off in no more than ten minutes. What's the chances you'll be missed? Slim. Or more than likely. Take the back way up around and be lying in bed when or if the fuzz shows up, make like nothing. Tell em the phone didnt ring through, that you never stirred. Maybe it works, maybe it dont. Be right nice and groggy and sleepy-sounding and polite. Naw, they'll know then for sure. Give em hell Johnny! What else? Give em all manner of sauce cause that's the way youd be if you was really in the right. That's the only way to be. If youre in the wrong too.

Consistency, that's the rule, that's the law.

Always, always give em hell.

Here comes little Susie again now, running back down over the hill with a new spring in her step alright. She looks to have been crying, but man she's a whole lot steadier on her feet. Catch her Johnny.

Hey! Little Susie! Hey!

She looks up Johnny's way for a split second and hooks her toe in the pavement and almost does the big tumble down over the hill. Some sight that'd be, her face all a mangled mess scraped into the road, sobbing and bawling there, bleeding and needing a knight in shining armour.

Fuck off!!!

This is what she wails at Johnny, the little torment, and we can see clearer when she passes under the streetlamp that she's got a fresh reddish swelling up around her left eye. Fuck man she cant be a day over seventeen. But ya gotta live up to the nickname, hey Shiner, even if it means battering the merchandise like that. Little Susie picks up speed then when she shouts that at Johnny. Cause she's met his eyes and she knows. She knows she'd be devoured if she let herself get two steps closer. Cause Johnny'd pounce, he would, fly right out the window at her. Wouldnt he? Drag her into his lair, toy with her till he was good and ready to feast wouldnt he?

No, not really.

Well maybe.

But no.

Fuck man, no.

Legal aid. Cramped, sour cubicle office. Johnny sat around fiddling with his nuts for near on half an hour. That's true. Lookit here, Johnny says he's gonna be somewhere and he's bloody well there. Different thing if he wasnt. This crowd—and dont bother tellin me they're not all the same crowd neither, legal aid lawyers and piggywigs and prosecutors and judges—they're all right up each other's holes. And they lives and breathes in their own time zone altogether. Making you wait for months on end. Rescheduling, cancelling. Coppers coming for you at all hours of the night. Legal aid with their overseas conferences and vacation packages. Over two fucken months since they picked me up. And sure cant it all be said and done in a matter of fucken minutes? Punch in, punch out and fuck off. Lock me up or cut me loose. Different thing if *Johnny* dont show up somewhere, well then everything goes straight to fuck. Just say, just say he never showed up to sign in yesterday, up at the cop shop, sure the SWAT team'd be out lookin for him, infrared dots combing the sidewalks, tear gas, bullhorns. Fucken news bulletin and everything. Truth. Twice a week, Mondays and Fridays, he's scratching the old John Henry down for the coppers. They're only up over the hill though, a short jaunt. Couple of weeks ago when Johnny signed in he was still half cut. Took a couple of them dumb-dumb pills too. Very reckless Johnny. Here's the thing, if he never showed up at all they'd come lookin for him, and if they didnt find him right away there'd be the big manhunt and then he'd be locked up anyhow. Same if youre caught with booze on your breath, locked up until your court date at least. And you never knows, you never fucken knows, but you might end up gettin postponed for weeks and months and doing all this remand time and end up gettin off with the original charges when you finally do get your day in court. So there's all this time served for nothing. All's it does is get you better connected and more pissed off. So Johnny figured he'd go sign in with the booze on his breath and take the gamble that they wouldnt smell it off him. Woulda served him right though, all the same. Up at the station he lucked into this wheezy old bastard all stuffed up with the flu. And Johnny made like he had the same flu.

Jesus man, some bad flu on the go.

Fuck em. Johnny laughed all the way down over the hill. Johnny never ever gets the flu. The flu is for mice.

Imagine though, Johnny, gettin off with this. Off and gone, vamoose. Kiss my hole you dirty old shantytown. Up north, maybe. Johnny's good old buddy Paul is up north now this three years making all kinds of bucks, forty and fifty an hour, clearing something like four grand a week. A *week* now. Youre lucky to see that in six months around these parts. Four grand a week. Well ya knows now, you knows Johnny wouldnt be all riled up to get ripped right outta the head. Get out on a great big tear. Or no, maybe do up an old Charger, like the old man, Stevie, used to drive. Burn down into the States somewhere, cruise down around the coast of California with a nice missus in the passenger seat. Leather seats all slick with suntan oil. And get hammered besides, hey Johnny? Crash out in the little motels and fuck fuck fuck till youre rubbed fucken raw, trash TV and a hot shower and away again, wandering. Yeah, that's what Johnny and Madonna were planning. Right Johnny? Right? Well not that exactly, but something like it. Go off and make a bit of money and do something half sensible with it. She got some cousins way out on the west coast. Yeah, we was gonna go crash there for a while, get on our feet. Typical. All talk hey Johnny? All fucken talk. Start up again with no one knowing a goddamn thing about no one. Where's he from? What's he all about? What's his story? Fuck ya. Johnny and Madonna, just living, doing alright. That was before all this though. It was all different. Before she turned. The dope, ya know, I guess. I dont know. It brought something else out in her, no mistake. Almost overnight she was hell-bent on running Johnny into the ground. As if. Nothing and no one running our John-John into the ground, cause he's like a fucken machine once he gets going. I mean, what have they got on him? Nothing. What have they got? Sweet fuck all. Johnny's the one armed to the teeth. And what's his weapon of choice? What is it? The fucken truth, man. The cold hard truth. And if that dont go over like a goddamn house on fire then who the fuck knows? Who knows? There's no sayin. Have to rethink, restock, rearrange the arsenal. Dorchester. But what have they got? Johnny's word against hers. Hers against his. Nothing to it. Yeah, youd like to think it goes down that way, but look at the state Johnny's old fella is in. Fuck. And for what? Nothing. *Nothing.* Old Stevie wasnt even in the room, in the house, on that street, in the same part of town for shit sakes. He had what's-his-face, that biker fella who used to be down around Shiner's, what's his name, who got busted for armed robbery, he *told* the fucken cops Stevie was driving the car that night. The get-away car. Ratted him out right away. Stevie admitted it to the cops him-self. So, shit, if admitting to being a fucken accessory to armed robbery, and having a witness to back it up, if that's not enough to prove your whereabouts, well Christ the system is fucked. It's evil. And he's hardly the only one either, Stevie. Lots of fellas goes down for nothing. I mean it's hardly the States but mark it down, there's fellas out there serving full-on murder raps for doing fuck all. Lives ruined and wasted. Some of em, the lucky ones, are out now, names cleared, compensated, and still everyone around thinkin they got away with murder. Lookit that banker fella from Central sure, they put him away shortly after his little one's kindergarten graduation and they let him out in time enough to watch her graduate fucken high school. Her entire childhood. And he never done sweet fuck all neither. Down the line on a shit beef, like Johnny's old fella. Nothing. And they sent the banker away sure and he's, or he was, a goddamn *bank* manager with all kinds of reputation on his side and good people and good references and a clean record and the truth, yeah the cold hard truth on his side. Like Johnny's old fella. Like Johnny. But they locked the banker up anyhow didnt they! So what chance have Johnny got? Christ sakes. If they digs into his youth record it's all fucked. With your old fella gone away for life for what they says he done. Up with the dangerous offenders in Kingston. That dont look so hot for Johnny. And you knows they're slick enough to bring it up.

Jesus. Like to believe there'd be something come of that whole house fire business, but other than that you got nothing and no one on your side Johnny, except legal fucken aid. And that's a toss-up right there, hey b'y, if he's on your side or not. A job and nothing more. Same thing if he was workin in a slaughterhouse chopping the heads off cows, that's how much of a fuck a free lawyer gives about whether or not Johnny goes down the line.

Here he is now, Mr Legal Aid, nearly an hour late gettin to his own office.

Good morning Mr *Ke*ough. I'm sorry to keep you waiting, I was in a meeting.

Yeah, in a meeting alright, hey Johnny, cause he got one of them fancy big-city coffees in his hand, one of the ones you sees zombies lined up for a fucken hour to get a sup of, that costs near on five bucks a cup and that still tastes like burnt horseshit. Think he brought one for Johnny though? Think Johnny woulda drank it?

That's alright, Johnny goes, I'm not here long.

Legal Aid huffs over a few papers. Sets his briefcase on the top of his rickety desk. Barely much older than Johnny, really. Except for this fat greying moustachio that gives him this sorta air of learning and book smarts. Or that's likely the look he's going for anyhow. Books? Fuck off.

Johnny can see right through it all. No fooling Johnny. Reeves, his name is, like Superman. No doubt he likens himself that way too. No mistake he latched on to that little connection when he was a young fella. Like ya would. I mean, if yourself and the fella who plays Superman have the same last name, youre gonna try and cash in on it. When youre a young fella. But he's a far cry from the build, this Reeves. Skinny as fuck, all spindles and knobs. Go for his knees Johnny! Yeah, he's a fine sight, his eyes always bugged out of his head like something just blew up in his face, or he put a bag of money through the wash, or some wild animal pinned him down and blew a load in his face. Ha! Shoulda mentioned too, this is something else, he's got his office set up like what way a prison counsellor would, with the desk in the middle and *his* seat facing the opposite wall and Johnny's on the other side. This is the way they does it on the inside, in case things goes amiss, so that the counsellor or the assessment officer is the one closest to the door, in case they have to make a quick break for it. Plus it's got something to do with trust and psychology bullshit too. Stupid, high notions. Or maybe he's being smart about it all. Cause by Christ there's been a few times Johnny would have liked to pin him into the corner and snap his collarbone. Cool it Johnny, cool it man, cause you never know the way it's gonna go. Some day not so far away now they'll have these sorts of gizmos that read your intentions and then we'll all be fucked and fucked. Imagine that Johnny—going on trial for the thoughts in your head, for the things no one knows about. How many back-to-back life bits would you have to plug before they opened the gates again?

Okay, Mr Keough, I have to say that it isnt looking very promising.

Fuck sakes Johnny man, dontcha hate the way he has to go pronounce your name like that, dontcha feel like screamin it into his face? But what can you do? Pick your battles, choose your weapons wisely hey Johnny?

How so?

There's been some developments. Your girlfr . . . Ms Dale . . . although she has yet refused to give a statement, which is partly why youre out on bail I presume, unless of course youre . . . ahhh . . . but youre not . . . ?

Unless I'm what? Spit it out man if you got something to ask me.

No, no, I didnt . . . of course not . . . it doesnt matter . . . ahh . . . but Ms Dale has otherwise agreed to testify in court. Which is not good. Until recently the Crown's case was weak. I'd expected without either her statement or testimony you would have walked. But . . . not only has she agreed to testify, Ms Dale has consented to the submission of her medical records, and it's been brought to my attention that the Crown will be submitting a series of photographs that were taken on the day of the arrest . . .

Yeah, so?

Bruising around the breasts and hip area, and the shoulders . . .

I've told you before . . .

Not to mention the cut on her forehead that was made with the . . . ahhh . . .

He shuffles through some papers cause he aint even looked at Johnny's fucken case since two weeks ago. Feed it to him Johnny.

Teapot. They're sayin I hit her with a teapot. But I never. She . . .

Yes, yes, it says you hit her with a *teapot*, that you broke it on her head?

No, but listen . . .

And when you were searched they found fragments of the *teapot* on your person?

Yes but see . . .

And that you still had the handle of the *teapot* gripped in your hand?

Listen for . . .

Plus these photos . . .

Fucken listen to me! Alright? Listen to me. Now I dont mean to have to shout. Alright. But I'm after tellin you a dozen times, we've been through all this. I told the cops and I'll tell it to the judge. She fucken walked into the teapot and then she made out that I struck her with it. I held it up to protect meself cause she made a run at me. I was *defending* myself. She was pounding on me too, with her fists, for about half an hour before the teapot business. I just dont bruise as easily as other people.

Reeves sits back for a minute in his maggoty swivel chair and does that thing with his hands, puts all his fingertips together like a church steeple or whatever, and puckers his lips and ruffles his fat grey moustache. He thinks he's Johnny's head doctor now or something. Ya get what you pay for Johnny my son.

Okay yes, alright, okay. I hear what youre saying. Self-defence. But you have to understand that these photos, these bruises . . .

They're sex bruises alright?

Excuse me?

Sex bruises for Christ sakes. She has em all the time.

I'm sorry I dont . . .

They're bruises you gets from bangin like a savage, alright? Is that what you wants to hear? She's tellin me to slap and squeeze and pinch, beggin me to beat the hole off her! Alright? It's rough sex that leaves the marks. Do you get it now? And she's . . . now she's fucken . . . now she's sayin that I'm after slappin her about. And she's pale-skinned too, you know, so everything, every little bump shows up on her skin. Alright. Jesus!

Reeves sits back again and does that thing with his fingers and swivels his chair. Finally that perma-shocked expression on his face is grounded in the right moment. He clears his scrawny throat and leans in like he's some kind of doctor about to give Johnny six months to live.

Would you be willing to talk about this in court Mr Keough?

It's Ke*ough*, alright? Ke*ough*. Not *Ke*ough. And yes, yes of course I will, if that's the way she wants to play it. I'm hardly gonna sit there and let her say I beat the shit out of her on a regular basis. Fuck.

Johnny takes a swipe at some papers on the desk but they're stuck onto it. Prolly glued on there, for looks. Superman dont like that.

Please calm down Mr Ke*ough*. This is something you'll have to be careful of. The courtroom is no place for a display of emotions, I shouldnt have to tell you. If a judge sees you lose your composure for even a moment, no matter how trifling the moment or the circumstance, then youre offering him a glimpse of your capacity to anger and he will almost without a doubt form a mental image of your behaviour at the time of your alleged crime. Once he's formed that mental image you'll be as good as done for. With your record, you'll have to keep this in mind. It's one thing to throw a hissy fit in the confidential company of your lawyer, but dont expect to throw a similar tantrum in the courtroom and have it go by unobserved. Okay?

Well. Now whose turn is it? Now it's Johnny's turn, now Johnny's the one must look like a bull caribou jerked off on his face. Finally, after nearly four weeks of drivel and technical slop and phone tag and high-notioned big-headed legal lingo, the skeletal bastard decides to grow a set of nuts and say it like it is. Well now. Wonders, Johnny, they never cease. And you gotta take it, have to let him say them sorts of things too, cause he's all you got. Yessir, Johnny's been down that road—representing his own self like he was some sort of Charlie Manson wannabe or something. Yeah, done all that and dont it have a way of blowin up in your face? But here, Johnny's smart enough to know that he dont know everything. But he wasnt always, smart enough to know. And it's one thing knowing nothing, but it's another thing altogether when you dont know that you dont know nothing. That's what fucks fellas up, thinkin they knows something they dont, thinkin just because they can crack someone's head apart with their bare hands while they're out on the street somewhere that they can march into a courtroom and tell the judge what's what. Fuck that. Johnny's not going down that laneway this time of night.

Very well sir, Johnny says, very well. Youre the boss. Youre the man with the briefcase. It's just, what I'm sayin is, it's all bullshit. Alright? Are you listening? It's lies. Filth. That's the best way I can put it. She's an evil liar. She's a drug addict. She's . . .

She's a drug addict?

Yes, she is. Or she was then, two months ago. All of her life, on and off. So I assumes she still is. I mean, things were different when we first . . . Why? What's that got to do with anything?

It's a means of discrediting her testimony. And without that . . . was she . . . ahhh . . . did you mention . . . using drugs on the day you were arrested?

My God man, how many times . . . yes, she was sweatin it out of her pores, that's what I've been tellin ya. You coulda wrung her ponytail out into a pipe and got all of Buckmaster's Circle wrecked until Labour Day. Haul a paper across her twat and . . .

Well okay, good. I mean not *good*, of course. But good for us.

Well you already says before that they're gonna question me about my drug use. So fuck it. Yeah, fuck it, why not. Especially if it gets me off the hook.

Reeves gives Johnny a sly look then, ever so briefly, a flicker over the top of his papers. Like he knows something that Johnny dont. Like he already knows in advance that there's no way Johnny is walkin away from this one. Funny that is, how fellas can talk you blue in the face, all these words and gestures and the imparting of information and such, but then they can give it all away in one tiny minuscule passing glance like that. He knows something that he's not tellin. Or maybe Johnny's gettin paranoid. Or maybe he knows something that Johnny dont. That he's not fucken tellin.

Do you know something that I dont know? That maybe I should know?

Pardon?

You heard me. Are we on the level here? Am I walkin aboard a ship that sunk yesterday? Am I? Be straight with me, cause if I finds out youre fucken . . .

Mr Keough, please, the outbursts, they wont help.

Reeves lets out this long dramatic weary sigh and Johnny almost feels sorry for the scrawny skin-and-bones little knob. Come on, sometimes you gotta wonder what home life must be like for fellas like that.

Be straight with me, Johnny says again.

Is your father, your biological father, is he Steven Puddester? Stevie the Scar?

Ahhh . . . well . . . well yes, yes he is. Why? What's that got . . .

Serving life without parole?

Yes . . . well . . . yes he is . . . but he's . . .

First-degree homicide?

Jesus. I mean, how do I answer that? Yes he's in jail, yes that's what he's in jail for. But he's there in the wrong, see. He's not supposed to be there. He never done it. Just cause he had a record . . . What's that got to do with me and my case? Come on man!

And do you also go by the same nickname? Johnny the Scar?

What? What the fuck are you on about man? That's some whopper aint it? Where in the name of Christ did you hear that?

That's information I've picked up Mr Keough. But if youre telling me that's not the case, then that's enough . . .

Fucken right man, what do you think I'm off me head? I mean yes he's me father and yes he's doing time . . . but I'm my own man here you know . . .

Okay. Fair enough. I dont think it's going to be an issue. I dont believe it's admissible during the trial. I'll have to double-check . . .

What do you mean you'll have to double-check? Youre a fucken lawyer aint ya?

Yes, well, I'm reaching here Mr Keough, because I'm still more than a little baffled that you made bail, that you didnt even have a bail hearing . . .

Look. I knows what youre thinkin. Okay? So choose your words wisely before you goes accusing me of anything like that.

I'm not. I'm not Mr Keough. It's nothing . . .

What difference does it make to you to know why I made bail anyhow? Maybe the prosecutor had a soft spot for me. Ever think of that?

Could be any number of reasons. Maybe they just were hoping I'd fuck up my conditions and knew that I'd be definitely going down then when I did. Make their case that much easier. Cause they havent really got nothing on me without . . . without. I mean, what odds? It looks that much better dont it? Say I comes up against a different judge for some reason and they sees that I wasnt deemed a flight risk or a danger to the victim, and that I abided the conditions . . .

Of course, youre right of course. We'll move on.

Reeves with a little bronze key opening the drawer to his desk. He slips a package of peppermint knobs into his lap. He tries to pull one out of the bag but they're all stuck together in one congealed glob. Johnny snatches the bag away from Reeves and slams it down onto the face of the desk between them and the candy shatters like glass, and slivers and dust spray across the floor. Reeves says nothing, reaches into the bag and pulls out a jagged little pink piece of candy shaped kinda like a baseball cap with the peak cut off. He pops it in his mouth, slides the bag towards Johnny, then leans back in his chair. Johnny eyes the bag of candy then slowly reaches out for one. He selects a piece that doesnt resemble much other than smashed stale candy. Reeves shifts the hunk of peppermint from one cheek to the other, gawps drearily at Johnny.

When did you get those teardrops? Are they new?

They were new three years ago.

Arent they supposed to represent . . .

Yeah, yeah . . . that's all bullshit.

Can you conceal them somehow? Some sort of makeup?

No. I cant.

And these are the two teardrops Johnny had tattooed, one under each eye, down at HMP during a stint for trespassing and breaches. Christ. I cant say what was going through my head. Pills most likely. No regrets anyhow, no regrets. Fuck it. Not like you can see em clearly from across a room or nothing.

They each sits there then for a while, Johnny leant right back in his chair, suckin his peppermint, gawkin at the cheap ceiling tiles. Reeves leant in close across his desk, staring right straight at Johnny, who feels like smashin him now, his smug moustache, the sunken eye sockets. Briefcase. But it's not his fault. No. Not his fault. It's hers. Or maybe it is Johnny's fault. Your fault Johnny. Mine. Alright? *My* fucken fault. My fault for takin up with her. Christ. Johnny's fault for going in for that sort of skirt. Johnny's fault for being too fucken pussy-whipped to be able to see clearly enough that he was bedding down with a god-damn . . . with . . . with a bloody deviant. I dont know. I dont know. She's not. She's not. She's just Madonna. She's just a girl that turned, got scared, got talked into talkin. And she'll show up in court lookin like she do, prolly wear that pink thing she's got, and do her eyes that way she does em. That's Johnny then, done for. As good as gone. But Johnny aint done for now is he? Not yet. No not yet. What have they got on him? Just, just . . . ahh fuck it.

What about the fact that I aint been in no trouble in a while? It was over a year since I had any run-ins before all this.

Well we can certainly make a valid claim that youve been attempting to get yourself on a better path, but . . .

Well what about this business with the fire then? Supposed to be some sort of ceremony next month. Supposed to be giving me a medal for fucken *bravery*.

Yes. Yes. That wont hurt at all. That's certainly crossed my mind. We could argue that you were under ahhh . . . emotional duress, stress, like a sort of PTSD situation after the fire incident and that may have contributed to . . .

Naw man, that's not what I mean, that's pretty much comin out and sayin that I clobbered her. What I mean is, cant we use the whole fire story as a kind of testament to my, you know, me character or something?

Well yes, yes. I suppose we could. But I'm more than a little curious about your youth record as well, Mr Keough, because given the circumstances . . .

What about it?

Well, it's quite varied and lengthy . . . destruction of property . . . ahhh . . . theft over five thousand . . . indecent exposure . . .

I shook my cock at some party! Come on, it was a party. Crowd there from the university. There was fellas there too, not like I cornered some little girl and shook it at her.

. . . unlawful entry, arson . . . countless disturbing the peace . . .

Well how can they bring that stuff up?

And I've heard, I mean there's obviously no report, but I heard about some chickens, your neighbour's chickens?

Who told you that? That's not . . . no no no. Listen . . .

Did you kill someone's chickens?

There was never any charges for them fucken hens . . .

Regardless, Mr Keough, even if they dont go back that far, the adult record alone . . . three petty thefts, possession, assault . . . break and enter . . .

Jesus H. Christ Johnny man, will it never cease? How many times do Johnny have to explain that fucken hen story? Never even any charges and still it rears its head. And how many times with the story about that party in the Goulds with that uppity university crowd carrying on like that until you had no choice but to whip it out? Indecent exposure? Sure I was barely fifteen! Pius and his jeezly Cavalier too. Course I fucken burnt it, no question. But it's not like I *set out* to burn it. Arson? Christ.

Okay. Okay. Listen Mr Reeves, what am I lookin at here? I mean, what's the likelihood I'll be walkin away from this? And if not, what kind of time, realistically, am I lookin at?

If you do go down, youre looking at three to five. We talked about this. The Crown will push for the maximum.

So I'm going down, for sure . . . ?

Well Mr Keough, I'm not in a position to offer false hope, so I wont.

So there's absolutely no chance I'll get two-years-less. No chance it'll go provincial.

We're building as strong a case as we can. This incident on Barter's Hill, with the ahhh . . . fire, and the fact you havent had any trouble in a while, they'll take all that into account. Meantime, keep your nose clean, abide the conditions of your curfew, sign in on time . . .

Yeah, yeah.

Well it cant hurt to be seen as having obeyed the court orders . . .

That's what I said to you! Look, be fucken straight with me, alright? Cant you . . .

The bruises, the photos, the cut on her head, police notes, your record, her testimony, your father's reputation. Come on Johnny, do the math!

What's that? What did you say?

I said do the math.

No, you called me Johnny. That's the first time you said my name. In four weeks.

He just stares at Johnny then, with that shell-shocked expression. Like he's surprised suddenly that he's sharing the same breathing space with another human.

Cause that's what we are, all of us, humans.

Even Johnny.

It's a funny concept though, an odd notion, Shiner goes, in a way, when you thinks about it. I mean, lookit Johnny, here we are being policed right? There's people out there, other *people*, with blood coursing through their veins and hair growing out of their heads, with dicks and pussies and fingernails and brains and hearts and such, all the same makeup as you and me here Johnny, and they're specifically trained to *police* us. They're *policing* us. Us! I mean, think about it for a second. Not to say that I dont believe in right and wrong, but who gets to pick and choose who's who, that's what I'm most concerned about right here and now. Who gets to pick and choose? Cause when you thinks about it Johnny, most of us never had a fightin chance, did we? I mean, it's a goddamn bloody miracle when you thinks about it, how ones like us, with the shit kicked out of us from day one, can sit around the table here now and carry on a decent and sensible conversation. Think about it. None of us ever had a fightin chance. Look at the shitheap youre in tonight. Yeah. They're policing us, they're on patrol, monitoring our actions, how we gets on with other people, where we're off to and how we're gettin back, keepin watch over how we're gettin by. Alarming isnt it?

This is Shiner going on. Night before court and Johnny thought he'd kill his last free hour, before curfew kicks in, listening to fucken Shiner yammering on about the ways of the world, how it's put together. As if none of the rest of us knows nothing about it. That's the thing about the blow, it's the best kind if *youre* the one running your mouth off. Oh he's a smart enough fella, Shiner, just when he gets a few lines in he gets all wound up like he's suddenly after uncovering some huge conspiracy and now feels he has the responsibility to fill the rest of us in. Shiner. Spose Johnny coulda picked worse company tonight.

The ashtray rattles on the table when what sounds like a big beefy pickup rumbles down the street outside. Some rigger's cock extension most likely. The flash of the headlights on the kitchen wall. Shiner darts over to the window to see who it is. He stands there gawping through the ratty curtains, breathing through his teeth, then he whips back across the room and slumps back into the chair across from me.

I mean, think about it Johnny my son. Here you are, never done nothing, best kind of a fella, going at it clean as a whistle, for the most part, hunkered down all nice and cozy, pulling old folks out of burning buildings, turning a new leaf, as they says, and the missus gets it in her head to go running to the cops about you. And for what, right?

Shiner's after shaving his goatee and he looks older somehow. Aged. And with the weight gone off his face these days too, he looks kinda apish. Really though, he looks like an ape with his chin jutted out like that and his bottom lip almost lapping up over his squat little nose. Toss that in with the way he hunches about and there you have it, the Missing Link. Yeah, it's an odd thing, facial hair. Johnny wouldna recognized him if he'da run into him downtown somewhere. Christ, remember Shiner had the *massive* beard years back, braids in it and everything, useta pull joints of weed out of it. Everyone calling him Moses on the sly.

And for what Johnny my son? Youre what, twenty-two, twenty-three fucken years old? Whole life ahead of you. Who's to say you wasnt gonna straighten yourself right out? Everybody's entitled to a few rough-and-tumble years, arsing shit up and gettin in a bit of trouble, having fun. It's not right is it? They just looks at who you are, that's all. And they sees who your father is and that's you fucked. Same way it was for me back in high school—the older brother gave the teachers fucken hell years before I showed up but they went and tarred me with the same brush. I never had a goddamn prayer. And that's what's going on with you, cause of your old man. And like I said, your old man is a good man, a good man. Done me a solid on the inside. It's not right. Cops rolling up and snatching you, roughing you up and mocking you, slappin all kinds of bullshit conditions on you, puttin you on a curfew like you were some kinda youngster, and then they runs and tells the goddamn judge on you! And what's he gonna do? He's gonna fucken *judge* you? He's gonna listen to everybody else's side of the story and then he's gonna pass *judgment* on you. And he dont know nothing about you. I mean, it's not like he can see how you are here and now sitting at my kitchen table good as gold and not hardly making a peep. And youre prolly gonna be gettin a goddamn *medal* for fuck sakes! That's how best kind you are. And even without all that hype, sure, there's lots of other things. Remember that time you helped what's his name with that couch? How's that hit you by the way? Feelin it yet?

Ahhh . . . yeah, spose I am.

This is a couple of low-dose perks Shiner hooked Johnny up with about a half hour ago. Johnny's just now feelin it in the knees, that dizzy shaky burning in the joints. That's where it always hits first, the knees.

Shiner's bell goes off, one long and three short. Someone lookin to score. Shiner walks over to the window and looks down to the street. He snatches his little bag of goodies off the table and brings em back to the window. He holds up the bag and dangles it at whoever's down on the street below.

Fuck you Penny, he shouts down. Fuck you. Six hundred bucks.

Come on Shiner man, I told you . . .

Fuck you. Six hundred bucks.

Shiner snaps the blind closed and ape-swaggers back to the table. He's lanky and gaunt from all the dope, but with this sorta funny-lookin potbelly poking out, like them pictures of starving youngsters you sees in magazines. As soon as he's sat down the bell goes off again. He jumps up and goes for the stairs. Johnny can hear him talkin real low and menacing down there. Must be young Rodney. Johnny dont even try and make out what they're sayin. Couldnt care less. Nothing new around these parts. Technically youre not even supposed to be here Johnny my son, not supposed to be in the same company as anyone else with a record. But fuck it. They're watchin Shiner, they're watchin Johnny, fuck it. They're watchin the whole goddamn street, watchin the whole fucken planet from some space station out there. They can zone right in to watch you humpin your pillow in the nights. Perverts. Fuck it Johnny. Get on home before curfew and keep the fingers crossed that Shiner's gonna offer another few perks for to take in the morning before the showdown. Why the shit not? Wouldnt be the first time some jailbird was fried in court. Walk in in a big jellied haze and get carted down for processing and by the time you comes around youre on the bus and it's all over, the waiting. Plus it'll keep our John-John from losing the cool in court. Cause youre going down, and ya fucken knows it Johnny. And the last thing you wants to give her is the satisfaction of seeing you losin the cool. So, a nice buzz on, float through like nobody's business. No room left for meltdowns Johnny boy! Three to five. Fuck though, what has he to worry about? Really? If he dont care about gettin smashed and banged around a bit, then what odds is it? What fucken difference does any of it make? Who cares if someone jumps him? Who gives a fuck? No one. Not Johnny. But if they thinks he's not gonna come back at em, sometime, no matter how big and hard they are. He's hardly gonna go up there strutting like the bigshot or nothing, but there's no way he's gettin run over neither. Fuck that.

This fella Johnny heard about, fella named Nuts, a couple of years ago he got sent down for seven years for manslaughter, or criminal negligence causing death if you wants to get specific. He's dead now, Nuts. Caught a cold, as they says. He got smashed, lasted three months inside.

He was after taking up with this young one, a one-night stand that lasted all weekend or something, and come Sunday morning she saw his motorcycle out in the backyard. This was early in the year too, he never even had the bike out for a good run yet that year, no insurance or registration or nothing. Anyhow, she starts in asking Nuts for a ride, and he dont really want to cause he's all hungover and strung out and wanting to take her back to bed, but she keeps it up and keeps it up, how she's never been on a bike before, pestering him until suddenly they're out on the arterial doing something like a hundred and seventy and Nuts is thinkin *Well she wont bloody well torment me the next time cause she'll be too fucken shitbaked.* That bike could go, too, Suzuki 850 or some such beast. Only thing, when he stopped at the lights going into Kilbride and shifted himself back in the seat, well she wasnt on the bike no more. That's that. I mean, Christ it's awful when you thinks about it, she was barely outta high school. Nuts freaked the fuck out, like ya would. But to his credit, he went straight to the cops to say what happened. He had no clue where he lost her to, so going back and combing through the bushes on the side of the road woulda been pointless. Cops found her though, way the fuck down on the other end of the arterial. Musta been when he hit a bump, or the wind took her or something. Little thing, she was.

Imagine though, he went the whole length of Pitts Memorial not knowing she wasnt on the bike no more. She died instantly, they said, she wasnt mangled or nothing, so that was good for her, and prolly the best-case scenario for whoever she was belonged to. Of course it turned out the girl came from a bit of money, slumming it for the weekend to be knocking about with Nuts. And she was just after turning eighteen, her whole life ahead of her and that sorta tear-jerking stuff the media goes in for. Not sayin it wasnt fucken awful, like I said, but you knows now what that newspaper crowd are like. And it was said that booze mighta been a factor. Not definitely, but maybe. And Nuts didnt even have a licence or nothing. And he was married then, separated, but still married. This all came out in the news and such. It was a right circus for a while. Christ, he had it all stacked against him. Anyhow, Nuts still held his head high cause as far as he was concerned it was all an accident, that he done the right thing by going straight to the cops, how he coulda easily drove on and no one'd be the wiser. He wasnt going playing the sorry sap with plans to mend his ways just cause of the way the cops and the news crowd made it look. He told the papers that yes, what happened was tragic and unfortunate and he wished it never hadda happened, but it did. And that's all he said. No apologies.

Course then he went up away, doing federal time and all, and got on like he was different from everyone else, like he was better, like he didnt belong there. Not that he was innocent, that's different, but that he was above it all and not there to do the same kind of time as the other lads. And he strutted that attitude. And he got smashed for it. Dead and dead. Money talks, yeah. No one ever did get the rights to how it went down, but you can gather it was none too pleasant for old Nuts either way. But there you have it, such is the way. So no, you wont catch Johnny running his mouth off and lording around. He's not that stunned. But not to say he's gonna let some fucker tromp him into the floor neither. Fuck that.

Shiner comes back up the stairs and takes his seat.

Business, he says, business.

He dont look too pissed off. Kinda looks in good spirits. Musta given Rodney a smack. He roots out a pack of papers.

Three to five hey Johnny, he goes, three to five. Yup . . .

Might go two-years-less though, it's possible, at least then . . .

Nah, fuck that Johnny. Better off up away my son. Better off.

I dont know . . .

Well lookit, say you got two-years-less right? And you hadda go down by the lake doing provincial time right? Well youre fucked altogether then cause you knows what kinda hellhole that place is. No fancy programs or school, drugs are the shits, no gym, no fucken *conjugals*, the place literally crumbling down around you. Right? Cant get to see a doctor. No jobs, unless you licks enough arse to get a spot in the kitchen. The food is nothing but grease and slop you wouldnt feed to a dog. That's HMP. Grey filth and dirt and scum, banged up with all sorts, fellas who by rights should be in the Mental. Squat in with the stink of shit and piss and sweat. It's a pigsty and it's not gonna change and everybody knows it. And it's even worse down there now since all the talk about a new jail being built, cause now they *really* dont give a fuck, now there's *nothing* being done. And, worse than that, more than likely you'll do your whole bit, right? Cause you'll be drove cracked with the way things are run down there. It's fucken burnt out. Soon as you gets onto a routine or whatnot they fucken switches everything around on ya. Takes forever to get to see someone or talk to someone or get into a program. You'll be drove mental Johnny my son. You'll crack right up. You'll get the fever and you'll start fighting everybody on everything and you'll end up doing your whole bit. But see, you goes up away and so long as you keeps your mouth shut and all that, well you got lots of programs, if youre into that. I mean, you might as well if'n youre lookin to get out early, you might as well do a few programs right? So say you gets three years right? Well sure you'll be out in one, or less. Even if you gets five years you'll prolly do less time than you would if it went provincial. And the drugs are fucken A-1. A-fucken-1.

Shiner takes a big haul on a fat freezie he's twisted up, hands it across the table to Johnny. Johnny feels like running off into the corner with it.

Thought there was the big crackdown on dope nowadays?

Oh yeah sure, the pills and stuff. They dont like that. They dont like the hard stuff, the oxy and the blow and stuff. The E. Cause it throws everyone out of whack when they cant get none, drives the lads fucken mental during the dry spells. And they're even worse about booze, homebrew and stuff. You knows all that. If youre caught with a brew on youre fucked, straight to the hole. But they turns the blind eye to the hash and weed, see, in the federal joints, that's the thing. So you can smoke as much of that as you like. The bulls figures it keeps everyone settled and peaceful. So you knows now, the weed up there, and the hash, well it's fucken laced with everything right? Cause the boys knows they can get away with having it. So it's specially cut. I remember a block of fucken hash as big as your head and when you sliced into it you could see these squiggly white lines running through it. Fucken *laced* with opium. Twelve hours out of a blast. Man, never see it like that no more. Gym, they got a fucken wicked gym on the go. Soccer teams and hockey teams. Newfs on the one team, darkies on their own team, Capers on their own team. Christ man the Capers are a fine bunch. Newfoundlanders with their brains kicked in, that's all the Capers are. I mind of the time . . .

How long of a bit did you do anyhow Shiner?

Me? Well lets see, I done what? See I had a few scuffles. Cause that's the other thing, you dont wanna go up there lookin like the goody-two-shoes neither Johnny my son. Doing fucken programs and talkin to the chaplains and taking a job and shit. Not right away. Cause they'll think youre soft if you goes about it that way.

Yeah . . . I mean no . . . yeah I wasnt going in for none of that, not right away.

Ya gotta be mindful Johnny, too, what sorta jobs ya do go in for. Dont take just anything. Stay clear of the fucken library. They think you thinks youre a smart fucker then. Stay clear of the laundry too, if you gets offered. They'll think you pulled a few strings, if you hears me right. Or they'll think you got the bucks. Better off mopping a floor and minding your own business. Dont let no one see you reading a book or nothing, not right away anyhow. But here . . .

Shiner holds up his glass.

Stop lookin so whipped young feller. You never knows Johnny my son. The gods might take pity on you yet. Maybe she dont even show her face b'y. Maybe she gets struck down by a bus on her way to the courthouse and you'll be off with it. Never know do ya? Never know.

Johnny raises his own glass but he already drained it half an hour ago. Juice though, didnt trust himself with what Shiner's havin. A glance at the clock says he's got ten minutes left. Rain is starting up now, supposed to fucken piss down they says. It all feels so set up somehow, hey Johnny? Lets turn on a bit of rain for Johnny's sake. Let's send him off with a good drowning. Fuck ya. Johnny pulls on his jacket to go. He's got one sleeve in and Shiner's bell goes off again. One long, three short. Shiner darts over to the window. He turns back and gives Johnny a look that tells him to stay right where he's to.

I gotta go Shine, I only got a few minutes left.

You sit there now Johnny. I wont be a second.

Johnny stays where he's to. Not going crossing Shiner tonight. Shine takes his goodies down the stairs, right enough too, cause Johnny wouldnt trust himself with all them in front of him now. You can only get so fried on the perks though, then you gets sick. But Johnny dont mind that, kinda likes it, heaving his guts up. Good for you once in a while. Lots of water you needs.

Between the gusts of wind and rain on the window, Johnny can catch little snippets of Shiner's talk down there. Cant make out no words, just his manner, right soft and cooing and musical. Must be a looker down there. Shiner gets all sorts these days, wont be long before he's hot on Johnny's heels for the clink too. Never know who's who coming to your door. The rain and the wind drops off again, and fucked if Johnny's spine dont about crawl out through his neck when he hears that laugh, that sharp little giggle that flips in on itself and comes back up as a full-throated lusty roar. It's her, Madonna. Make no mistake. Johnny hears Shiner shushin her, tellin her to keep it down. Then there's nothing, the wind. Johnny digs his fingernails into the underside of his chair to keep from lunging at the door and bolting down over the stairs and . . . just to see her. Talk. Talk this out. And not just all this shit with the courts and this legal shit neither. Just . . . me and her, you know. Johnny and Madonna. Talk this shit out man. Never even gave ourselves a chance to see what mighta become of us. Things were tight, they were solid. Right before they stopped being that way. Before the streets were awash with all that dirty crystal. Once in a blue moon do a little hit of molly and stay up all night laughing and chasing each other around the kitchen and flopping down into the bed and *not fucken sleeping* for hours. Let's talk this shit out, come on. The very gal, Madonna, who can make or break the course of Johnny's coming years, with only a matter of hours to go before court, right down there now at the bottom of Shiner's . . .

But wait now Johnny, wait now. What the fuck is she doing here now at Shiner's? Sounding so buddy-buddy. Cause Johnny might not be able to make out no words, but there's that familiar tone perched in the air, that ease, that intimate leaning that lets the spurned know, in his gut, that another man's hand has been up under his woman's skirt. No matter that there's court in the works, no matter about no fucken teapot and no backward glances, no matter. She's still, for now, in Johnny's head at least, Johnny's girl. And he's belched and roared and snotted it all up here at Shiner's table since the whole thing went south how many weeks ago? What the fuck? What the fuck?

Johnny digs into the underside of his chair and pulls up, up, up until he can feel the screws in the chrome legs buckle under the pressure and the plywood seat starts to splinter and crackle and a staple that keeps the plastic coating in place digs into the tip of his finger and slips and gouges deep into his fingernail and the blood comes quick and drips in mute scarlet splendour to the cheap linoleum tiles and there's that laugh again, that shrill little half snigger that never quite plays itself out before morphing into something you might hear out on the barrens some foggy night when youve been wandering in circles for years, and Johnny knows, Johnny knows, knows that there's no man focused enough, no man hard enough, no man sturdy enough. He fucken knows where Shiner's been. And so much of it makes sense all of a sudden that none of it does, and for a moment Johnny feels an ecstasy and a white-hot blinding surge of righteousness that sees him reaching across the table for a crusty metal fork left over from Shiner's plate of Ches's that he didnt even bother to offer Johnny a fucken chip from. And Johnny takes this fork and watches the whole scenario play out in his head—Shiner monkeying up the stairs with all his plans, his own greedy waiting game almost played out. Waiting for Johnny to get sent down so he can have an easier crack at Madonna. And Shiner might try to nod, might try to smile, might try to muscle his way past when he finds Johnny waiting at the top of the stairs. But who are these blowhards, hey Johnny? Who the fuck are these *types* with their mouths and their little blue bags and their steady supply and their phantom connections? Who are they when they're truly and utterly called out on what they *really* are? They're fuck all Johnny. Even Shiner, who knew your mother, who claims to know things no one could know. Even Shiner, who swung at Big Jackie with a pry bar that night over in the Circle parking lot after Jackie had Johnny down and shithauled, and one more smack woulda rattled your brain Johnny, and you woulda never been the same again. Even Shiner.

Johnny watches all this play out, the confused and flustered look of inverted betrayal in Shiner's eyes when he knows the jig is up, when he feels the cold filthy cantankerous teeth of the fork plunging into his tight jugular and smells the hot blood spewing in thin streams across the walls and into Johnny's hair and across the little glass end tables. And Shiner knows his time is up, that the credits are about to roll. He knows he's breathed his last.

Johnny sees all this as he takes the fork and buckles the two middle teeth down flush to the handle so that there's just the outside teeth like a miniature pitchfork, and he has a flash of a sticky summer's day in the lower meadow making hay with Pius, the man he called Dad for sixteen years. Young Johnny's hands blistered numb and the sweet smell of slaughtered wildflowers, the constant stabbing itch from the dried dead root-ends of the hay sticking in under Johnny's shirt, and that perpetual grimace on Pius's sunken, miserly gob, that ceaseless sneer shattered by the pale rumour of a smile when a little calico kitten backflipped up out of a haystack and caught a butterfly in its jaws and clamped down, crunching the fluttering alien thing until it was gone, nothing but the shimmering yellow wing dust smeared about the kitten's mouth. It was the only time Pius had set the prong down all morning. Johnny and Pius stood there watchin. And Johnny thought he saw Pius smile. And that was the one kitten from the whole litter that never met its end off the head of the government wharf.

Johnny hears Shiner shoulder the heavy storm door shut, then buckles the teeth of the fork back in place and tosses it across the table. What good? What good now when the rain is pelting off the siding like salt shots and Madonna's really only up to get her own kinda fix before the big day? And what's it to Shiner but another day, another dollar? And if Johnny's going down then aint it easier, in a sense, not to be wondering who she's with and what she's up to? If he knows, knows, that she's just back home slumming around with Shiner for a scattered free bump, then dont that make it easier than wondering all the time? Wont that be the quicker pill to swallow come this time tomorrow when he's on the bus for the mainland? Fuck it. And besides, hey Johnny, if even ten percent of Shiner's bullshit is the truth then wouldnt you rather be going off to the Big House on good terms with him, rather than having to look over your shoulder waiting for some punk who owes Shiner a favour to slink up behind you and make good?

Shiner lomps up the stairs and wheezes past Johnny to the bedroom.

Business, Johnny my son, business.

He huffs past Johnny again and back down the stairs, and Johnny looks at the crooked fork on the table and wonders at how softly and quickly we're all here on this small ball of spinning dirt, and how some of us has it all fall from the sky the moment they comes into existence and how the rest of us are sitting here, hands gripped to the lip of this greasy edge, waiting for the bottom to rise up to meet us.

Johnny hears no more laughs and giggles from down on the street, fancies he feels a goodnight smooch on the wind, but he's got a slow leak now and cant be bothered with it all. You come into the world freezing and fucked and alone and why should any of us expect to go out any different?

Shiner comes back up to the kitchen and flicks off the dull orange porch light below that lets folks know it's still not too late in the night to come a-knockin for a fix. He tosses Johnny a little blue bag with what feels to Johnny like half a dozen perks knotted in the corner. Shiner wont meet Johnny's eye. Johnny knows anyhow that he cant hide what he knows to be true and that it'll only make for an awkward scene if Shiner has to acknowledge what Johnny knows. It'll all be said and done with tomorrow anyhow. Shiner tells Johnny to have a stiff upper lip, and Johnny nods gravely and agrees with Shiner's wisdom as if he'd walked a thousand miles to receive the words, and there's no eye contact between them because there would be no avoiding the admission that neither of them have any fundamental understanding of what this old cliché means. Have a stiff upper lip. Christ.

Outside on the street, in the blistering rain, Shiner takes Johnny by the hand and offers a sweaty, pathetic shake that to Johnny sums up all the contradictions and duplicity of the total charade of their association. There, fuck ya. But, for all that, Johnny feels suddenly protective of Shiner, and cant say goodbye, turns and saunters down the hill in the rain and drops his eyes to the pavement as he scuffs past the red glowing window frames of his cozy upright neighbours, his dopey brain feebly tussling with the notion that by knowing something he shouldnt know he's let down his only halfways real friend on the planet. Ah fuck off Johnny.

Three to five, three to five, federal. This spinning in Johnny's head as he tucks himself into the far corner of his single cot to avoid the drip, drip, dripping splash from the paint can he's set on the opposite corner of his mattress. He sits up once more to make sure his alarm is set. When he slumps his head on his ratty yellow pillow he can feel each drop in the can pounding through his skull like a stubborn four-inch nail. He looks across the room and his slitty eyes latch on to a warped and water-stained framed pic of Jesus with his open hands and bleeding sacred heart, and for the first time in years Johnny makes the sign of the cross and clasps his hands together and closes his eyes and offers up a feeble hello to the Big Man upstairs. Johnny knows it's all a bit pathetic, yeah. But what have we got, any of us?

God, it's me, Johnny. I knows things must look rough. I knows I aint been one of the good guys, not lately, and not for a long, long time I spose. But I can change all that. I can. I can find a way to make good. I dont know where to start or how to go about it, but if you turns one of them knobs up there, if you finds it in yourself to maybe shift things around a little and help me out of this situation, then I'll make good. You look down at me here now and you knows I never done nothing bad enough to be going down federal. Things got fucked up, things got shagged up, but I was trying, I was. You saw me, you had to see me runnin into that house and you knows I didnt give a fuck. I mean, *yes* I was already . . . but what difference? Even before all that, I was tryna be in the world, I tried to be one of them types. Maybe I wasnt ready for it, maybe I didnt clip along fast enough. And I'm not sayin she brought it out in me. But she did. I mean, no, she never. It was me. I slipped back. I did. I knows I did. I got up to the old ways. I'll admit that. But if you can, like I said, put the brakes on and kinda rethink this for a second and let me walk out of that courtroom tomorrow a free man . . . well, I can make good. I'll try. I'll try. I'll try . . .

By this time Johnny's vaguely aware that he's bawling his face off and he passes out like that, still sobbing, with three more perks melting in his stomach and holding on for dear life to the little blue bag. Almost immediately he slips into a barren dream that he's drifting a hundred miles from shore and suddenly latches on to the slimy, rotted end of a rogue anchor's rope that he knows by no means will keep him afloat, but he's got nothing else to keep ahold of, and at least if he hangs on tight he'll keep from washing farther away and might stay in the same place, for a time.

It aint a long trek from the Hood to the courthouse, and Johnny's been up early, scratching and tossing and scrubbing the stink of sweat off in the busted rusty sink in his room. He wont miss that pissy shower down the hall. There's lots he wont miss. He packs a few pairs of socks and some drawers and tee-shirts and a pair of jogging pants and a hoodie and his old grey boots in a black duffle bag. There's nothing else in his room that he ever wants, or expects, to see again. The blankets were here, the pillows, the clock radio. He wolfs back the last of Shiner's perks and he's out the door by half past eight, in his only pair of jeans and sneakers and a ragged wool sweater over the light blue collared shirt that Madonna always said brought out the light in his eyes. Black denim jacket. Not necessarily courtroom attire, but what good is a suit and tie now Johnny? What good is it now?

The rain musta let up sometime around daybreak. The street's got a sweet, fresh tang going on. Johnny stands at the crossroads at Cabot and Lime and looks down over the harbour, hears the gulls, thinks about Pius's old twenty-two, nods at one-lung Tom who's feeding the pigeons near Leonard's Convenience. He walks on down the hill and breathes deep passing by his and Madonna's old dwelling. The old pad. Nice that was man, for while it lasted. Sitting down at a table and eating something that you cooked yourself, or she cooked for you. Matching pillowcases. Fuck.

Crossing up Central towards Livingstone he takes a shortcut down through the housing units. He tromps down over the steps where he first met Madonna, and he tries not to conjure up the memory of that strange ghostly pull, that brawny tug, that otherworldly *drawing in* he felt that morning nearly two years ago. She was sitting on this step where Johnny's standin now. It was dawn, with the first of a new day edging up over the Narrows, and Johnny'd been out, and free, for over a month and he'd been down at a late-night bar and drank himself sober and left, like a good lad, when the bartender said so. And when he stepped out onto Queen Street his feet started moving up towards New Gower even though he lived way up on the west end of Water Street near the Station Lounge, and he felt his eyes clear up with every step, watched, from some great height, his legs dash across the road by city hall and felt that rising sense of anticipation like that feeling youd get when youre after gettin some long-awaited care package from the outside world and it's left back on your bunk, waiting to be opened. Like walkin home with the dope in your pocket, knowin youre gonna be fried for the rest of the night. Kinda like that feeling, only tenfold. Like one of them kids in some wholesome holiday movie who's lying in bed on Christmas morning before anyone else in the house is awake. Whatever that feels like. Only a thousand times that. Something is happening, something is comin your way, something good, something you needs and wants. Something that's gonna change everything. Johnny stoppin outside a mirrored shop window to check his look, fix his drink-battered hair, tuck his shirt in, zip his coat, take a slug from the flask he'd been hoardin in his inside pocket all night. His heart is pounding and some part of him knows why, but the conscious part of him has no clue. He picks up his pace and almost sprints up through Carter's Hill Place. He sees the graffiti-marred concrete steps leading up onto Livingstone but he knows he's meant to turn left and carry on through the courtyard behind the housing units. By the time he makes it to the last set of steps he's winded and his stomach is burning and there's sweat dripping into his eyes, and when he sees her sitting there so casually, with her hands clasped around a forty of white wine and the thin tie-dyed hippie scarf wrapped around her head like some unruly Virgin Mary, and one of her bare knees skinned so bad the blood's trickled down into her skimpy canvas shoes . . . When he sees her there like this . . . well it's like . . . he feels . . . more acutely than ever in his life his limited vocabulary. He feels his face flush red. Like he's been caught out. Fucken jailhouse stench rising off his skin. But a real stirring in his pants too, for the first time in what seems like months. And he wants to speak, he wants to sing, he wants to lunge, he wants to lie down and howl at the coming daylight.

But he throws up instead.

She pulls her feet out of the way and nudges his shoulder with the wine bottle and lets out a tiny giggle that seems to Johnny to cut itself short before it's finished, like she's almost giving something away and then checks herself. She sits quietly sipping from her bottle, and when it seems Johnny is finally finished choking and sobbing and drying his eyes and sucking on his teeth she offers up that half giggle again and asks him if he feels better now. And Johnny looks at her long and hard and says *Yes, yes I fucken do*. And she stands and screws the cap back on her wine bottle and takes Johnny by the arm and leads him up over the steps and says *Alright then, lets get you to bed*. He brushes his teeth while she sits on the edge of the bathtub cleaning the blood from her knee, and he's got his mouth between her legs before she even asks him his name.

On Water Street Johnny stands in the alleyway across from the steps to Atlantic Place and watches his lawyer, Reeves, toss his head back and laugh rowdily at something the Crown prosecutor is sayin. Oh Johnny knows em all. And they all knows each other. And they all knows Johnny. The early-morning sun glinting off the fresh-polished toes of Reeves's brown leather shoes. How far removed, hey Johnny? A couple of motor-cycles rip past, drowning out everything in their wake, and Johnny watches them weave up the length of Water Street, and when he cant see them anymore he can still hear them in the distance roaring through the gears and maybe taking the turn onto the arterial, and from there, who the fuck knows? Maybe BC or California. Maybe New York City. Johnny squeezes his eyes shut and tries to imagine his hands gripped to them handlebars, burning into NYC full throttle in the rain with all kinds of money in his pockets, fated for some cheap motel on the outskirts with a dollhouse on one side and a liquor store on the other, and he feels that thick dull lump of pain welling up in the back of his throat, and when he opens his eyes again he sees his arresting officer scooting up the steps behind Reeves and even though there's no grand guffaws between them, there is a nod that only Johnny would have reason to take offence to.

Johnny knows it's time to cross the street, but his legs are a frozen, trembling, jellied mess and there's an icy sweat on his spine, a tight fluttering burn in the pit of his stomach, and he thinks if he takes one more step that his knees wont do their job but could very well snap back the wrong way and he'll hit the pavement, writhing and gasping his last breath while his guts come streaming out the leg of his pants, and, hey Johnny, that wouldnt be so bad anyways, considering. No? He keeps waiting to see her face. He takes a few wobbly steps, then leans his head against the coffee shop and finds some comfort in the idea that if he wanted to, right this instant, he could smash his face off the gravelly brick wall, over and over until he split his skull in half and there was nothing left of his life but a splatter of grey brain matter and his filthy broken-down frame. Ten-minute cleanup job for some poor City fucker. He squints up to the open sky and has a vague recollection of the pitiable bargain he tried to strike up with the Big Man the night before. What's that they say about prayer and the doomed man? Fuck sakes Johnny.

A plaid, greying man in his late forties holds open the door to the coffee shop for his perky teenage daughter and when she passes through the doorway Johnny hears her say *Well then, if not there Daddy, how about my bellybutton?* Just fucken kill me. Or give me something innocent to destroy. Johnny eyes the brick wall again, gives his cheek a little squeeze, realizes the skin on his face is as numb and dead and useless as his legs, realizes he's well stoned out of his gourd, and feels better straight away.

Johnny straightens his spine, belches out a terse laugh or moan and flicks what might be his last cigarette for a while into the bowels of a grimy manhole, takes a deep breath, shoulders his bag and strolls out into the fuming morning traffic, and there, waiting on the steps of Atlantic Place, shifting the bloated shell of herself from foot to foot and chomping down on the top end of a chocolate muffin, is Johnny's older sister. Johnny's mother. Johnny's sister. His mother. The woman he called Tanya for the first sixteen years of his life. Until the day he didnt know what to call her anymore, or how to look her in the eye. The day everything made sense, finally, and nothing did. The day his *father* became Pius and his *mother* became . . . fucken . . . Pius's missus. And Tanya, big sister Tan, became nothing more to Johnny than another ignorant, craven slob.

Not to dwell, hey Johnny?

And not to come down too hard on her either, cause fuck knows when you gives the situation a good sizing up, well, she was raised under the same fucken roof as Johnny, wasnt she? Not like she had it any better.

But you know now, you hear these stories of this one or that one finding out they were adopted or whatever the case might be, finding out that the ones who brought em up are not their real folks, right, and so they hits an age and tracks down their *real* mother, or their *blood* father, whatever, and finds em living alongside a swimming pool somewhere, doing alright for themselves, halfways waiting for the day when their long-lost child takes it upon themselves to come sniffin em out, lookin for answers, connection. And how it turns out life was hard back then and there was no choice in the matter. But they've pined after you and thought about you all these years, hoping you were safe and living good. And welcome home and lets get to know each other. You hear them kinds of stories, right?

Yeah.

But no.

That's not the way it went for young John-John.

Johnny stops dead in the middle of Water Street before Tanya registers his presence. He stares across at her dumpy rolls, the way she slams the bottom of the muffin into her gob. The dancing, cornered-animal eyes. Empty barrel of a Bic pen twisting her greasy hair into a bun. Folded under her arm is a cheap mouldering garment bag with the tip of a coat hanger jutting out through a busted zipper.

Tanya suddenly notices Johnny and gives a frenzied flap of her arm without moving her shoulder. The left lens of her dated egg-shaped glasses slanted towards her eyebrow. He swallows back the rigid edge of an ancient rage as he steps up onto the curb beside her.

Waft of deep-fried something or other.

Johnny cannot believe he slid from this woman's womb.

Please Christ dont try to hug me.

By way of greeting Tanya sighs and unzips the musty garment bag and inside it there's a beige suit that Johnny recognizes as Pius's Sunday best. Tanya says she's had it taken in a little, and cuffed. Johnny keeps staring at her, waiting for her to meet his eye, but she wont.

Christ, that's . . . does Pius know you took his suit?

Tanya pops a cough drop into her mouth and holds the suit out by the hanger.

Pius dont know nothing much about nothing much these days John-John.

She still wont meet Johnny's eye.

Here, take it John-John, fuck sakes. Dont be so stubborn. God knows, it might do a bit of good. You knows what that crowd are like, lawyers and them.

Johnny spies the thin, patterned silk tie poking out of the pocket of the nicotined shirt and remembers the long-ago afternoon of some Kinsmen's banquet when Pius had the very suit on. There was a creepy, grainy cartoon on the old TV about a smiling spider that ran a hotel for flies who meets his match when he ensnares the innocent bride of a burly fly with a faint Irish accent. Johnny's heart pounding, not knowing whether to root for the spider or the fly. Pius jangling his keys, leaning on the counter lookin out over the harbour, grumbling under his breath about Mart Roach's new truck and slamming back a double shot of Crown Royal. Never went far without his Crown Royal did Pius. God love the old sleeveen. He opens the front porch door and as an afterthought he turns and bawls at Johnny to turn that goddamn shit down. But Johnny doesnt move quick enough and suddenly Pius is across the room towering over him.

Is there something wrong with your fucken ears? Are you deaf? Are you fucken stupid? What? Come here, bastard . . .

He lifts Johnny off the floor by the shirt collar, drags him, kicking and wailing, to the crumbling wood shack behind the house. Johnny begs and pleads and frantically tries to cover his legs and backside all at once, hunching his shoulders, making himself as small and tight as possible while he's whipped and lashed and battered with the busted cord from a power drill until Pius's curses give over to a low, dry gravelly grunt and the sweat runs oily down his forehead. Johnny snivelling in a pool of his own piss with his pants down around his ankles and not knowing why or what it's all about until Pius clears his throat and says:

That's so you wont act up while I'm out. So you wont crucify your mother. Now pull up your fucken trousers.

And when Pius is gone and Johnny's managed to pull his pissy wet pants up over his red, burning, welted backside, he sees the half-full flask of Crown Royal in the sawdust beneath the wheelbarrow where it must have fallen from Pius's pocket. Johnny waits until he hears Pius's truck make the turn at the end of the lane, picks up the flask, brings it to his nose for a stately moment, then drains it. The heat rushing to his knees. Lungs heaving with the hunger for authority. Any trace of self-pity nipped dead in its tracks. And the rest of the day is foggy, confused, a muddy shitstorm of skinned knuckles and bloody noses in the west meadow and Mikey's mother screamin across the lane that Johnny is some kind of dirty bastard that belongs in the boys' home.

Fuck it, listen. What odds is any of it? No complaints. You make the most of it, no? You make the best play with the cards youre dealt.

Johnny takes the suit from Tanya's hand and folds it over his arm and they stand there, not speaking, until Johnny nods towards the mirrored glass entrance doors to Atlantic Place.

Well you knows I cant come *in* John-John. You knows I cant watch all that. I wanted to see you off, is all, and to say . . .

But she cant finish her sentence. It rises up in him to let her know that it's all a fucken farce anyhow, all a big load of slurried bullshit, whatever slant Pius likely put on it: *Didnt I always say?* That whatever she's heard, whatever she mighta read, some skewed clip in the newspaper, well, cant she see what a trumped-up pile of pathetic shit it is? Ah but fuck it. What difference now? All the cards are marked already and Johnny's been guilty until proven guilty more than once in his day, make no mistake.

We were all some proud to read that story about the old couple and the fire. We were some proud then. That's our John-John, I said, I always knew you had . . .

Yeah, well, thanks for the suit Tanya. Say hello to your mother for me.

John-John . . .

Johnny notes the watery swell in her eyes, the quiver in her nostrils, and gives her a look that tells her to not say one more fucken word, which she doesnt. He spits into the street, grunts and winks at her—his sister, his mother—as he lurches up the steps to his imminent slaughter.

A shocker for Johnny, but the suit fits fine.

He can smell Pius's best drinking years baked into the underarms and the pockets are lined with a dry powder of Drum tobacco.

Johnny half expects to find money tucked away inside the lining. But he does not.

The docket's got him scheduled for half an hour's time. Johnny scans the list of names, recognizes a few. There's that young one who drove her car out over Signal Hill a few weeks back, tryna do away herself. All fucked up. She jumped at the last second though, let the car go on. It was all over the news, emergency crews dragging the car back up over the cliff, all the houses down below evacuated. Everybody was right livid with her, about the damage she done to the grounds near the castle and the money it cost to get the car up out of it. She was charged then with mischief and reckless endangerment! Imagine that. Poor fucked-up girl. I mean, get her some goddamn help, ya know? Whatcha gotta go dragging her through the courts for?

Johnny spies that evil cunt from CBS who burnt his house down with his five-year-old daughter inside. Left a shitload of messages on his ex's phone beforehand. He's being led through in shackles and chains and there's a few reporters taking pictures of him. Evil motherfucker. And here's young Leo Davis, up for another car theft and joyriding and a dozen breaches. Leo's girlfriend is hiccupping through the tears and mumbling and clung to his sleeve but Leo is stone-faced with his brows scrunched in that hard way and pushing her away, tellin her to go on home if she's going gettin on like that. Johnny waits until Leo catches his eye, then gives a nod to let Leo know that he knows he's just putting the face on, that face you gotta wear, the face that Johnny hopes he's wearing himself. The face that says *I couldnt give a fuck for no man here,* when in truth youre just about ready to shit your pants. Yeah, Leo's gotta go federal this time too.

Reeves passes up through the gaggle of drunk drivers and sleep-deprived mothers and anxious girlfriends and pill-heads and small-time teeny hooligans. He scurries right past Johnny with not a spark of recognition. Johnny thinks for a flash that it'd be fun to boot Reeves's legs out from under him and send him sprawling across the floor in a flurry of papers and a splatter of scalding coffee, but instead he shouts out *Reeves!* Reeves turns and clocks Johnny in the dated suit and gives a little nod, not of approval, but a nod that says *Well, at least you tried.* He takes Johnny by the sleeve and pulls him to a cubby corner and asks if he's seen the victim? And it takes a moment for Johnny to realize Reeves is talkin about Madonna, and not him.

No, no I havent. Why? Is she here?

Well, we have another few minutes, and she might be hanging back . . .

What would that mean? Like if she dont show up?

Johnny lets Reeves lead him by the arm into the congested, stagnant little courtroom. A tight whistling sound and the manic pulse pounding in his wrists and neck and chest and the sweat trickling down his back and his teeth loose from the late-night grinding and the taste of metal in the back of his throat. Fuck. Johnny sees a bottle of water tucked under Reeves's arm and grabs it and has it almost drank before Reeves notices it gone. Johnny scans the pews, but no sign of Madonna, and he thinks again of his offering to the man upstairs last night and his pulse quickens to a genuine breakneck speed. Reeves sits Johnny down, leans in conspiratorially to burble in Johnny's ear:

Well if she doesnt show, and that's *if*, the Crown can still press forward. But the meat of the case hinges on her appearance and testimony. I know Victim Services couldnt reach her. And you do have the ahhh . . . did you say you were applying to trade school? Computers or . . . no that's not you . . .

Look, what do they got on me, if she dont show?

But before Reeves can respond, that flaccid, jowly-eyed Judge Roberts hefts into the court and all hands have to rise and then sit back, like fucken schoolchildren. Reeves instructs Johnny not to speak anymore, to sit there and be quiet and not to fidget and to take that scowl off his face. And the rest, for Johnny, is a jittery blur of dirty looks and heads huddled together and murmurs about a recess, about a possible holdover. A scrap of paper slipped across the bench. Judge Roberts's bloated flabby bald head staring down at the scrap of paper for what seems like forty days and forty nights. Teeming drone of the digital clock. Reeves's biting garlic breath. The musty, closeted death stench of Pius's old suit. Throbbing itch on Johnny's shoulder that he cant reach without prolly rippin the armpits out of the suit. Officer Norris catching Johnny's eye, nodding ever so discreetly, a nod that offers Johnny the first crumb of hope he's known in months and months. A nod that says *You were lucky this time, Johnny boy. But there'll be another.* And then Roberts shaking his head and shrugging his shoulders at the CP and more shrugs and the termination of Johnny's conditions! What the fuck??? Then Reeves nodding at Johnny with this semi-apologetic hue in his eyes . . . and Johnny not feeling quite as light as would be expected. Not feeling quite so unburdened as he woulda thought. No, something . . . something . . . Johnny does not have to reach out for the bench in front of him to keep from floating up to the ceiling.

It's over, Reeves goes, it's over Mr Keough.

But there's no victory jig, no gloating legal aid smirk, just Reeves's jaw set with something more, a looming pronouncement stuttering on the tip of his tongue as he leads Johnny out into the main lobby and Johnny's sayin *What? What is it? Spit it out!*

Well, she, Ms Dale, ahhh, Madonna, she was . . .

What? Fuck sakes man, what?

She was found this morning . . .

Whaddaya mean she was found? Where the fuck is she then?

She's ahhh, she's dead Mr Keough. She's dead.

Johnny makes an instinctive grab at the lapels of Reeves's suit but Reeves slips eagerly back into the horde of doomed hopefuls and is immediately swallowed up by a thick herd of sheriff's officers. Johnny's left to boot at a garbage can. Grinding his knuckles off the cheap stucco coating on the support beam. Roiling, foaming at the top of the escalators where he sees Leo Davis shoving at his girlfriend, sayin *Fuck off will ya girl? Go home!* And when she finally gets it and bulldozes, red-faced and puffy-eyed, towards the escalators in Johnny's direction, Johnny can see the dull yellow bruises on her neck and the tender swell of her pregnant belly beneath the taut pink wool sweater.

What's left Johnny? What's left? Quarter flask of Crown fucken Royal. Neighbour's framing hammer. Shiner. Shiner's left. Left over. Madonna's gone. Madonna. Gone. Capital G. Not. Coming. Back. Gone where? What did you see girl? What did you feel? Peace and ease? Bright light? Or do you sink into the darkness like going off to sleep. Suddenly there's nothing, as if there's always been nothing.

This is Johnny, back now, back only hours from Caul's Funeral Home and Crematorium with a ceramic urn of Madonna's ashes on the table before him. Shiner's table. Back from a week of wandering about town pounding on doors at four in the morning, roaring mad and smashing bottles and kicking at parked cars, his knuckles scabbed and swollen from lacing into brick walls. Feet all a-blister, cracked and bleeding when he bends his toes a certain way, the grey leather boots gone bust. And not a cop in sight, for all that. Jesus, try and lay low and they're up your hole every time you takes a piss. Go out and pull a fucken armed robbery and boot the drunken shit out of the town for the week and they're nowhere to be seen.

Madonna.

Shit man, no way. No way. This is not . . . this is . . .

Johnny aint shaved, aint showered since the evening before court. And there will be no shower forthcoming. No more need for showers.

As far as Johnny's head is workin, the dirt and filth on his knees and under his nails and between his toes, the blood in his boots and the pus on his knuckles all belong to a time when Madonna roamed the same town, breathed the same air. And he'll be good and goddamned if he scrubs it away. Johnny finishes the flask and hops the bottle off Shiner's mantel. It's plastic, bounces to the floor. He twists the urn, dull beige pimpled ceramic, each one handmade with inconsistencies supposed to promote something original. Like something youd keep tea bags in, the cover suctioned on with an inner plastic fucken . . . circular fucken thing. Johnny weighs it in his hand, a whole lifetime scorched down into a ceramic bottle. Could scatter her to the wind with a flick of the wrist. Twenty-three years. Madonna is in there, Johnny, in a glass bottle. Miss Madonna Dale. That first week. Lying there, pressed against her, sober and raging to fuck and wanting it to be different and tryna work out how this moment right here, with this lovely new gal beside you, tryna grasp the concept that . . . that . . . all these moments of your existence are all strung together in such a way that they winds up being the one youre in, here and now. With this fucken beautiful woman here. Christ. Tryna sort it in your head so it dont come out of your mouth sounding like crazy talk. Wanting to show her that you got other thoughts going on besides what's between her legs. How you had all that on the tip of your tongue and afraid to say it to her cause you knew you wouldnt get it across the right way, and when you tried anyways she grabbed your balls and jumped on top and started that tight slide up and down, and the second she knew you were gonna blow she jumped off to catch it in her mouth! Sweet Jesus. Lookin at you all the while with those smoky grey eyes hemmed in with the boozy black mascara. Reaching for her beer. And then that night when you had her face down, grinding yourself off the small of her back, her giggling, *Youre bad Johnny Keough, I know what you want* . . . rubbing baby oil into her shoulders and when you got up to close the curtains, because the bedroom window was level with the old doll's next door, how she told you not to, that she hoped when she was eighty-some-odd years old she'd have at least a live sex show across the street to tuck her in at night, and what did it matter? And then the long stretch of downtime, when there was no need for the pills and no need for the booze and neither of you even noticed or missed being stoned and fucked up, and then so much sober time passing, with the stories, and that mad rush to outdo one another's pasts and Johnny's first utterances of Pius and Tanya, and that night at the boys' home in Whitbourne when that cunt guard McGregor told him all about it, all about how his sister was really his mother, and that his real father, well . . . and, hey Johnny, what about McGregor laughing while they led you down to the observation room? What was it you done that time?

How Madonna never strayed from your eye while you told her about Shane Chalk blowing an air gun off into your ear until you bawled, until you had no choice but to swing out at him, and then how he held you down and pounded your nose in until there was just this squishing sound when his fists landed. And how she laughed when you told her how you waited and waited and then got him back so long after he didnt even know it was you. Madonna coming into the room with teardrops drawn under her eyes in black pen. Madonna from out west with her beach parties and paper lantern festivals and the time a black bear got into her house, and rented limos for prom night and all that strange food and all those drugs, and dens in Chinatown where you could go and smoke opium, how she wouldnt go see her father on his deathbed and how she still didnt regret it, and people reading poetry on the streets. Madonna, hopping aboard her rusty grey Volkswagen Rabbit that died the very minute she pulled into Tulk's parking lot at the top of Lime Street. After chasing a young guitar player right across the country, only to be ditched and left at some hash party in Shea Heights not two weeks into it. Walkin down Blackhead Road at two o'clock in the morning and meeting a gang of rowdy teenagers and how she took off down over the bank, slicing her ankle on a broken bottle, *Here look at the scar,* and crying while the lads tossed rocks in the bushes up ahead of her, scrambling down over that gravelly bank of alders and having that strange feeling that she was walkin over a grave and finding out later that that very bank was where they found that other girl's body with her throat stabbed in four places and her underwear stuffed down her throat. How she found that out a couple of weeks later outside Tim Hortons and how her knees went to jelly and she collapsed into a herd of young cops and how one of them suggested she might want to go in for a pregnancy test.

Johnny's story about smashing out the windows of all the teachers' cars in the school parking lot when they wouldnt let him come into a dance, even after he won second place in the day's races, winning a banner for the school. Sleeping in the government twine shed after knocking the last of Pius's yellow teeth down his throat. The cops cruising around the harbour shouting his name into the loudspeaker, Johnny rolling over into the twine and yawning, feeling easier and lighter than he'd felt in years, the print of Pius's teeth gouged into his left hand.

Yeah Johnny, them first months: tell-all grace period of fucking and sucking and drowning and falling and letting go of everything. That deluded sense of having arrived somewhere. Delusions of arrival. Going out to NA meetings together. Johnny building a bookshelf as big as the wall. Sunday mornings and he'd wake up with Madonna's head bobbing down there under the blankets and a hot cup of coffee on the night table beside him. Sipping hot coffee while she sucked him off, laying it down before he got there, for fear of slopping it off the ceiling. Out on her balcony afterwards with a cigarette, Madonna reading a book in bed, him standin there lookin out over the town and wanting to roar something out, wanting to chew the railings away, smash something in half with his face, not knowing that it was a good, happy feeling ripping through his veins, not knowing that this was what it felt like to be welcome, and home, and welcome *at* home. Not wanting to face the fact that it was all gonna blow up in his face at the drop of a dime, any day, any hour. Stood there, smoking. The sensation that she'd stopped reading and was lookin out at him. The feeling that if he turned around she would be gone. The notion that if he turned and looked now there would be someone else in the bed with her. The feeling she was laughing at him behind his back, making faces. And when he finally gathered up the courage and turned back to tell her all this, she was asleep. A dark puddle of drool spreading across the page of the paperback she was reading. Sunday mornings. Coffee and a blow job.

And what's any of it matter now Johnny? What difference when here's Madonna in a fucken bottle on the table in front of you?

Johnny's conditions were dropped, of course. All charges dropped. Like none of it even happened. Walkin back up over the hill that morning in that dragged-out, drug-addled daze, weighted down with the big news and wanting nothing more than to be able to share it with Madonna. Who else? Johnny racking his brain for who to pass it on to. Who would she want to know? Who knew her? No one here in town, not really. Her junkie mates. There was her sister out west. Dana or Danielle. Last seen by Madonna on the corner of Main and Hastings in the back of a cop car almost five years ago. Who to run to? Johnny found himself wishing, wishing he was in that holding cell, waiting to go on down the line. He'd trade it up in a flash.

That morning, the news fresh and burbling in his gut, walkin back up past the housing units where he'd met her and crushing a burnt-out light bulb under his heel while the sky seemed to blacken and then buckle in on itself, compelling Johnny to look up to where the sun should be, and seeing that face, that sorta blurred presence lookin down at him. The feeling that someone or something was up there waiting on him to make a move. His desperate little prayer of the night before swirling in his head, rallying for room and priority in the new horror of Madonna's death and Johnny's new-found freedom. Make your move Johnny boy. Pony up. Grinding the light bulb into the concrete and screeching up at that woolly face to go fuck itself, that's not what he'd meant, not what he'd wanted atall. And then the burning madness in the gut as he put all the pieces together, with her comin around lookin for Shiner.

It was Shiner's dope that did it. Shiner killed Madonna. Focus Johnny, focus.

Johnny made it back to his room that morning after court just in time before Mike Quinn changed the locks on his door. Nine days left in the month anyhow and didnt Quinn wanna make the most of that? Johnny's sheets and pillowcase tossed out on the sidewalk. He had a few words with Quinn. Quinn had this look, this fucked-over expression, like he'd had big money on Johnny's odds of gettin sent down. Johnny got rid of Mike, then lay on his cot, knew there was a funeral coming. Knew there'd be finger-pointing. Knew how it looked, knew what the word out on the street and up at the shop and up at the club was gonna be. How Johnny got off fancy-free after smashing Madonna's face in with a teapot and she was so screwed up and heartbroken that she took to the dope and didnt know how to handle it and went too far. How Johnny got her into the dope in the first place. How now suddenly she'd be foremost on everyone's minds, scrambled into the talk for the next week and how loved she'd be. How Johnny'd have to watch his back in a whole different way. And how Shiner'd be at the heart of it all, the talk, if only to deflect the blame from his own self, even though all hands would know he dealt it out to her that night before. No question. But who's gonna cross Shiner, who owns every heebie-jeebie, shaky-handed, tooth-grinding morning after on Cabot Street? Johnny lay on his bare cot that first morning after court and let all this spin in his head. And came to the conclusion that he'd see it all through to some end. That if he got off with this, like he'd begged for the night before court, that if he got off and Madonna paid the price, this price, for his spineless prayers, then he'd make it right by doing Shiner in, at least, he'd even it all out and go down the line once and for all. Three to five or thirty-five, what difference did it make, with Madonna on a cold metal slab in the Health Sciences morgue?

Johnny hadda hit the bottle then, somehow. Hadda score a few perks, anything. On the verge of huffing gas if that's what it came down to. Checked his options and waited till dark and brought a couple of cases of empties up to Jackman and Greene's and bought a pair of women's nylons, then slunk down through the shadows to Queen's Road Store. He sat for ten minutes in plain sight on a step across the street, waiting for some old fella to finish with his Nevada tickets. There was a husky blond skirt behind the counter. Johnny felt bad for her already. No need that it comes down to this. Johnny hauled the nylon over his head. He still had the suit on, Pius's suit, but a dusty black windbreaker he'd found on the rail outside the room opposite his, he had that on over the suit coat, to bulk himself up. He shoved a piece of one-by-three strapping up his sleeve, wrapped his hand tight around it. The feeling of drowning under the nylon, his eyebrows squished down, couldnt breathe through his nose. Johnny held his breath until his vision blurred, then burst in through the door of the store and slammed the strapping down on the counter. He bent his knees and managed to take about a foot off his height. He made his voice really deep, like the big bad wolf he was. Told the girl he had a hammer and that he didnt want to use it but he would and that he didnt give a sweet fuck if he got caught, that he did not give one sweet fuck for nothing in this world. She stood there frozen, shocked. She was not a bad-lookin woman either, and Johnny caught himself wishing the circumstances werent quite so grim. Take her out on the town and show her a time. With the money he robbed from the cash register! Jesus.

Open the fucken register! Hey! Fucken money, come on! Smokes too!

His heart racing, his legs shaking, the sweat on his back. The girl froze, her jaw gawped open, staring at the nyloned maniac. Johnny slammed the strapping down on the counter again, hard enough to prolly sprain his wrist. He smashed a plastic bottle of five-cent gum, the ones with the stupid comics inside, the ones that taste like rubber dogshit after a minute's chew. Bubble gum went everywhere. She stood there. He let out a roar, grabbed her by the shirt collar and pulled her towards him, her string of wooden beads bursting and bouncing, scattering all over the counter and onto the greasy floor.

You think I wants this? Do ya? Think this is where I wants to be tonight?

She snaps out of her stupor then and when Johnny lets go of her shirt collar she falls back onto the cigarette stand. It's not . . . ah fuck, there's nothing graceful about none of it. The impulse is there to go around the counter and help steady her on her feet. But the clock is ticking. Johnny told her a carton of Rothmans kings, the blue ones, even though that's not what he normally smokes when he's flush. He knew what button to push on the mouth of the register, cleaned out all the twenties and tens and fives, a few rolls of loonies. A couple of fives hit the floor. She handed him the cigarettes. She didnt blink. She didnt cry. Johnny grabbed the cordless phone and smashed it in half on the edge of the counter. A piece of the plastic casing struck the poor girl in the forehead and she made the first sound since Johnny'd stormed the store, a low masculine grunt, very unladylike, thought Johnny. But she didnt cry. At least she didnt start blubbering.

I'm sorry girl, about that, about all this. I am.

And Johnny ran then, ducked down with his legs bent like a man crossing a battlefield, or the way you see folks in the movies running towards a helicopter. Hauls that nylon off his face. Down over Bates Hill first, then up the alleyway to his right where he ditched the black windbreaker. He split the carton of cigarettes in half and tucked each half into his left and right pockets. One thing about the old suits—lots of deep pockets for stashing stuff away. Johnny knew there might be a dog, and that he had likely less than ten minutes. He crossed Duckworth and took his time on the steps to George Street. George Street was hopping with young university White Russian guzzlers and a few business suits and hey, that bouncer outside the Sundance must have really messed up his hand on that guy's forehead. Gaggles of smokers out on the street.

Hot dog guy. Johnny kept from making eye contact with anyone, and at the end of the street there was Gulliver's cab stand and Johnny jumped in the back of a minivan whose driver was nodding off at the wheel and only snapped to attention when Johnny slammed the door. Johnny wanted LeMarchant Road, near St Clare's. The sleepy-eyed cabbie talked about the coming weather. A scratchy story on the radio about human feet washing up on the shores in BC. Johnny shot the driver a ten outside Christine's Place on LeMarchant, made like he was going in for a drink, then crossed the road to the bus stop as soon as the cabbie was out of sight. Johnny waited in the glass shelter, waited. Here came the sirens. A cruiser burned down the road with lights a-blazing. Maybe eight minutes had passed since he left the store. Maybe a little more. Johnny dropped the nylon into a recycling bin. There was a thick, healthy dark hair off Johnny's head tangled in the mouth of the nylon. Lucky Johnny, lucky you never ditched it with the windbreaker. The bus arrived and Johnny jumped on, cool and calm. Number 4 headed downtown. Johnny sat in his seat, his face pressed to the window as the bus cruised past Queen's Road Store. Four rigs—two cruisers, that matte-red Charger and the paddy wagon. Johnny saw an all-black German shepherd crossing the road towards the top of Bates Hill. He caught a glimpse of the big blond girl crumpled against the side of the store, crying. An officer was holding a cloth to her head and Johnny thought there might be blood. Wrong shift girl, sorry about that. The old guy with the Nevada tickets was back, yakking at a female cop, shrugging and nodding and waving his arms. Johnny felt the crumpled wad of bills in his pocket and knew they had nothing. He let the bus do the loop up Portugal Cove Road and down Prince Philip Drive until it came to the mall, where he got off.

There was a random cop car outside the entrance to the mall and even though Johnny instinctively knew it had nothing to do with him, as a precaution he tossed the cigarettes into a dumpster outside the gym. Then for a meal of real Italian pasta in a dark little booth. When he reached for his money he found in the corner of his pants pocket one little brown wooden bead from the girl's necklace. He pinched it between his thumb and index finger and then began to shake all over, a deep telltale crash and burn shake that started in his ankles and shot violently up his torso until his teeth chattered. He tossed the bead into the light fixture above his booth. He counted out the money and laughed out loud. Fucken right man. Three hundred and twenty-five bucks. Six vodka and orange with his meal, doubles. Steady the nerves. Then to the liquor store with not five minutes to spare. Large bottle of Grey Goose. Large.

Five, six days later and Johnny's slumped at Shiner's table with a framing hammer, huffing for breath. Swear a bomb went off in Shiner's apartment. Glass coffee table and end tables are smashed in bits. Shower curtain speared into the TV screen. Johnny even opened up the fridge and started bludgeoning the shelves of mouldy Tupperware containers and cruddy ketchup, mayo, mustard bottles and Eversweet butter, Tang. He pounded and roared until the light was gone and big gaping holes showed through the inside walls of the fridge. Then he saw the dozen eggs and closed the fridge door, softly. He slung the eggs across Shiner's living room, slammed the whole carton off the far wall. Most of the mess stayed inside the carton. Poured a full gallon jug of Javex onto Shiner's black satin bedspread. Slung chairs at the walls, gouging big trenches in the plaster, and smashed the breadbox into the dirty dishes, picked another chair up by the seat and jammed it, legs first, into the sink. Kicked the cupboard doors in, booted the back of the toilet until it cracked and gave and exploded across the floor in one cold wave of rusty sludge water. No pills in the cabinet. Shiner too slick for that. Johnny'd already been more quietly through the place lookin for Shiner's stash. Nothing. Not so much as a rum bottle under the sink. He ripped the cabinet off the wall and slammed it into the bathtub.

The funeral blurs in Johnny's head. Cant remember what was said about her, cant remember what the priest had to say. Some people nodded at him. Wasnt hardly no one there anyhow. McFlabberguts in the corner bawlin her eyes out and lookin around every once in a while to see if anyone was payin attention to her. Johnny drooped at a table with a tray of sandwiches and eating every last one of them and then out heaving the works up in the grass off Gear Street. A bottle belonging to someone snatched out of Johnny's hand before he even had it to his mouth. A hard shoulder to the back and Johnny is on the pavement in Caul's parking lot. A good crisp dart to the small of his back and someone muttering something about Johnny not showing his face at the club and something else about his time coming around. Walkin down Barter's onto Cabot and hearing Shiner roaring laughing in someone's backyard. The smell of roasting hamburger. Cops shaking him down somewhere on Duckworth Street and pretending they didnt know who he was. A seat at Ches's and reaching into his pocket to pay for his feed and coming up a dollar short, thinkin he was three hundred bucks ahead the whole while. Lookin out the window at the cops crawling up Freshwater Road. Johnny knockin on the window at the cops after they were gone and some young family gettin up to change seats and the waitress asking him to please go home. Johnny falling into her shoulder and asking for one kiss, one kiss. *Just let me smell your hair.* Asking for a cigarette outside the Peter Easton and some battered granny spitting at him from between the gap in her teeth. Having some kind of slurred talk with his next-door neighbour, the one with his shit together, taking out the garbage, that fella. Johnny stuttering and blubbering, sayin how sorry he was for getting on with all that shit, how he never meant it, how his girlfriend died, and have you got anything to drink? All the while the ceramic urn under his arm, and then suddenly the big twenty-two-ounce framing hammer in the other hand, pounding down on Shiner's doorknob until it fell to the porch floor, shouldering the heavy door in.

Now here at Shiner's table, pretty much the only piece of furniture in the house left in one piece. Holes everywhere, in all the walls. Every one of Shiner's tacky mall shirts and three leather jackets slashed to ribbons with a utility knife. A pair of men's one-piece woollen long underwear, Stanfield's, still in the package. Might come in handy Johnny? Shiner's stereo bashed into a thousand and six pieces in the corner, stomped into the floor and finished off with the hammer. Digging the claw of the hammer into Shiner's four-foot speakers, ripping at the fabric and thinkin about Shiner's throat.

Shiner killed Madonna. He killed Madonna. *Killed.*

Not much longer now, before someone shows up to find out what all the racket is about. No one's gonna call the cops, that's one thing for sure. But someone's sooner or later gonna come lookin. And think our John-John's gonna budge? *Go get Shiner, go tell him what I'm after doing. Tell him I'm waiting here for him.* And then, and then . . . well they'll be scraping Shiner off what's left of the walls and it'll be Johnny on the steps of the shop down the road, covered in blood and skull bits with a half case of beer at his feet, waiting for the fuzz to take him away for good. What difference now, hey Johnny?

Only a matter of time before Johnny goes down for that robbery. Cant even hardly remember the details no more. God knows who he ran his mouth off about it to. What fucken difference does any of it make now?

Johnny fixes his tie, Pius's ancient brown silk tie, and waits. Nothing but his own breathing. Water dripping in the bathroom behind him. Big diesel passing on the street below. Gurgled groan when the fridge tries to cut in. Johnny waiting there, knuckles white around the hammer handle, thinkin about what song he'd like to have playing for when Shiner comes home. Something hardcore, some old Metallica. *Kill 'Em All.* Or maybe not, maybe something nice and light and feel-good, some old twangy Hank Williams tune. Pius's Saturday night go-to. *Why dont you love me like you used to do?* The perfect murder song. Shiner dead and dead before the fiddler scrapes out the final note.

Johnny waits. Waits, pushing voices out of his head. Pushing reason away. Pius's gloating, constipated hate face. Tanya's jowls flappin in Johnny's head sayin: *Johnny wait, Johnny wait. It's not gone too far. So you smashed his place up, so what? It's not murder at least, not yet. It's not murder. You can take off. Go on and hide out for a bit. Shiner's just a friggin drug dealer, a pimp. No one got nothing on our John-John. It's not murder, not yet. Youre a free man. Someone somewhere musta been watchin over you for some reason. Certainly not to go mashing someone's brains out with a hammer?*

And then Johnny's on his feet, demolishing the face of the table with the hammer, screamin *Shut up! Shut up! Shut the fuck fuck fuck up!!!* And from the bottom of the stairs he hears a woman's voice, a real woman, a real voice, sayin *Hello??? Is someone there? Hello?*

Johnny takes the stairs like a bull moose, but then stops halfways down when he sees in the porch at the bottom a fulsome older missus in a business kinda suit, with gold earrings dangling and some sorta silky floral scarf around her neck. She backs out onto the street when Johnny approaches. The lingering perfume in the porch enough to gag on. Johnny looks down at his hand and sees no hammer. Madonna's ashes in his other hand. Package of long underwear tucked under his arm. Johnny hovers in the doorway about to tell the old gal to go fuck herself when she thrusts a thick white envelope into his hand and says: *Now, this is more than what he owes you, our Rodney. Now please leave him alone. Leave us alone. I dont care who you are or what youre all about. My husband knows people. So you leave Rodney alone.* And she spits at Johnny's feet then and darts back across the street to heft herself into the passenger seat of a spanking-new F250, her sour-faced husband waiting at the wheel with the engine running. She shoots Johnny the middle finger and the truck tears on up Cabot and Johnny is left flipping through a stack of twenties the likes of which he aint laid eyes on in too long, too long. Easily a thousand, at a glance. Young Rodney's mother paying off his dope tab! Must be nice.

Johnny's mind starts a-swirling. Right across the fucken country. *Me and Madonna.* Right to that beach she always seemed so smitten with. Toss her into the wind, hey Johnny, out there on that beach she was always on about, what was the name of it? Something religious? Jeremiah? Maybe track down this sister Dana. Danielle? Go Johnny. Go now. Go. Right across the country. Run to a cab stand and get out on the TCH and bloody well vanish.

Me and Madonna on the road, disappearing.

Johnny stands in the street, gawks up at a crow on the pole on the other side. Puts Johnny in mind of old Wally B's school bus, down by the slipway. The crow laughs and sniggers down at him and some distant part of Johnny's head toys with the notion that the crow sees more than Johnny's gangly form, more than the look on his face, more than the clothes on his back. The crow sees . . . the crow sees . . . Johnny shivers in the drizzle, looks left and then right, checks for bodies on foot or familiar cars coming down Lime Street, then darts onto Cabot towards Goodview.

How the tables have turned, hey Johnny?

Have to risk passing the backside of the housing units.

As he cuts the corner he runs face first into Shiner's girl, little Susie. She almost falls down over the steps, and when Johnny reaches out to steady her he drops the envelope and the twenties fan out the mouth of it and he sees the look in little Susie's eyes at the sight of the money when he's scooping it back up. He shoulders himself around her and as an afterthought, as he passes, he slips her a couple of twenties from the stack and nods gravely, conspiratorially, pleadingly, even though he knows that she's well armed now, with information that she cannot wait to spew into Shiner's lap.

And then he's gone.

What's this, four hundred kilometres or thereabouts? None too shabby, Johnny. Still, gotta get in off the road again soon before you catches your death. Soaked to the bone now, eyeing this four-door Dodge outside the Gander Hotel. Nothing to it Johnny, nothing to it. Start one of them with a fucken Popsicle stick. Cold, mucky fall day spluttering out ahead of him. Calling for flurries later on tonight. Best be in off the road then. Big-rigs thundering past. Compact families with wipers flapping, gawking through blurry windshields, the long spider-web glow of headlights, and then them cunt taillights.

Johnny in a suit with a fucken urn tucked under his arm! Not that they'd know.

First ride was the best, right to Clarenville. Passing by Whitbourne Junction and Johnny spies the battered old Whitbourne Youth Correctional Facility sign and it all comes rushing back. Johnny felt like tellin the driver to pull over so's he could burn the place to the ground, but he kept quiet instead. A full year in that hellhole when he was fifteen. Turned sixteen inside. Theft-over-five, that time. And that cunty-eyed screw, McGregor, with his sickly, pedo eyes following Johnny down the corridor, and Johnny decking him that night outside the observation room after McGregor had the fucken gall to go and say what he said, about Pius and Tanya, and some guy name Puddester.

* * *

Pork chop dinner at the Irving Big Stop in Clarenville, not bad, not bad. Cant beat Caines down on the east end of Duckworth though, no by fuck. Big shit in the can, then a tidy ride as far as Glovertown with some stuttering wombat from the Northern Peninsula, some bookish type who saw Johnny eating at the restaurant. Years of speech therapy never done much help. Johnny barely could understand a fucken word, robbed a pair of cotton gloves out of the side pocket in the door. A story on the radio about a fella that chopped off some dolly's head in Corner Brook twenty years back, and now's up for parole. The wombat says *L-l-l-let him r-r-rot.* Johnny gets thinkin about his *real* old man, rotting away in the clink for something he never done. Thinkin on things that happened ten years ago, twenty years ago. Things dead and buried in the ground and still hopping mad alive. The blast from a thirty-ought-six. Cousin Mikey. *Fuck.*

An hour on the side of the road in Glovertown with the drizzle eating through Johnny's stinking long underwear. The beige suit gone a chocolate brown and his hair pasted to his forehead in thick black strands. From there to Gander with some old salt-and-pepper couple who thought Johnny was a fella they knew and so took pity and broke their golden rule about picking up rapists and murderers. The old fella driving, a wiry mess of grey and black hairs sprouting out of his ears. Taking grooming tips from Pius by the looks of it. Johnny let the old couple go on calling him William for the first five minutes, asking questions about his Uncle Dessy in Calgary.

Is he still driving trucks? Is he still with that same woman?

Johnny with his yes and no answers until the old fella driving finally gave a good look in the rear-view. An awkward moment or two, then mostly a quiet ride. The old girl never knew the difference first nor last.

That's near on two hours ago now, and here's Johnny stuck out like a sore thumb on the side of the highway in jeezly old *Gander*, and wanting to be moving on. Too many eyes. Too many fucken baby-boomer gawkers. Next thing the pigs are gonna be swingin by lookin for some ID. RCMP too, out this way. Whole different kinda bastard. Not that Johnny's got nothing to worry about. There's the record, yes, but nothing outstanding, no conditions no more. Nothing no one can say. Travelling. *Here's my dead girlfriend's ashes, right here. Yes sir officer, gonna scatter em into that other ocean, on the other side. Minding me own business, grieving along. Cant get far enough gone. Now, if you'll excuse me, officer.*

Johnny watches the steady onslaught of Sunday afternoon coffee junkies gushing in and out of Tim Hortons. The drive-in cars lined up all the way into the hotel parking lot across the way like some nullified serpent. Two girls tucked in under the one umbrella, wolfing back a smoke. A man with a small boy on his shoulders and the boy cracks his head off the doorframe on the way inside. Johnny watches through the front windows at the boy screeching and the gangly man, the boy's father or uncle or something, tryna quiet him down with a five-dollar bill.

Some dolled-up skirt jumps out of a brand-new Toyota Tacoma, a black one with chrome bumpers, tinted windows. She clicks inside and leaves the motor running. Make short work of that truck, Johnny would. Enough gas money to get him across the rest of the way. Speed limit. Dump her outside Port aux Basques, maybe set a fucken match to her. Dont tell Johnny about burning cars, dont bother.

Fifteen years old. Pius and his wife, or Johnny's mother and father back then, gone out to some banquet, down to the Legion for a dance and a drunk. Pius with a brand-new Cavalier in the driveway. First ever new car he owned. Only ever used her for going into town. Takes the truck when he's having a drink. Sister Tanya off whoring somewhere. Johnny sitting there, sitting there, watchin *NYPD Blue* and wishing someone'd crack Jimmy Smits's face open with a maul. Spare keys to the Cavalier in the big glass bowl on the table, buried under light bills and last year's birthday cards, hair elastics, nail clippers. Johnny on the phone then, with that saucy little Rhonda from Fermeuse.

Did you really kill all those hens Johnny?

Is it true you found Mikey?

Johnny tellin her no to the hens question, ignoring the other. Tells her what short work he'd make of her if she came down the Shore. Rhonda giggling, sayin she's never seen one before. Johnny says come on down the Shore girl, come on down if you wants to see it. No. No. She's not allowed out of the harbour on a Sunday night. If Johnny wants to see her he's got to come up her way. But her folks are gonna be home in an hour. The big glass bowl on the table. Johnny's cock out, throbbing pain in his balls, tryna get her to talk dirty when she dont know how.

Come on up Johnny Keough. Are you scared Johnny? I think youre scared.

The fuck I am.

And then Johnny's behind the wheel of Pius's car racing like a fiend towards Fermeuse with his lad still out. Two feet for the pedals—one for the gas and one for the brake, his knees like rubber. He pulls onto the side of the road in Ferryland to haul on his seatbelt cause he does not wanna die before he's got Rhonda's nipples in his mouth, and when he pulls out again he knows nothing about rear-view mirrors or what's coming behind, his mind clouded and fevered with the possibility of that hot wet slit between Rhonda's legs, and there's the screech of tires and headlights blasting across the dash and Johnny's burning up the road again with some fuckhead tryna rape him in the bumper and flashing his headlights and blowing his thin girly horn. But Johnny drives on and on, putting more and more distance between himself and Fuckhead and no thoughts of moose along the black roadside. Skid Row's *Slave to the Grind* jammed into the Cavalier's top-notch tape deck, the sparks flying from his cigarette. Johnny catching on, somewhere outside Aquaforte, that he only needs to use one foot now, one foot. And poor sweet Rhonda when he gets there. And the less time he's got before her folks are due home then the better and the worse she's gonna get it. If that's what's on the table? Please Christ she wants what Johnny hopes she wants, what she's more or less came right out and said she wants. I mean, if a fella says he's got his cock in his hand and she says well come on up the Shore and show it to me, that kinda sets the bar right there, dont it? A fella can reasonably expect some sort of action, no?

Outside Fermeuse and just when Johnny spies the lights of the snack bar next to where Rhonda said her house is, he swerves too late to avoid a toppled road sign and there comes a booming, clunking, murderous crunch under the car, and one of Johnny's headlights is gone and there's the sudden fragrance of gas from the back seat and Johnny's nerves are just about shattered in bits but he's afraid to slow down because Fuckhead seems to be picking up speed again. Johnny burns past Reddy's Pub doing about ninety and then hauls off by the old bridge and tucks himself in behind the big rock where Mikey had himself a bit of a meltdown during a school dance the year before. Out in the parking lot punching himself in the head, swinging at everybody, screaming vile shit at this quiet girl from Town, someone's cousin, who'd been dancing with him all night. Snapped, Mikey did. Right outta nowhere. Johnny had to give him a few taps that night, to set him straight. Dragged him off before the cops showed up. Mikey muttering nonsense the whole way down the Shore.

Johnny, with the Cavalier tucked in behind the rock now, sits and watches Fuckhead blow past the bridge and latch on to the taillights of another rig that's pulled out of the gas station. Johnny sits and waits, waits, tang of gas stronger now, beautiful fumes swooning in his head, that folding echo growling in his brain. He rests his shrunken head on the steering wheel. And then Johnny's at Rhonda's door, pounding on the screen like a lunatic and the fresh air almost making him heave and she's sayin he cant come in, he cant come in, that her folks are coming any second and Johnny starts to undo his belt and she squeals and slams the storm door and Johnny hears giggles and laughter from her girlfriends inside and when he turns around Pius's Cavalier is parked askew, still running, in Rhonda's driveway and the cab is full of thick grey-white smoke that's leaking and curling, wisping in cartoon spectacle up through the edges of the doors. And then a green flame licking up the back seats and Johnny staring, staring, waiting for the boom, his hand around his cock and the raw, sickly gas-huffer's loose-tooth muscle cramps, the burning whore-sludge in his sinuses, and he's lurching across the shiny black asphalt of Rhonda's driveway with the girls howling in the background. Scrambling through some icy river of slime up to his knees, up to his waist, and clawing his way up a bank of alders behind the church with the desolate screech of a fire engine moaning down from the heavens.

No clue how it burned. No explanation to this day. Maybe a stray spark from a cigarette wound up on the floor in the back when Johnny thought he was tossing it out the window. Maybe wiring got ripped loose when he hit that road sign. Maybe Johnny stood in Rhonda's driveway and tossed a lit match onto the back seat. Just for shits and giggles.

No explanation.

In any event, Pius's precious Cavalier, his baby, up in fucken flames.

Johnny made it back down the Shore somehow that night, smoking hash in the back seat of a Camaro with some lads from Witless Bay. Holed up by hisself in Big Tony's drafty old hunting cabin for three nights, listening to *Sex with Sue* on a windup radio and sleeping with a hatchet in the bunk, the funnels on the stove too fucked up for a good fire. Shivering and shaking in the bunk and eating Cup-a-Soup straight from the package. Talkin out loud to Mikey. Going to the door and shouting his name into the night woods. Mikey dead and buried not six weeks even. Johnny sobbing himself to sleep. *Where are you man? Where did you go? Where the fuck are you?* And then waking up around midnight on the third night to Big Tony, with a full-faced helmet on, tellin young Johnny to get the fuck up and come on, that the cops were after sending him in. And Johnny so fed up with the hunger and the cold and the freaked-out noises in the woods, and wanting to be back in the land of cigarettes so bad that he just got on the back of Big Tony's trike and went on out to face up. Fuck. The racket waiting at the house. Pius, God love the wily old fuck, way too sly to lay a hand on Johnny this time.

There, anyhow, dont tell Johnny about burning cars, no by Christ.

Johnny's kicked back in the passenger seat of a cushy eighteen-wheeler, a dusty black Kenworth. Somewhere past Grand Falls and the hopped-up hippie named Saul in the driver's seat with his greyed-out mutton chops is droning on about some *puckbunny* called Sass that he knows who works a Comfort Inn near the US border and who better be waiting for him come Tuesday night. Old Saul hammers his fist into his thigh every time he says the name Sass and the heat is blasting so vicious Johnny's nose is feeling like it might bleed. But his suit is good and dry now and it's coming on seven o'clock. Saul thinks they'll make the one o'clock ferry in Port aux Basques, and when he says this he upshifts and gives a roaring shot of gas and Johnny entertains no misgivings about making the one o'clock ferry.

The heat in his face, his hand wrapped tight around the wad of bills in his pants pocket. Madonna's ashes tucked up against his balls. *She'd be mortified.* Saul flips on the radio for the evening news. Johnny's chin is just about rested on his chest, puddle of drool collecting behind his bottom teeth, when he hears the broadcaster spew something about the police lookin for a John Joseph Keough, only the bastard pronounces it *Ke*ough, instead of the right way. They say Mr *Ke*ough is wanted in connection with an armed robbery on Queen's Road. No mention of the other thing, how he pulled that old couple outta that flaming inferno. That's old fucken news, hey Johnny. Still and all, they give a pretty goddamn accurate description, of the suit Johnny's wearing, his height and his looks, the teardrop tattoos. *It's believed Mr Keough is in the St John's area.* This is the only part that brings a smile to Johnny's face; old Shiner ripping up every flophouse in town tryna get to Johnny before the cops do. Saul glances across the cab at Johnny smiling like that, and gives him the once-over. Too much of a fucken coincidence, fella in a beige suit, Johnny's height, with the teardrops tattooed on his face, out on the highway like a stray cat. Johnny knows Saul knows.

Shit man, says Saul, they nailed you didnt they?

Johnny, in his state, thinks first to feign ignorance, but what with the heater blastin in his face and the burning blistered feet on fire, and that pork chop dinner burbling nasty in his guts, he just dont have the energy to lie to old Saul. Johnny eyes the rusty, oversized tire iron on the hump between the two seats and thinks, hey, if it comes down to it . . . if it comes down to it. And he pictures himself in Saul's seat, the captain's chair, plowing through the sidewall of the Kingston Pen in a flurry of barbed wire and bullets and blowing the horn for Stevie, his old man, Stevie the Scar. Cause you cant just let an innocent man r-r-rot away like that?

Johnny eyes Saul coldly until Saul tosses his head back, for a laugh, and dips into a little pouch attached to the front of his seat. Johnny eyes the tire iron. No way to use it without putting the big-rig into the ditch, at this speed. Johnny watches Saul's hand grip and pull and slide a twenty-six-ounce bottle of Beefeater into his lap. Saul takes a big slug and then passes the bottle to Johnny. And sometimes, hey Johnny, sometimes you just gotta take a risk on some folks. Sometimes the good guys are in disguise and you cant very well go about with no faith in no one, none of the time. Johnny drains about four ounces of gin.

I guess they did, Johnny says, I guess they fucken did.

Well, you can always change your outfit somewhere along the way, but I dont know what youre gonna do about them teardrops . . .

Not much I can do. Burn em off. Not like I flaunts em.

Yeah, still though, it aint in your favour . . .

The bottle slips back and forth from Johnny to Saul, thirsty slugs. Silence, the wide road unfurling in the dark.

Well, I pulled my fair share of smash-and-grabs when I was a pup, 'fore I got myself into the long-haulin. So long's you never hurt nobody.

I never hurt nobody, says Johnny, and he has a tight flash of the cop with a towel held to the head of that big blonde from the shop on Queen's Road.

Not no one who never asked for it anyhow.

Well, says Saul, it can get pretty messy out here on the road sometimes too. I aint none to judge. So you relax young feller, you relax . . .

Johnny feels the gin do that nauseous churning devil's dance as it passes his stomach and scurries on into his parched veins, down to his smouldering shins and feet, waits for it to hit his battered brain, only to realize it likely hit there before he even had the bottle to his lips.

Saul starts in again with some story of an old-time trucker that helped him across a weigh-in scales outside Saskatoon years back. Saul says how he was nearly three thousand pounds overloaded, and the old-timer told Saul to follow up behind, and when the old-timer pulled onto the scales he hits his kill switch and makes the truck stall out. Made like he couldnt get his rig started for love nor money, until the guy at the desk came out, all pissed off, and waved everybody else around. Saul says this was back when you could take another trucker on his word alone, but how it's dirtier out there these days, lots dirtier. Johnny nods and listens in the dark of the cab, the mute squelch of Saul's two-way and the first of the night's predicted flurries clinging like ash to the corners of the windshield. He strokes the urn between his legs. *Madonna in there, in a ceramic bottle between my legs, incinerated.*

A gas station. The parking lot thick with a fluffy layer of snow. Johnny's neck is stabbing stiff from having it slumped against the window. A notice taped to the pumps about how gasoline theft affects us all. Fuck off. A sign at the edge of the parking lot pointing towards Stephenville. Johnny thinks, from any maps he's seen, that Port aux Basques cant be too far down the road. Saul on a pay phone near the doors to the station. Johnny thinks he might have to bolt, his hand on the handle, then he sees Saul throw his head back and laugh, so he knows it's not the fuzz he's on to.

Some crazed young bayman in a bright orange floater suit bounces up out of the ditch on a red quad and burns across the road into the parking lot, nearly slamming head first into a passing pickup. The pickup driver toots his horn nice and friendly like and the young feller on the quad winks back at the pickup driver and simultaneously does that reverse grinning chin-wag thing like youd see the old men outside the fish plant do when you were a young scrap. The feller on the quad tilts the handle bars and his body to the left and hits the gas until the bike is spinning like a top up on one wheel in a fuming powdered flurry of snow and gravel. The pickup starts blowing its horn and someone somewhere starts whooping encouragement as the quad spins faster and faster until it and the driver are just a red-and-orange blurry little tornado that lifts off the parking lot and floats on out over the black treeline, vanishing into the storm. Something, that. Christ. What you wont lay eyes on.

Johnny hears himself mumble something when Saul climbs aboard. The sound of Saul laughing, like that giant, that wrestler in that movie where they were lookin for somebody with six fingers. *No my son there's no tornadoes around these parts.* The big door clicking shut, the sound vague and outlying like the snap of branches in the woods at night, far off, ricocheting over the tops of the trees, away out there in the darkness.

Johnny raises his head for a moment, then nods off again. Rumble of the rig vibrating up through his toasty toes. The faint growl of some waiting hungry creature. A brittle laugh on the wind and the grinning face of Johnny's old friend Mikey, Cousin Mikey, flickers and dances briefly across his mind.

Dime-sized black hole in Mikey's throat.

Fish flies.

The gravel black with blood.

Look I'm fucken sorry, man. How could . . . ?

Johnny tries to push it away, reaches out for the image of this nurse in a smutty book that got passed around down at HMP. The nurse is leant at her desk lookin over a clipboard, bursting out of her tight white skirt. The edge of her nipples heaving out of her low-cut blouse. Heels and white fishnet stockings. There's a knock on the door. She looks up and sees Cousin Mikey floating towards her holding a chunk of his own skull in his hands. FUCK! No, no, no. Come on Johnny. Let it lie. Leave it alone. The snapping echo of a thirty-ought-six rolling down across Gorman's Hill. Pius sayin how someone musta got their moose. Fuck off Johnny, shut up now. No one wants the juice Johnny. No one wants the real meat. Keep it nice and light and easy with your bleeding-heart shit about gettin pussy-whipped and thinkin it was fucken love. Where's that nurse gone? Where did she go? Who wants to think about brains and blood and bits of skull and hair splattered halfways across that gravel pit? The nurse Johnny, the nurse, I believe she was reading over your chart . . .

Johnny climbs down out of the bunk behind the seats in Saul's rig. Saul's not in the driver's seat, and the only view is what looks to be the back end of another trailer. It's cold, Johnny's breath little explosive wheezes of blue-grey. The thunder and grumble of a far superior engine pulsing through the rig's cabin, rattling the little beaded dream catcher dangling from Saul's rear-view. A net to catch your dreams in. Johnny cant help but wonder how long it's been since he was on a swing set, at a playground, doing *that*. Did them days ever actually take place? Fuck it all. The truck dips in a drawn-out list to the left and Johnny staggers gently towards the driver's side. This must be the ferry.

There was a commotion, that's what sent Johnny back to the bunk. They were parked in the lineup outside the ferry terminal and suddenly there they were, the fuzz. Johnny scrambled into the back and buried himself in Saul's bunk, hauled a greasy duffle bag up in front of his face and went about settling his heart down. Routine check, what have you got on board and what kinda load are you lugging tonight and what's your destination and can I see your papers and is there any alcohol on board? Flashlight beaming across the dashboard, lingering on the passenger seat where Johnny was planked not ten seconds before. Johnny so dead tired, peeking out through the crack in the curtains at the outline of the cop, the tip of his RCMP cap barely rising above Saul's foot. Nice boot in the face, if it was Johnny in the driver's seat. Cop handing Saul back his papers, making like he was finished up and then, almost as an afterthought, asking Saul did he pass anybody hitchhiking or did anyone approach him for a ride anywhere? And then the moment of truth hovering in the air and Saul shaking his head in a nice laid-back way, no way of knowing how tight the grip Johnny had on the neck of the old-fashioned Coke bottle he pulled out of Saul's duffle bag. Johnny figuring, well, if it comes down to it I'll have to bag me a hostage, sort it all out as we goes along. What difference?

A thick, dry heat with a faint bilge stink sets Johnny's stomach churning as he makes his way up the yellow iron steps leading to Deck 7 where the signs say there should be a restaurant and gift shop and the like. Johnny cant remember ever setting foot aboard anything bigger than a trap skiff his whole life and here this boat claims to have a fucken movie theatre on board! Jesus. He stumbles out into a right clusterfuck of strung-out travelling families and screamin youngsters and burly truckers and old fucks with white hats and big oversized sunglasses seated around squat bolted-down tables sharing sandwiches and sipping Pepsi from straws gawking out at the windows into the black night and pointing at Christ knows what. The eyes on Johnny when he stumbles past.

He has a look around for old Saul but no dice. Johnny sees another sign and figures it's for the bar and so straightens his tie and tucks in his shirt and smoothens his trousers and feels the wad of bills in his coat pocket. Free man, Newfoundland somewhere out there far across the water behind him. There's fiddle music a-blastin from a big-ass set of speakers. The place is only half full. Saul is there, leant up against the far corner of the bar making the grand big gestures at this young barmaid. Like he's tellin this elaborate story. He shouts something towards the ceiling that Johnny cant make out and the barmaid laughs and blushes a bit and looks around like she's afraid to be caught laughing. Johnny starts to walk over and join Saul but decides against it. Dont wanna go gettin drunk and running his mouth up and shagging up his ride off the boat. Johnny nods to the barman and orders up a double shot of rye. He asks for a certain kind, but no dice, no dice. Just as well. He spins on his heels, sippin his drink and feeling like the Man, feeling like a free man at last. Without looking in Saul's direction, he scours the bar, hoping to latch on to any sweet gals who might be looking for trouble, or not. Cant write em off just cause they're *not* out looking for trouble, hey Johnny. They're the ones turns out to be the most trouble anyhow, the ones who aint out looking for it. Mostly because of the added details to the game you gotta play. Good girls. Underneath though, Johnny knows he's got the edge on the lot of em, cause they're all, underneath it all, looking for a fella like Johnny every once in a while. They likes that false bottom notion that they can always say they were tricked into it when it all goes south. Cause it always goes south, that's one rule. *He seemed so sweet.* Yeah yeah, he seemed so sweet when he was tellin me how he'd as soon crawl under the table right here and now and suck my lungs out through my pussy. He seemed so sweet. *God, what came over me? I never do anything like that.* No, never, hey Johnny. Dont try and say you dont know what a fella like Johnny got on his mind, little mama. What do any of us got on our minds ninety percent of the time for fuck sakes? The house the car the job the new policy the drinks the drugs the money the face in the paper the music the new gadget the clothes—you name it and it all comes down to the prospect of a decent fuck. Or somebody's idea of a good fuck. Or the satisfaction in the notion that someone wants to fuck you. No need to go pointing no fingers at our Johnny just cause he's got a handle on what's behind the smokescreen. Good girls and bad, no big difference. Take Madonna, hey Johnny . . . Johnny suddenly looks down to the hand that's not holding the drink and realizes the urn is not in it. He bolts from the bar and back out through the doors and down the stairs the way he came. He shoulders open the heavy iron door leading out to the car deck and almost flattens a young couple carrying a scrap of a dog, little black-and-white wiry thing, in some sort of bag with air holes. The *man* of the two looks about to say something in defence of his dolly and beast but then gets a good look at Johnny's face, maybe sees the scars and the teardrops and decides against it. Johnny is out running mad down towards the back of the deck in between cars and SUVs and pickups and minivans, but no sign of Saul's truck, no sign of any big-rigs atall. He darts back to the stairway and down another greasy flight of steps and out onto the deck below, but again there's no big-rigs in sight. He spins and screams a torrent of bloody oaths in the thick diesel air and then there's a worker in an orange vest with his hand on Johnny's shoulder tellin Johnny that passengers are not allowed to return to their vehicles! And Johnny squaring off with him, tryna convey, trying to fucken . . . impart, to make this *motherfucker* understand that Madonna is . . . that her ashes are . . . *Fuck*, Johnny wails. *Fuck*. Two more fellas in orange vests poke their heads out through another chunky steel doorway and Johnny realizes he's got no ticket and no ID or nothing and there's a warrant and it prolly wouldnt be such a smart move to burn the fucken boat to the gunnels. Best he can do is sigh and shrug in mock-defeat before disappearing back up the stairs into the stale chaos, determined to keep a low profile and track down old Saul and stay close to his good side and wait this one out.

Roadblock on the outskirts of Truro. Johnny with a Molson Canadian cap pulled down to shadow the teardrops as best can be. Baby-faced RCMP with his shit-brown middling eyes skimming through Saul's papers and asking Johnny his name and Johnny casually offering the first words that comes to his head: *Mikey. Mikey Puddester. This morning. Yes officer. Meetin my brother in Halifax. Work lined up in Fort Mac. All my papers are gone ahead with me brother's girlfriend. I ahhh . . . I got drunk on the boat and they sorta dumped me.* Details Johnny, details. Toss in that little confessional tone, make yourself look stupid, make the fucker feel superior. Baby-face holding his gaze on Johnny with those dead churched-out eyes. Johnny smiling back, neutral, blameless, hands on his lap, not a twitch, not a sniffle, delivering every word to the cop's eyebrows, feeling the teardrops on his own cheeks practically glowing.

Big-rig rumbling on down the highway and Saul sayin how in five years he aint been pulled over and now twice since he picked Johnny up. And the implications of such happenstance thick and rigid in the air between the two and Johnny suddenly surly and allowing that he'd as soon jump ship if his presence is a hindrance. Saul shrugging, humming through the morning's anxiety and looking to diffuse the tension with the last of the bottle of Beefeater. Johnny with the urn back tucked safely between his thighs as he drains the final three ounces of gin, brazenly handing the empty bottle back to Saul.

Well I'm headed down towards Saint John in a bit. The road forks off. Gotta cross into the States, so . . .

Johnny bats drowsily at the beaded dream catcher strung from Saul's redundant rear-view, hums a dreary melody that's been spiralling through his head for years and years and years.

Birch. Maple. Ash, maybe. Trees Johnny dont know the names of. An endless ocean of blood and fire the likes of which he's never laid eyes on. Cause where's Johnny been? Almost as far west as Clarenville that time. No farther. Until now.

Rickety truck stops and greying family diners, rust-streaked gas pumps and ramshackle vegetable stalls and crumbling miniature golf courses, deserted campgrounds and boarded-up information booths and desolate little wooden churches. A brilliant white billboard screamin for miles in six-foot black lettering: *John 15:23.* Johnny with his head slumped against the foggy window, hears Saul announce theatrically:

He who hates me hates my Father also.

What?

That's what the sign says. New Testament. I looked it up last year.

Johnny's poisoned now, fed up, resentful, wanting to cut loose on his own, struggling to suppress something in him that wants to fucken . . . smash everything. He looks across at Saul, who's supping one of them meal-replacement drinks that smells to Johnny like meat-flavoured milkshake.

Dont tell me youre one of them fucken God freaks are ya?

What? No, no. I was just curious. I pass by it so often that . . .

Cause I aint got no time for fuckers like that, man.

Saul thieves a timid glance across at our Johnny, as if he's only now considering the real risk of Johnny's capacity for chaos and carnage. But what's to be said now, clipping through the Maritimes doing a hundred twenty? You knew Johnny for an armed robber not five minutes after you picked him up.

Seen me fair share of fuckers like that, says Johnny, God freaks spewing Jesus and forgiveness and turning the other cheek and all that shit. We had this *prick* come in and give us a talk one time, this big old fat fuck whose daughter was run down by a drunk driver or some such bullshit. This is me doing a five-month bit for possession of a prohibited weapon, ya know. I was what, twenty, twenty-one? Prohibited fucken weapon they said! Christ. Hardly two inches sawn off the tip and they calls it prohibited. Anyhow, we're all called into the multi-purpose room this day to hear this *prick* go on about how fucken full of, ya know, rage and hate and stuff he was for so many years. How this drunk ran down his daughter when she was on her way home from school, last day of grade five, skipping home with her report card, ya know. Gettin ready to go on the family vacation and shit. Buddy on his fourth drunk driving offence and got himself ten years for vehicular manslaughter. And he comes up for parole after five years anyhow, and this fella whose daughter it was, he kicked up the big fuss with the media and everything. Anyhow, there was some sorta meeting arranged between the two of em, him and the fella up for parole. By this time his wife is after packing her bags and he's after losing his job and all that cause where he's so consumed with hating this drunk driver and putting all his time into that MADD shit and letting the rest of his life fall apart. And he goes in to this meeting with the parole board and the drunk driver with the intent of spitting in buddy's face. He got this big statement drawn up about the state of his life and the insult to his daughter's life that this fella should walk early, ya know. But anyhow, he says he walks in and he sees the scrawny little fuck with these blasted-out eyes and they gets talkin. And buddy, the drunk driver, tries to say he's sorry but the little girl's father, big tubby fucker, he wont hear it. He starts firing these questions at the old drunk, about what he remembers and all that cause he figured where he was so drunk and all. Turns out the drunk fella remembered everything in the most minuscule detail, the kinda haircut the little girl had, whatever kinda cartoon thing was on her school bag, the colour of her lunch tin. Said every night he closes his eyes and every morning he wakes up, for five years, that's the last and the first face he sees, the little girl's. And I guess when the father saw that this drunk fella was just some guy, ya know, some guy who fucked up, however bad, well he said he let it all go. He forgave him, so goes the tale. Gave his consent for him to have an early parole. And they're even friends nowadays, if you can believe that. Anyhow, the father, he comes in and he tells this big dramatic story to all of us lads on a Sunday morning who are mostly just there for the free donuts, and next thing he's going on about God and penance and that, and how we're who we *are*, not what we *done*. Tryna say how us crowd, inmates, how we're all the same, dont matter what we done. And after a time we all realizes that he's tryna get us to take pity on the fucken skinners, is all he's at. Fucken diddlers. I looked at him and I asked him straight out, I said, *Are you tryna tell me that I'm no better, me in here on a prohibited weapons rap, that I'm no better than some pederass who sticks his tongue up little boy's holes? Is that what youre tryna say?* And he started to get a bit tongue-tied then I think cause he was used to talkin in the high schools and the church groups and shit. He tries to stay on course though, like he's got this spiel that he usually gets out because no one ever calls him on nothing, he goes on about how forgiveness of them that wronged you, even if they dont *want* to be forgiven, is the way to fucken Christ and all that slop! Can you imagine? *That's* the way for us all to overcome everything like addictions and self-destructive behaviour and what have ya. But I aint fucken listening to that shit, I says, *Hey, lookit here prick, youre here tellin us to share our smokes with the fucken skinners when half of us are after being diddled ourselves? Tellin us we'll stop using dope and shit and there you are and your legs can barely hold you up, half a fucken honey cruller jammed into the folds in your chin and bacon grease brimming up under your eyelids and you says all's forgiven? That youre healthy and happy and carried on? Bullshit,* I said. *Bull-fucken-*shit.

Saul gears down at the bottom of a long winding hill on the outskirts of a town called Fort Lawrence, rubs his eyes and checks his watch, glances nervously at this fresh menacing version of his passenger.

Sounds to me like he was trying to . . .

An eye for a fucken eye, that's what I said to him. Cause that's about as much religion and God as I can suffer, man. A tooth for a fucken tooth. *Look here,* I said, *if some fucker slaughtered my daughter or my son, or my little nephew or my cousin or brother or something, and you put me in a room with him to help weigh in on his fate? Fucken hell man, I'd weigh in alright. I'd suck his goddamn eyeballs out and fuck the sockets with the leg of a chair.* That's what I told him. Anyhow, what's the good of him to be going around and not gettin called on nothing he has to say, never met with a challenge? How's he gonna *learn* anything? Fuck that. Anyhow, he went home grumbling and nearly bawling and he musta said something to someone cause I got sent down to special handling for a week. Prick.

Gruff, dense silence in the cab for the next half hour and Johnny chain-smokes from Saul's package even though they both know Johnny's got a full pack in his jacket. At some point Saul makes to reconcile, asks Johnny if everything's okay. Johnny glowers across the cab at Saul, smiles forebodingly.

Is everything okay? Yes sir. Everything has never been better.

Just outside of Sackville. Saul needs to gas up. He pulls into an Irving and Johnny slips inside for a leak and a Coke and when he moseys back out to the parking lot Saul's rig is nowhere to be seen. Johnny whirls around in pending panic, smashes the Coke into an empty garbage bin, notes the coming roar bubbling in his guts, thick heady impotent outrage pulsing in his forehead, throws his claws into the air and raises his throat to the heavens . . . and then he sees it, the urn. Madonna. What's left. Abandoned perilously on the lip of the diesel pumps at the far end of the lot. Madonna, out here in a ceramic bottle in the Maritimes, scorched down to a litre of grit and ash and her only hope for a proper send-off hinging on the crazed impulses of the hot-blooded creature that is Johnny Keough.

Not a clue, not a clue how far he's come, how far he's yet to go. How big is it Johnny, out here? Dont know do ya?

This is Johnny, hours down the road, having hoofed the most of it except for a couple of lame-arsed rides. First one was with some fella coming back from visiting his father somewhere in Nova Scotia. Told Johnny all about how his father is nearly dead and all his brothers and sisters are gone to war over who's gonna get the money. He got a bit emotional and everything and Johnny was starting to feel a bit bad for him. Then he bucks up and gets ahold of himself and tries to do the small talk thing. He wants to know where Johnny is from, and when Johnny tells him he roars laughing and thinks it's great and right away says how he heard a wicked *Newfie* joke not long ago and starts tellin it to Johnny. As if Johnny looks like the type who's gonna laugh at a fucken Newfie joke. Johnny cuts him off though, wont let him tell the joke, but instead asks him if he heard the one about the fella who picked up a hitchhiker and got his face smashed in for tryna tell a Newfie joke.

Do you know that one? Stop me if youve heard it already.

That ride didnt last too fucken long.

Next one was with a deathly gaunt sales rep for a garden supply shop who would not shut the fuck up about a new attachment for trimming hedges that was gonna change everyone's lives overnight. Like he was tryna talk Johnny into running out and buying one or something. Likely chance of hookin a ride then, hey Johnny, on the side of the road revving up a hedge trimmer in Pius's old suit. Could hide it up your hole I spose. Imagine though Johnny, there's folks out there whose lives would change overnight if only they had the right kinda attachment to trim their bushes. That's the world we're livin in. Big wonder the jails and mental hospitals are bustin at the seams.

***

Could not let it slide, could ya fucker? Hadda go gettin all power-trippy and psycho with yon Saul after he pretty much saved your ingrate hide and got you off that sinking rock back there. Nothing to do with him. Old burnt-out hippie trucker who dont give a fuck for much else aside from some *puckbunny* named Sass. Some little thing, little twitch in the jawline, maybe when he rubbed salve into his hands, that showy biblical namesake, or them sickening menthols he was smoking, women's cigarettes, or the way he carried on with that barmaid on the ferry. Something, something struck a nerve with me, with our John-John, something as petty as all that. Something always does.

Hunkered on a guardrail outside a Best Western and Johnny's in mind of the last time he sat on a guardrail cursing the weather and done in for a ride. Made the papers that time. Not your name, but the deed, the deed, the great escape—*Resident Escapes Whitbourne Youth Correctional Facility.* Ha! Fucken *resident* they called me, the papers. Resident. End of March it musta been. This is the stint for theft over five thousand and arson, all that nonsense.

No choice, no choice Johnny me son. Insurance tells me if I wants to collect I'll have to press charges. I hates to do it, you knows now, I hates to do it. But I got to. Time enough you went somewhere to get a bit of help anyhow.

Pius, God love the big lumbering old prick, smirking over the delicious string of charges on Johnny. Sending his own flesh and blood off to the boys' home for the sake of collecting on his burnt-out Cavalier. Tanya bawling and wailing in the courtroom like one of them Italian funeral women when they carts Johnny away for a full fucken year. And not a word out of any of em except Tanya, who couldnt ever get a ride out the highway but sent lots of useless fucked-up letters about what was going on up on the hill or what happened the other morning down by the fish plant. No money though, no tobacco, not a measly visit, not even

Christmas. Fuck em Johnny. This was the little dilemma too, when he finally ruptured out of the woods and onto the highway that night with the sole busted out of his left sneaker and his hood shredded to ribbons, deep gash in his forearm from where he slipped in the pleading dark and landed with a full-bodied thud into a deserted bottle pit, this was his little dilemma then, to go east or west. But what was east? Home? Fuck that. Last place he'd be welcome, but where they'd expect him to run to, young and stupid, back to familiar turf. So he went west, towards fuck knows where. Sixteen-year-old Johnny couldnt think of a single town he knew the name of except Corner Brook, and he wasnt even sure if that was in Newfoundland or not. He got one ride, then dropped at the turnoff to Adeytown, middle of nowhere, next to an angry black pond and a sign that said *Clarenville 18 km.* And he sat on the guardrail and pondered the wound on his arm, coated with rusty dirt and slivers of green glass, and his feet were blazing cold and wet and the zipper of his hoodie was torn away so he huddled and shivered and waited, waited, almost jumped out into the road when the first beam of headlights came blinding round the turn. Young Johnny, not hitchhiking but dancing jumping jacks on the side of the road like he's crawled up from some wreck at the bottom of the pond beside him, desperate, desperate to put as many miles as possible between himself and that beige hellhole and that chunky McGregor fuck. Johnny jumps and shouts and dances and waves and the first car pulls over and stops a few yards ahead of him and as he's running to catch up a second car pulls in behind and before Johnny can even sort out what's happening he's making a scramble over the guardrail and tumbling arse over kettle down the gravel embankment and landing with a mute sludgy splash into the stinking bog below. He tries to push himself upright onto his feet but his freshly bleeding arm sinks to the shoulder in the muddy shit masquerading as the bottom of the pond. His head goes under and he tries to kick free, find a foothold, grab hold of something, anything, a soft memory, the icy water like black knives in his ears and eyes, and next it's McGregor's sneering pug face at the gates and the cops are driving into the gravel lot, McGregor shouting *You little bastard. You little bastard.*

Thinkin back, hey Johnny, think they mighta sent you to the hospital or something? No. Arm infected for weeks afterwards. Headaches, fevers. All the feeling gone in three of his toes. And McGregor then, sitting on the edge of his bunk while Johnny's lost in a blistering haze of sweat and terrible voices and wall sprites. McGregor gleefully tellin Johnny all he's heard about a man named Steve Puddester and another man named Pius Keough.

And this *sister* of yours, Johnny? This Tanya Keough? Well youre lucky youre lying down, that's all I have to say.

Black SUV pulls up outside one of the units at the Best Western and a sharp-dressed mama gets out, forties, trim and slim, long black hair, black coat and slacks, white collared blouse, high heels. Fucken hell. She keys open the door to her unit and strolls inside, confident, at ease. Comes out a minute later and unloads a suitcase and travel bag from the back of her rig, big forty of white wine tucked under her arm. Johnny watches all this, without lookin like he's watchin. He squeezes the wad of bills in his pants pockets and wonders on a room. Mind of the time himself and Madonna took a room up at the Greenwood in the Pearl for over a week and went fucken mad. Madonna. This was months into it, two of em coming off a dry spell. Johnny came and collected Madonna on the steps of the Health Sciences where she was chairing a goddamn Narcotics Anonymous meeting. Fuck sakes. Not like he twisted her arm though. There was just this look between them. An understanding. *Sharing.* One day at a time. Serenity now. Christ Almighty.

Let's get fucked up girl.

Youre bad Johnny Keough.

Couple of bottles of brandy, her favourite. Couple of bottles of vodka. A drop of Crown Royal of course. A dozen Black Horse, little bag of E, Xanax, them speedy little yellow pills, chunk of hash, enough rock to flatline an elephant, lots of codeine. Go big or stay the fuck home, hey Johnny? Johnny after playing getaway driver for the brothers, Darren and Pat Janes, after they lifted two ATM machines right off a downtown street that Sunday morning. Took the ATMs out to the White Hills and went at the fuckers for about an hour with mauls and pry bars and a blowtorch and finally Pat takes out this fucken massive industrial-strength grinder and cracks it open like a peanut shell. Forty-five hundred bucks, cut three ways. And nothing ever come of it. Wasnt in the news, not a word about it around town. Like they werent even missed, the ATMs. That's just twisted, what? Johnny took Madonna to the mall, decked her out with all that La Senza gear, makeup and the like, then off to the Greenwood. Not because it was the cheapest place on the go, but you gotta keep a low profile after pulling a job like that. Not going checking into some ritzy place downtown and have everybody wondering how you got so flush all of a sudden. Plus you cant get away with nothing in the fancy places. And everything has to be on a fucken card. But the Greenwood, you know, it's tucked away up there in the woods and you can jump into the pond naked and howl at the moon and smoke in bed and no one gives a fuck. By the end of it Johnny was shooting straight vodka up his arm and Madonna said she couldnt fuck anymore because she was too sore. She just couldnt handle Johnny's cock no more. And she was so serious, hey Johnny, and so beautiful beneath that red lampshade that Johnny thought he could search the world across and never lay eyes upon a worthy likeness, that he might as well marry her.

But I did not.

No. If we coulda just left it at that, left it all behind at the Greenwood and got back on the straight and narrow the way we'd been trying to live.

But we did not.

Then an evening not long after when she told Johnny she was going to an NA meeting and Johnny said he was going to an AA meeting and he met her walking down the stairs at Shiner's place with half the month's rent worth of rock in her hand.

Oh, are we gettin fucked up?

We *are* fucked up Johnny.

And they stayed that way, Johnny and Madonna, back and forth between the crack and the oxy, the good old cottonballs. Up and down. Flush and busted. Holding your breath behind the curtains while the landlord pounded on the front door. Vicious, screamin rackets. Sex was just sex. Two strangers fucking the DTs out of their systems. That's the way it went, the way it stayed. Until the teapot, that day. Until she just never woke up that morning, never made it to the courthouse. The doctors said she took a few too many Valium on top of the cottonballs, lay down on the couch and her heart just fucken quit. Never felt a thing. Never knew she was going. And who knows if that's better or worse, really.

That McGregor fuck, see here Johnny, sure he was only in his twenties back then. He was only a young feller, a pup, not much older than you are now. Funny when you thinks on it, the way you remembers folks towering over you like that and how they stays that way in your head. But that's hardly the case now is it? McGregor, he's likely a greyed-out pasty-faced obese bald-headed bag of nerves these days. Assuming he got more than one smack in the face over the years aside from the one Johnny gave him that night. That was some fucken crack Johnny gave McGregor. Top teeth rattling around in his gums, laid out on the floor of Johnny's cell with blood bubbling out of his nostrils. And Johnny coulda made a go for it then too, McGregor's gear all there, his keys and everything. But that smack was all the strength he had in him. Everything Johnny had in him—the insides of Mikey's head splattered halfways across the gravel pit, his new John Deere cap hanging from a branch in a big black spruce almost twenty feet away. All Johnny's whole life under Pius's roof and rules. Kicked around and turned out in the yard like a stray dog from the time he could walk. Never smiled at, never picked up into anyone's arms, never read to, never told he was nothing other than a fucken thief and a burden. And now here doing a stint for arson and theft-over-five after Pius pressed charges.

And then to find out that Pius's not even his fucken real father? All *that* went into that punch. Burnt him to the fucken ground, did young Johnny. McGregor was in the right place at the right time, for Johnny. Cause that's the only proper way to send the message, by taking out the messenger. And nothing ever come of that neither, hey Johnny, come to think on it. Nothing come of it. Johnny on his feet for the first time in a week after the big escape and all the lads treating him like a fucken god, that's all that come of it. Started calling him Steve McQueen, but Johnny didnt like that so they stopped. But this is the boys. The guards simply never mentioned nothing to him. Johnny kept waiting to get hauled out of his bunk in the middle of the night, or slapped with a dozen charges—assault, escaping custody, unlawfully at large—but nothing. McGregor took sick for about six weeks, and the week he was back on the job Johnny walked out the front gates, released to the rest of his fate.

Rain is picking up Johnny, drizzle's not good enough. And not a car excepting a string of million-dollar motorhomes twenty minutes back. What to do, this hour. Must be near on nine o'clock in the night now. Colder it's gettin too. Here's that missus again Johnny, standin in the open doorway of her room, big tumbler glass of white wine in her hand and some sort of novel or textbook tucked under her arm. She eyes Johnny up and down, the sight of him, hair stuck to his forehead, layer of drizzle shimmering on the shoulders of the suit. Johnny looks over, offers a nod, but that other kinda nod, the quick raise of the chin that's not sayin *Hello, hi, nice night, nice to see you*, but more or less the kinda nod that says *What the fuck are you lookin at? Have I got something on belong to you? Take a fucken picture.* And Johnny cant stand that he just done that, but it's done now and that's all's to it. Johnny Keough, ladies' man. This class dolly with the shiny black hair and skin-tight business suit, she glares back at Johnny, flicks her smoke out across the parking lot, shifts her book from under one arm to the other, then turns and purposely, however subtly, offers up a soft swing of the hips. Eases the door closed behind her without a sound.

Fucken hell Johnny, there was something in that.

Here you are Johnny, grown man. Aside from the fact of that niggling warrant youre free to roam too. Able-bodied. Add subtract multiply and divide. Read and write. All them battered HMP books, whatever you could get your hands on—*The Waste Land, Country Wisdom and Know-How, Peter Rabbit, Far from Shore, The Morality of Law, The Handmaid's Tale, The Outsiders, That Far Greater Bay, Shake Hands with the Devil, Addiction by Prescription, A Guide to New York City Restaurants, Do It Yourself Home Wiring, The Stranger beside Me, The Artist's Way, The Weekend Mechanic.* Fuck, Johnny read em all. That one about that burnt-out motherfucker in Alberta blowing up oil rigs. A whole bunch by that fella, bleak as fuck, from somewhere in New Brunswick, somewhere around these parts, with the big long titles where everyone always turns against this one family and someone ends up fucked around in the backwoods or wrongly accused or some such shit. And no one ever gets their revenge until years and years later when it dont matter no more. Books? Fucken hell, Johnny ripped through thousands. Anything you needs to know about proper chain tension, fucken vapour barriers, Lee Harvey Oswald, where to eat in Manhattan. All kinds of *knowledge* and info logged away in the old noggin, hey Johnny. Useless, the lot of it. None of it changes nothing. None of it mends nothing. You can scour every bookshelf on the planet and you wont come up with not one fucken phrase that changes where you comes from or what youve been up to, been through, who you fucken *are*. Blood is blood is blood. Youd think you could only contain so much in that soggy old brain of yours. Think after a time youd force all that other shit out. Or burn it off, what with all the chemicals and pharmaceuticals and booze and draws. But no, it all keeps bubbling back up, stuff that went on twenty-odd years ago, ten years, last fucken week. Old scars and open wounds. Everything always spinning in the head, bullying you to the brink of madness, stuff you cant do one fucken thing to change. It's still there, all of it, always. And wretched fucken woe to the weak, flimsy, brittle motherfucker who wants to take a hard look at it, sort it out somehow, *talk* about it.

This is Johnny with his head spun back to a night in another hotel, when he was somewhere around four or five. Pius gone to some fisheries meeting and his missus, Old Bat Shit, gone to bingo. Only thing that steadied her nerves apparently, blowing wads of cash at bingo. Sister Tanya was babysitting and Johnny fell asleep in the living room chair with a He-Man colouring book, and when he woke up he was lying across the back seat of a massive car, like a Crown Vic or a Lincoln, one of them real cushy smooth and bouncy ones, but one that stank to the high heavens of salt fish and damp tobacco and something else Johnny couldnt quite pinpoint, something sweet. And a man, an older man, somewhere around Pius's age, maybe younger, in the driver's seat, and no big sister Tanya in sight until Johnny let out a holler from the back seat and she suddenly appeared, like she was asleep across the man's lap or something. Fuck sakes Johnny.

Go back to sleep John-John, we're going on an adventure, we are. Close your eyes love, we're going on a trip.

And Johnny lulled, soothed back to sleep by the big springy car, and comes round again when the man, the driver, is hefting him from the back seat and into Tanya's arms.

Waiting at the counter in a smoky lobby in the stifled dead of night until a shadow slips Tanya a key. Up a muffled set of stairs and down a dank gloomy hallway, an aquarium with no water, a fake tree, the sounds of a small dog yapping and whoops and shouts and music coming from behind the numbered doors they pass. Johnny trails his index finger along the wall as they walk and his fingertip comes back coated in a greasy grey gunk. Then into their own room with a bathtub and sink right there in the room, and a TV at the foot of the bed, a telephone, a rickety desk and chair, flowers on the walls.

An adventure John-John, just me and you.

Johnny is asleep again within seconds of his head hitting the pillow and when he wakes sometime later he needs to pee so badly but lies paralyzed in the big bed and doesnt cry out in the dark for fear of finding out that he either is or isnt alone in the room. From his pillow he can distinguish the shadowed blue outline of the toilet in the adjoining room and he imagines himself walkin across the floor and standin before it and relieving himself of this stabbing burn in his belly, hot reprieve flooding out into the bowl, and when he wakes again the pain in his belly is gone but he's cold and wet and Tanya is yelling at him for the love of Christ to get up out of the bed, but she's laughing and there's a presence in the far corner, seated at the small desk, and there's bottles and a sweet metallic smoke in the air and Tanya is stumbling and falling about like she was aboard a boat as she peels Johnny's pants to his ankles and slings them into the corner at the dark figure seated there. Pajama bottoms from a duffle bag, the bed stripped of its sheets and a thin green towel laid across the wet spot and then Johnny laid across the towel, the comforter thrown back over his head, moans and grunts and giggles and hushes and the bed rocking, slamming, thump thump thumping against the wall, the lamp of the bedside table tumbling to the floor and more hushed giggles and then the thumping and slamming gets so that Johnny thinks the ceiling, the roof, the sky is gonna come crashing down on top of him and then nothing. Quiet. The room door clicking shut. Tanya snoring and a cigarette smouldering in the bottom of a whisky bottle on the desk across the room. Then daylight, morning, and Tanya gives Johnny a Pepsi and the biggest bag of cheese balls he's ever seen. *Mighty Mouse* on the TV and Johnny sits up in bed and eats his breakfast and watches Mighty Mouse rescue a flock of sheep from a wicked starving pack of wolves while Tanya sits on the corner edge of the mattress with a can of beer and sobs and moans and guzzles the beer and sniffles and wails, and over the heroic roar of the end credits and between the hiccups and snots Johnny hears Tanya say, *Listen to me, listen to me John-John. Listen to me. Youre not my brother. Do you hear me? Youre not my brother . . .*

Next it's Pius, God love his rotten drawers, in the doorway barking orders and stompin around, flingin clothes and kickin bottles. The bag of cheese balls explodes off the far wall in a flurry of cheese dust and leaves a greasy orange streak across the floral wallpaper. Tanya crouched in the corner, howling, her hands flailing manic out before her as Pius beats her about the head with one of Johnny's grubby sneakers.

And then the long silent ride home.

The long ride home, hey Johnny.

Youre not drowned yet!

What?

I said youre not drowned. Not yet.

This is the classy gal with the coal-black hair standin in the doorway of her room again, clutching about the neck the clunky forty of white wine that's already over half gone.

You wanna come in an dry off?

Johnny dont think twice, tries his best not to sprint across the rain-slickened parking lot towards her, ends up somewhere in between a walk and a run, a sorta gimpish, fruity skip which he loathes the reality of but finds himself useless to bring under control. But no matter anyhow, cause as he gains ground towards the hotel she steps inside her room and closes the door very quickly and Johnny stops dead in his tracks. Fuck sakes. The door opens a few inches and Johnny sees she's got the security chain fastened. She peeks out at Johnny and he can feel the dry sterile heat emanating from her room.

What's with the teardrops? Youre not a murderer are you?

What?

Not a mass murderer? Not a travelling rapist are you?

What? No . . .

Cause I wasnt planning on being raped or murdered tonight.

Well that's, that's not . . . I dont . . .

Good. I'm Joanna.

Ahhh . . . Johnny.

Ohhhh, big bad Johnny. Where from?

Wha??? Well . . . originally I'm . . .

Actually, you know, it doesnt matter.

Joanna stands scrutinizing, contemplating, mullin it over. The sudden hard rain slashin sideways across Johnny's face and hair. What's to see? Teardrop tattoos, pulsing Adam's apple. Pius's battered old suit from some other lifetime, folded beef jerky packet jutting from the handkerchief pocket. Strange, oddly luminous ceramic jar tucked under the armpit. Prayers in hell, hey Johnny. She giggles and steps back into her room and Johnny thinks it's a giggle and a motion that says *Fuck no, I must be off my head,* but for reasons beyond reckoning—shaky, dicey reasons known only to Joanna—she unhooks the security chain and allows Johnny full passage.

You probably think I'm crazy dont you?

Yup.

What??? No you dont! I felt bad for you, that's all. You looked so lost and lonesome out there. You looked like a drowned rat out there. I'm not crazy, I'm good, I'm good, I'm a good girl, goddamn it!

You keep tellin yourself that.

Ha!!! I know right. This is crazy . . . this is . . . I dont know . . . I never get to curse and carry on like this, you know. Usually I'm having to either smile and goddamn nod and yes sir no sir, or I have to be a total bitch. That's a government job right there in a nutshell. I never get to, you know, be me, cut loose. Fuck! Fuck, fuck, fuck!!! Hey do you have any pot?

Pot? You mean weed? No ma'am, I wish . . .

Ma'am, dont call me frigging *ma'am*. Makes me feel . . . how old are you anyway?

How old are you?

I asked you!

Well I'm asking you.

How old do you think I am?

I dont know, maybe thirty-four, thirty-five?

Ha! Good answer! Sounds like someone's trying to butter me up.

Yes ma'am, I confess.

Fuck off, I said. Seriously though, how old do you think?

Maybe thirty-six?

Fuck you! Youre a tease Johnny . . . hey what's your last name?

Ahhh, see now if I told you that . . .

Youd have to murder me! Ha! But make sure you rape me first, that's all I ask!

And with that Joanna flops backwards onto the bed, slops a drop of wine onto the carpet and giggles and roars and guffaws for a good five minutes with her knees tucked up to her chest and rocking back and forth like an inmate at some trauma centre, streaming tears trailing pink streaks in the pale powder on her cheeks. Johnny sits coolly, serene, in the cheap upholstered chair in the corner across the room and takes it all in, one ear to the cold rain battering off the room's lone window, tryna decide on his next move, cause if she's crazy or not, drunk or not, he's in for a penny in for a pound and cant think on the last time he was in the company of a woman in fucken high-heel shoes. Christ.

Joanna catches her breath, sits up, flicks her tongue inside the rim of her glass, stifles another giggling fit.

Oh my, that's bad. That's bad talk. I thought you looked so lost out there, and lonesome. That's all. I have a husband, you know. I do, it's true. I do.

Oh yeah? Should I be scared?

Fuck no. Fuck him. I dont want to talk about him. Nothing worse than a limp prick that's what I say. You know he was almost a hundred pounds lighter in our wedding pictures? A hundred pounds. That's like strapping a hundred blocks of butter onto your body. A hundred blocks of butter. And he blames me that he cant get it up, or keep it up. Me! I mean, look at me. His friend Gerald, his best man, he's a multi-millionaire these days. Owns half the west end of Saint John. Investments, real estate, some landscaping deal thing. Millions. Fit too, in great shape, like someone carved him out with a chisel. I coulda had him too. The offer was there. Bet he's got no trouble keeping it going, Gerald. So hey, tell me about these teardrops Johnny the mystery man. What are they supposed to mean? Or are they decoration or something?

Kinda. I mean, they means something. But when I got em I wasnt thinkin much about anything. I just wanted teardrops on my face. Nothing more to it than that.

But what? Now they mean something?

Well yeah, that's kind of the nature of a tattoo aint it? They can mean whatever a person wants them to mean. Makes no odds what the original intent was, or how fucked up you mighta been when you got em done . . .

Ha! Were you drunk?

No. I was bombed on morphine.

Oh . . .

In jail.

Oh . . .

Yup.

Sooo . . . should I be scared or something?

Up to you. All's I'm doing is being honest.

Fuck fuck fuck Johnny, dont blow this now. Fine drunken piece of gear like her who aint seen a hard cock in who knows how long, dying for it, wants it bad enough to cajole some derelict hitchhiker in off the road. Warm, dry hotel room, out of the rain. Wine. Right out of a bloody movie or something this is. This doesnt happen, shit like this. So dont fucken blow it Johnny, with your surly psycho shit. Let her blather on about the husband and then make your move and let her know what she's missing, wasting her time with some bloated dipshit who cant fuck her, or wont fuck her. Stay the course Johnny my son, stay the course.

Well I'm *not* scared. How's that Johnny Teardrops? I'm not scared. You dont *scare* me. How's that? Now tell me what they mean. Right now! Or I'll shout rape! Ha ha ha!

Jesus Christ girl, enough with the rape. Startin to spook me out over here . . .

Ohhh, now Johnny is scared, Johnny Teardrops. Now . . . hey we need more wine . . .

So do you wanna know or what?

Yes! Yes I do. I'm sorry. I wanna hear. But we need more wine. Okay, tell me. Alright. I'm listening. Go . . .

Jesus. Well there's not much to it really . . .

I love your accent. You killed someone didnt you? You did . . .

No I never fucken killed no one. But . . . they're like, for people that you lose. People who died. But when I got em I wasnt thinkin that. I guess . . . I guess I was thinkin how I hoped people might *think* I killed someone.

What?

Yeah, I was stupid, a stupid punk, locked up, you know. I was young.

How old?

Eighteen or nineteen, I don't know.

How old are you now?

Old enough.

I'm old enough to be your mother, I'd say. So who'd you lose?

Well, I lost me buddy, my cousin. Fella I grew up with. He lived across the meadow. We were the same age and all.

How did he . . .

Shot hisself. Thirty-ought-six. Fifteen years old. I was talkin to him that morning like normal. Said he was going after rabbits in on back of Gorman's Hill.

Where's that?

A hill back where I'm from. Going after rabbits, he said. He had snares out but he brought the gun anyhow, just in case. We had a smoke. He brought me back these tapes he had belonged to me. Skid Row, Guns N' Roses. And . . . small talk, stupid shit. He never gave nothing away, never let on. I guess when you racks your brain afterwards and thinks it through then you can talk yourself into believing that the *signs* were there, but other than them cassettes I cant think of nothing. Everybody knew he was fucked up in the head a bit. He was after going to doctors the year before and taking pills for . . . stuff going on in his head, you know. But I figured that was all done with, like a one-off thing. He seemed normal enough, that day anyhow. I dont even think Mikey, that's his name by the way, I dont think he even knew his own self, the *why* and all that. Anyhow, sometime that afternoon we heard a shot. But I mean no one thinks nothing of a gunshot up around our way, not in the fall of the year anyhow. Later on that evening I swung round his house and he wasnt home yet so I went on up Gorman's Hill lookin for him. Not like he was missing or nothing, just, he wasnt home. And . . . I came upon him . . . Mikey . . .

Hey Johnny?

. . . and he was parked on the quad over at the far end of the gravel pit lying back on the bike, like he was stretched off sleeping, or so I thought. I sang out to him but he never answered, never, like, woke up. And I thought then that he musta come up in the woods and got drunk or something, went off by hisself to go get hammered, and I remember thinkin you dirty fucker, greedy bastard never offered to share the wealth with his best buddy . . .

Hey Johnny?

Next thing I sees his cap, brand-new John Deere cap that he was all smitten with. Well, that was way the fuck up in a tree behind him. And I stops then, cause there's the gun on the ground beside the quad, and the way his arm is limp like that . . .

Johnny you dont have to . . .

Then I saw the hole in his neck, little black hole under his chin, powder burn, and the blood all run down. A real neat, thin streak down his chest . . .

Hey ahhh . . .

But his shirt was black, ya know, so I couldnt tell from far off. Anyhow, blood and bits of brains . . . flies . . . the back of his head was . . .

I dont know . . . one of his eyes had this film, a sorta milky bubble . . .

And then Johnny feels a gentle, very purposeful hand sliding up his thigh and looks down and here's Joanna on her knees before him, foolish tears brimming in her eyes, the pasty sympathetic shadow of a smile.

It's okay. It's okay Johnny. I shouldnt have . . .

What girl? I'm just talkin, just . . . tellin you . . .

But Johnny cant quite get the rest out because his sinuses are all slogged up and his eyes are hot burning blurry and he makes to leap from the chair in sudden outraged disgust but for Joanna's glistening grey-blue eyes fixed on him as she hoists herself tipsy to her feet and takes Johnny's head and cradles it to her belly. The smell of her, hey Johnny, the smell of clean clothes, a woman's clothes, thin tanned strip of bare flesh between the lacey end of her blouse and the smoothened edge of her leather belt, fingers snaking through your hair as she bends down to kiss the top of your head, your eyes and nose and forehead nuzzled luxuriously to her hardy cleavage.

Well now Johnny, not bad, never even made it to the second teardrop for Christ sakes! But enough of this cuddly nurturing shit. One second she's on her knees with her hands running up your legs and next she's doing the whole *come here you poor lost soul* sorta deal. And what are you up to in the meantime? Fucken bawlin? What the hell man? No no no, we're supposed to be doing the blow job thing right about now. Enough of this psychotherapy shit. Johnny aint lookin to be *mothered* goddamn it. He aint lookin for compassion, fucken sympathy. Fuck all that. You learn to live without, dontcha? Learned not to expect any of that kinda shit from the world a long time ago. That summer's day Johnny fell in the bog and nearly sliced his finger off on a broken bottle, ran home bleeding and screamin, panicked. Five, maybe six years old. No one home except Old Bat Shit, who was still supposedly his mother back then. She was kneading bread at the kitchen table. She stopped for a second when Johnny busted into the house, saw the blood-soaked tee-shirt wrapped around Johnny's hand, saw the tears streaking down his cheeks, heard the panic in his voice . . . and then turned back to her bread dough, humming a little tune. Never said a word. So, not to dwell, not to dwell, but right then and there, hey? You learn to go without. You learn to stitch up your own cuts and clean your own wounds. And you dont go out into the world pining for something you never had in the first place. Not like Johnny lost nothing, so. No. Fuck all that. Not lookin to be mothered thanks very much. He's lookin to get his mouth on someone, lookin to get fucked and sucked and put to bed with a bellyful of dirty wine. Still, Johnny cant figure why he went there, why he blurted all that out about Mikey, or how he was even able to. Maybe the rain, the sudden unexpected haven of this room with this woman who's drunk enough not to remember, not to judge. Maybe youre just that fucken tired Johnny.

Next Johnny's on his feet with his talons clutched at the small of Joanna's back, her legs instinctively locked about his waist, almost violently ferrying her from chair to bed where she makes a smallish sound confused somewhere between a grunt and a giggle as he bounces her down on her back. With one hand he pins her wrists behind her head and then his mouth is on hers, sucking her cold boozy tongue and thanking the heavens she's wearing one of those front-clasping bras. Her fleshy hefty jugs spilling out of her blouse and Johnny scooping the left one up and sucking the soft pale inverted nipple into his mouth with a slight pang of disappointment cause Johnny's always been a nipple man, always had a thing for the dark stiff salty nipple. But beggars and choosers, hey Johnny, beggars and fucken choosers. The backs of his fingers spidering beneath her thin panty line where Johnny is surprised to find a clipped and trim landing strip in place of the snarly unkempt bush he'd expected. You never can tell, hey Johnny, never can tell with these married ones. They're either after giving up giving a fuck because the hubby wont touch it either way, or they're after putting the extra effort in just in case, just in case, just in case some teardrop-tattooed layabout comes wandering past on the highway in the rain with an urn and a criminal record to rival the length of the cock she's suffering to get her mouth around. Just in case.

Joanna humps her pelvis a touch to meet Johnny's hand until the frenzied tip of his middle finger finds the swollen nub and he joggles it with his knuckle back and forth, back and forth, faster, faster, probing frantically downward in search of wetness, harried pursuit of slick snug suckling heat and it's been too long, too goddamn long, and Johnny cant help but muse at the bizarre turn of events visited upon this night. How one minute you can be left for dead in the middle of arse-fuck nowhere on the side of the road in the pissing drizzle and rain with nothing and no one for company save for your own twisted thoughts and your dead girlfriend's ashes, and the next minute, the next minute . . . fucken hell Johnny my son.

He finds the very sweet spot, slippery fevered heat far in excess of his expectations. Two fingers right to the knuckles and her whole body clenches and convulses in a spasm of bucks and jolts and shivers and he watches her face contort in abandoned rapture as she arches her back, pressing her shoulders deep into the mattress, mouth gaping as if to cry out, scream, as if to moan, groan, growl or howl—but no sound escapes her, nothing more than a barely audible whimper. And how's the old poem go? How's that old poem go Johnny? How's the world supposed to end? *Not with a bang but a whimper.* Always liked that line, our Johnny. But it cant hardly apply tonight, no, cause we're not ending with no fucken whimper tonight are we Johnny? We're ending with a fucken *bang.* Yes by Christ.

Johnny reaches down to undo the old-fashioned fastener at the waist of his pants, his head spinning off again at how curious, how peculiar, how strange indeed how he's lived this whole life, with that other life under Pius's roof. Countless itchy insomniac nights in musty damp jail cells, and not in a million years can we any of us have the foresight to see ourselves elsewhere, in some other life. We can hope and we can make spiteful plans and we can even fucken pray to be done with where we are, to be onto some other path, somewhere better, different, out of the tangle, free from the muddle and the maze. But aside from wallowing in the past or wishing for better days ahead, we cant sink our teeth into fuck all beyond the moment we're in. Because that's all there is, the moment we're in. We barely have a say over the next ten seconds. And we have no fucken say whatsoever over the ten that just passed by. But then one day Johnny finds himself in Pius's Sunday best, rooting to get his cock out of the pants and into some classy civil servant type missus in a roadside hotel!

And out it pops, Johnny's cock, glossy and stiff and ready to go go go and he's tugging at the waist of Joanna pants but Johnny dont even know if he'll make it, cant say for sure if he'll hold off long enough to send it home cause here's that tingling numb swelling in his balls and aint it funny, the mind, how sometimes it takes all fucken night and there's absolutely nothing you can do to get there, but then a strange bit comes along, or you finds yourself somewhere youre not supposed to be, and all she's got to do is literally give it a few smacks with the back of her hand or barely dangle the prospect of it or fucken look at you a certain way and youre ready to splooge and gunk and mess all over everything, no control. Nothing like a strange bit, hey Johnny. And nothing like it when it's not where youre supposed to be. But this is exactly where Johnny's supposed to be tonight. The very moment he left town, the *way* he left. Young Rodney's mother showing up at Shiner's door with a fucken envelope of cash! Every ride. The way he turned on Saul back there. That short-arsed run with that fucken garden supply rep. The timing of the rain. How she dug into that bottle. Every happening, however petty, however minuscule, has escorted Johnny right to this lovely gorgeous woman's famished pussy. Tonight.

Wait. Hold up a second. Hold up.

What?

Just, I need a breather. Hold up.

This is Joanna bumping Johnny off and rolling onto her side to let her feet hit the floor and she's sitting now on the edge of the bed with her feet on the floor swirling the empty wine bottle before her with a mournful, reclusive sigh, her head wheeling on her shoulders, the blouse flapping open from the blast of the heater and a sudden metallic tang in the air, strong enough to take your breath away.

What? Dont say it's your fucken husband. Cause that's . . .

No, not . . . fuck him. No. I need a breather. Really. It's been a while. And I want more wine. Dont you worry Johnny Teardrops.

Johnny's back in the chair and he's turned Joanna's room into a smoking room without her protest or seeming notice. She lights one of her own. She's called a taxi for another bottle of wine and Johnny thinks she's coming dangerously close to pooping on the party if the fucker dont get here soon. She tries to talk about the situation with her husband but Johnny's enforced a *no talkin about your goddamn husband* rule and so shuts her down anytime she brings him up. Her talk turns to all the red tape in government and she wanders through a confused, fervent ramble about policies and amendments and the dipshit she has to answer to until Johnny enforces a *no talkin about your cunnyhopping job* rule and she laughs and says she likes these rules and tells Johnny she likes him even though she knows it's all a passing lark.

She asks about the urn and Johnny tells her the tale in as clear-cut and simple a manner as he can muster, leaving out the court business and the teapot nonsense and just laying it out as it is, that he's travelling right to the other side of the country to scatter Madonna's ashes on some beach where she used to go when she was a girl. Joanna tells of her brother, her older brother who died when she was seventeen. He'd just gotten a job at a lumberyard, his second day on the job, engaged to his high school sweetheart, got his skull split open, struck in the head with a swinging apparatus, maybe a boom. Took him three weeks to die. She tells of her sister's boyfriend who was thrown from his motorcycle and got trapped under a car and burnt to death up against the converter because the paramedics took forty-five minutes to get there. All these people standing around, lots of burly men, and none of them had the guts to band together and lift the goddamn car off him. But, she said, he was an asshole to my sister, so . . .

Johnny listens to Joanna's stories of calamity and sorrow and rising up out of the slummy backwoods of New Brunswick to put herself through university when everyone told her again and again that she'd never add up to shit, and Johnny does not enforce any sorta mock rule against this kind of talk, but rather feels a twinge of . . . something . . . deep down or right there on the surface or even outside of himself, a twinge, a vague sensation of knowing what she feels, of feeling for what she feels, of feeling connected to something, an experience that doesnt originate within. And lookit alright, Johnny knows the *definition* of the word empathy because Christ knows he's heard it tossed around often enough in courtrooms and counsellors' offices and fucken rehabilitation workshops, but he aint never measured it beyond a word, beyond a bullshit *word* until this moment. Now, Johnny, doubling back to that line of thought about how all these perfectly timed out occurrences led me here, to this woman, but, well, maybe there's something even more to it than a piece of skin, maybe I'm supposed to feel . . .

C'mon Johnny for the love and honour of Christ! Snap the fuck out of it brother. Unless youre planning on going soft or something? Turning into some sorta sissy-boy? Cause that's how it's starting to look. Of course it's all about a piece of skin. Everything is, everything comes down to a piece of fucken skin! And youre tired, wiped out, and as much as you wants that bottle to arrive so Miss Woe-Is-Me over there can feel easier about dropping her fucken trousers once and for all, as much as you wants that, a nice warm dry bed that doesnt rumble and lurch and move at a hundred-plus kilometres an hour, well that's pretty appealing right about now too. So fuck off with the flouncy self-analysis slop and get her head back around to the matter at hand, namely your rod in all her inviting love-holes.

So when was the last time you and your husband . . . you know?

I thought there was a rule against that?

Well it's different when I asks . . .

Oh yeah, so what are you asking? When was the last time he fucked me, or half-fucked me with his half-hard prick? Wow, that sounds kind of bitter doesnt it?

Yeah. No. I mean whatever, youre allowed to be pissed off . . .

I am! I'm allowed to be pissed off. I'm allowed to be vicious, arent I? I can be as goddamn . . .

But you dont have to get all pissed off *right now*? I was just askin how long.

Too long Johnny Teardrops. Too long. And you know what? You wanna know what? I'm not going back to it. I'm not. Christ I cant talk about it! I mean I'm going back but not to that. I'll give it a month, that's what. And if nothing changes and he doesnt come around then I'm gone, I'm done. Cause you know something, you know I caught him jerking off one night? Sitting there in front of the TV with his prick out and hard as a rock beating it off to some little anorexic slut barely out of high school. So it's not like it doesnt work, not like there's something physically wrong with him, is there? Oh, but that's different, he says. That's not the same because there's no emotional expectation or whatever. Horseshit. I mean think about it, fresh out of the bath and lying back with my legs spread wanting to get screwed. That's all. I'm not looking to be cuddled or boosted up or made to feel loved and beautiful, this is what I tell him, I'm not looking for any of that. I'm looking to get nailed. Take your prick and stick it in me. Where's the emotional expectation in that? Horseshit. Oh hey, betcha that's our bottle . . .

A rapping at the unit door and Joanna seems to catapult from the bed to the other side of the room without touching the floor in between, one bounding leap and the door swinging open and there's a grizzled cabbie shielding himself from the rain with a scrap of cardboard and passing the prized bottle to Joanna who stuffs a crisp fifty into his hand and tells him to keep the change, and all in one motion she slams the unit door, unscrews the cap from the bottle and sucks back about two standard glasses worth of gut-rot wine.

Oh, that's amazing. God I needed to get drunk. Where are the glasses?

She skips through to the bathroom and returns with a couple of plastic glasses and fills them both to the brim, hands one off to a mute Johnny, who's still grappling with the notion of Joanna fresh from the bath, spread-eagle on the bed and some fella cant or wont fuck her. Beyond comprehension when you thinks about it, especially from a jailbird's perspective. Sure the last time Johnny done a stint at HMP there was that Harnum fella from around the bay who was in for banging a cow. Really, up on a stool in the middle of some meadow where all eyes could see him, slamming it home. The cow munching on a bit of grass, hardly any the wiser. He missed his wife, that's all he said in court, he missed his wife since she left. Fucken hell. And that time Johnny's cellmate got a week in solitary after he was caught doing his mattress. His *mattress*. Ripped open the vinyl fabric and burrowed a hole in the cushion enough to fit his cock and he had away at it, gawking and drooling at a picture of some other inmate's girlfriend. But they gave him solitary for destroying HMP property, not for twisted sex with an inanimate object or nothing. And then there's the ones that gets so hard up they starts having a go at each other. And they're not *gay* or nothing, at least not when they're on the outside, just closes their eyes and makes like it's a woman. Well, come to think on it, one of em would have to be a bit more bent than the other cause it's not like the fella on the receiving end is closing his eyes and pretending it's some skirt pounding him with a strap-on. But anyhow, from a jailbird's angle, the notion of a class gal like Joanna and a fella cant get it up? He should be fucken shot.

Johnny flattens his wine, tries not to grimace at the acidic metal aftertaste, but then considers the vile concoctions he's poured down his throat in the past—Lysol, Old Spice, ketchup brew, rubbing alcohol—and has a little chuckle to hisself. *The past.* Joanna tranquilly refills his glass, smiling idly, her eyes glassed over with drunken satisfaction.

You know my husband shit his pants at a Christmas party a couple of years ago? Can you believe that? Try taking that home and getting a rise out of it.

Johnny snorts scornfully at this, hooks his fingers into the waistband of her pants and tries to pull her down into his lap but she slaps at his hand and staggers a little as she tips another half glass down her throat. Johnny wonders then if there's anything behind all that rape talk she was gettin on with earlier, if it's some sort of twisted fantasy of hers. Lead Johnny to the brink and get herself plastered with the notion that he'll just take her when she's too drunk to change her mind. If that's the case Johnny wants nothing to do with it, no thank you ma'am. Not that foolish. He might be hard up for a piece tonight but he'd sooner jack off onto the guardrail out there. All bad enough. Cause who are they gonna believe if she decides it didnt go down the way she set it up to go down?

She peeks out onto the parking lot through the blinds.

I gotta take it easy Johnny Teardrops. I have to give a presentation tomorrow. You have to keep me out of trouble . . . But hey, they've got a whirlpool down the hall somewhere! We could . . . yes, lets . . .

This is Johnny now, Johnny fucken Keough, kicked back in a goddamn Jacuzzi in a hotel on the mainland, glass of wine in hand, waiting to be accompanied by some married drunk government missus who's dying for the meat. Or at least that's the vibe she's giving off, hey Johnny? Hard to know. Fucken hell. But who fucken cares? Where was Johnny a week ago? On his way to Dorchester for Christ sakes. *Yeah, and where was Madonna?* Hey now, none of that talk. No fucken downers allowed in. Not that kinda party. Madonna, the old Madonna, she'd be tickled pink at the notion of Johnny pulling something like this off. Cause that's the way it was sometimes. Out on the town and they couldnt be bad enough, wandering from bar to bar on George Street and Johnny sucking the face off some old cougar while Madonna went through her pockets and cleaned out her purse. Madonna luring that young feller into the alleyway behind Liquid that night and then Johnny shaking him down for a month's worth of E. Good times Johnny, when they were good. A team. A unit. And then back to the bedroom for an all-night romp on E and neither one of you able to get off but going at it all fucken night and maybe sleeping with his cock inside her and the next day he couldnt hardly look at her but she was coming in her panties. All day. Like you build it up and build it up the night before and almost get there so often but the E wont let you and then the next day it's constant, constant. Johnny too.

So yeah, maybe tonight's proceedings might not be something Madonna woulda been all that enthused about when her and Johnny were *together*, like if he fucked off to a hotel and got loaded with some sugar mama, but a story she'd have loved to hear, something from Johnny's old life, his past, anything. She hung on every word. *In the beginning.* How real, how valid she made it all seem, hey Johnny. First time in your life someone looks at you and tells you youre *allowed* to be pissed off, that youre entitled to your rage, that even though there's nothing can be done about it, the way things were werent necessarily supposed to have been that way, that the knot in your guts is real and that you were reared up by stupid ignorant backwater fucks and kicked around by a stupid ignorant backwater system and that for the most part you were a fucken child.

The day we went downtown to that coffee shop and sat and watched people after I almost got caught swiping CDs from Fred's Records. CDs neither of us had no interest in listening to. Madonna laughing, sayin I was a right klepto, and I got thinkin out loud about how Pius, God love the old cunnyhopper, bloodied me lip one time for taking a peach from the fridge. Cause where peaches were special or something. Johnny the thief, stealing from his own fridge. Lookin up at Pius, peach juice dripping from me chin and sayin *I never took no peach*.

See what I'm sayin girl? I was always a thief. I was always a liar.

No. You were *told* you were a thief. It's different. And you were told you were a liar. So what are you gonna do? Youre gonna lie and steal. Think about it Johnny love.

And then a little blond boy, a boy of about eight or nine, walking across Water Street holding his mama's hand, and Madonna points him out, says *Look, look at that little fella Johnny. He's a child. He's a little boy.*

Johnny sips his wine and lazes back in the rumbling water, sweat beading his temples, keeping an eye on the women's change room for a sign of Joanna, who stayed behind in the room to check in with her sagging husband, let him know she's alright, safe and sound, preppin for tomorrow's presentation, watchin trash TV and havin a quiet little nip of wine. Yeah, fuck.

What a night, what a night Johnny this has turned out to be.

Johnny's naked in the Jacuzzi. The sign says swimsuits are required, but all he had was his long one-piece woollen underwear and they just werent up to scratch somehow, something very unromantic about them. Besides, doubtful Joanna brought a fucken swimsuit to a roadside motel, so that means she'll either be in the buff herself or she'll be wearing her bra and panties. Which would be just as awesome, says Johnny, soaking wet bra and panties. He leans back against the force of the jets and glances over to the white plastic lounge chair at the mound of his crumpled suit, his filthy wool socks, the grey boots, Madonna's ashes, and considers the road in the coming days, his money, his health, his sanity, his freedom. And then what? Once he's there and finds that beach that he dont even know the name of and scatters her to the wind and makes his peace? What then? Where to?

Johnny notices a faint murky quality to the water around him and realizes it must be dirt coming from him, that this is the first hot water to touch his skin since he showered before court. Fucken hell. Might as well give it a good scrub, soap or no. Maybe there was a fucken reek off him and Joanna was too polite or shy to ask him to take a shower, maybe that's why she wanted for the whirlpool. Johnny claws at the bottoms of his feet, gives the toes a good squeeze, rolls back the old foreskin and wrings the head of his lad, cups his hand down the crack of his arse and scrubs for all it's worth, dunks his head into the bubbling heat and grates at his scalp, kneads the cheekbones, temples, then sits back with his wine and tries to settle his lower back against the powerful jet but he cant seem to hit the sweet spot. He raises himself slightly off the tiles and the vigorous stream shoots down the crack of his arse and hits his balls with a blissful humming gush that he likes very much and so tries to raise himself farther up to meet the jet but to simultaneously keep his shoulders under the water so it wont look like he's doing what he's doing—frolicking with a Jacuzzi—to anyone who might be watchin, or who might walk in at any moment.

That's good, that's really fucken nice, hey Johnny. Imagine if you had one of these whirlpool set-ups one day. The days of chasing women all said and done. Johnny feels himself stiffening, the jet purring and droning heavenly against his nether regions. He lets his head fall forward and wonders vacantly if there's a name for that square inch of flesh between his balls and his arsehole. Betcha there's some sorta weird, hard to pronounce clinical name Johnny, just like there's a name for that thin strand of flesh that joins your foreskin on. Busted that off more than once . . .

Are you doing what I think youre doing Johnny Teardrops?

Near lethal shot of adrenalin surges through his body at the sound of her voice and he looks up to see her stepping down into the pool. His heel slips off the edge of the submerged tile seat and as he tumbles backwards, his spine rasping painfully against the edge of the pool, he feels a severe burst of pressure swelling in his guts and realizes only once it's way too late that he's somehow flooded his bowels to the brim with steaming hot Jacuzzi water. He hears himself moan, piercing jolts jabbing agonizing dull knives in the far reaches of his insides, deep mincing electric groan in his lower back, his suddenly bloated belly, knees weak and rubbery. He squints past Joanna to the door of the men's change room. Maybe twenty feet away. Fucken hell Johnny Keough, this is madness. Joanna with her bra in one hand and glass of wine in the other, smiling, laughing, *Youre a bad boy Johnny Teardrops, I know what you were doing*... Johnny's puckered asshole winking and twitching, desperate to expel, eject, banish, cast away this nuisance violation of alien hot tub juice. He squeezes the cheeks together, thrusts his hips forward as he rises to his feet, his eyes focused desperate on the door to the men's change room.

I gotta . . . I need to . . .

Oh my, what have we here?

Johnny waddles tentatively across the tub as Joanna reaches for his midsection and he looks down to see he's standin at full attention.

Mmmm . . . I know what you want me to do Johnny Teardrops . . .

No . . . I have to . . . just let me . . .

Johnny gets his right leg up out of the hot tub beyond Joanna's shoulder, his toned abdominals twinging and heaving, shuddering hysterically, searing balloon spasming in his lower back, his cramped and trembling asshole.

Joanna's cold lips around the head of his inflamed cock.

No wait . . . I got to get . . .

He hoists his left leg towards the edge of the hot tub and he knows it's all over.

Joanna's eyes wide with something near terror as a torrent of slurried hot meaty shit explodes from Johnny's backside. She lets go of Johnny's stiff member and cries out and backs away as if there were some foul demented creature in the water, which there is. She lunges to the other end of the pool to escape the onslaught but it's everywhere, Johnny's shit. Scraps of undigested lettuce from some gas station burger, stringy goops of what mighta been beef jerky, unidentifiable chunks of . . . well, shit, swirling in the bubbles, clinging to Joanna's hair, spattered onto her chest, lapping against the sides of the pool like so much stinking putrid flotsam.

Minus the urgency of his original intent, baffled and slack-jawed Johnny staggers off towards the change room. Stops and turns to see Joanna struggling to pull herself up out of the whirlpool, gagging violently, thin splash of grainy shit spattered across her back.

Do you . . . do you need help?

Fuck off!

We can shower . . .

Fuck off . . . sick fuck . . .

He trudges across the room to the sound of Joanna throwing up on the wet tile floors, moaning and hacking, not quite sobbing but more like . . . more like . . . whimpering Johnny. The woman is whimpering. Johnny Keough, fucken ladies' man to the bitter end. He bends to scoop up his tattered outfit and notes dazedly that the urn seems to have a bit more glow to it, a touch more shine, dark, translucent sparkles in the ceramic he hadnt noticed before.

Couple of lads from Halifax, Gavin and Trevor, round about Johnny's age, one half of a reggae-type band. *Ska,* Trevor calls it, but more like *World* says Gavin. They been blasting their latest demo for the past half hour, looking back to Johnny and shouting and nodding, fishing for his approval, but Johnny cant decipher one song from the next, cant tell which is the verse which is the chorus where one song ends or another begins, cant make out the lyrics, and the ones he does make out dont sound like they're sayin all that much of anything. Scratchy muffled nonsense drone. But Johnny, having spent the previous eight or nine hours limping and scuffing and cursing and bitching his way along a dismal and desolate stretch of highway with all hope for a ride, and subsequently all hope of that west coast beach, all hope in humanity crushed and mulched and dashed to hell and back, grateful to be in off that fucken road, Johnny nods his enthusiasm from the back seat of the swank Ford Explorer that must belong to one of their daddies because no way in fuck could either of them be making a buck off their shoddy music, or their looks, or their fashion sense. Frazzled dreadlocks and filthy Mexican-style ponchos and rainbow bandanas and the sour stench of garlic enough to knock up a dead nun. And hey Johnny, you could be the band manager! Johnny in his shabby and shithauled ragged old suit with the cuff of the left leg stained almost to the knee from some mystery fluid he stood in near a gas station outside Edmundston, and the elbow with the gaping hole from where it hooked on the broken door handle of a prehistoric Volkswagen driven by that wild-eyed old trapper type who couldnt or wouldnt speak a word of English. Johnny's face and hair is that greasy he's half afraid to light a cigarette. Cant even remember what colour his shirt was. No amount of scratching to appease the itch. Incessant grungy damp in his boots. Manage these hippie Rasta fuckers right into the ground, Johnny would.

All the way to Kingston though, so say the lads. Meeting the other half of the band somewhere outside Montreal and then motoring on to Kingston. That's a good potent run, hippie stink or no. Scraggly Trevor, the one with the dreadlocks, from the front passenger seat passes Johnny a huge joint as thick as Johnny's middle finger and Johnny sucks it back and coughs and hacks and shouts over the blaring drone that his father lives in Kingston, perfect, perfect. Johnny nods drowsily when he's asks what he thinks of the weed and the two lads start laughing, laughing.

Dude, there's lots more where that came from, lots more.

Trevor produces a small black canvas bag and holds it up and thumps the side of it, supposedly to show how packed full of weed it is. Johnny's fuzzy nod of approval. The lads start giggling again. The evening sun sinking leisurely behind the distant treeline. Gavin flicks on his driving lights, turns the music down. The weed hits Johnny like that pink milky hospital anaesthetic shit and he feels harmless and cocooned, dog-tired and stunned, buckles his seatbelt and huddles deep into the soft leather upholstery, taps the urn jutting bulky and cumbersome from his left side pocket, saltwater smell, a cavern out there, a cave, ghostly heart throbbing from some great vast distance within . . .

. . . north side of the harbour. Me and Mikey and my dog Scrapper, shaggy little terrier, fucken savage. We're hopping the coves. There's one scanty inlet we can never get to, one spot we can never get past. The bank around it is all loose shale and rotted roots and moss, so's you gotta hug the cliff good and tight and sidestep with your back to the harbour.

Past that there's a narrow, slimy landing where you can turn around. Lookin down from the ledge there's about a ten-foot drop, straight down to a little rocky beach. Wave comes in and the beach is gone. Draws back out and the beach is there again. Wave crashes in and the beach is gone.

Timing, Mikey, that's all's to it.

We can see across to the other side and there's a cave. A real cave. Had our eyes on it for the past two summers. Old stories and treasure and all that foolishness. This day we meant business, brought a length of rope, a hatchet, pocketknives, matches. Mikey got half a dozen Rothmans he swiped from his nan's cupboard. I got us nearly a pound of bologna, two bags of Hostess plain, two Big Turks, only one can of Pepsi. Marked it down at the shop in Tanya's name. This is all jammed into a green army knapsack I found down by the twine shed last summer. We're going for it, we're making it over to that cave and hunkering down and having a feast and trying out them cigarettes.

This is the day.

Here's how I got it sorted, how I explains it to Mikey:

You gotta jump when the wave comes in, when the beach is full of water. Are ya listening to me? Might feel like youre jumping into the water, but by the time you lands the wave should be back out again. Then boot er on up over the rocks to the other side. No dawdling, less you wants to get sucked out the harbour. All about timing, see? Sound decent?

We flips a nickel for who's to jump first. Comes up tails. Mikey gapes out over the edge, dread-fuelled excuses dancing in his eyes. But I'm standin right there and he'd have to push his way around me to climb back up the bank. But I aint budging, and he knows it. He wants to flip again, two out of three. I looks at him. He watches the wave below crash in on the thin strip of beach. Four or five feet deep when it's full. Over either of our heads. And savage, angry, violent, the way it smashes against the rocks. The beach drains and he shifts his weight to his right leg and starts to push off but I grabs him by the arm and holds him back and explains the timing again, how he needs to jump the moment the beach is swamped, no later. We waits and watches, letting the wave do its thing. He makes a couple of false goes, then retreats with his back pressed against the cliff face and I can tell he lost the nerve, if ever he had it in the first place. He wants to go back up, take the cigs and grub down to Murphy's old smoke shack where he says he heard there was a stash of skin magazines. He's been obsessed with skin mags ever since we found a bunch of fucked-up ones down in old Wally B's bus. He's starting to get that high-pitched whine thing he does when he's sookin. Says it's not safe. Says he's not *feeling* good. Jesus. He wants me to listen. *Listen, hear that?* But there's nothing only the waves on the rocks. *Listen Johnny. Sounds like someone* . . . But I aint buying that shit this time—people calling out from the woods, weird noises, people laughing out in the meadow in the nighttime. He's been getting on with that shit all summer, lookin for attention. I gives him a little nudge with my knee. He says he'll go if I goes first but I knows that to be bullshit. He puts his hand on me shoulder and gives a little shove and I whops him in the guts and grabs his jacket at the same time so's he dont fall over the ledge. He stands there gawkin out across the bay holding his belly and tryin not to look winded. *Shit,* he says, *shit Johnny*. He knows he's got no choice. He makes another false go. Cant do it. Next time the wave comes in I gives him a bit of help and down he goes, hollering, squealing like a girl, nine feet, six, four feet above the water. But no splash when he lands, the crunch of his feet on the glistening beach rocks, then a mad scramble up the rocks to the other side. Perfect timing. But then I sees he's turned around, Mikey, searching, dazed, panicked. He's only got one sneaker on. His left sneaker is slammed in against the mouth of the beach and the wave sucks it halfways out when it draws back. He's having trouble on his feet. Scrambling, half crawling back down the rocks and leaning out to grab at the sneaker as it passes, and then he's screamin, rooting at his sock and his gob is like a blood blister, pleading up at me with this agonizing twist to his face and he gags a bit, dry heaves, then falls head first into the swell and he's under. All's I can see of him is the pale blue stripe on the shoulder of his windbreaker. His head comes spluttering up and he roars something I cant understand. The wave drives him back in and he stands for a moment and screeches and falls and then he's snatched up and jerked back under again. I've got the rope out now and I wraps an end three or four times around my wrist and hand and aims the heavy coil towards the centre of the beach and drops it, and when Mikey comes back up again his arm by chance snags on to the coil of rope. And dont he fucken cling to it.

Hard for me to keep good footing on the slimy ledge and I slips at first and the rope goes slack but then it tightens again and I'm almost pulled over myself. Scrapper is pacing back and forth underneath me too, whining and shit. I makes a roar at him and he cowers off around the corner. I digs my heels in and leans back against the cliff face and starts heaving and hauling on that rope for all I'm worth. And Mikey aint light neither, soaking wet as he is and thrashing and twisting about and crying and moaning and still pleading and begging me to help, *C'mon Johnny, c'mon, help me Johnny, help me.* And I roars back at him that I am fucken well helping, that's he's gotta help me! Corner of me eye, I can see his sneaker is well out into the open water. Me hands are numb and my arms and shoulders are flaming, burning tired, but Mikey's only about three feet away from me now, dangling above the swell. He manages to get his hand up and I reaches for it but both of our hands are too slippery. Next thing I got a good grip on his hair and he's shrieking and yelping and I hauls him up like that, by the hair, onto the ledge and out of danger. But he still wont stop with the bawling and yelping and I'm shouting at him to shut up, *Shut up Mikey. Youre up now, I got ya, shut the fuck up!* He peels his sock off then and we sees his shattered foot, the bone splintered out through the side of a massive gash running from his ankle to the tip of his little toe. Blood. Mikey howling. His arm around me shoulder as I hoists him around the tight landing and drags him up across the snarly bank of trees. Sour, vinegary smell, something goopy and hot runnin down me back and I turns to see he's hurled into me collar and I wanna choke him so bad. His head is lobbing forward and his eyes are half closed so I slap him hard across the face and he comes to and moans, cries out like a youngster, wailing, *It hurts, it hurts Johnny. Oh my God, oh shit, it hurts Johnny.* I smacks him again and pulls more of his weight onto me shoulders and there's grass under my feet now, solid ground, and I tries to set him down but he clings to me neck and so I got no choice but to trudge and slog on up across the Reddigans' steep boggy meadow with Mikey across my back like some scene from a war movie. Scrapper yipping and yowling up ahead of us. At some point I slips and falls and we both tumbles to the ground and Mikey is howling in me ear how much it hurts. I cant take it, the grating noise of Mikey's snotting and Scrapper lickin at the barf on me coat and the panic in Mikey's eyes. My fist jabs out three or four times square into his lips and now they're bloodied and Mikey is worse and then someone's coming running down across the meadow shouting for us to *break it up b'ys, break it up!*

Sitting on the Reddigans' porch when Mikey's father, Uncle Austin, Pius's brother, pulls up in his old brown Chevy and he dont so much as glance in Mikey's direction but marches right towards me, his hands clamped around me throat.

Little bastard. That's all you are. Little blood of a bitch. Bastard, they shoulda tossed you out with the goddamn afterbirth.

Reddigan sayin *C'mon Aus, save it,* pulling Austin off Johnny. Mikey is moaning and howling as he climbs into the cab of the truck. Austin tellin Johnny not to dare show his face across their yard for the rest of the summer.

Youre trouble, nothing only fucken trouble.

Johnny tryna make eye contact with Mikey as the truck burns down the gravel road, anxiously willing him to come to his senses and relay the heroic tale of how Johnny fished and lugged him from the water with a goddamn rope and then carried him on his back all the way up the cliff! Johnny turns to old Reddigan, who's wadding a hefty chew of tobacco into his cheek, and young Johnny, sobbing now, young Johnny says *I saved him, I did. It wasnt my fault.* Reddigan spits ominously across the dirt yard and shakes his head and nods in the direction of another approaching vehicle. Johnny looks up to see a dark churning cloud of dust sprawling behind Pius's pickup as it fishtails onto the lower road. Johnny stares dumbly as he catches Pius's savage blazing eye through the filthy windshield. The pickup grinding to a gritty halt outside Reddigan's fence and then Johnny scuttling, scurrying over the porch railing, Scrapper hot on his heels, pounding the sod for all hell back down across the meadow beneath the hastily darkened skyline, damp gloomy gust of wind blustering under the waistline of his putrid coat.

More anguished groans, shouting. The sensation of being tased. Big Turks. No need to wonder if Johnny knows what a taser gun feels like. Like feeling more awake than youve ever felt in your life while youre crazed to stay awake. Every muscle in your body. Pounding. Searing. Useless. It's fucked, *We're fucked, ahhh dude, we're so fucked . . .* Rothmans kings. A bristly thing, thick and warm, earthy, kicking and twitching next to Johnny's cheek. Sweet, thick grassy stench of shit. More shouting. The edge of hysteria. *Check and see if he's dead.* Hostess plain. *You check. Dude, you were fucken driving!* Dark figure silhouetted on the road, limping, holding a rag to its head, hobbled. *Am I bleeding? Am I?* Chalky white film dusting these leather seats. Old Scrapper. Pius on Reddigan's porch waving some sorta tool, a mallet maybe. Sliver of glass gouged into Johnny's palm, the thumb dead and useless. No pain, never any pain. Antlers? Airbags. Fur.

Hey . . . ahh . . . hey buddy . . . are you alright in there? Can you hear me? Hello?

Moose. Struck a moose Johnny. See that lump of mangled guts and grizzle and fur on the hood? That's a moose Johnny. On the mainland somewhere. Middle of nowhere. Quebec. Who knows. See the light near that little farmhouse down the road a ways? That means people. That means cops. French ones. Heading this way.

Hey buddy? Did he say his name? Hey . . . are you alright?

He's dead. Dude, he's dead. We're so screwed. Dude we're so fucked.

I didnt see it. It's like it appeared there. I didnt see it walking out . . .

Dude, I said, I screamed at you, I said moose, moose, and you were like . . .

That guy's dead in there. Hey!

You can get sued if you touch someone and they, like . . .

Sirens Johnny. You know what that means. Johnny chokes off a groan as he unhitches the seatbelt, bats a splintered hoof away from his face. His left hand settles on the urn, intact. Thank Christ. Madonna. No one said it was gonna be a breeze. Johnny lifts his right leg and boots the crumpled passenger door and the door falls open but keeps swinging out and drops from its hinges into the ditch. Sirens. Gavin or Trevor, one of these clowns, helping Johnny out of the doomed and done-for rig.

Youre alive! He's alive.

Johnny pulls the glass from his palm and the blood spurts across Gavin or Trevor's poncho. The two of them standin there gawp-jawed and stupid while Johnny bends down and scoops up a wallet. Sirens. Two sets. Police and ambulance. He pulls a driver's licence from a sticky leather folder.

Hey that's my wallet . . .

Gavin Patrick Gallant. 410 Woodland Avenue. Dartmouth, Nova Scotia. January 12th, 1991. Hello Gavin.

Hey . . . ahhh . . . that's my . . .

That's your full name and address and date of birth . . . How many passengers did you have tonight?

Wha . . . ?

Was there anyone else, besides you and your boyfriend, riding in the vehicle tonight Gavin Patrick Gallant of 410 Woodland Avenue in Dartmouth?

Wha . . . ?

Was there anyone fucken else . . .

No! No man. No. Just me and Trev. No.

Good. That poncho you got on, that's the same one here on your licence?

Wha . . . ?

Give it to me.

Wha . . . ?

Give me that fucken shawl or cloak thing youre wearing, now.

Gavin almost graciously struggling out of the poncho and handing it across to Johnny. Trevor staring blankly out the highway towards the looming sirens.

Where's that fucken bag of dope?

Wha . . . ? It's ahhh . . . it's behind that . . . see the white stump . . .

You fellas took the time to stash your dope and never bothered to check and see if I was alive or dead or dying?

What? No man . . . no . . .

Fuck you fucken both.

Johnny slips Gavin's licence into his bloodied handkerchief pocket and claws his way up out of the ditch in the direction of the stump. He rummages around in the dusky light until his hand latches on to a thin canvas strap. He hefts the bag, grins at the lads, nods towards the wreckage and whistles. The crumpled accordion of the front end, stinking black river of blood spilling down over the fender, mammoth garbled creature splayed across the hood with its hind legs and left rack speared through the windshield, broken skull twisted the wrong way around. One bulbous martyred eye failing, failing.

Thanks for the ride fellas. Hope your daddy's got good coverage.

And with that Johnny spins, almost elegantly, on his heels and saunters into the thick black woods and disappears.

Two Rasta hippie boys left shell-shocked and baffled.

Spirits broken, weed pilfered, road trip dead in the water.

* * *

Fuck that, hey Johnny. Hang around and let some French coppers drill you for info and then find you got no papers and suss out the teardrops and you knows they'd find some bullshit reason to haul you in and run your prints and then youre fucked altogether. Locked up in some French jail where no one knows how to fucken talk. And youd be weeks or months waiting on an escort back home, then banged up for another few months before youre standing trial for armed robbery and fuck knows what else. Shiner with the whole of HMP turned against you. Right back where you started, only worse. And for all the word about French cops? Fuck that.

This is Johnny's rationale and he staggers and stumbles warily, sightless down a haggard meandering old Ski-Doo path in the blackest pitch night deep in the middle of the backwoods of Quebec.

Vague, listless rumble somewhere to the left of him, or maybe ahead, seems to be gettin louder, rowdier, as he tromps along.

Might be a river.

Scouring his memory for any maps he mighta grazed over in the HMP library, but comes up with nothing. Tries to remember the name of whatever town that hairy trapper dropped him on the outskirts of, started with *Drum*, some burnt-out French name that Johnny's brain wont even let him attempt to pronounce.

No idea how long he slept before the crash, no inkling how many miles.

Remote, hazy flash of Gavin or Trevor at a gas pump.

Winking lights of industrial sprawl through the tinted glass, a toll bridge.

Powerful fucken weed, hey Johnny?

And hey, old Scrapper. Aint thought about that dog in years. Mind of the time he got into all them Russian hens. Good dog he was, rabid little savage.

The night is cold but the air is dry, hardly a breeze.

Johnny stops and turns back and combs the skyline but can no longer pick out the flashing red and blue lights, no longer discern the direction of the highway, cant decide how long he's been walking, ten minutes or two hours, and it dawns on him that he might just be headed nowhere.

We're lost Johnny, we're lost . . .

Rambling overgrown woods path that sometimes disappears altogether so that Johnny is leaning forward, using his body weight to urge and thrust his way through dense scrags of brush and knotted branches, stumbling over rotted stumps, slopping through puddles of muck.

Back out to open trail for a few minutes, now hacking and clawing his way again.

Nowhere.

Woods.

We're lost Johnny, we're lost . . .

We're not Mikey, how can we be lost?

Where's the track? Where's the bridge Johnny, what's that? Listen . . . what's that?

Stop it will ya . . . it's a loon . . . I dont know . . .

With Mikey, troutin. First time ever in the track on our own. Eight or nine years old. We were told to be out to the road before dark but the trout were savage, going after the bare hook and everything. All nice pink bellies. A string of about two dozen each slung over our shoulders. Time they let up feeding we could barely see our bobbers. We'd turned down to the pond by an old slab bridge, followed the river down. Nothing we loved more than troutin the rivers. So we figured to follow it back out to the track, like we were told. But we'd trouted all around the pond, and there's more than one river running in. The one we followed out looked right. But it kept going, and no bridge, no track. We're laughing and foolin, Mikey bragging about catching the biggest trout, fighting over a bag of chips. The river thins out, weedy and feeble. It becomes another pond. We see the darkness. Mikey goes up past his knee in the marsh, fills his rubber. Then I do, only I gets mine stuck and I falls and drenches me jacket too. Mikey sayin *This way, this way, we never went this way.* Tromping through the marsh in circles and coming back to the edge of the pond. Walking along another river, knowing it's not the right one, that it's too low, too tame, but going it anyhow. Then woods all around. Mikey tryna catch his breath.

Listen Johnny, what's that?

What? Nothing, there's nothing Mikey . . .

That! Do you hear it? Someone . . .

Stop it Mikey! Alright. There's no one . . .

There's only three trout left on my string, three of the first ones I caught, wrinkled and crusty with moss. The rest are gone. Mikey starts to cry and then I starts and we're running in the dark and I've got ahold of the hem of Mikey's coat and when he trips and falls I falls right on top of him and we're huddling there sobbing, terror-stricken in the night with the horrible woods enclosing us, heavy with evil, teeming with the worst of our fears. Things live here, unnamable perverse shadowed beasts that stalk and prey on children and carry them away screaming to some putrid lair where their arms are torn from their sockets and devoured raw right down to the marrow in the bones. No trace. Two young boys who went into the woods and didnt pay heed and were never seen again. Something got them. Some thing.

What's that Johnny? Listen . . . what's that?

Mikey dont . . .

No listen . . .

And then we hears it, a voice, a man's voice off in the distance, calling, calling our names. Mikey bolts to his feet and howls *Daddy! Daddy! We're here . . .* Then I'm shouting through the sobs *Uncle Austin! Uncle Austin!* and we're rushing, jostling towards the voice but there's no path so we stops to listen again, the voice askin where we are, but we dont know, we dont know, the voice tellin us to walk towards the sound, *Walk towards me voice Mikey! B'ys youre alright, walk towards me voice . . .* The voice singing, an old party song, an Irish song, beautiful booming echo, closer, closer . . . something, taking the train to Belfast, what was that song?

I'm right here b'ys, right here on the track . . .

Uncle Austin standin on the track with his arms outspread as Mikey leaps into them and buries his snotty face in his father's thick shoulder.

I gotcha now. It's alright little man. Daddy gotcha. It's okay little woodsman. You got a fright didnt you? Youre alright now . . . c'mon little buddy . . .

Johnny trailing behind, snivelling. Mikey snug in his father's arms, big hand thumping his back, rubbing his hair.

Shhh . . . it's alright little man . . . Daddy gotcha.

One of Mikey's trout slips from his string, the big one, the biggest one.

Plump speckled pink belly gleaming in the moonlight.

Johnny stoops to pick it up, then decides against it.

Dull pop as he twists and grinds the fleshy moonlit thing beneath his heel, slick, scarlet innards spewing out through the trout's glossy gills.

Wandering through the backwoods somewhere in fucken Quebec? Jesus Christ Johnny. Stealthy black flutterings of bats or fucken flying rats or something criss-crossing the path, swooping. Johnny reeling back from a soft flapping shadow grazing his cheek. The urge to shield his eyes warring against the fear of not seeing what he already cant see.

Icy, hostile sludge seeping through the sole of the left boot. Wasted emaciated leather click-flopping with each mindless step. Johnny's blistered heels long since layered numb with highway calluses, but limping now anyhow. Flexing and squeezing his throbbing hand where the glass punctured. Wheezing and cold sweating and wanting to lie down, wanting to stop and rethink, regroup, reassess, but afraid to look too closely, stare the lunacy in the face. For fear of turning back, then turning back again. For fear of throwing his hands up. *What the fuck am I doing here?* The thought to smash the urn on the rocks down over the banks of the nearing river. Or stand at the river's edge and say a little few words and scatter Madonna into the roiling current, black snaking creature with its faithless destination. *Madonna.* Johnny Teardrops standin with an empty urn, miles and years from everything he's ever thought himself to be, no further obligations to this world, nothing pressing, anonymous, stranger, face with no past walking through woods. Wander deeper, deeper. Fashion a shelter. Carve a point on a stick. Track something. Stalk it. Kill it. Eat it raw. Something with blood. Big, small, squirrel, rabbit, beaver, stray dog. Hot blood. Dig a hole and crawl into it and never utter another foolhardy word. Telephones and pavement. Forms to fill. Glass things. Motors. Identification. City folk. Procedures and checkpoints. Lineups and meters. Money. Having. Not having. Showin up and takin off. Party girls. Bull queers. Classifications. Ketchup beer. Dope. Bad ink. Door buzzers. Piss tests. People and their fucken cameras. People. Police. Being *policed*.

What's it all for Johnny? Live your whole life. Live your whole life to find out youre not who they says you are. That they're not who they made themselves out to be. Live your whole life to find out something you knew in your bones the first moment you opened your eyes. That they're not who they says they are. And to start from there. Or not there, but here. Start from here, now. Start from then, even, *not* being what they told you you were. Too late now, to start *new* back *then*. Have to start *now*. Being what? No bloodline, no past, nothing to show but a file thick as Pius's dimwitted skull. Marks and scars with no stories to go along with. Bones that crick and pop and grind where they shouldnt.

Johnny home from Whitbourne. Back in that house. Hardly a word spoken. No special dinner, no welcome home, no welcome, not fucken welcome. Tanya off at Jimmy Dawson's shack, coming home to change her clothes and shower once in a while. Grungy stink of weed and jizz and Charlie perfume. Dopey glaze in her eyes, hugging Johnny on her way out the door and wishing she had a bit of money for him. Johnny on his own with Pius and the missus, *her*, Old Bat Shit, who once was his mother, who mighta looked him in the eye twice in her life. *Her* with her stories of UFOs following her in by the pond on her evening walks. *Her*, barred off in the bedroom muttering Hail Marys for days after running into her father's ghost in the old churchyard down the harbour. With her past lives and bad nerves and horse tranquilizers and weekend excursions to the Mental in St John's. Fucken burnt, tellin ya. Gone, she was, gone long before Johnny was ever spat out into the world. And now the three of them sat around the living room watchin that show on CBC, what was it, that one with the cop who walked around crime scenes and had flashes and visions. Bald-headed fella with glasses, moustache. Who fucken cares what it was called. Sat there, pumping TV slop into their brains, and Johnny walks to the fridge and pours himself a half glass of Pepsi. Then to the cupboard for the bottle of Crown Royal. Pius, God love the sodden old shithead, not registering what Johnny's doing until the glass is just about topped off. Johnny with the drink gone before Pius makes it across the kitchen floor. Tossing the glass into the sink where it shatters into the supper pots. Pius dead in his tracks. Johnny, for the last six months steady go at the weights, and a foot taller than when he went away. Pius's hand on automatic, fiddling with the buckle of his belt, his jaw tight, quivering. Johnny laughing, delighted.

Whatcha gonna do with that belt old man?

The old girl catching the scent of violence and shouting at the two of them that the program is back on:

Come on, lay off that nonsense!

You shut the fuck up in there *Mother*. Nothing to do with you.

Pius? Pius? Mind what the doctor said! Pius???

Pius with his fist clamped tight to the buckle, waiting, waiting like an old burnt-out gunslinger. Johnny casually twirling his head on his shoulders, grinning, his right hand drawn back behind his torso, down, out of sight.

You listen here my son, you dont talk to your mother . . .

She aint my *mother*. She belongs in a fucken straitjacket . . .

Pius??? Pius what's he sayin???

I'll call the cops on you, little bastard . . .

And with that word Johnny grounds his left foot forward and throws the punch he's been waiting his whole life to throw. Breakneck uppercut that pancakes Pius's nose with a staggering bloody crunch of failed vertebrae and mushy cartilage. Ah Christ, hardly any way for family to be gettin on, what? Then a straight left jab to the mouth and one of Pius's teeth clacking into the far corner of the kitchen. Old Bat Shit howling blue murder out through the living room window. Johnny casually slipping into his jacket, tucking the bottle of Crown Royal under his arm. Scooping Pius's tobacco and papers from the kitchen table. Pius on the floor dazed and gurgling in a puddle of blood and the old girl jumpin on the couch in the living room screamin for help, *Help, help us!!!!* Wouldnt know but Johnny was some sorta home invader, some stranger in off the road.

Johnny raises the bottle of Crown Royal and grins at the scene, walks out the door into the crisp fall night, thinks about going back for the Pepsi, then carries on towards the lower path to the Gut Pond. Where else to wait out the shitstorm? A grand lifting, a new weightlessness as he pushes through the reeds towards the twine shed down by the Gut. Fresh absence of dead weight. Johnny feels faster, stronger, even smarter. Dangerous. Not to be fucked with. Ever again. He pictures Pius in the deafening slow-motion moment before the first punch destroyed the middle of his face. The flash of fear, the dawning panic, the reluctant passing of the torch. The twinkle of new knowledge that what once was will never be again. And then the tumbling of that old man onto the faded and scarred linoleum. Johnny replays the scene again and again, flexes his left hand where the knuckles are indented with the pattern of Pius's teeth. And he tries to feel something other than glory, tries to conjure up something soft, something lenient. But he cannot. McGregor sayin *I know you Johnny Keough, I know your kind. Youre the kind who doesnt know that other people feel. Youre the kind who doesnt feel for other people. Youre a fucking little sociopath. That's what you are. And you dont even know what that means do you Johnny? You dont even know what you are.* Johnny tracking the word down in a dated medical text in the library—*referred to as a personality disorder characterized by the inability to form human attachment and an abnormal lack of empathy, masked by an ability to appear outwardly normal.* Having to look up the word empathy too—*the capacity to recognize, and, to some extent, share feelings with others in society.* Johnny slamming the heavy text shut when he feels McGregor's eyes scanning him from across the table. McGregor grinning, peeling an apple with a pearl-handled pocketknife that Johnny woulda given his left nut to get his hands on at that moment. Lying in his bunk that night and thinkin *So that's what I am, a disorder. That's why I never shed tear one at Mikey's funeral. Cause I'm a disorder.* Uncle Austin, Mikey's dad, with Johnny held up by the lapels of his Sunday jacket:

Fucken abomination! That's what you are!

Shaking Johnny back and forth like a scarecrow outside the funeral parlour, and not speaking words, groaning through his teeth, boozy spittle blasting Johnny's face and neck. Then Austin on his knees in the gravel parking lot, big bubble of snot bursting onto his moustache. All the gang from school leant against the back wall of the parlour pretending not to see, not to hear. And what did any of em know? Voices? Women crying. Pius, God love the old pasty-faced prick, standin at the edge of the parking lot trying with the toe of his shoe to stand a bottle cap on its edge.

Johnny bending to pick up a button popped loose from his jacket.

Not feeling.

This bitter, long-gone scene, the numbness of those hostile days that followed Mikey's suicide, all that slicing through Johnny's head as he booted open the heavy wooden door of the government twine shed the night he dropped Pius. Flopped down in the corner on a rank pile of capelin nets and sipping at the Crown Royal. Listening to the familiar wail of sirens echoing across the harbour. Drifting off to sleep to the sound of his name crackling through the cruiser's loudspeaker. Not feeling a fucken thing.

And you went quietly that night didnt you Johnny? No fuss, no hassle. Group of gawkers out on the beach road, the flash of the ambulance lights on up over the hill outside Pius's. Down to the Ferryland lock-up for a couple of days, transported into Town then, fast-tracked to your very first adult trial.

Given the brutal nature of Mr Keough's crime Your Honour . . .

Two years less a day. HMP. Johnny barely seventeen, half shitbaked, not knowing who to talk to, where to sit, who to look at. Big burly fuckers eyeballing you. Guards treating you like a youngster. Roaming the block wondering when he was gonna get called out and who by. But how quick they changed their tune, hey Johnny? The fucken mileage when word got around that Johnny was Steve Puddester's son, Stevie the Scar, who was away in Springhill then, tail end of a five-year bit. However that got around. Johnny wondering who in the fuck this Stevie character was. Pack of tobacco waiting on your bunk that first night. Fellas nodding at you walking down the hall. This fella named Shiner shaking your hand like you were old pals and taking you down to the rec room and setting you up with a workout, nobody daring to give you any hassle. Coming back to the cell that evening and someone's after leaving a radio and a wicked set of headphones on Johnny's bunk. Job in the kitchen where you ends up in on every scam, no matter how big or small. Everything passes through the kitchen—cigarettes, cellphones, all the dope, titty mags, endless messages. Yeast pellets and little packets of sugar. Brewing ketchup beer in a garbage bag, a few gallons enough to get the whole wing plastered. Good times, a lot of the time. Like when what's-his-face, that Harnum fella from out around the bay who was locked up for screwing a cow, came along in the lineup to get his supper and Larry Morgan laid a handful of hay on his tray. Harnum swiped the hay onto the floor and Larry Morgan says: *What? It's good enough for your girlfriend.* How the place went up. And where did the fucken hay even come from? Shiner slipping Johnny an address and he starts writing letters to Stevie, his *father*, in Dorchester now. Johnny's heart pounding, the pen shaking in his hand, full of something like hope, tellin Stevie all about Tanya and Pius and Old Bat Shit. About that cunt McGregor in the boys' home. About what happened with Mikey, Mikey hearing nasty voices inside his head. Johnny askin all sorts of questions that he never got no response to. *How did you meet Tanya? What's the story? What do I call you? Do you even know about me? How?* And nothing, not a letter in return. But grateful as fuck for the stuff coming down the line. Pricey new pair of sneakers and a hoodie one day waiting on the bunk. Davey Alyward slipping Johnny an ounce of weed the day before Christmas Eve. And next thing Johnny's going on nineteen years old and the gates are swinging open with no one waiting for him on the other side, no girlfriend, no Tanya, no fucken Pius. Nowhere to go. Not knowing hardly a soul in the city except for a few lads from the inside he didnt really care to see no more. And then Shiner pulling up outside Erin's Pub on Water Street. Johnny hanging with some travelling kids from the mainland, kids with matted hair and German shepherds and everything camouflage and sun-blasted and stinking. Shiner literally grabbing Johnny by the scruff of the neck and heaving him into the truck. A room waiting for him in a boarding house on Brazil Street. A little job. Go over and kick a door in and smash everything in sight. Hundred bucks. Another little job. Wait outside this gym on Elizabeth Avenue and give a certain dipshit a few darts in the face. And dont say a word, dont make a sound, no threats, no names, dont take nothing off him. Dont lose your cool. Two hundred bucks, enough for six green monsters back then. Johnny back on ice in less than a year for assault and uttering threats. Well looked after on the inside though. Well looked after. Going back wasnt too hard atall. Johnny thinkin, nights lying in the bunk, the first time he was in, that there's no way, no way, never again. But then you finds yourself back inside and it's not too bad, really. Easier, knowing the ropes, knowing the shortcuts, familiar faces. First time in Johnny's life he felt like he had a bit of community for fuck sakes. Making up lies, tellin all about his trip to the Mainland to hang with Stevie the Scar. *Toughest motherfucker ever tried on socks, man, no question.*

Day is breaking over the tips of the trees by the time Johnny sets himself down on a rock not three feet from the river. Cant remember having gotten off the path, if ever he was on one. And the odd notion that's he's turned around, been travelling back the way he came. Slumped and staring stupidly at the rushing water, flings a rock into the grey foam collected near the shoreline. Tries to think, tries to conjure up a coherent thought, the seed of some kinda plan. Counts his money. Three hundred twenty and some change. However that happened. Seven hundred bucks' worth of beef jerky and cigarettes? Drinks on the boat? Fucken hell. He hefts the bag of weed, tries to figure what it might be worth, and where or when in fuck he'll offload it. Sitting pretty though, when he finds a buyer. Offload the works of it the one time, none of this grams and quarters shit. He'll know his buyer too, soon as he spots him. Johnny feels for his smokes then, cant hardly believe he's gone the whole night and never reached once for them. He finds them in his front pants pocket broken and damp, tries to salvage a pinch but then tosses the lot into the river. Cramp in the guts again, Johnny frantically whips the trousers down for the third time in as many hours and squats over the rocks but nothing comes, nothing's been right since that hot tub fiasco. Joanna. Jesus Christ Johnny youre losing out, losing out.

See here though Johnny, get yourself outta these woods and make your way down to the Kingston Pen and find some way to get in and visit. Look him in the eye. Let him see who you are. Talk. Maybe make some plans or something. Maybe Johnny could help wrangle up some interest in his case, be Stevie's man on the outside. Get some decent lawyer handling things, that wrongful conviction crowd who got that banker out of jail. Get Stevie sprung finally. And they'll have to cut him the big cheque. The big fucken payoff for locking him away without a shred of goddamn evidence. With a witness sayin he was somewhere else. After confessing to an armed robbery for fuck sakes! Come on. Johnny and Stevie rolling in the dough. Maybe get a place together, settle in, be some sort of family. Dysfunctional? Yeah, more than likely. But that's gettin ahead of yourself now Johnny. Gotta get in somehow first. Walk on into a maximum security pen with no papers or nothing? Filthy as shit with needles and moss and rotted leaves and slimy creature bits. Blood and mystery grease and sweaty road muck caked into your clothes. And they're gonna throw the gates open for the big father-son reunion? Make no mistake. Gotta figure something, somehow.

Johnny spies a little overhang, mossy, halfways dry, tucks hisself in under the mound and lays his head against a cool bank of beige sand. Ancient snarl of roots. Something digging into his back but he's suddenly too shithauled to even adjust his position by an inch to ease the irritation. First ray of sun creeping up the riverbank towards him. The river's monotony. What was Stevie in for that time, back then? Something no one wanted to talk about, something bad enough, and no fucken armed robbery or none of that shit. Something bad. And then not two years later he's out for less than six weeks and lands himself a life sentence. For something he never even done. But see how the distinction, the reverence, see how the *respect* for Johnny fell away once Stevie landed himself a life bit? No threat to nobody no more see. No chance of him gettin out and coming after nobody no more. Smoke and mirrors, the lot of it. Fuck it, Johnny said, chin up, chin up. By that time Johnny could hold his own anyhow. As if there ever was a time he couldnt.

Johnny slips away to that nowhere gap between sleep and dream, watchin the river through his eyelids, the rocks gurgling, small matted creature eagerly digging in the mud near his shoe. A huge ugly bird, hideous kinda chicken with no feathers on its neck, pecking in the brush below the bank to his right. Radio waves, signals, patterns out there. An older man. Groomed. Important-looking. Receding hair, greying. Spectacled. Walks out of the river. Dry as ash. Stands before Johnny. A dog's leash and collar strung over his shoulder. Johnny tries to stand, reaches for a knife he used to carry as a child, but the man eases him back down with a subtle sweeping hand gesture. Johnny relaxes. The man calls for his dog, Maddy. *Maddy!*

Have you seen her? She's not quite your height. Dark hair, tattoos on her shoulders? She's been gone now, gone a good while. She can crawl on her belly across the kitchen floor, for a treat. She took off. She fell in with a hard . . . You think . . . you think you'll see your own out of harm's way, that the world might hold off, that what we know will stay that way until the bloodline is settled away at least, until we're all either on our feet or in the ground. But that's ego, I guess . . . Maddy!

The man pulls a bottle of prescription pills from his pocket and rattles them over his head.

Here girl. Here Maddy. Come get a treat!

Johnny tries to open his eyes but the man brushes and sweeps at the air with his hand again.

You keep those closed young man, for as long as you can. All this wont last, you know. We got what, ten, twenty years tops? And then we'll all starve. Mass starvation, that's what's coming, that's what'll do it. Who youve been, where youve been, teardrops and case files, none of that will make much difference then, when we're bashing each other's skulls in for a sliver of red meat. All you need to sort out is who loves you enough to place themselves beside you in the end. That's all. That's what we need to figure out. Maddy! Here girl! Here my girl! Come on get a treat!

The man drifts on up over the embankment behind Johnny, rattling the pill bottle over his head. He knocks loose some gravel that tumbles down the neckline of Johnny's coat and Johnny squirms away from a stinging pinprick itch that spreads across his neck and shoulders, and when he comes to and sorts his coordinates he starts in scratching furiously at the side of his face that was settled against the sandy bank. He claws at a scurrying in his hair, flaming little pinches and needle jabs. He roots at something crawling across his ear and finds beneath his fingernail a tiny brown fire ant. Plum-sized burning welts throbbing, screaming, pulsating from down the inside of his neckline all the way to his scalp. Johnny stands with the sun blasting full onto the other half of his face and tries to gauge how long he's been lying there, the sun high in the sky now. He touches the right side of his face, the side that's been baking in the sun all morning, well into the afternoon. There is no immediate feeling. Raw suggestive numbness. Johnny staggers over to a docile pool that's collected behind a rock at the river's edge, gawps down at his reflection, the one half of his face a distorted swollen chaos of lumpy bites and welts and then a border running perfectly straight down the middle of his face where the other half is a broiled and blistered beet-red sunburnt mess. Johnny drinks greedily from a faster-moving part of the river, fills his belly with icy water, his teeth aching with the shock. When he's had his bloated fill he splashes water onto his face and grits his teeth against the little girl's snivel that rises in the back of his throat. Fucken hell Johnny, walk on.

Seen worse, been through worse, looked worse. Well, maybe aint *looked* worse, but been a sight out there, no mistake. That time Big Jackie and the lads cornered Johnny outside a party in the Circle, everybody on them speedy bombs that made you wanna chew through the pavement. Everybody except Johnny. Johnny with a few drinks in, and thinkin everything was grand, that it was all settled away, that shit about Big Jackie's little brother. Johnny hadda give it to him, young Shane, who ran off at the mouth about how the video lotto machines up at the Big Easy were rigged to pay out on a timer. None of his fucken business. Not like he dropped a dime in. And so Johnny hadda set him straight, young Shane. And maybe he went a bit hard on him there, but it's all about the message. Then Big Jackie shows up home from Renous and it's this foolish sing-out, retribution and that. But it got sorted, it got sorted. Shiner sorted it. And so Johnny was at that party a couple of months after and here comes Big Jackie and his crew, hopped up on the bombs, lookin to rip Johnny's face off. Nearly almost did too, no question. Big

Jackie hammerin a chess piece, one of the important ones, the king or the queen, into the corner of Johnny's face. Then Shiner showing up. From somewhere. Crowbar. Big Jackie, like he was waiting to be told when to stop, hey Johnny? Come to think on it. Fucken hell. Not worth thinkin about is it? Not worth it. Cause youd snap, youd lose your goddamn mind Johnny. If you had a good hard look, sometime, at who's really who, as opposed to who they says they are, or appears to be. Lose your cocksuckin mind. Shiner prolly arranged the whole scene for fuck sakes. Not worth thinkin about. But Johnny was a sight after that beating. People coming up to him on the street and barely recognizing him. Cheekbone cracked, lip busted open, forehead all purple and yellow, eyebrow stitched back on, fucken detached retina, coulda went blind. A week in hospital. What doesnt kill ya though, like the fella says. Yeah, our John-John's been a sight. Not like now, this is a different kinda sight. But fuck it, never felt better, truth be told. Out on the highway, few dollars in the pocket, drifting along, free as a bird, on a fucken mission. Never better. Never better. Get yourself hooked into a good run now and see if you cant work out some new duds somewhere. Gavin's poncho's warm enough but Johnny's not traipsing across the whole country lookin like some sorta escaped Mexican convict. Bad enough they might spot him for a Newfoundlander. Some hardy boots we needs, whatever you were thinkin to be hoofin across the country in these old things. You werent thinkin Johnny. You were not thinking. You wore a suit for Christ sakes. Gotta get yourself dolled up for the shitstorm, that's what. If youre gonna be off wandering in the woods in the middle of nowhere, sleeping in ant banks, youre gonna at least need decent boots, wouldnt you say?

Fucken Shiner. Bastard. That night after Reddy's going-away party, down at the Piccadilly, only it had another name on it then. Still, same stretch-marked flabby lap dances though. Scattered time youd even catch a glimpse of a tampon string. More of a laugh, that place. Local talent.

See some missus walkin the street sellin ten-dollar blow jobs, some baygirl, and you wonders who she is and then finds out she's strippin at the Pic too. Go on down for a gawk. They'd all end up workin for Shiner then. Down there that night to toast Reddy's latest trip to the Big House. Christ, how many going-away parties for that prick? What kinda people goes out and raises their glasses for a fella who's after beating the living shit out of some old man who had the audacity to wake up while his house was being robbed? Fucken hell. Shiner, yak, yak fucken yakking all night, pinching that girl's tit like that and you could see she was trying not to cry. But you were laughing and snorting along with the boys all the same Johnny. *Fuck off.* Shiner chopping out a big line of baby powder and Johnny fool enough to snort the works of it back, nearly fucken blinded himself. Everybody at the bar in on it, laughing. Johnny knocking over a table and breaking a pool cue across Reddy's back. Reddy booted out of his own party. Come closing time and it's Johnny and Shiner again, thick as thieves, strolling along the waterfront passing a freezie back and forth, tanked on Slippery Nipple shots and two hits of MDMA. Johnny's head full of tell-all visions and useless insane cartoon formulas and flashes of some dimwit summer afternoon from back as far as his fuzzy toddler days. Confessions bubbling up everywhere. Blinkered, intricately detailed ideas, brilliant scams and master plans—all gone straight to hell the minute you closes your eyes for the night. Johnny after pissing on his own boot. He hears Shiner grunting and laughing and whooping and searches for him all around the wharf but dont see him nowhere and then finally spots him dangling some fifteen feet above the water swinging two-handed from one of them big fucken mooring ropes attached to some Russian freighter. Shiner, with that fucken epic beard back then, beads and braids and everything dangling from it, shimmying as far up to the boat as he can and then sliding back to the wharf again, laughing at Johnny for not being able to handle his booze and dope. And then Johnny, the fool, on the rope, shimmying along, Shiner roaring from the wharf, goading him on. And Johnny's made a mental note how far up the rope Shiner got, how close to the boat he came, and that's the mark Johnny's gonna beat.

Smouldering death in Johnny's shoulder muscles and forearms. Palms of his hands cramped and stiffening from holding up his own weight. The cold, noxious stink of the open harbour water beneath him. Dangling there. Three, two feet from the mark, from Shiner's best. And then a jagged tremor shooting up through the rope and down through Johnny's wrists, elbows, into his tight, dead back muscles. The rope swaying back and forth, back and forth, Shiner laughing all high-pitched and psychotic. Johnny shouting at him to stop, *Hold the fuck off Shine, come on!* And if it was anybody else Johnny'd be making all kinds of threats but instead he finds himself hollering as if it's all a bit of late-night fun and he's not hanging fifteen feet above the filthiest body of water in North America. He tries to wrap his legs around the rope and misses the grip and one of his sneakers falls and slaps against the surface of the water and vanishes. His arms useless and worsening. Tryna shimmy back as close to the wharf as he can get before he falls, cause he knows he's gonna fall. Catches a glimpse of Shiner's coked-out drunken sneer and knows full well he aint gonna take no pity on Johnny this night.

Hope you can swim Johnny my son, hope you can fucken swim! Ha!

Johnny finally managing to hook his legs around the thick rope and at the same moment his arms giving way and he's hanging there not knowing where or how he's got the rope gripped, scrounging and flailing to get his hands back around it, feeling stupid, passed over, Shiner's shrill laughter echoing up the harbourfront, and half a second later comes the gummy black harbour stew. No word to describe the taste, the texture, putrid clogging rot in the sinuses. Fresh decay. Dense gritty sludge. What dont go through your mind? How many toilets flushed down into this even in the past hour? Two hundred thousand pisses and shits. Used frenchies and flushable tampons. Poison stuff from the bottoms of cans and containers. Filthy fuckers taking baths and showers and washing arse sweat and scum from the folds of their bodies. Runoff from the abortion clinics. Fucken dead bodies even, people gone missing. Whatever they drains out of folks' bodies in the morgue after they dies, hospital waste. All stirred up into one big hepatitis soup. And Johnny down in it. Johnny down in it. As suddenly sober as a man gets. Some heavy senseless sunken thing, firm but mushy, bumping Johnny's hand as he gropes for a way to the surface. And what else goes through your mind? Once youve taken on the fact that it's in your ears, settling behind your eyelids, seeping into that cut on your knuckle, that it's up your nose and in your mouth and that you think you mighta *swallowed* a teaspoon or two, breathed it down into your lungs? What dont go through your mind? That fella a few years back who fell off a longliner one drunken night and hadda go in quarantine for six months, healthy as a horse and then afterwards all kinds of trouble with his lungs, skin problems, scabs that wont heal. Divers who goes down cutting ropes tangled in the propellers of boats who comes up with their lips all broke out in sores. Christ almighty. What goes through your head is if I lives through this, if the cold dont get me or if I dont suffocate down here, then my life is never gonna be the same anyhow. I'll never be the same again. Better off if I dont make it out, better off. But then you makes it out, Johnny. You makes it out. Clawing your way up that scum-ridden iron ladder, hands and feet numbed out, trying not to open your eyes or breathe. Hauling yourself over the mooring and rolling onto your back, hearing yourself moan, calling for Shiner. *Shiner!* Lookin around and he's nowhere to be seen. How he musta took off lookin for help, he must be gone lookin for a phone, a cop, an ambulance, blankets, a few lads to help fish him out. *Shiner!* And then the cold really setting in. Middle of March, snowing earlier. A different kind of burning cold, your neck seizing up. Johnny on his feet, sopping wet with chunks of harbour sludge in his hair and caked into all his creases, limping and shivering wildly towards the giggly rumble of George Street with the one sneaker on and the shirt plastered to his frame, the jeans glistening, painted on, the cold. That cop next to Ziggy Peelgood's, lookin Johnny up and down and whistling, pointing him towards an ambulance that was pushing its way through the drunken chaos towards Christian's Pub. Johnny mumbling to the paramedic, about the harbour, the toxic stuff, the cold. The paramedic askin Johnny to step aside. *Please sir, step aside, we're on an emergency call.* Johnny pleading. *How sick am I gonna get? Shouldnt I be going to a hospital? I'm gonna freeze.* The paramedic not lookin at Johnny, propping up some drunk little MUN dolly whose gut was bursting out of her blouse. Johnny at the cab stand outside CB's sayin he's got no money, askin the cabbie to take him up over the hill, take him to the hospital. The cabbie locking all the doors and staring straight ahead. Johnny wandering onto Water Street begging to use someone's mobile, for someone to please call an ambulance, *Someone please gimme a quarter for the love of fuck I just fell into the harbour I'm gonna freeze, I'm gonna get sick and fucken die! Come on!* The crowd backing off, backing away, girls squealing. This drunken fool with one sneaker on, soaked to the bone, shivering with chunks of shit falling to the pavement all around him.

Two weeks later down at the East End Club and Shiner is tellin the tale, how he climbed down the ladder and grabbed Johnny by the shirt collar and dragged him up outta the harbour. How Johnny woulda been a fucken goner. Johnny sat at the other end of the bar, still feeling the chill, nodding, grinning. Watchin fuckers buy Shiner drinks.

Funny thing, for all the tromping and tumbling and walking Johnny done through them woods back there, by the time he made it back out to the highway first thing he sees is a tow truck hauling the Rasta boy's busted Ford Explorer up outta the ditch. Came outta the woods hardly twenty feet from the crash site. Fucken hell. Couple of runs a while back. A half hour here, an hour there. The stink of Gavin's weed rising up outta the bag and Johnny coulda sworn the driver of the last ride, this righteous young fella who was supposedly gettin bloody well *married* to a gal on New Year's Eve in fucken New York, Johnny coulda sworn buddy could smell the weed and was right on the verge of calling Johnny out. Johnny had a story all worked out, about how he'd borrowed his brother's jacket and his brother had a prescription for the medicinal stuff because where he was a paramedic and suffered from PTSD because of all the burnt-out shit he'd seen out there, car accidents and gunshot wounds and suicides and shit like that. But he never even got to spin his lies because the righteous fucker decided he just wanted done with Johnny and so dropped him at a gas station long before where he said he was headed. Just as well to be rid of cunts like that, full of judgment, hey Johnny? Never know, never know.

Johnny's feet barely touches the ground though when a big white van that just finished gassing up at the station pulls up alongside of him and in Johnny jumps. This ride was short-lived too. Some oily bastard with thick Coke bottle glasses who kept rubbing his nuts while he went on about the long hours on the road and how he feels so distant from the wife and family. Johnny didnt even have the energy to pop him one. And when he put on his signal light and made like he was gonna pull down this gravel road leading into the woods Johnny just laughed at him. *You might as well drop me off right here now, motherfucker.* Buddy was all apologies then, and Johnny told him not to worry about it, not to bother, just that he wasnt like that. To each their own, yeah. Tons of fellers like that on the inside, strutting around straight as whips, tough as nails, but this look underneath it all, this desperate plea in the eyes. To each their fucken own. Loneliness, mostly. That time Johnny gave it a go when he was in on remand on a possession charge that never went nowhere. And here's this young punk from down in Placentia somewhere goes right to town on Johnny, sucking for all he's worth. Johnny with his head laid against the mouldy brick, keeping watch out across the unit, tryna picture that new young blond guard on her knees in front of him instead. That one who always looked so scared and saucy all the one time, what was her name? But he couldnt hold her there, in his head, couldnt get out of the moment, couldnt get past the fact that it was some young punk from Placentia Bay down there, doing that. No good, no good.

Young punk lookin up at Johnny with this half-crazed *purpose* in his eyes, like to say, *Oh no, oh no, I dont care which way you leans, I'm not stopping till the job is done.* Johnny felt bad then, and let the poor scrap finish. Dark times Johnny, dark times.

Christ.

Spose there's no need to be bringing that up now is there?

Not like there's any question when it comes to our Johnny. Been a goddamn ladies' man since he was twelve years old. Lizzy what's-her-face, O'Neill. Down by the beach in an old twine shed. Fucken *twelve* I was, so, you know . . .

Johnny scuffing along the roadside. Scuffing along. Cars blowing past. How many days is it now, since court? Since the funeral? Christ. Madonna. Since he done the job on Shiner's pad? Three, four? Five days almost? Is it? A full day crossing the Island. All night on the ferry. Old Saul. All day on the road as far as Joanna and that whirlpool business. Fucken hell. Not with a bang, no, not at all. Woke up with the hoof of a fucken moose barely inches from your face Johnny! Lost a bit of time wandering through them woods afterwards. Cant quite figure if it was hours or days or what. Fuck it. What odds? Johnny scuffing along, scuffing along, tryna figure how much money he can make on the weed if he sold it in one go or sold it in bits and pieces. Out with his thumb for the nine hundred and ninety-ninth time this hour. Some sorta midsize SUV pulls up. Finally. Scrawny, friendly-lookin old feller at the wheel. Jesus, you know, where's the lonesome wayward travelling gal from the movies who's taken to the open road in an old convertible, hair blowin out behind her, lookin to take a gamble on an old road dog like Johnny? Pick him up and tease him into a frenzy and pour cold beer down his throat and fuck his lazy brains out in a gravel pit somewhere? She is not out here. And if she is she's not stopping for the likes of Johnny. That ship sailed when you dumped that load of shit in the Jacuzzi back there. Joanna. Stop, stop!

Johnny slips in beside the old feller. Well, not really an old feller, fifties maybe, or late forties. Yeah friendly enough. Pleasant, warm kinda sad-lookin pale eyes. Brand new Blue Jays cap and one of them blue zip-up cotton blazers. Neither wedding ring. Inside of the rig clean as a whistle, that thick heady new-car smell. Right away before Johnny's even settled into his seat he holds out his hand and introduces himself as Jerome something-or-other, from Timmins, wherever the fuck that is Johnny wont pretend to know. He dont ask Johnny nothing about the state of his clothes or his face. If there's a smell he dont seem to notice that neither. He eases back onto the highway and turns on some old George Jones album. Pius's faithful drinking buddy, Jones. Jerome lets Johnny get comfortable and they drives along for a good half hour before he asks Johnny how old he is. And Johnny tells him. Jerome cocks his chin and nods thoughtfully, opens his mouth to say something more and then doesnt. He taps his breast pocket, roots around for a bit and then pulls out one of them nicotine inhalers. Chews on that. Turns the radio down low and Johnny knows something's coming but he cant for the life of him sort out the vibe. Another few minutes and Jerome, staring straight ahead at the car in front, clears his throat and tells Johnny how his own son would have been just turning Johnny's age next month. His voice sorta cracks a bit on the word month, so it comes out right high-pitched and ragged. He dont elaborate though and Johnny's thankful for that but still feels kinda set up to ask the question, backed into a corner. He lets a long minute pass and still Jerome dont offer up no further info so Johnny asks the question he's supposed to ask.

What do you mean *would have been*? Is he dead?

Oh yes, he's gone. He's gone now. Would have been your age next month.

What ahhh . . . what hap . . .

He drowned. It's all in the past. Around this time of year though, I tend to have to work it out a little, all over again. It's not something you ever quite get over, you know.

Jerome stops himself there and pats his pocket again, only to realize he's already got the inhaler in his mouth. He plucks it out from his teeth with a little snap and rolls his window down an inch or so and lets the little plastic bat fly into the wind like you would the butt end of a cigarette. Johnny sits soaking up the warmth from the heater.

I was still drinking, those days. My boy was ten. Myself and the boy's mother had called it quits. So, he was shuffling back and forth between the two of us. He was fine with it. I think things were better, from where he was standing. No more shouting matches. This was back in . . . we were living in Cape Breton then, that's where my ex-wife is from. Glace Bay. I dont know if you know it? Well anyway, the drinking, my drinking, tore the marriage apart. But of course I was too . . . well . . . too drunk I suppose, to see it at the time. Everything was always someone else's fault. And so when we finally called the marriage off and I didnt have to go sneaking around with the bottle anymore, I suppose I got myself in a bad way. This particular weekend, when it happened, well she knew I'd been up to no good all week long and she didnt want to send him with me. She was not having it, kicked up a hell of a fuss. And I knew the truth in what she was concerned about, but like I said I was too stubborn and too stupid, always in a fog. I fought with her for a good hour until she relented. I'd spent the better part of the summer fixing up an old camper and I had a campsite reserved in the park. This was the middle of August. Really hot summer that year. And the plan I had in my head, roast a few marshmallows, a few wieners. Let the boy do what he pleased. Let him have a good weekend roaming around the woods, sw-swimming. While I got myself good and plastered. That was the plan and I stuck to it. The first night was perfect. We had our fire and he did funny dances while I plucked at a guitar. After a while I was too drunk to play and we crawled into the camper. The next morning I was sick as sin. Horrible headache. I burnt his eggs and then I snarled at him for not eating them. He went off with some youngsters from another campsite while I nursed a beer. Later on that morning he wants to go swimming.

I'd bought him one of those rubber dinghy boats. But I was in no mood for it, in no mood for going down to the pond. I was desperate to go back to the bunk for another nap. I tried to convince him that it rained overnight, that the water wouldnt be warm enough until later on, but he wouldnt listen. So I'm grumpy and huffy as hell driving across the park to the pond. He was talking gibberish and making these silly noises and it was grating on my nerves and I was telling him to stay quiet and when he wouldnt I got to shouting at him. I think about that sometimes, more than other things. His little voice and the foolish way he had about him. And me talking to him like that. Like his personality was some sort of inconvenience to me. His little voice. So, I'm sitting up in the truck with my cap down in my eyes, half watching him wade out into the water. I told him not to go past the rope. There was no one around, no other kids. I could tell he wouldnt be in long anyway because when he got in up to his shorts the way his little shoulders hunched together. I knew the water was freezing. But he takes the rubber dinghy boat and launches that and the wind takes it right away. The dinghy brings up on the rope about five feet away from him, but he wont budge to go get it, he's standing there huddled up looking back at me hoping I'll run down and strip off and swim out after it. Sure enough then the wind blows the dinghy over the rope and it starts sailing away across the pond. And he stands there watching it, looking up towards the truck at me. Sometimes I can get all messed up about that part, this time of year. Around his birthday.

I dont know why I'm telling you all this. Maybe because I dont know you. Maybe it's selfish of me. But I know there's no point keeping quiet about it, not talking about it. That doesnt do anything. Every once in a while it helps me to talk about it, that's all. I hope you dont mind. It's a hard thing to even mention around people youre close with. Youre supposed to just . . . well you learn how to shoulder it. Drive yourself nuts if you dont learn. You start remembering things differently, workin it through as if there's going to be some other outcome, this time. You go back, you go back and see yourself sitting there in the truck and tossing the bottle aside and running down and wading out and grabbing up that little dinghy. Having a splash and a dip and mucking off back to the campsite when he had his fill. God in his heaven, you know. And all the years ahead then . . . But, like I said, you can drive yourself bonkers thinking like that. You have to learn to give over. Took me a long time to accept what I did. Or didnt do. I even tried to kill myself that next winter, after it happened. I had a two-year-old Ford Ranger, decent truck, never a spot of trouble with her. I jammed a potato into the exhaust and shut the garage door, got behind the wheel, locked the doors, just in case. I lit up a cigarette, turned the key and she wouldnt start! Brand-new battery, full tank of gas, never a problem with the truck before. She just didnt want to help me out that day. Not for that. Spooky, when I think back on it. But I took it for a sign, you know. I couldnt accept that it was just a coincidence. And I got sober. Not right away and not without a lot of stopping and starting. But I eventually got sober. And here I am. Here we are. Who knows why the truck didnt start that day. Maybe so I could come along and pick you up out here. Maybe it had nothing to do with me. Maybe it's all about you, about your story, your journey. Who knows how things work and why. Or maybe there is no design. Some people find that to be the easier version to contend with. Most folks shy away from looking too close at that sort of business. I guess you can drive yourself mad that way too. You need to balance it out. Anyhow, all I know is that, for some reason, something or someone wanted me to stick around for another while and that same . . . *being* or force or what have you . . . *God*, maybe, that same force decided my boy's time was up when he was hardly ten years old. Because if I believe one thing I have to believe the other. Make sense?

What happened?

What's that?

Your boy, you never finished. What ahhh . . . how did he . . .

Yeah, I danced around it with my high notions, didnt I? I have that tendency, to be full of shit when I need to be anything but! Look he drowned, you know. And it was my . . . it's my responsibility.

Were you charged?

No. Never any criminal charges, no, no. But there should have been. I would have welcomed something like that, a jail sentence. At least then you can have some kind of closure or something, put a time frame on your . . . penance. Sit with it. There was an investigation, but it was an accident, I guess, or that's how it was written up. My wife, my ex, for some reason she never . . . she just wanted it to go away. I mean, I was hungover a bit but I wasnt drunk . . . there was no booze or nothing in the truck by the time, you know . . .

What happened to your boy Jerome?

Ahhh shit . . . shit. I dont . . . well . . . I settled back in my seat, you know. Hauled the cap down in my eyes. Just under the brim I could see that dinghy boat drifting across the pond. He came running up out of the water and making his way up the beach where it looked like the boat was going to land. As far as I knew he was out of the water and just running along. I remember fiddling with the radio. Then I looked up and I couldnt see him. Lost sight of him behind some trees. I guess he had to climb over a few rocks and around some bushes and that. Those old snarly junipers that grow along the edge of ponds. I could see the dinghy where it came to rest up against the far shore. And I sat there and I waited for him to come around the bend. Sitting there waiting for him to come out from behind those trees. But he never did. He never did. I got out of the truck and started calling out to him, all annoyed and put out. Hands cupped over my mouth, calling his name . . .

What was his name?

. . . but ahhh . . . so I made my way over to where I last laid eyes on him, calling out to him the whole while. I thought maybe he was hiding on me, teasing me. And I remember shouting out about the trouble he was in for making me come looking for him. And I was thinking that too, you know, bitching at him under my breath for getting me out of the truck. But by the time I came round to where that patch of trees was, I guess I was thinking other things, hoping and praying he really was just hiding out, playing some game, making a fool of me.

What was his name Jerome?

. . . then I seen the little legs in the water. Little orange shorts with the yellow and white stripes down the side. That's all he'd wear that whole summer, those shorts. He was face down. And I, you know I tried to do all the things youre supposed to do. But he was gone. He slipped and hit his head on a rock and fell into the water and that was that. Sometimes I work through that part a bit much, how he fell. The little twist in his hips, his arms reaching out, grabbing at the air. If he made a yelp I certainly didnt hear him. There was a gash on his forehead that was bleeding a little. So he still must have had a bit of a pulse. I tried, you know. But they said even if I had to have been standing right there . . . But you cant know that for sure. Ambulance. Police cars. Hospital. His mother . . . Jesus Christ. He would have been your age next month . . .

What was his name?

. . .

Jerome?

. . . Brian. His name was Brian. He would have been . . . would have been your age . . .

Johnny reaches out and lays his hand into Jerome's. Jerome nods and wipes at his eyes and doesnt look at Johnny but gives a shot of gas and lets go of the steering wheel for an instant to slap his breast pocket once more. Jerome squeezes Johnny's hand until Johnny feels the tips of his fingers go that tingling numb way, but he wont pull away, he wont pull away cause it's the closest he's been to . . . something . . . in a long time. He wants to tell Jerome about Mikey. How Mikey woulda been the same age too, how things might be different if Mikey was around. But how fucked it all was and is. Voices. And Madonna here in a fucken urn. And all the shit that went down that led her there. He wants to tell Jerome everything, all of it, like . . . but . . . fuck, he knows it wouldnt come out right. It'd all come out sounding desperate and crazy and tangled up.

Jerome gives Johnny's hand a hardy shake and smiles brightly through his red-rimmed eyes.

I've never really told that story. Thank you.

No man, thank you. I needed some cheering up. I mean, just look at me.

Ha! That's what I thought when I saw you, I said to myself, there's a man who could use some cheering up. So there. My good deed for the day!

Johnny and Jerome have the big laugh then, and it's alright, it's . . . it's . . .

Something about Jerome's story. Something eases up in me, in Johnny. I looks down at the urn shimmering in me hands. A jolt of . . . something . . . shoots up me arm and the cold shivers rip through me whole body.

Someone you loved?

Johnny looks up to see Jerome pointing at the urn, at Madonna.

Wh-what?

Well youre carrying an urn . . . I just thought . . . if you want to talk about it . . .

No, no I dont.

10

Fucken hell man, going around the country holding hands with old booze farts. Dead youngsters and haunted Ford Rangers. What next? Just as well youre back out on the hoof Johnny. Another stream of gawkers passing round the bend now, to slow and stare and then slam that pedal down once they gets a good look at our hero, wouldnt know but he might run and catch up and jump aboard if they hangs around the speed limit too long. There's a headspace to this shit, this thumbing racket, a psychology to it. Cant take it personal. Once you starts taking it personal, that's when you loses your steam for it, that's you fucked. Big case of the *why me's, what's wrong with me? If there's a God gimme this one break*. All that nonsense and you knows the jig is up. Soon enough youre laying down on the side of the road and not going nowhere. Gotta be prepared to hoof it the whole ways, wherever it is youre off to, even if it is the other side of the country. Cause what odds, really. What difference? But Johnny's only an hour, hour and a half from Stevie now, so, a little stopover. Look the man in the face, the man himself, somehow. Maybe put a call in from a pay phone and see if you cant get him on the line, fill him in on the situation, enlighten him. He's hardly gonna not wanna see you Johnny, flesh and blood. Curiosity at the very least. And he'll get you in somehow. Stevie Puddester? Prolly give the nod to the guard and Johnny'll breeze on in, no trouble atall.

* * *

Jesus, Jesus, Jesus. Who wants to buy some fucken dope??? Holy sweet fuck. I'm like that fella in that movie, that one about all the junkies over in Ireland or Scotland someplace and the lads gets their hands on this big bag of heroin and goes off and sells it, makes a fortune. Then this one lad robs the works of the money right out from under the rest of their noses and takes off. That's me right there, motoring off into the future with a big bag of dope. More I thinks on it I cant fucken believe how lucky I am. First off, walking away from that moose business with hardly a scratch except a bit of glass in me hand, and then next off, I got a bag of dope must weigh about seven or eight pounds! I could go set up shop somewhere couldnt I? Or unload it all the one time. I mean, youd easily get ten grand for it. I'd let it go all the once for about six, maybe even five. Just to turn it into cash. And I'll know to. Not gonna see Johnny out tryna peddle it off to different fuckers, tryna convince fellers to buy fucken quarter bags. I'm offloading the whole works the one time. Cause I'll know, I'll know me moment. I'll know a buyer the moment I lays eyes on him. Fucken right.

Next run was alright. It was a run, you know. Point A to point B, big fucken deal. Quiet older fella with bloated, beet-red ears so hairy youd swear a sparrow might take nest in there. From away out on the west coast somewhere, this old fella, living in Prescott now, Johnny remembers cause of it being the same as the street downtown, back home. The old-timer, he's quiet for the first while, then he starts on about drugs and being the man, all that stuff, how he useta be the real go-to fella back in the day, how there never was a party started but he was right in the middle of it, dealing dope, all the women on the go, everybody knowing his name, everybody wanting him to party all the time. Then suddenly he says he turned around one day and realized he never had a friend in the world, and that's when Johnny lost interest cause he knew right where it was bloody well going, how buddy then had this revelation that he had a friend all along, *And he can be your friend too, he can be your friend, do you know who I'm talking about stranger?*

Ah fuck off will ya.

Excuse me?

Yeah, no offence or nothing but I heard it all before, all that stuff about Jesus and gettin saved and everything. I'm in no fucken mood for it.

Half felt like flashing the bag of dope at him.

But a nice quiet, civil ride again. Johnny glancing across only once to see a couple of maggots squirming outta the old fella's blood-red pulsing ear, plopping down onto the shoulder strap on his coat, twitching and flipping around. What have any of us got for brains anyhow?

Johnny hopping out nice and cheery on the 401 down from Prescott. Some arse-fuck town in Ontario. Away to Christ from underneath all that French shit at least, all them woods, couldnt even read a bloody road sign. And now hoofing it again. Long time since anyone even slowed down and threatened to stop. But not taking it personal, that's the trick. Nothing personal. Bunch of fuckers racing along towards your lobster pot lives without thought or heed to who might be out there needing a bit of a boost. Suck me hole. Johnny flips off the last line of cars and kicks at the dirt and roars something even he dont understand. And when he turns around again he hears a rig pulling in onto the shoulder, the crunch of rubber on gravel, then sees the long white ominous snout of a police cruiser rolling up alongside of him. Jesus Christ there's no end to it. Halfways across the country and they're still lurking about. Johnny does a quick scan but it's a good haul to the woods and even then he'd have to cross over the divided highway and up over this bright-orange fencing and there's no tellin how long the woods are gonna last cause there's the sense of a slope beyond the treeline and maybe a town down there. No guarantee he'd get away. And you knows what it looks like when you runs Johnny. So, staying put. But no fucken way is Johnny sitting in the back of that cruiser. Not this day. Only the one cop, sure. Maybe Johnny might be in the fucken driver's seat when all this is said and done, whatever it turns out to be. Go big or stay home, hey Johnny?

Miserly drone of the power window on the passenger side and Johnny dutifully bending down to give the cop a good look at this lanky and ramshackle poncho-sporting burnout who's after doing God knows what to fuck knows who to get to where he is right now. Black duffle bag full of weed slung over Johnny's left shoulder. *To the death Johnny. To the fucken death.* An almost human expression flickers across the cop's lack-lustre mug when he gets a good look at the mangled sun-blasted mess gawping in through the window of the cruiser.

What in hell's name happened to your face son?

And Johnny unloads the whole story, how a couple of French punks picked him up hitchhiking and pulled off somewhere and roughed him up and tried to roll him but how Johnny fought them off good and proper and then got lost in the backwoods and ended up spending the night. Ants and sunburn, the cold and the wet, horrible, officer, just horrible. Johnny even senses that telltale swelling in the back of his throat, the brimming moisture in his eyelids. Lawdog shaking his head, shaking his head. When Johnny finishes his story the cop sighs and stares out across the highway at the moaning traffic, one arm draped across the steering wheel. Shaking his head, staring.

Yeah those Frogs son, take and take and take. Never satisfied. Cut your throat for a glass of wine. I should know, since I married one.

Well, I wouldnt ahhh . . . I dont . . .

Lucky they never tried to fuck your ass too. Still, puts me in an awk-ward position if they got away with your wallet and such. I get a call about some vagabond on the highway making his way into town and I let him pass on through without checking his background and next it turns out he's a wanted killer. Travelling rapist. Sex fiend. That wouldnt be too pleasant, in my opinion.

So . . .

So unless you got yourself some proper identification I'm going to have to ask you to come for a ride.

Johnny fingering the corner edge of Gavin's ID card in his front pants pocket. Moment of truth now Johnny. Make or break the rest of your days. Warrant out there, big bag of dope slung over the shoulder.

Well I got . . . I got my licence on me here somewhere . . .

That would be what we call proper identification son.

Perverse reflection of Johnny's scorched and seared features in the window, his spirits rising half a notch to note that the teardrops are at least muted somewhat beneath the recent carnage. Tryna steady his hand as he slips the greasy licence through the cruiser's passenger window. Lawdog plucks it from the outstretched hand and scans it beneath a fuzzy blue light attached to the underbelly of the dash. Johnny waits. There comes a long shrill beep. Lawdog fingering a keyboard, scrolling through a small touch-screen set-up. All very high-tech, hey Johnny. Gone are the days, gone are the days. Lawdog drumming his digits across the steering wheel, watchin the road, the bone-grey skyline beyond. Johnny flexing his stiff cold calves, thumping his busted heels, waiting, waiting to find out if maybe this Gavin fucker is the wandering rapist type, or some wanted dope-slinger, and which the better scenario then, to own up to being Johnny Keough or to go down as some fucken grubby Bluenoser? Waiting for the cop to compare the picture on the card to Johnny's vile rumour of a face. The screen flashing pale orange. *Gone are the days.* Lawdog leaning across the front seat with the card pinched nimbly between his knuckles.

Youre a long way from home Mr Gallant. What's your intended destination?

Wha . . . ?

Where are you headed?

West coast . . . Vancouver.

Vancouver. My, my. You got a few miles ahead yet. What takes you out that way?

Johnny tugging the urn from the depths of his knotty poncho then, holding it up for the cop to see.

Ashes . . . my ahhh . . . gonna scatter em on a beach over there.

Uhmmm . . . well . . . you get in off the road as soon as you can, okay? I'll be back this way in an hour and I dont want to see you out here. Okay? And watch out for those bloody Frenchies.

And with that Johnny's left trembling and choking in a dead dry cloud of grit and dust, shackled to his treacherous shadow, staring down at the photo of the bright-eyed and hopeful hippie mama's boy tucked into the corner of the impounded licence. Save for the poncho and the snarled shade of the hair, no resemblance, no likeness whatsoever.

11

Steady stream of cars and trucks and empty minivans rippin on past. Burning on down the line, paying no heed atall. Not a sweet fuck do any of em give about young John-John, our hero. And why should they? And where in Christ's name are they all off to anyhow, when you thinks about it, hey Johnny? Racing off to pick up piss-arsed youngsters they didnt hardly want in the first place. Accidents, like the rest of us. Waiting for em to grow up and get out so's they can get on with their lives. Scrounging for change in their sparkling ashtrays to make the price of a coffee that tastes like it was strained out of a dog's arsehole. Must be nice. Lining up for that then too. Talkin slop, nonsense, on their five hundred dollar phones. Maybe. I dont know. Meeting people they dont even wanna see. Going off to jobs they dont even want or dont like. Is that what it's like? Taking shit from fuckers who're good for nothing only giving shit? Every last one of em wishin they could keep on driving off into some other life. Maybe. Home to watch the hockey game. Supper table. Bagging up leaves. Hosing down the driveway! Ripping their eyebrows out over their youngsters' homework. Going down on the same old cock, heaving it aboard the same old pussy. Constantly in the hole. Going on and on about that thing they always wanted to do and knowing in their guts they're never gonna get around to it. Terrified of making a wrong move. In-laws and daughter's shady boyfriends. Icy morning walking some prick of a dog that couldnt give a fuck about you unless you got a hambone in your pocket. The frantic stench of monotony. Holy Mary Mother of Fuck. Is that what it's like? Is that the alternative? Well slam that pedal down missus. Run it right out over a cliff somewhere.

Lay your head down in the oven and breathe deep.

Wrap a cord around your neck and tie it off and kneel and lean.

Put a bullet in your brain old man.

Bite down on that barrel and squeeze that trigger like Mi . . .

Go on, take the whole bottle, girl.

I wouldnt blame you girl.

I dont.

Wait for the cottonballs to kick in and toss some old-school Valium in on top.

Fuck court, fuck those greasy lawyers, fuck Johnny Keough.

Big glass of brandy to wash it all down.

Go on in and lie down now.

Turn on your favourite song, count the years between the heartbeats.

Give over to that staggering dark.

Goddamn it, Madonna.

Shit man, ugly metallic taste in the back of me throat. No smokes. Half tempted to pick up an old butt from the roadside there about half an hour back. No fucken mistake. I mean, I likes me smokes but I aint no slave and I aint no scumbag neither. Mind you now, there was a time. Like that time up around Mayor Avenue when I was in the rooming house for a few weeks, crashing with a bunch of students and tryna scam a student loan. Busted flat and trying not to be ripping shit off all the time, tryna do it different for a while. To think I coulda done anything else but what way I went. Anyhow, yeah, the night I busted the passenger-side window out of a little Jetta. Passing by and gasping for a smoke and there's the ashtray all lit up under the streetlight, overflowing with butts, most of em snipes, like half-cigarettes. Out goes the fucken window of the car anyhow. Johnny racing up the road with some big wheezing beer-bellied monster shouting after him, almost keeling over with a heart attack after running ten fucken feet. Johnny whooping it up to have a bit of tobacco on the go. Home to his little room with the filters and the roller and dont even notice till he lights up the first one that all the butts are bloody menthol. Cameo. Christ almighty. Bashing out a fella's car window for dirty old dried-out menthol tobacco. Fuck that. Two nights later Johnny and some punk from out Grand Falls way ripping off a bar up on Ropewalk Lane. Lotsa smokes that night by Christ. Premiums too.

Musta been twenty fucken miles crossing that causeway into Kingston. Dipped in under the overpass and dropped the trousers yet again. Boots are shot altogether. Cannons and sailboats. Buncha arseholes standin around some glass shack with Styrofoam cups, all stopped gawking at Johnny when he passes. Johnny foolish enough to shout out and ask how to get to the Pen, Kingston Pen, and some smart fucker shouting back how there's dozens of ways to end up at the Pen. The big roars out of his buddies then. Ontario Street. That's creative. Fucken K-Rock Centre! Swanky brick houses. Edge of town. Gulls overhead, floating and gliding and circling like vultures, the way they do sometimes. You wonder about that, about what they're up to. Gulls. They gets the whiff of something and waits up there in the air to see if some goodies are gonna materialize outta the stink. Circling over some rich bastard's garbage, waiting for the pit bull to fuck off to sleep out of it. Gulls, fucken rats in the sky, no character. Seen one in by the old dump one time making off with a shitty old Pamper. Crows now, them are the smart fuckers. What's-his-face, down by the slipway, Wally B, lived by hisself in a gutted-out school bus up on blocks. People used to call him the Jap, I think cause he had jaundice when he was younger. Dirty old fucker, shitting in bread bags, pissing in bottles. Me and Mikey'd get in the bus sometimes and flick stuff around and rob his empties, when we were young fellers. Wally off on a jag somewhere down the Shore. Fucken stink of the place, the whole last ten feet of the bus blocked with garbage and blankets and damp old cardboard boxes stuffed with pictures and postcards and engine parts and busted capelin nets and frayed-up lengths of ropes and little metal mechanical bits and fucken everything under the sun, all junk. Me and Mikey in there that one time and found one of them inflatable sheep with the little slit in the hole. All covered in duct tape from where Wally was after busting it up so often. Inflatable sheep! Dirty fucker. Stacks of weird girly mags in some foreign Nazi kinda language with pictures of women shitting in fella's mouths. Fucken burnt, man. Lookin at that stuff and we only eight or nine years old. Mikey wide-eyed and quiet, not knowing quite what to think, face flushed red. And that pellet gun. That was a find. Taking turns shooting bottles under the Gut Bridge until I staggered under a gust of wind and lost the gun over the side of the wharf. Mikey fished it up with a rod the next evening but it was useless. Fuck man, it was always Johnny and Mikey, Mikey and Johnny, them days. Taking turns with each other's shadows. And then, I dont know . . . he got . . . I mean . . . you just hit this age . . . and suddenly Johnny Keough was bad news and poor young Mikey was having to take pills and everything was all hushed and weird and fucken fragile.

Anyhow, old Wally, for all his filth, he was good with the animals. Youd hear tell that he had a tame fox this one summer, eating out of his hand, or a weasel that useta come in and pick around and sit across the table from Wally when he was having his supper, waiting for a few scraps. And sure a weasel, them things'll rip your fucken throat out. But one summer Wally had this crow that he got in a nest when it was still small enough. They says he was watchin the nest and knew when to take the chick. Raised it up, taught it to catch stuff out of the air, like he'd toss up a bit of sausage or something and the crow'd pick it off. Never another rat down around the bus for that whole year neither. Even taught the thing to laugh and say hello, or hi, or something. And it'd steal anything it could fit in its beak, didnt matter if it was shiny or flashy, like you hear, just anything it could carry. One of Wally's drinkin buddies one time, the crow swoops in and swipes a lit cigarette right out of his mouth, brings it up across the marsh and drops it in the dry grass and the upper meadow goes right up in flames. Took about twenty bodies to put the blaze out. And there's the crow perched up on top of a telephone pole the whole time, watchin everybody fighting the fire. Squawk. Laugh. Hold a fucken grudge too, them crows. Feller from Ferryland one time, who ran a little fish truck, he was down by the plant and kinda casually tossed a rock up over the roof of the plant and struck Wally's crow. And every time thereafter when the little fish truck showed up outside the plant, there comes Wally's crow shitting all over the windshield, dive-bombing at buddy. Smart fuckers. They never forgets a face. Wally even useta tell how he woke up one morning with the crow on his chest squelchin and squawkin at this ungodly pitch. Wally shoos it away and the crow perches on the sill of the open window and squelches some more, starts circling the bus then, swooping down and rapping on the glass, gone fucken mad altogether. Wally looks around for a fire but there's nothing. Finally he goes out and follows the crow to see what the fuck is going on, follows it right down to the breakwater where the crow is circling over something in the water. Wally sees a dog then, old waterdog, splashing around a bit, his snout barely up over the surface, not able to move, gettin tired. Crow swoopin around and screamin. Wally sees what's up and wades out up to his neck towards the dog, and here's the dog's leg all snarled up in a bit of rope. And the tide rising. Wally works the dog's leg free of the rope and the dog with barely enough strength left to swim ashore. Crow saved the dog's life! If you can believe what you hears. Whatever came of that crow I dont know. Heard tell that a cat got him, cornered him in back of the bus. Someone else said he took off with this massive flock of crows that passed up along the Shore one year. Thousands of em, crows, big black cloud coming over the hills like something out of the Bible. One year that happened, this colossal migration, and never after. Wherever the fuck they were all off to.

Standin here lookin at them gulls circling, scavenging rich mainlanders' garbage bins, and you wanna fucken shoot em all. Remind you of home in a different way, before they told us we couldnt catch a fucken fish no more. When there was money on the go, good work on the go, and people seemed settled and content. Not what came after, after even the gulls fucked off—fucken misery. Whole other level to the booze. Like the whole town shifted overnight. And then there's nothing to do, no way to scrounge up a dollar. Johnny, since he was nine years old, never short a pocketful of change, always with twenty or thirty dollars tucked away somewhere. Knew his way around a skiff better than he did his own bedroom. Take a fish and bleed it out, gut it, fillet it, cut the tongue, ears, sound, sculps, cheeks, napes, whatever bit someone was lookin for. Want them fillets skinned and boned? Not a fucken problem. And then nothing. Nothing to do, no way to make a bit of money, all this stuff that youre good at, fast at, and it's no fucken good to you. So what do you do? You starts kicking up shit, robbing stuff, scamming. Crawlin in through windows lookin for booze, lookin for anything small enough not to be missed that can sell for a quick dollar.

Scavenging.

Like them bastard gulls.

How else?

Kingston Pen, there you have it. The Big House. Oldest, meanest, dirtiest slammer in the country. No fucken thank you. National Historic Site says the sign on the front wall. That's how old the place is. A National Historic Site. And they complains about HMP back home. And look at the likes of the ones youd be banged up with too, that bigshot army fella who went around wearing women's drawers while he was rubbing shoulders with the Queen, what's his face, and Bernardo, another fucken wackjob, then that twisted old kiddy killer from out west who went around screwing and slaughtering youngsters, fucken Olson, crazy old Clifford. He was fucken burnt. Heard he was in KP too. And them're only the famous ones. The rest of the pop is made up of the hardest, most vicious, rabid motherfuckers in the country. Hell's Angels. *Real* skinheads. And my old man amongst em. My old man in there now these years for something he never even fucken done. And still holding his own, no doubt. Chin up. I mean, not likely that he's running the show or nothing, but I'd say he's bloody well holding his own.

Here Johnny finds himself shifting around, tippy-toeing outside what looks to be the main gates, lookin for the buzzer or call box or some sorta sign directing visitors where to go. Nothing. Concrete. Razor wire. Half expected to see armed guards strutting their stuff. No. All cameras these days. Johnny about to start shouting and slapping at the big iron gate when he suddenly remembers the backpack full of weed slung over his shoulder. That's one sure way of gettin in Johnny. Them boys back on the bridge, they'd get some kick outta this. Fucken dunce.

Johnny stashes the backpack behind some bins outside the entrance to a prison museum directly across the road. Imagine that, a fucken *prison* museum. Next he's inside, in the squat churchy lobby that stinks of some sort of cleaner, ready to rip the living shit out of a battered phone book dangling from a pay phone when some nerdy pimply-faced student type sidles up and asks if there's something he can help with, something he can do. I turns and looks at him and he nearly goes arse over tits tryna put a bit of distance between us. He reaches out for the wall to steady himself. Forgot about me snarled up face.

Yeah, I'm lookin for the number for the main desk across the road there, the Pen.

Excuse me?

But I dont bother repeating meself. I lets my request hang in the air for a few seconds until it penetrates his thick skull. Finally he goes:

You mean the prison?

Yeah. What's it under?

I . . . I dont know . . . I guess it's . . .

You works right across the street in a prison museum and you dont know how to get in touch with the crowd across the way? Christ man.

We . . . we're not affiliated . . . we're . . . but it's probably under government, in the blue pages, here, let me look.

No time flat Johnny's little student helper got the number wrote down on back of a museum brochure and even got Johnny hooked up with a quarter to make the call. None too shabby. Johnny dials the number and drops the quarter in the slot and stands there listening to the options until he's offered one about regular visiting hours and visitor information, number seven. He lets it ring and ring and ring and ring and ring until some crackly far-away voice says hello. Not *Kingston Penitentiary* or *Hello, front desk* or *Visitor Information* or nothing like that, just this gruff *Hello*. Like you could picture the guy splayed off on a couch watchin cartoons hoping the phone is gonna stop ringing.

Yeah, hello.

. . .

Well, is this, is this Visitor Information?

It is.

Crackling, thin, faraway voice like I was making a phone call to another century or something. Right across the jeezly road.

When are regular visitors' hours?

Not for another two hours.

Okay. So . . .

So?

So, well, I'd like to arrange a visit. With a prisoner.

Name?

Me? Ahhh, Joh—ahhh Gallant, Gavin. People calls me . . .

Is that your first or last name?

Gallant is my last name and . . .

Inmate's name?

. . .

Inmate's name?

Puddester. Steve, or Steven.

Nature of your relationship with the inmate?

He's me . . . he's my biological father, I guess.

You guess?

Well he is, you know, but I never . . .

Have you ever visited a federal penal institution in the past?

No . . .

Have you been sentenced to serve time in a federal correctional facility?

No . . .

Is the inmate expecting a visit from you at this time?

No, he's . . .

Hold the line please.

Johnny left scratching his nuts in the museum lobby while the line goes dead. Gavin's licence. Spose if it worked with the fuzz back there a ways, who you knows now was fucken itching to haul me in, well there's as much of a chance of slipping past the pencil pushers at the visitors' desk. Just as much of a chance. Christ, half nervous here. Coming all this way and hardly a thought to what I might wanna talk to him about. Let alone that, but *why* in the hell I *wants* to see him even? Like you cant shake the notion that you owes it to him or something Johnny. But why would you? Warrants and bags of weed and stolen ID and lookin like you do. Stuck out like a sore thumb in the bright midday mainland sunshine. Squeaky-clean streets, all this grass and trees and shit. Goggle-eyed old fuckers in their little eco-friendly cars slowing down gawking at you, wondering what in the name of Christ youre doing out walking along the road? A real live hitchhiker? What sort of abomination? No, it aint quite the grungy, fuck-it-all, rock and roll biker town they makes it out to be, is it? Young nerdy crater-face lurking in the hallway beyond the lobby, giving everything a sizing up, memorizing Johnny's getup. Most excitement he's had all fucken year—fella come in to make a phone call! What's the word for all this Johnny? *Con*-spic-u-ous. And not only that, but you knows the stories, how fellas gets tracked down. How fast the word travels when it wants to. Fella gets jumped in Springhill and even the fucken skinners at HMP knows about it before the guards in Springhill do. Small little world. You knows goddamn well someone's gonna find out you were here and no question it'll get back to Shiner's crowd. Assuming Shiner gives a sweet fuck. But you knows he do. Gotta save face. And what would *you* do if someone busted into your swanky skin pad, someone you knew and knocked around with, and demolished the place and then ran off with a wad of your cash? Dont say you wouldnt hold no grudge Johnny my son. So why bother showing your face *here*, of all places? Think Stevie the Scar is gonna . . . what? Approve of something? Give you some sort of nod? That you'll get some kinda clearance out there? Father and son, at long, long last. Why? *Just. Fuck. I do. I gotta see.* What, are you supposed to go your whole life and not *see*? Pass through the same town and not try? Maybe this is one of them moments that everybody talks about. One of them points in a person's life when things gets turned around, or things start unravelling a different way or whatever. One of them things you gotta do so nothing is ever the same after. Or maybe nothing comes of it. Who knows if even he'll want to see me? Some feller he never heard of named Gallant who's claiming to be his son for Christ sakes. Who knows? Maybe this is where I'm supposed to be right about now. Who the fuck knows what's waiting out there, between here now and the other side of the country? How likely that I'll be passing this way again? Unless it's in handcuffs and I'm thirty thousand feet in the air. So who gives a shit? So what if I goes down anyhow? Johnny Keough. So what if they storms him at the gates and tackles him and slaps the cuffs on him? Not all that foreign now is it? So fucken what? What else do I know? Fuck it.

Yes hello, Mr Gallant?

This is not the same voice atall, this voice is all solemn and careful, in control, present, very present. Not the same line either, clear as day, the line now, no buzzing or humming or nothing. This might be not good Johnny.

Yes?

Yes Mr Gallant, it appears Mr Puddester is no longer with us . . .

Dead? Holy shit man . . .

No, no, he's been transferred. Quite some time ago in fact.

Transferred? Why? He was . . .

Well I dont have that information before me, and it would be confidential regardless. Is there anything . . .

Well . . . where was he transferred to?

I'm not at liberty to disclose . . .

Come on man . . . I'm just lookin to meet him. I never met him. I'm after comin a long . . . a long ways . . . You cant tell me where he's at, where to look for him?

Long pause on the other end and the line goes all muffled for a bit, distant underwater murmurs, and then he's back on, the big dramatic submissive sigh, milking the moment, hey Johnny? Cause you gotta believe some of em are halfways human, at least on the administrative end.

Mr Puddester was transferred to the Frontenac Institution about five years ago.

What? Okay, well where . . . can you . . .

It's a minimum-security facility. Get on Bath Road. Not far.

Minimum? That cant be . . . Bloody hell. Okay, well . . .

Thank you for your call Mr Gallant, good luck.

Pickin through a second-hand clothes store, a Sally Ann on Bath Road, and Johnny finds a practically brand-new pair of army boots, perfect fit. Little gems, like Madonna called em. Walk into one of them dreary old thrift shops on Kenmount Road back home with Madonna and she'd walk out lookin like a fucken superstar. Johnny's never been one for clothes and shit. But he knows a good pair of boots when he sees one. Aint worn army boots since he was thirteen. Make ya feel like stompin the shit out of something. Might as well go in for the pants too, considering the state of the ones he got on. Hauling on a heavy pair of washed-out army-green cargo pants and registers a pang of guilt or nostalgia or the rumbles of an old anger as he stuffs Pius's suit pants into a garbage bin. Pius, God love the old bug-eyed fucker, on the news that time when all the TV cameras came to the Legion for some coalition thing, askin the fishermen what can be done to keep the bottom from falling out of it all. Pius in the very suit, roaring about how Newfoundlanders are supposed to be a gentle people, and how maybe it's time we showed em a different side of ourselves, cause sure as there's shit in a cat no one's gonna do the fighting for us. The crowd in the old Legion cheering Pius on. Young Johnny lookin back and forth between the proud and passionate fisherman on the TV and the red-faced, drunken, far from gentle lummox sat on the couch across from him and Johnny thinks *I hopes it all goes under,*

I hope we all starves. Phone ringing off the hook that evening, all hands from up and down the Shore praising Pius to the high heavens for tellin it like it is. Johnny too young to grasp the politics, bewildered somewhat by all the recent chest-thumping around town. Everywhere you turned it was like something was gonna happen, like someone was gonna take *action.* Johnny just about old enough to know that no one ever would. Watchin Pius that evening while he grumbled into the phone, something about how the lot of em should storm the Confederation Building, hearing in his voice that no one ever would. And in that moment, listening to Pius's liquored bravado on the phone with his mates, in that very moment, all Johnny's boyhood fears of Pius's loose moods and looser fists, and despite the fact that he wouldnt be old enough to really swing his own fists for a while yet, all those fears fall to the wayside. Pius, a couple of weeks later, walloping Johnny across the backs of the legs with a busted work boot, and Johnny standing and taking it, not a flinch, not a peep, watchin it all from somewhere up above, observing the onslaught from up in the farthest corner of the room. Pius, God love his woolly socks, wheezing and panting, waiting for Johnny to start in with his telltale snivelling and pleading. Johnny after being caught down on the wharf with a load of grub, Pepsi and chips and canned sausages, robbed out of the cabin of the Ledwells' longliner. Pius finally slackening off with the boot long enough to catch his breath, askin Johnny if he's ever gonna do it again. Johnny crumpled on the porch floor, the backs of his knees and thighs throbbing numb and swollen, lookin straight into Pius's bloodshot eyes and sayin *Yeah, more than likely.*

Three stinking blistered hours on the road tryna beat in them army boots until Johnny's finally outside the main gates to the Frontenac Jail in the rancid muggy mainland evening. Minimum security. You dont even wanna think about what that means, the why. Like why would some hardass bastard like Steve Puddester, in for a life jolt, get transferred to some country club on the edge of town? It dont make no sense and you dont wanna think about it Johnny. Cause it certainly aint the kind of benefits you gets from leaning on a guard. Some heavy-duty paperwork tangled up in all that, a transfer. And if he sold someone down the river, which is fucken impossible, well he'd go into PC or get sent off to a super-max like Renous. Cause once they tags you a dangerous offender there's not much chance of gettin out from under it. Ever.

Johnny thumbs the buzzer at the front gates. The voice on the other end cackles back that visiting hours are over for the day. Come back ten o'clock tomorrow morning. Who is it youre wanting to visit? *Steve Puddester.* Nature of relationship? *I'm his son.*

Sun going down and Johnny so dead tired on his feet, sitting on a stump next to a burnt-out Ford tucked into the woods behind the prison. Could walk back into town and snatch up a hotel room or something, but the money is gettin low. And the town makes him half paranoid anyhow. Nine fucken prisons in this town, and other than gettin a gawk at Stevie in the morning, well Johnny wants fuck all to do with a mainland jail. Half afraid to hit the road again for fear of that copper spotting him too. And he got that strange look, from the old gal at the second-hand place, she looked too close. How some people sees you but they really dont, and then there's the ones who fucken sees right through you. Well that old girl was somewhere in between, and Johnny couldnt tell if she was simply eyeing him for the stranger that he was or tryna figure whether or not he already had them pants on when he walked in. Musta took her ten minutes to ring the boots in. Kept mucking up the register. Distracted wasnt she Johnny? Tryna sort out whether she recognized the pants. She was on to *something,* that's for sure. Like she could smell Johnny's past. And sure how hard is it to go back through the security cameras and check and see? Flip back through and there's Johnny walking in in the grey suit pants and walking out with the army pants on. And then call the cops with his description, right? And then what, he walks the road lookin for a place to stay?

And for fuck sakes Johnny the pants were something like seven measly dollars. And why the pants when the boots woulda been way fucken easier. Christ man. Why take the risk, here and now? Are ya stunned? You still got three hundred bucks in the wad for Christ sakes. But I dont know, I dont know. I was after opening the urn. Standin in some parking lot after I left that museum, and whatever came over me I whipped out the urn and took the top off. And I realized it was hangin over me all the while, the thought of lookin inside it, of touching what Madonna's been reduced to. And it's not like youd think it'd be either. You think of stove ashes or cigarette ashes, all smooth and even, dusty and silky. But that's not what Madonna is like. She's grittier, lumpy. Little bits, pebbles of bone. It's more like gravel than ash. Johnny let about an ounce sift through his fingers and then a slight gust of wind took some out of his palm so he put the cover back on cause he was pretty sure Madonna had no desire to hang around these parts any more than he did. And then he's in that shop, that second-hand shop, and it's like she's there with him or something, and he wants to show off or he's not thinkin on his own, or like she's goading him on, the grey-brown dust of her under his fingernails keeping a lookout while Johnny comes out of the change room and stuffs Pius's pants into the garbage. All the shoplifting they did. Going into the mall or Sobey's or Shoppers with duffle bags and coming home with em chock full, dumping them out on the bed and sorting through stuff neither one of them could hardly remember stealing. Madonna with whole honey-baked hams, pre-roasted chickens, hundreds of dollars' worth of cologne and perfume, razors and makeup, jackets, jeans, books, videos, CDs. One time she even had a fucken DVD player from Canadian Tire. How in the hell she even got it in the bag was beyond Johnny. But then to walk around the shop lookin so casual, and walkin out without trippin the alarm? The fucken queen, she was. Sell off what we didnt want or need. One week she tucked away almost fifteen hundred bucks. Jesus. Until that time she got busted in Cash Converters, of all places, the pawn shop. Some gal's engagement ring.

Madonna leaning over the glass askin to see this one and that one, trying a couple on, then changing her mind and walking on in through the store, picking through the DVDs when she gets the tap on her shoulder from a uniformed RNC officer. Turns out the ring was the most expensive item in the entire shop. Go fucken figure that it caught Madonna's eye. But she talked her way out of it somehow. She had the ring in her pocket. And gave it up right away and made like she'd forgot all about it being there. And here where she technically wasnt after leaving the shop, well she wasnt technically shoplifting then was she? The cop was young see, didnt know enough to wait for her to leave the premises. Madonna all embarrassed, then pouring on the outrage. Standin there so bold-faced, making the clerk feel like shit for calling the cops, making the cop feel lower than shit for trying to arrest her. Still barred from the store though, the two of us. Madonna was some pissed. But that was it for her and the five-finger discount all the same. She always said she'd go until she got caught, and near the end there, like I said with the DVD players and stuff, it's like she was wanting to get caught. It's what you hears about serial killers and them sorts, how they gets clumsy cause they wants to get caught. Like she couldnt handle the stress of it no more. Cause it is stressful, ripping shit off. I mean, it's prolly not as stressful as serial killing, mind, but it wears you down all the same. Anyhow, that was it for the shoplifting spree.

Come Christmas though, I was all bent outta shape about what to get her, then me and a buddy got our hands on a video camera and he taped me while I smashed out all the windows to that shop. Great big six-by-six picture windows and me with the fucken mason bricks over me head and slamming em in onto the floor amongst the guitars and amps. I had a mask on too, but then I walks right up to the camera when I'm done with the windows and the alarm blaring in the background and I hauls the mask up past me eyebrows, looks right into the camera and says *Merry Christmas little mama*. Christmas morning she opens her card and finds the little DVD in there, gives it a spin, and dont her lovely face light up once she figures out what's going on. Fucken hell. Johnny, now here's that same girl caked in under your fingernails, egging you on to swipe a pair of fucken cargo pants from a goodwill shop. Or, maybe, more likely, once a rogue always a fucken rogue, hey Johnny? Maybe it's as simple as that. The leopard and his spots. *Or maybe it's that youre wanting to get found out too Johnny, maybe youre* . . . ahhh fuck off.

Coming to, stiff and cramped and cold after crashing the night in the passenger seat of the old Ford. Springs from the seat jabbing into his shoulder. Still and all, likely the soundest snooze Johnny's had now since . . . fucken . . . Anyhow, not the first time he bunked out in a wreck, no sir. Booted out of Pius's house so often, or too spiteful to come home. Slept a whole week one time up in the Tuckers' woodshed, right there on top of the junks. No more than twelve or thirteen. So an old Ford is like the penthouse suite now aint it, depending on your reference point. Woke up once, the whole night. Dreaming shit. Other than that, hardly budged from the moment he shut his eyes, and here the sun is well into the sky now, must be going on nine, half past. Madonna in the front pouch of the poncho, safe and sound. Bag of weed stashed down in the abandoned den of some dead creature. Well you cant risk keeping it on your person or in the goddamn rig in the seat alongside. Never know but some dipshit lawdog could come along in the middle of the night sniffing about. Never know but you were spotted beating around the bushes after you left the front gates. Likely cameras around the perimeter anyhow. Cameras fucken everywhere these days, even in the woods.

Yeah, woke up the one time last night. Got out and had a little look around the woods, a listen, tryna work out this dream and at the same time tryna shake it off. Black snaking patterns. Thick, clogging stink of hot tar, dump trucks and graders, steamroller. It was the pavement, wasnt it? The day they paved the roads in the harbour. I mean, the dream was pretty vague and wonky, feelings, smells, and likely it only lasted two or three seconds. But that's what they says about dreams anyhow, how they feels a thousand times longer than they are. You could have this big old epic dream with all these twists and turns and details, and the telling of it takes five or six minutes, but in reality they says the dream takes place in a split fucken second. The details are just triggered memories or something, your mind tryna rationalize, sort things out in real time. What a load of shit. Still and all, they paved the roads one day, all the little back roads and side roads that used to be gravel and potholes. Big gang of us up on the hill lookin down on the harbour, watchin the colour of the roads change, waiting on our bikes, waiting for the machines to hurry up and fuck off back where they came from so we could take over. Like the real world came to town, or we stepped up a couple of rungs on the ladder or some such shit. The roads all led to the same shithole spots, same ragtag houses, same dead ends. But they were smoother werent they? Mikey sitting out on his step with the clunky cast on his leg pretty much that whole summer while the rest of us whipped around the harbour flying ramps. Poor sook.

That's the summer his father brought home them hens Johnny?

Shut it, fucken shut it about them hens.

Big stretch. Dog barking. Kids whooping it up somewhere. Be nice to scrounge up a cuppa tea. Piss. Crows squawking. Starved, fucken famished. Mass starvation, hey Johnny? Cant remember when was the last time I sat down and ate something with a fork. Big old feed of eggs and toast and bacon, hey Johnny. That'd be nice round about now. One of them mornings, that's what I wants. One of them peaceful and dopey mornings, no past, like you just arrived here, only now showed up in the world in this form. No ghosts clinging to you, no luggage weighing you down, the heavens still deciding what species youre gonna be. The way the sound leaps around, the way the head settles right down, nothing racing, nothing urgent. Ahhh but even if you could get there Johnny, even if you could shake it all for a time, you knows it dont fucken last. The old heart dont be long skipping a beat when you thinks on the day ahead, walking in through that jailhouse and laying eyes on your blood father for the first time in your life.

Well, they says minimum security and by fuck they means it. Never even asked me for ID or nothing, never searched me. I could be packing all kinds of dope or a blade or anything. Hardly even glanced at me, lookin like I do with the face all scrabbled up. Signed a disclosure agreement and then I was told to wait in this indoor-outdoor shabby cafeteria kinda room with the far wall opening out onto the yard. Past the yard was a regular old rusty fence, hardly six foot high. No razor wire or nothing. And beyond that the woods. Dont make no sense now do it? Dont even look to be any cameras in here, in the goddamn visiting room.

I showed up at ten on the dot so I'm the only visitor yet. Whole place to meself. A buzzer groans from somewhere deep in the building, doors sucking open. There's ashtrays around so I sits at a table near where the wall opens up and I lights up a smoke. Fucken hell, they got er scald in here dont they? Down in HMP it's all the same now if youre caught with tobacco or fucken heroin. It's all contraband. And mind you, tobacco is worth about as much as the best dope on the inside too. Fellas selling their nicotine patches for Christ sakes. One New Year's when I was inside I got me hands on a level-one patch and a fella showed me how to heat it up with a lighter and draw the nicotine out of it. Run the lighter back and forth underneath it, couple of inches away, until all that brown juice bubbles to the surface. Wipe it off with a bit of tissue or bible paper or whatever you got, then toss in a pinch of loose tea and spark her up. Three or four cigarettes out of the one patch, if youre careful. What we're reduced to sometimes, hey Johnny? Get a good fucken hit off it though.

Voices down the corridor, doors clangin, another buzzer. Christ, the old heart poundin in me chest. All this way, all this time. A low, deep voice says *Come on now Pudding, got yourself a visitor.* Pudding? That's funny aint it. Soft and sweet like pudding! Ha-fucken-ha. *Youre not gonna try and make a run for it now I hope?* And the voice this time's got a little bit of sarcasm in it, so that you cant help but expect it to be told to batter to fuck. Still tryna wrap me head around the situation here when a gnarled and twisted little scraggle of a man is wheeled in through the door at the far end of the room. Wheeled in. *Wheeled.* What the fuck is going on here fellas? I stands up, takes a step towards them, then I steps back, sits back down. The little scrap in the wheelchair sorta looks at me from out the corner of his eye, like the way youd eyeball someone youre planning to fuck over. He wont look at me directly. The guard wheels him right up to where I'm sitting so that one of the footrests on the wheelchair is touching me shin. And not a word from the guard, nothing, doesnt even so much as look at me, turns and walks back to from where he came, whistling low under his breath. And then it's me and . . . well . . . me and my father. Except this is not . . . I mean I got just as open a mind as the next fella . . . but . . . and it's not the wheelchair, it's not . . . yes, I mean the wheelchair is a shocker, no question, but it's the man in the wheelchair that does me head in. Or the shadow of the man. Cant be no more than a hundred and twenty pounds for fuck sakes. I could wrap me whole hand around his fucken biceps couldnt I? I could. I'm searching his face for the telltale scar, or scars, but he's so wrinkled and lopsided . . . He's supposed to be in his mid-fifties or so, but swear to fuck he looks to be seventy-five. No joke. Maybe he's sick?

Are you sick or . . . ?

He sits there kinda bitter and dopey with his head tilted slightly so the right-hand corner of his mouth glistens with spittle. This is not . . . this cant . . .

Got a camera under that getup?

This bit sorta snarled at me from out the corner of his mouth, like it was all forced out of one side of his body, gravelly and cavernous.

What? No . . . it's ahhh . . .

Oh, see I thought you were wanting to take a goddamn picture.

I'm not . . . well I thought . . .

What do you want?

Me . . . ?

No, the fucken chair there.

I just thought . . . it'd be nice to meet you . . .

Who the Christ are you to me?

What? Well youre my . . . you mean you dont know who I am?

All's I motherfucken know is I havent had a visitor in over ten motherfucken years, and never in this place, and I'd be content to go another ten without one if I make it that long. So whoever you are and whatever you want, spit it out.

After the effort of this tirade he gives over to a wretched, rib-cracking coughing fit that rattles his rickety old wheelchair and raises thick blue worms all over his forehead and temples and neck and I'm about to reach out for him cause he really dont look like he'll live through the next minute if I dont, but then he works a dirty gob of phlegm up out of his lungs and cannonballs it across the room where it splats dead centre on a poster about domestic violence. The poster's got this blurry image of some hefty dude off in the background and this missus up front with a black eye and the caption underneath says *He said he'd never do it again . . . twenty times.* The big chunky glob of chest scum jiggles on the poor dolly's forehead. I glances back at Stevie. My father. My biological father. He sits there and wheezes and hacks for a little bit. I lets him catch his breath until he juts out his chin and arches his eyebrows at me as if to say *Get on with it, out with it.* Gotta catch me own breath now.

Well . . . I'm Johnny. Keough. I'm your . . . youre my . . . ahhh fuck . . . I dont know man, I dont know . . . I'm passing through town and . . . so I thought I'd drop in to see . . .

I can feel me weight shifting in the chair, my body tellin me to bolt for the door. I dont fucken need this. Some things, some people, they're best left up to the imagination. Youre better off not knowing, better off making it all up as you goes along and then sticking to it. Take your delusions to the fucken grave like everyone else. Like Tanya and Pius and Old Bat Shit, all that crowd. Better off. I feels me hands on the armrests of the chair and I'm pushin off, eyeing the far door, measuring how long the distance. But I cops his expression then, old Stevie, the bubbling realization of the true nature of this visit. One side of his face slackens, softens, the left corner of his mouth bobs open like he's gonna say something, but then he's close-lipped all of a sudden, nods his head about a half an inch and leaves it there. I settles back into me chair, takes a breath.

They tells me youre my father, I mean biologically.

Well now, lucky you. Who tells you?

What . . . I was told . . . my sister . . . or mother . . . you knows the story . . . I was brought up by my grandmother and grandfather, right, I thought they were my folks, but it was my sister . . . and anyhow . . . well I was told that you and her . . . I wrote you some letters . . . I dont know b'y . . . I'm here now . . .

Youre here now, yeah, and what? I dont got no cocksuckin offspring that I know of. How old are you?

I'll be twenty-four next . . .

Well how in the Christ am I supposed to remember some bitch I tapped twenty-four years ago? What's her name?

Tanya. Tanya Keough. She was nearly sixteen, I think.

Tanya Keough. From Town?

Well from up the Southern Shore . . .

Holy fuck! I do remember, I do . . .

Yeah, she's . . .

. . . and I tell you why? Wanna know how I remembers?

I'm on me feet, suddenly. A stale waft of piss and sweat off him. I'm willing him not to say what I knows he's dyin to say. And I dont know exactly how I knows. I just do. It's in his voice, a glee. It's in his eyes, this nausea. And in my head, some long-lost piece of a jigsaw puzzle suddenly being snapped into place. I backs up towards the corner edge of the table to put the right amount of distance between us. Anchor my feet. A pulsing in my skull. Hands balled into cold and sweaty fists. He dont seem to take much notice, or if he does he dont seem to care.

. . . yeah . . . she was a sweet little thing, your mother . . .

. . . alright old-timer . . . that's enough . . .

. . . come to think on it, I met her shortly before I done my first federal bit . . .

. . . shut your fucken mouth, I'm tellin ya . . .

. . . yeah, little Tanya, little baygirl . . .

. . .

. . . always thought she'd keep in touch too, but nope, not a visit, not a phone call, not so much as a postcard when I got sent down. Wanna know what I got sent down for that time? Forcible confinement and ra . . .

So fast shit happens, so fast. I'm already over on the other side of the room watchin it all go down. His gaunt, bony neck snapping back like a toothpick and the chair tumbling over and over until it rests upright on its wheels again and gives a little creaking half spin back and forth, back and forth, while he lays folded in half with one of his legs twisted up under his torso and the blood trickling out the side of his temple. But he's laughing aint he? Cocksucker. This deep gaping chuckle full of lung and grit and beach rocks. But he'll be howling for a guard soon enough now and I'm not so far gone to say it wouldnt bother me to be hanging around to explain this whole mess. But Johnny could end all this right fucken now. He could. I could. Go down for life. Charge across the room and stomp that scrawny fucker's throat into the floor. Christen the new boots, hey John-John? Splatter his sick brains out with that wheelchair. Thumb his eyeballs out the back of his skull. Ahhh, but that's exactly what he wants now aint it? That's exactly what Stevie Puddester wants.

I opens the door. He growls out, still chuckling away:

Some fucken hero you are. I'd say you were already in the house . . .

This bit rattles me. Just his way of letting me know that he knows a fuck of a lot more about me than he was letting on. But I dont take the bait. I cant. I wont. Gone, me, Johnny, scuttling along the tight crumbling corridor towards the cold grey light of the outside world. I slows as I passes a guard on me left. He's tucked into a little stall, hunched over a copy of *Mad*. The guard grunts at me, nothing more, no signing out, nothing.

My hand on the door to the entrance, old Stevie roars one more time, a snarled and throaty and muffled cry for help that I hope never fucken arrives.

The left eye is completely swollen shut now. There's a headache, a sharp one. Still seeing two of everything, although it's not as bad as it was this morning. The foot too, fucken killin me, toes on the left foot bashed and crunched in. However they managed that, through these army boots, big old shit-stompers. Some fucken tough guy Johnny is. Four fractured ribs, they says. All the fingernails on me right hand are shredded off like someone held my fingers against a grinding wheel. You can see the bone of two of me knuckles. Honestly no clue how that came about. Me arm is black and pocked with bits of asphalt. And my mouth, three of the front teeth gone and three or four more barely hanging on. My face. Me jaw. They'll be wiring that shut soon as the swelling goes down. Fucken hell. It's a strange feeling, I aint never had me jaw busted before, like a door off its hinges. Try to open and shut my mouth and one side of the jaw cant catch up and then finds it has nowhere to settle. It dont fit no more. Six stitches above me eye. The rest of my body, what's not bandaged up, is one big bruise. It fucken well burns and throbs and stings and pulsates all over, but it dont hardly hurt unless I thinks about it. What hurts, I guess, is the *how*. How it happened. Live your whole life on the edge of the battle, waiting for some fucker to get in your face. You learn to be ready for it. But how in the Christ was I supposed to be ready for *that*? Fucken teenage *girls*?

* * *

What do I remember? This is what they wants to know. *Tell us what you can remember . . .* Since when? Since that lanky Reeves fucker? Caul's? The hoof of a moose? Since fucken Kingston?

I dont.

I do.

Remember.

Too fucken much I remembers. That look she gave me, headed up over the hill with the blood spilling down her forehead. Madonna. *Youre so fucked Johnny.* Yeah I know girl, I knows that. Aint we all? And I knows that no matter what went down or how it happened, what kind of spin you put on it all, you just needed a way out. Cause where was any of it going? Feeding off each other's misery. I knows what that look meant. It meant *Goodbye Johnny, this is my ticket out.* And I cant hardly blame you. We're all lookin for a change of scenery, at the very least. We're all lookin for our ticket. Who's not lookin to claw their way out from under what they're tangled up in? Who's not, underneath it all, desperate to let go of what they're hangin on to? And what's really worth hanging on to anymore?

Fuck you, that's all I have to say.

We're all gonna fucken starve anyhow.

Mass starvation, so says the man.

What do I remember? From the moment I first opened my eyes, being looked at like I was the spawn of some fucken evil happening. And not allowed to question it. Not allowed to talk about it. Not allowed to feel a bit bad for yourself, lest someone accuse you of dwelling on the pity pot. Try hauling yourself out from under that. Try *letting go* when there's nothing you can do to alter the hate, curb the revulsion.

Until you *become.*

I remember reaching for a lock of hair, my hand too weak, fingers too pudgy and stubby.

I remember a smell, sweet and heady, a mucky texture smeared across rungs, all up and down my arms, streaked along my thighs, grainy film pasted across my teeth. The horror-struck wails and moans of that old bat shit cunt, calling for someone named Tanya.

Tanya??? Tanya??? Come clean this up. I draws the line at shit-eaters!

I do recall being rushed, rushed out the front door, one of my boots barely half on, a thick callused hand on the back of my neck. *Move it, move it.* My toe hooking in the battered canvas curled near the door-frame and then tumbling face first over the step, my head cracking on a big white rock shaped like the island outside the harbour. Blood streaming into my eyes, head forced under the scalding flow of the bathroom taps, the water pink and steamin, swirling into the drain, then cold, the shock of the cold, me forehead with the fast ice-cream feeling. That hand on the back of me neck the whole while. Not a word spoken.

Walking into Mikey's house, calling out, finding no one home. A bowl of five-point apples on the kitchen table. Starved. Insatiable. Tossing the stumps, one after the other, into the culvert at the top of the lane. The case of the missing apples.

Dump trucks and graders and steamrollers.

The first of the longliners moored off at the wharf.

Monstrous fish from the no-go zone, 3NO, with tongues weighing half a pound, three quarters.

Chasing Lizzy O'Neill down across the track and cornering her in an old abandoned twine shed, she after cracking me in the face with a rock.

Thousands of gulls stalkin Pius's little grey skiff, sunk to the gunnels, puttering in to the wharf like the homecoming of some king. Me and Mikey and a few lads waiting at the wharf, me with my hand held out to catch Pius's line. Pius cursing me out for missing it, red-faced and spitting: *Are ya fucken stupid or what? Are ya stupid?*

Guts and gurry and the shit-rot stench of rubber boots in the porch.

Mikey, all out of breath, delighted to announce: *Dad says we're actually second cousins or something, not first . . .*

Johnny rummaging beneath the seat of Austin's truck and finding a half-full bottle of liquor with a plastic sheriff's badge stuck above the label. The case of the missing whisky.

You suck mine first. It's okay.

Tell anyone this and I'll burn you in your fucken bed.

She's not really your sister Johnny! You were adopted! Johnny was adopted!

Youre *dead* . . .

Christ. What else is even worth fucken mentioning, worth dredging up?

I tried to tell Madonna, what happened. I wanted to. I tried to tell her. About the fire. About what happened. That night. But I never got to. The bandages and the eyebrows and the shaved head and all that. Me, chock full of raw codeine. Needing her to nurse me in the middle of the worst of our times. Fucken garbage. I never got a chance to tell her. I clung to that new status, the one good thing I ever heard the world sayin about me. A big announcement about it in the papers sayin how I saved people's lives, an old couple. How lucky it was that I was passing by when I was. And I wanted to tell her, Madonna. Fuck, man. I thought . . . I thought it'd maybe bring us back to where we were, some scam to share and laugh about. Us against the fucken the works of em. I wanted to tell her. How I was already in the house. How I was casing the place for over a week. Watchin the old couple come and go. The two of em in bed by nine-thirty and lights out by ten. How I knew the old feller got up like clockwork every night at two o'clock to have himself a piss and thereafter he was too hard to predict, up every hour, half hour. So, the four hours between bedtime and the first piss. Timers on the lights, one in the downstairs hallway and one in the living room. Johnny staggerin up the street at midnight, swaying and lurching, rambling, tellin sweet nothings to himself, singin a Pogues song. Just another harmless downtown drunk blubbering home. All an act though, not a drink in him, not a sup. Ducking up the alley around the back of the house and tapping out a small cube of glass in the back door, hearing the shards thunk onto the mat inside. Waiting, watchin the windows of the neighbouring houses. Inside then, keeping to the edges of the stairs, avoiding the middle, where the squeaks are. Bathroom first, to the medicine cabinet. Bottle of expired Demerol. Bottle of them speedy blood thinners. Bottle of anti-inflammatory meds. Fuck all else. Into the bedroom, straight for the jewellery box, tucked that up under the arm. Then the old feller's wallet. Canadian Tire credit card. Forty bucks in cash. Just about to slip me hands in under the very mattress they were sleeping on when I caught that smell, this bitter electrical thickness in the air. Then the smoke alarm, shrill and deafening. Johnny frozen at the head of the stairs, black smoke billowing through the open living room doorway. Johnny down the stairs and out onto the back step. The needling scream of the smoke alarm in the background. Stashing the jewellery box, the wallet. Breathing, breathing. Wanting to run. Then inside again, the fire licking up the stairway now, snaking down the hallway towards the kitchen. A calendar with a picture of a map of Fogo Island raging into flames next to his head. The nauseous odour of burning hair. Back to the bedroom and shakin the old man and woman from their drooling slumber. A lot of good, that smoke alarm. Clapping his hands, shouting, *screaming* finally: *Get up! Get the fuck up!!!*

The two of em terror-stricken, horrified, to see this crazed hoodlum looming above their bed in the middle of the night, half his hair gone, one of his eyebrows.

Your house is burning!

What??? Who . . . ?

The house is on fire!

Hauling the old girl out of the bed, lifting her gently over his shoulder. Trying not to shove the old boy tumbling head first down the stairs to his pajama-clad death. The old doll moaning for *Charlie*. Smell of mothballs and fruity perfume wafting off her nightdress. Nothing to her, maybe ninety pounds. Standin out on the street, lights coming on in the house next door. The fire blasting out through the living room window like some demon belching. The gust of sudden madness. Tears rolling down the old boy's face, his mouth gawped open, reaching out for his wife in the firelight. Sirens. Johnny back inside shouting for Charlie. The street all a-buzzing with onlookers, folks wrapping blankets around the old two. Shouts and cheers and clapping when Johnny stumbles back out over the doorstep.

Our John-John, fucken hero.

Lucky for everyone, that he was happening by.

What else? What else can you remember. A doctor no older than Johnny. The here and the now, hospital bed somewhere in the middle of nowhere. Flat, incessant nothingness, I remembers. Never-ending waves of dead grass, fields trodden and trampled. Roads with no bend, no rise, no fall for miles and miles. Stumbling into some scuffy little prairie town. Gas station. Fat litre bottle of Labatt 50 with the last of the cash. Drinking that. Drank the rest too. How quick the money turned on me. Days, a lifetime away from the Frontenac Jail, away from that bastard. Ran down through the woods, back to the old Ford to snatch up the bag of weed. Waited there and watched the road. Watched to see if any cops pulled in through the gates of the jail. Nothing. Who gave a sweet fuck that Stevie Puddester was splayed out on the floor with his head busted open? No one.

On down the highway with the urn and the weed. Pissing the last of the money away. Sudbury. Thunder fucken Bay. Coffee shops, gas stations. Lookin for real dope, cottonballs, Percocet, anything . . . Trading weed, big packed handful of it, for a forty of rum outside a hotel in a place called Richer. The Richer Inn Motor Hotel. Johnny tryna make it with the girl at the desk. Her scoffin, tellin Johnny to move along away from the truck stop, *for your own good.* Sluggin back the rum on the side of the road, tryna remember the words to that old Skid Row album. Singing at the top of his lungs, diving into the bushes when he spies the approaching headlights of a new-model Charger. Not even the cops, not even a Charger. Losing it Johnny. Drunk and running the mouth off, flashing the weed at these suit-and-tie boys. Man in a pale-blue sweater busting out of a townhouse to ask Johnny if he needed help with something. But not really asking, more like can I help you with something *fucker*? Johnny like some sorta creep standin transfixed on the sidewalk, staring in through the man's kitchen window, watchin his young family eat and squabble and laugh and pass around plates and bowls.

Hey! Can I help you with something?

Sitting on a sidewalk at the edge of someone's lawn in a cul-de-sac, watchin the light change, the new day breaking. Dry-heaves. Throat raw and sore like youd swallowed a pack of thumbtacks, too fucked to even raise your head, desperate to lie down. Passing a greasy bottle back and forth with a bunch of Natives who kept tellin Newfie jokes, Johnny laughing at em all for some strange reason. Sometimes they're just funny. Waking up on the cold concrete floor of a gazebo somewhere on the outskirts of Winnipeg. Throwing up all over the back wheel of some girl's bicycle, a fucken fine-lookin woman. Trying to apologize, hating himself. How quick she mounted up and took off, not even bothering to try and get the sick off her wheel. Bug-eyed and horrified like some snared creature. Wouldnt know but Johnny was in any state to make a play on her. Force himself on her. Make a rape baby, hey Johnny? Carry on tradition. Fucken hell, everything turned upside down, in the old noggin. Everything you thought you were. Going around for years spewing off about how Stevie Puddester was wrongly convicted. One fucken look at him though, one look and Johnny knew he done it, that Stevie killed that poor girl. You just *knows* that kinda shit. Everything you thought you were. Johnny Keough, rape baby. And now, sure, when you think about it, no wonder they looked at you like that, reared you up like that. What a fucken offering Johnny. Fifteen years between you and your sister. And what choice did *she* have? Tanya. Just as much of a choice as Johnny. No wonder she stuffs her face. Two of us shackled to Pius's house. Beholden to him. Not just Johnny. But what in Christ's name would she hang around as long as she did for? For me? For young John-John? That time she jumped in front of Pius's belt when it was cracking hard across the back of Johnny's head over something to do with grass stains on a pair of Mikey's fucken hand-me-down jeans. Times Pius had her by the throat up against the wall or had her by the hair pressing her face into the kitchen counter and slappin her around the ears screamin that she was a whore. And Johnny the blood of a whore. Big oily clumps of hair all around the sink. Tanya sobbing in front of the TV, watchin *Three's Company* with a tub of chocolate ice cream in her lap. And who else musta known? All over town. The whole Shore. Everybody, fucken *everybody* knew it. Except Johnny. Even Mikey musta known. *She's not even your sister Johnny!* And think about it, Pius booting in the door of that hotel room in Town, dragging the two of us back up the Shore like slaves. Keep us around to remind us of how much of a burden he carries. Why not toss the two of us out on our holes and let us fend for ourselves? Cause we all needs some creature to lord over, that's why. You often wonder about prison guards too. What the fuck is up with a man, or a woman, who chooses to make a career, a life, out of *keeping* other humans? Cause there's something missing there, some crushing absence of control over people in the real world. Shortfalls and failures. The urge to rule, dominate. All stemming from weakness, fear. But here, take this job and take this big-dog uniform with all the trimmings and here's a couple of hundred men under your command and you can fuck em around and bully em and mock em all you wants to cause no one gives a fuck about em anyhow, not even their own mothers. And watch how good it feels when you punches out at the end of your shift and you gets to lumber on home to the free world and fuck your wife. What a goddamn power trip. Johnny, from the time he was fifteen, placing himself in the hands of fuckers like Pius? That McGregor bastard. How vulnerable we are, to who we are, to what we're born into. And when youre that age who are you aside from what they tells you you are? Liar. Thief. He'll steal anything you dont tie down. Not to be trusted. Bastard. Abomination. Bound for the boys' home. No reference point, nothing to measure it against except the way other kids have it. Kids with bowls of five-point apples on their kitchen counter. Kids with their trips to fucken *Florida*? Johnny trudging off to school in fucken Mikey's jacket and jeans, stuff Mikey hadnt even outgrown yet. And what did you do, when you measured your lot against his Johnny? Lash out and destroy. Blacken the eyes and bloody the nose.

Well there you have it then, lots to dwell on Johnny. Lots more shit to go gettin yourself in a drunken jail-bound mess over. But what odds now? Any of it. Not like you can change any of it, or control any of it. And what *does* it change anyhow? What does it change? Nothing. Changes fuck all. Nothing is any different is it? If anything, things are clearer now, aint they? At least there's an explanation for the way things were in that house. So what do you do? You take what you got, you start again right where you are and you carry on, move on, sally forth with your eye on the prize. And some fucken prize it is, hey Johnny?

Grade eight, this is what I remembers, cold, dreary day in early April, this is what jumps into me head front and centre when I sees that gaggle of young girls out back of the gas station in that ragged prairie town. I thinks on Mikey, on the ground, his remote control helicopter smashed. Coming back from Florida after Easter holidays with his bright tee-shirts and talkin Disney this and Disney that. Beaches with golden sand and women in bikinis and some with their tits showing. Swimming pools. Fishing for strange colourful fish that dont swim around *our* wharves. Who wants to hear about that shit in fucken April? Alright for some.

Johnny rallying the troops, some fellas who aint seen an orange or an apple since Christmas morning, goading Mikey about his father's money, fucken sook making a big deal out of Disney World. *Disney World is for fucken youngsters! Look at ya, showing off your fancy fucken toys. Gimme a turn, gimme a turn.* Mikey shoving at Tim Coady. Tim shouldering Mikey towards Johnny. Johnny sidestepping, his leg extended, catching Mikey in the shins, slamming him and his helicopter to the ground.

Mikey scrambling to collect the propeller, two halves of the windshield, his eyes brimming with panic and rage. Johnny kicking the remote out of Mikey's reach. Mikey swinging blindly at the gang, catching Johnny in the shoulder. Johnny standin back to let the other lads move in. All hands shouldering Mikey back and forth, slappin his cheeks, the back of his head. The neck tore out of his new Miami Dolphins jersey. Someone slams a handful of muck into Mikey's eyes. Johnny standin back and watchin, waitin, then swoopin in to the rescue as soon as the first real clout connects with Mikey's cheek. Johnny stepping in then, breaking it up, shoulder to shoulder with Mikey, ready to take em all on. Cousin Johnny to the rescue. Tellin Mikey's mother that evening how it all got out of hand, the lads teasing, how Johnny jumped in and broke it up before it went bad. *I never touched him, I only broke it up.*

Johnny told to get home out of it.

Mikey not allowed to go to the dance that weekend and then not showing up at school on Monday. No sign of him anywhere for a couple of weeks. A bit much, all over a little scuffle in the meadow. Johnny over knocking on the door, tapping on the windows. Mikey's father, Uncle Austin, sitting on a couch in the living room in plain view, reading his paper, and not even lookin up from it. Then one evening, twenty-fourth weekend, trouting season just opened, Mikey shows up on Johnny's doorstep with his rod and reel. Down to the Gut Bridge after sea trout, fuck it, no questions asked. Mikey's not sayin much, pretty quiet. I starts tryna get a laugh out of him with them old MacLean and MacLean songs but he's not really into it so I gives it up. After about ten minutes Mikey's line snaps taut and the rod nearly buckles in half. Something big on there. But Mikey makes no move to try and land it, just stands there staring out over the harbour, kinda dazed, like he's seeing something or lookin at something I cant see.

Reel it in Mikey for fuck sakes! Hey! You got something on the hook! Mikey!

Mikey dont budge, dont move a muscle. Finally I grabs his rod and starts fighting with whatever kinda beast he's after hooking. Never know what youre gonna hook into down around the Gut where the fresh water runs under the bridge into the harbour. Dinny Walsh caught a little shark last fall. I hauls and reels and wrassles with whatever it is but Mikey is still standin there. He dont move, he dont watch, dont bat an eye, nothing.

What the fuck is wrong with you? Hey! Mikey?

I gives another tug and as quick as that the line goes slack. Gone, whatever the fuck it was. I turns and gives Mikey a good hard plick on the ear to try and roust him out of his trance but I still dont get a reaction out of him.

Mikey? What's . . . what's on the go man?

I wasnt in Florida.

What are you talkin about? What about the jersey and the helicopter and . . .

My aunt was down there with me cousins and Mom got them to send stuff back.

What? That's fucken burnt out Mikey. Why would . . . where were you then?

I'm not supposed to tell anyone. You cant say nothing to . . . not anyone . . .

Say nothing about what? Jesus b'y. What about all that talk about Disney World and the beach and naked women and shit?

I was in the hospital in St John's.

Fuck off. Why? What happened? Are you sick? Is that why youre not in school?

Yeah . . . I mean no.

What then Mikey?

I had to talk to some doctors . . .

The Mental? You were in the fucken Mental?

Youre not supposed to call it that!

Mikey hauls off like he's gonna hit me, like he wants to. We leans against the bridge for a while, quiet, watchin the current. I reels both of our lines in. Mikey's spinner is busted off. Brand new Red Devil. I dont know what I'm supposed to ask him or what I'm supposed to say to him. He sets his head on the old wooden railing of the bridge and starts to cry. I just goes about tidying up the rods and the gear, listening to him hiccuping and sobbing. Finally he raises his head.

Voices.

I looks around and listens but all is quiet around the harbour. The faint echo of a chainsaw coming from the north side, that's it. No voices. I tells him I dont hear no one.

No, me. Voices. I hears em.

Where Mikey? I dont fucken hear no one.

In my head Johnny. Voices in me head.

Whose voice? Like your father's or . . .

No . . . it's not . . . it's strangers I guess . . . not anybody I knows . . .

Stuff you remembers?

No! It's just voices . . . mean things . . . sayin shit . . . tellin me stuff . . .

What stuff?

Just . . . bad shit . . .

Curses or stories or . . . ?

Nasty voices Johnny. Tellin me I should do things, sayin shit that's not true.

I dont . . . like now? Do you hear em right now?

No. Not always. Some days it's bad. They gave me pills to take, but . . .

Shit man. That's burnt, that's . . . that's just burnt.

He lays his head back on the railing and starts to sob again. I dont . . . I mean I have no clue what this is, what it means. I dont know what I'm supposed to say. I lays me hand on the back of his neck and leans in right close, my mouth barely an inch from his ear.

Hey! You in there! Get the fuck out of my buddy's head! Hey!

Mikey pulls away and winces, gives me a little shove.

Jesus Johnny! Bust me eardrum why dontcha?

I will if you wants me to, if you thinks it'll help. I'll drill a hole right into your head and march in with a big stick and kick the shit out of whoever's in there making a racket.

Mikey straightens up now, rubs his eyes. He's almost on the verge of a smile. He grabs his rod and sees that his new spinner is busted off.

That's three spinners you owes me now *John-John*.

Dont fucken call me that.

We trudges on up the hill in our rubber boots, not talkin much, neither one of us in any rush to get home to either of our houses. I'm tryna work through what it means but I cant figure which way to think.

That's why you never had no suntan when you got back!

Ha, yeah.

Youre a fine hand for the bullshit, I'll give you that.

Thanks man.

So what was it like, the Mental?

I said youre not sposed to call it that. But . . . yeah it was pretty mental. Crazy people everywhere. I was on the youth wing, I guess, but youd see the others. Some woman shit herself and rubbed it on the wall in the hallway. One guy chopped up his neighbour with an axe while the whole family was eating dinner. He cant even remember doing it.

The last of the evening sun sinks behind the trees. My head is spiralling. I dont know what to make of it all.

Hey Mikey, the voices, what do they say? What . . . what do they tell you to do?

Mikey turns and juts his chin forward as if he's about to say something, then he decides against it. He kicks at the gravel and stirs up a little cloud of dust, spits into the ditch.

It's just . . . nasty, messed-up shit Johnny, that's all. It's not even real. None of it is real.

The gang of prairie girls, at the gas station, they're pushing this one squirt of a girl back and forth in a circle, laughing and squealing, and the girl in the circle, a long shiny streak of bright pink cutting down the middle of her otherwise dark hair, she's sobbing, trying not to lose it, trying not to get mad. Cause that's what they wants. She's pushed up against one of the girls who shouts *Oh God, get her away from me, she stinks!* Then she's down on the busted concrete and Johnny sees the other girls, vampire bats, swoopin in and tryna get good grips on the waistband of her jeans. One girl, taller, her hair the colour of coal dust and her eyes shaded in almost to the bridge of her nose, she stands at the edge and watches the others, watches gleefully. The girl on the ground, she's no more than twelve, thirteen. None of em are more than fifteen. The tall one, with the painted eyes, she hauls off and boots the fallen one square in the guts, and then a total frenzy, total chaos as the others take their cue. Johnny's heart racing, shouts out *Hey! Let her alone! Hey! Get the fuck off her!* Running towards the pack of em, still half buzzed, hungover, half the bottle of frothy Labatt 50 swirling in his guts. All the girls stop and stare. The girl on the ground hiccuping, sobbing, her chin bleeding. One little tart sporting what looks like fifty-odd earrings and lip studs and nose rings, she's got the young one, the one on the ground, she's got her by the hair, lifting her off the ground. Johnny shoves her aside. None of the girls knows what to make of Johnny's sudden presence. Johnny bends down to look at the girl on the ground and when he does, out of the corner of his eye he sees the smile spreading across the tall one's lips, sees the nod, feels the rush of bodies closing in, and he hasnt far to go to hit the ground after the first direct kick to the back of the head. Boots and giddy hisses and claws from all angles. He pushes himself to his knees, catches hold of a sneaker and yanks it off. The outraged squeal from the girl who lost the sneaker. Johnny swings into the swirling pack of teenage fury, hoping to connect with the tallest one, the obvious leader. Johnny thinks if he can bull through the initial onslaught, muscle through long enough to take that big tall one down, well then it's game over, they'll all scatter. He struggles to his feet momentarily, catches sight of her. A boot to the nuts he barely feels. Then a thick whooshing sound and a flash of neon as the two-by-four takes him in the jaw. Johnny staggers backwards from the blow, weak-kneed and dazed, collapses into a putrid pit of grease and piss underneath some sleepy rusted propane tanks. He tries to crawl away, squeeze himself into the corner where the last tank meets the gas station wall. Hands on his ankles, dragging him back out in the open.

Get his bag, get that bag.

Down comes the two-by-four, speared into his ribcage. He feels the urn disintegrate in the front pouch of his poncho and when he tries to turn away from the next blow from the two-by-four he sees Madonna's ashes pouring onto the ground around him, jagged chunks of grey porcelain. He stuffs his two hands into the pouch to salvage what's left of the ashes and he curls into a tight ball and hopes for the best. He hears something about a *whole bag* of pot. Last thing he remembers is the young girl, the one they'd all been beating on, she stands over Johnny, blood streaked across her bottom lip, her foot raised high off the ground. The sole of her sneaker, patterned with different sizes of diamonds, all very intricately connected. She seems to hold it there for a long time, her foot in the air, hovering tentatively over Johnny's head, until Johnny almost believes the blow aint gonna come. Then the tall one ordering *Do it Brittany, do it!* Then a hospital bed. Flashlights in my eyes, stream of nurses. Pissing blood into a bedpan. Pain. Opening me good eye this afternoon, a doctor talkin to a man in a suit, looming outside the curtain that surrounds my bed . . . *This is not his card, no, this is not his ID . . . He told the nurse his name was Mikey . . . Multiple fractures . . . bacterial infection . . .*

Johnny eyeing the man in the suit, knowing, knowing. He reaches for the poncho, draped over a metal chair just out of arm's reach. A dusting of ashes, Madonna, clung to the fabric at the mouth of the big front pocket.

This one night, back in the old place, me and Madonna are lying there, lying around all peaceful and easy like, just after having a good romp. I was after sayin something during, something about not wanting to hurt her. We had this banter, ya know, when we were in bed. We were always talking, pretending we were other people, like as if we were younger than we were sometimes. She'd make out like she was right innocent and nervous and I'd have to talk her through it, all this dirty talk about how it's hard the first time but it gets better. We fucken loved that. And afterwards we're lazing around sharing a smoke and Madonna starts tellin me about her first time. She was sixteen. Her boyfriend was this big jock type of fella, basketball hero. He was leaning on her for weeks, tryna get it in her, but she dont want to. Finally they finds themselves in the shower together and he gets it in her. She says it hurts, there's blood. She dont like it at all. And then she dont see him no more. He dont come around no more. *That fucken prick*, I says.

What's his name? Want me to track him down?

He was a kid, Johnny. What did he know? What does a sixteen-year-old *boy* know except for what his balls tell him? What about you Johnny? Who was your first time? Who was your first love?

And of course I tells her it was her, that I never even knew what the word meant until I met her. I knows that's what they all wants to hear, the ladies. But the truth is I dont know if ever . . . well it's kinda like you feels what you knows youre supposed to feel, right? But you cant say for sure if what youre feeling is real or not. And it's always tangled up in sex. And the better the sex the more tangled up it is. But with Madonna it was, well I think . . .

Alright you fucken sap. Mr Casanova. What about your first time then?

So I tells her the story anyhow, about my first time. I was twelve, turning thirteen. The girl was a little older, maybe she was fourteen. Dont know if ever I uttered a word of it before. Once this psychiatrist, this decent, gentle old gal she was, like someone's grandmother, tried to drag it out of me in a group session, but I didnt, I couldnt. But you meet these people, dontcha, you meet these certain types and they makes you feel like it's okay to spill it. Madonna was one of them types, one of those people. And they're few and far between aint they?

Me and Mikey are in the woods above the track on the south side of the harbour. Blueberry season. They were scarce that year but we were at it for a couple of hours already. We each got ten-pound buckets and mine is nearly full to the brim. Only time I'd get a smile in the house from the old girl, Pius's missus, was when I brought home a few blueberries. I always picked em clean too, no leaves or white ones, no bugs or nothing. You could pretty much dump em right from the bucket on into the mixing bowl. This is the weekend before we starts high school, Labour Day weekend. I'll be thirteen the end of that month. Me and Mikey were right into this dirty MacLean and MacLean album that summer and I had the whole thing memorized. Filthy, filthy songs and jokes and poems and shit. I useta do pretty much the whole album for Mikey and he'd be in the knots. We're just there carrying on, having a laugh and picking our berries, when something whooshes past me head and lands in the bushes next to Mikey. Neither one of us seen what it was. Then we hears these raspy giggles from down on the track somewhere. I turns and sees Lizzy O'Neill, big townie girl, crouched behind a young cherry tree. She's only ever up around in the summertime but goes around sayin she's from the Shore and puts on this fake accent and everything. She bends and laughs and picks up another rock from a small mound at her feet and whips it up at us, but she misses. She starts to run out the track now and Mikey finds a clunky piece of old wood and flings it at her while she runs past. It dont come close. She squeals some more, lobs another rock while she's running. The sun is right in me eyes. Her silhouette lumbering past. She stops and stoops and picks up another rock and I sees her arm swinging towards me again. Then the dull crack of the rock above me left eye, knockin me back on my hole. I lies there for a few seconds, not quite convinced that what just happened was real. Golden flecks of dust floatin around in the corners of my eyes. The sound of a motor coming from somewhere inside me head. Lizzy screamin, horrified at the sight of the blood.

Oh my God, oh my God. Is he alright? Johnny?

The blood now, hot and thick, runnin into my eye, down me neck. I sits up and hears her scream. She's been running up into the woods towards me, stops when she sees the state of me face, the blood, the eye. I'm literally seeing red.

I'm sorry Johnny, I'm sorry . . .

Too late, too late. I'm on my feet, chasing her. When I gets down onto the track I starts scooping up handfuls of rocks and drilling em at her. She's fast for a big girl. Her house aint far, just down over the hill and across the road. I nearly gets run down by a bread truck when I crosses the road after her. I'm expecting she'll go running into her yard and barring herself behind closed doors and then that'll be me hanging about her doorstep waiting to show her father what she's after doing. But she runs right on past the path leading down to her house. Instead she carries on down the side of the road and ducks across the Stage Path at the top of the beach. All the while she's shouting back at me that she's sorry, that it was an accident. I dont say a word, dont even curse. I dont throw no more rocks neither. I just chases her. The left side of my teeshirt flapping in the wind, heavy with blood. We're on a little footpath that leads to an old twine shed that aint been used in years. The only way around it is to climb down over the rocks, and then she'd be stuck down in the cove below with nowhere to go except up the side of the cliff or out into the water. I'm not far behind her now. She stops and turns and looks at me, her face a mask of shock and disbelief, panic. She says my name once more before she thumps the door to the twine shed open and slams it behind her.

I takes me time now, coming up to the door. Rotted-out wooden boards. I leans against it, peeking in through the cracks, tryna catch me breath. She shoves an old splitting table against the door. She's huffing and wheezing in there, searching around for another way out. I realize

I've had my bucket in my hand the whole time. It's empty, not one measly berry left. I tosses the bucket aside and slams the full weight of me body against the door, my shoulder bursting through one of the rotted boards. She lets out a little yelp. I heaves once more and I'm in, the splitting table toppled off to the side. She stands there wide-eyed, staring at me. She steps to the side, like she's gonna try and make a run for it, but I stands in her way. I can feel something stirring. This new heat in the room. The smell of the damp. Salty and musty, earthy. Her grey tee-shirt darkened with sweat, clinging to her chest, heaving up and down. I bends and picks up a piece of board with a nail sticking out the end. Holds it up in her face. Blood crusting onto me hand. But I'm only wanting to scare her. I'm only wanting to teach her a lesson. Not like I had some sinister plot in mind when I was chasing her up the beach. I'm only wanting to make her see what she's done to me, to let her know that people dont get away with bouncing rocks off Johnny Keough's head. People dont get away with that. She mutters again that she's sorry, an accident, all that. I laughs in her face, this kinda laugh like the way the bad guy in the cartoons always laughs, this deep, forced belly laugh. I was right into laughing like that back then. She takes a step backwards. I takes a step forward. She looks back and forth between the piece of board in me hand and the blood drying onto my face. The wind sucks the door shut behind us and the room goes dark except for thin streaks of sunlight leaking through the cracks in the walls. And this part, this is the part I can never get me head around. I'm standin there, just tryna scare her and stuff, like I said, tryna put a bit of fear into her, and dont she just flop back down onto the mound of nets in the corner of the room. Next thing one of her legs is out of her pants. She was wearing these kinda baggy, thin jogging pants. She lies back, lookin right at me with her big wet brown eyes. But I'm more interested in that other wet spot. It's the first one ever I laid eyes on I think. Except for them twisted magazines and stuff that we seen down in Wally B's old bus. Lizzy O'Neill, from Town, with her furry little box all out in the open like that, offering it to me. I didnt know what it meant, what I was expected to do. I almost turned and ran and bolted for the beach. She looks up at me and nods then and next it's my body in motion and I'm doing that thing—watchin it all from across the room. I pretty much falls on top of her. I watches meself grind and hump against her. I tries to kiss her but she wont move her face towards me. Even after I gets it in she keeps staring at the far wall, not even lookin at me, not makin any noise, not sayin nothing. I knows enough to not let go inside of her so I hauls out and squirts all down the inside of her leg. I got blood all over the side of her face and on her shirt. Then we're on our feet and she's pulling her pants on. I got some gum in me pocket and I takes one out and offers it to her, but she wont look at me, scurries past and she's out the door and gone. That's the last I seen of her too. Her crowd never came up around for a few years and then I started doing time in Whitbourne or I was always off at something.

Madonna sat up in the bed looking at me. Her mouth wide open, and her eyes, her eyes bugged out like that, like she didnt recognize me all of a sudden.

What? You asked didnt you girl? What's that look for?

Nothing Johnny, nothing, I'm not judging, but I'm thinking . . . well it's kind of messed up dont you think?

What's messed up about it? She hauled her pants off and lay there . . .

Yes, Johnny, but think about it. Put yourself in her position for . . .

She fucken lay back and spread her legs! What was I supposed to do?

She was terrified Johnny!

The big racket then, me and her. Tryna get me to say that . . . tryna make me own up to . . . you know. And maybe I did! Maybe that's what it fucken was. Maybe . . . but the way you file that shit away, in your head. How we got this tendency to *reframe* things, I guess, as the head doctors and counsellors loves to say. Maybe I did. Maybe in truth I'm no better than . . . This is madness, tellin on meself like some fucken fool. The way Mikey went. That fire. So-called commendation. Stevie Puddester. This is burnt. I dont know. I mean, she lay there and offered it to me. Not like

I stalked her and forced myself on her. Maybe . . . maybe some part of me knew the difference. I dont know. It's grey and muddy, in me head, what I was thinkin. Cause you take what you can get wherever you can get it, when youre that age. You dont weigh it out, think about it. Right? I mean, am I to be held accountable for the rest of my days for a deed done when I was fucken twelve years old? Sweet Christ Johnny. What's it all about? And what good does it do to let it play out in your head anymore Johnny? Where's it get you? In the same boat. Father and son . . . Spend all this time likening yourself to the man, son of Stevie the Scar, then you sees him for what he is and finds out youre fucken nothing alike. Nothing. And then you go dragging this shit up and your conclusion in the end is that youre the very same. No difference. *He who hates me hates my father also* . . . The apple and the tree bit. Lizzy O'Neill. But it's *not* the same thing. Fuck off. Even if it is. But it's not. There's a difference. I just dont know what that is. Or maybe I do. But my fucken skull hurts man, it does. And they're closing in. They're closing in. Head full of this jelly sludge they pumped into me cause I'm all beat to shit by a gang of teenage girls. Busted flat with all the weed gone. What's left of Madonna is about two ounces in the bottom of Gavin's ragged-ass poncho. No turning back, no hanging about, nothing to do but get west, and whatever's waiting for me on the back end of that, so be it. But if I'm expected to buckle over and start pleading guilty to everything, crumbling in bits and falling apart and moaning over what a cunt I was when I was a youngster. Last year, last month, last night. Christ . . . and tryna make up for it all, like penance or some such shit. Well, if I'm expected to bitch out now . . . it's not gonna happen. You know what? If I *hadnt* been casing the place the two of them woulda burnt in their fucken beds. Just let me catch a breath for fuck sakes. Maybe it *is* my fault Mikey is dead. Alright? Fuck. Maybe it is. But it's not like I pulled the goddamn trigger. I mighta . . . I mean I mighta been . . . But what did I know about voices and shit going on inside someone's head? Sure I was a fucken youngster too. Bad enough tryna sort out what was real and what wasnt in me own snarled-up head. And more to the point, what in the name of all hell can I do about it now? What? So maybe Lizzy O'Neill *was* afraid of me, maybe she was. But it's like Madonna said, what do a fucken twelve-year-old boy know other than what his nuts tells him to do? What do any of us ever know? That we used to be children and now we're not. That what we are now is just a collection of our blunders and our missteps, a mashed and battered accumulation of all our wrongs. Sick as our secrets. And now we mainly gotta lean into the years and hope too much of it dont splatter back in our fucken faces.

Nurse comes in. She's humming a little tune. Broad, well-earned shoulders on her. She could pick Johnny up right about now and snap him in half. But a friendliness there, maybe warmth, even. She hums and smiles as she leans across me bed to check the drip bag. Smell of citrus off her that almost makes me mouth water. When she catches my eye and sees I'm awake she says pretty much that:

Youre awake! Okay! I'll let the doctor know.

Piercing, middle-of-nowhere accent that slashes into me head like a splitting knife, but pleasant enough all the same. Warmth. Lemons. Johnny's vision blurs momentarily. He wants to reach out. She places her hand on the back of Johnny's neck and gently pulls him forward while she adjusts his pillow. Goosebumps. A fiery shiver ripping down my spine.

Some people want to talk to you!

Johnny tries to protest, tries to speak, but has to sit there dumbly waitin for his body to do what his brain is tellin it to do. A low, gravelly grunt tumbles out of his throat as she turns on her heels and heads out into the hallway. A new bounce to her step, on a mission, knows exactly where she's going. No good, no good. People wanting to talk to Johnny Keough is not ever a good thing.

I wont get into the pain of it all. I cant. The heave outta the bed with the ribs the way they are. And landing on the foot, forgetting about the busted toes and almost keelin over into the garbage can. Having to stand there on one foot to wait for the room to stop spinning, me neck soaked with drool where it's after building up in my mouth on account of it not being too pleasant to swallow. I yanks the IV needle outta me hand like the way you sees fellas do it in the movies, like it's this big rebellious or symbolic act or something. But it's not. It's slips right out and I dont even feel it. Whatever they were filling me with, morphine drip, I dont know. But it was something good cause I knows as bad as it is I should be hurtin more than I am. I unhooks the clear plastic bag of liquid dope and makes a knot in the end of the tube and stuffs the bag into one of the nice deep pockets in the side of the pants. Right away I pricks me leg with the needle. Tryna haul them stiff army pants up over the hips with the fingernails gone off my hand. It's all I can do not to flop back into the bed and die. But after enough crashing around and falling into stuff, I manages to piece me outfit together. *Some people want to talk to you.* Knows what that bloody well means, hey Johnny? I stuffs the socks in me pockets and then drapes the one-piece over my shoulder. Force the boots on without passing out. Some fucker behind the curtain in the bed next to me clearing his throat real loud and then finally shushing me, right aggressive and pissy like. Next thing he'll be buzzing for the nurse. I'm picking up the pace a bit as me head clears and my balance comes back. But with that there's even more pain and like I said I dont want to get into it. Cause it's fucken *boring* aint it? Being in pain like this. Fucken mob of teenage girls? I'm careful not to spill any more ashes out of the poncho as I'm pulling it over me head. Blood caked into everything, but at least the poncho is patterned with different hippie colours. Stink of muddy piss off everything from where I was stuck down behind them propane tanks. Fucken hell. You dont wanna think about it Johnny. What the fuck can you do about it now anyhow?

Once I'm all geared up I peeks out through the curtain to see if I can see down the hall a ways, but it's pretty dark. Fuck it. Stay here and answer a bunch of questions and let em figure out who you are and where youre from, or chance it that you get away out of it. Better off skippering your own ship, like the fella says. I kinda hops towards the door to the ward, makes a sharp turn down the corridor in the opposite direction from the nurses' station. That nice nursey-nurse who was just in the room, she's on the phone, nodding and scouring the details on the clipboard in her hand. I dont look back, limping, hobbled and lame. Let's hope I dont have to make a run for it. I comes to the elevator and pushes the button for down and as I steps back away from it there's about eight or ten student types, nursing students or whatever, boys and girls, all in their early twenties, comes around the corner and stands there waiting. They were all giggling and joshing about until they stumbled upon me, then everything goes dead quiet. I looks down at this one girl's shoes and her whole body does this kinda wave, the kinda way you see it on the TV when the scene changes and moves on to, like say, a character having a flashback or whatever, or drifting off into a dream, all wavy and screwy. Like that. One fella cant keep his eyes off me, he's whispering to this other fella, whispering right close and concealed and discreet, gawkin at me the whole while, but as soon as I tries to make eye contact they each looks away. Typical. If I was in a stupider mood I'd have a go at the works of em right there in the corridor. But I wants out. And I dont wanna give any of em anything extra to remember me by, anything out of the ordinary, other than the way I looks, I mean.

Twenty years later the elevator light comes on, there's a little ding and we all piles into the box. Tight fucken squeeze for that crowd, but there's lots of room around me cause it's them that have themselves all squat together into the far corner. I spose there's a smell off me, yeah, and a look, and a vibe, I guess. Cant see why either one of em would wanna cuddle up to me. Still, they're studying to be nurses or doctors or something, think they'd be a little more at ease, think they'd even have a bit of compassion or something. *Says the fucken sociopath.* Fuck off.

I'm the last to shuffle out of the elevator cause they all bailed like scalded cats in a fit of giggles and snorts, couldnt get clear of me fast enough. But I'm close behind, moving as fast as my shattered frame will let me, cause I needs the cover. The old instincts are still sharp as fuck even if the rest of me is a disaster. I barely sets foot into the hospital lobby and it's like you can smell em, the fuzz, lawdogs, you can bloody well *smell* the fuckers. Sure enough, two plainclothes coppers waiting at the doors of the opposite elevator, gawkin up at the indicator lights with their brows all scrunched and impatient. The light dings and then the door slides open and they're muttering how it's about time and they're steppin into the box just as I'm passing by, trailing along behind the pack of interns. The fuzz aint noticed me and I knows I'm in the clear but I cant help turning back for a glance, cause I can be fucken stunned like that. I turns to see the elevator doors sliding closed and one of the coppers who's flipping through a little notebook, he's standin dead centre in the box and looks up and out and our eyes meet for that last split second and I knows he's pegged me. Maybe not that he's pegged me as the man of the hour, but I knows he sees what I am, the guy on the other end of the spectrum, the bad guy. He spots me for the jailbird I am, or used to be, for the criminal I used to be. You never quite shake that look, never quite leave it behind, like those boys, the fuzz, they can never quite cover up what they are either. All that student crowd made such a hasty dash towards the cafeteria, so I'm alone in the lobby, staring into this cop's eyes as the elevator door closes. His bottom lip gawps like he's about to say something and he reaches towards the display of buttons and then the door jams closed. I dont take off or nothing, cause I cant and I knows there's not a prayer in hell of making a quick getaway now anyhow, say if the door pops back open and yon Tango comes a-charging out at me. Where'm I going to? They'd burn me to the ground for not putting up enough of a chase. Play it cool Johnny, milk your grievances, work the limp. I turns and slaps the wheelchair button on the wall near the exit, stepping back while the door swings out into the bitter night. I'm waiting for the shout from behind, the ding from the elevator, the scuffle of feet coming across the tiles behind me, but . . . nothing. I'm out the doors then. Figure I got ten, maybe twelve minutes before they sorts out that I've left the ward and that they just passed me in the lobby, all this business.

The hospital parking lot is choc-a-blocked with cars and rigs. I shambles off the curb and into the road towards the lot, sweat dripping from me chin, trying hard not to grunt or moan or breathe too deep, fighting off the urge to stop and hurl. I dont know where I'm headed or how to get where I'm going or even where the fuck I am in the world. I seem to remember a conversation about someone being transferred to Regina, something about Saskatoon. I dont know, one of them towns then. I knows I'm the sight alright, left for dead, staggerin across to the parking lot havin to stop and catch my breath and steady me head cause I'm starting to see double again. I tucks meself on the other side of a black minivan, out of sight of the main entrance. Dodge Caravan, late nineties model. *Fucken right.* The gears in the old noggin, spinnin like mad. But I cant, I cant. All bad enough. *How else to get out of here? How else to get on with it?* Something catches my eye then, on the pavement near the rear tire. You wouldnt bloody well believe it. A Popsicle stick. It's excruciating, the stoop to pick it up, but I manages. It's a fresh and sturdy stick, one half stained orange. My favourite. Orange Popsicle. Madonna's was always the red, cherry. And man, you shoulda seen Madonna sucking on a red cherry Popsicle. Drive a man to the brink. Popsicle stick in hand, I peers in through the passenger-side window of the Caravan. Coffee cups and gadget chargers and take-away wrappers. A glance towards the hospital doors. Then a nod towards the skyline, for a sign or something foolish like that, but all is black up there. My good eye darting around the parking lot for a rock or a piece of concrete or something to take out the side window. Nothing. Checkin the pockets for a coin and I pricks me finger on the needle from the dope bag. Right where the nail is tore off. I dont even bother to feel it. Rootin deep down in the other side pocket of the pants and I fingers a hard damp wad of something that sets off a little light in me head. It's well stuffed down there, folded into a tight square. I works it out and finds it to be three twenties.

Dont remember stashing em there. Musta forgot em. Things are lookin up for Johnny, our hero, aint they? Things are lookin up. Popsicle stick, sixty bucks, possible getaway vehicle. Still, neither scrap of metal on me, no coin to do what more immediately needs to be done. Cant believe I'm out here on the road gettin shitfaced and shithauled and I've nothing on me that can even break a window, no weapon or nothing. Since when did I even walk to the fucken shop without a weapon? *Think you can lift that garbage can at the edge of the lot, heft it through the window?* Maybe. Nothing subtle about it though.

I takes a step in the direction of the garbage can and then I stops, turns to the van, reaching out for the door handle. I gives a gentle tug and feels the pop and grind of the side door gliding open.

Fucken hell, hey Johnny.

Armed with the orange-stained Popsicle stick, I climbs aboard.

Grand theft auto, nothing new about that, like I mentioned. Shoplifting, a while back. Old behaviour Johnny! Youre slipping back into old behaviour! Yeah. Slinging dope around in Northern Ontario, leaving the scene of an accident back there somewhere, swiping that young feller's driver's licence and threatening him, then passing meself off as him to the OPP. Pounding the shit out of Stevie Puddester, who's in a wheelchair and a federal inmate. That's Johnny, gone all straight and narrow, settled right the fuck down. Should see me when there's no warrants outstanding.

Grand Forks, BC. That's where I've landed this fine morn. Hardly a kick left in the old Dodge Caravan. Hardly a kick left in Johnny neither. Still, I got about twenty-four hours out of her. Gassed up only twice, and neither time did I pay. What can you do? Pull into a busy truck stop and wait your turn, gas up, then make like youre parking alongside the station, like youre on your way in to pay. Make sure your licence plate is muddied up, obscured. Not that it'd be traced back to me, but you dont want the plates coming up as stolen on top of all that. More reason to hunt for ya. So you park alongside the station, make like youre counting your money or something, then drive on out of the lot again, slow and steady, back in the opposite direction from where you were headed to. Drive back on up the road and find a spot to turn around and then carry on along your journey. Twice, both times I done it, I met cruisers coming towards me with the sirens blaring and the lights a-flashing. Coincidence? We'll never know. Our John-John was doing the speed limit, takin his time, maybe stoppin off once in a while for a milkshake at a drive-through. Milkshake is about all I can handle these days. Aint no chewing going on in our John-John's immediate future, that's for sure. Bad enough, the effort of sucking it up through a straw. Thank Christ me teeth are bashed out cause all I gotta do is move my top lip outta the way and poke the straw in the gap where the teeth used to be. Life is good. But Jesus Christ, passed a restaurant somewhere on the Alberta-BC border advertising a steak and eggs special for $5.99. I nearly bawled. I almost did. But the old mouth and jaw is too fucked, and that's me right about now, gotta live with it dont I?

Grand Forks. Pulled into the parking lot of a big-ass grocery store I cant pronounce the name of, like some Indian word. Hadda make me way in to the pharmacy to see if I couldnt find some sorta wrapping for the fingers and maybe some disinfectant cause the index finger and the one next to it are starting to turn yellow and there's this goopy stuff leaking out from under where the nails are snapped off. I knows that cant be good. The pain is changed too, my whole hand is a constant burning throb now and it's spreading up into the wrist and the shoulder keeps numbing out.

Been kinda blacking out too, I guess. It's like an hour passes on the highway, trees and mountains and trucks and flat suffering fuck eternity, and I'll suddenly snap to, snap out of it, or into it, back into the moment. And God knows where I've been, in my head, what I've been thinkin about—stuff that went on years ago, stuff that never happened atall, shit that *might* happen. Like I've been sleep-driving, but I'm hardly asleep.

Me head wandering off and I'm either freezing cold with the heater on blast or with me arm hanging out the window tryna cool off. Sweat pouring off me one minute, then the next I'm shivering so bad youd swear I was taking a fucken seizure.

Limping up and down the aisles of the pharmacy and I can feel all eyes on me, wondering who the fuck I am and where I'm from and what the fuck happened to me. So it's kinda difficult to pocket what I needs. Down to about twenty-five bucks now. Cigarettes and milkshakes, couple of cups of sweet tea. How much gas I got left, that's a mystery too cause the gauge dont work, always sorta hovering above empty. The battery light flashes off and on and the check engine light is blinking and spluttering. Big squeals out of the brakes and the power steering pump grinding and moaning, stiff as a diddler in a kiddie pool. Who knows but the rig is fucked. Get what you pay for I spose. Still and all, she handles decent on the highway and she got me the fuck outta that hospital parking lot. I'd say someone's out there in whatever arse-fuck prairie town that was and they're likely fucken delighted with me for robbing it anyhow. I never bothered to check for registration or names or nothing in the glove locker. Maybe someday I'll sit down and write a letter to the owner, anonymously, tellin all about the grand adventure I had with their van.

Ahhh fuck em.

I opens a bottle of Tylenol and dry swallows half a dozen, hoping maybe that'll level me off. Drop the bottle into the pants pocket. I got the bag of hospital dope with the IV out in the van, but I've been kinda wary of it, using it. I'm tempted to pop it into me leg but where I'm not quite sure what's in it . . . well some dope dont work through the muscles and you can get in an awful mess, big old blisters and shit, paralyze the nerves. I mean, I wants to kill the pain and maybe get a little buzz, but I hardly wants to fucken paralyze meself, not unless I got a good safe place to lie down for a while. And then of course I'm drivin and trying not to attract attention to meself on the road, so if I pops it in a vein I'm not sure how it'll hit me, or how much to take, and I dont wanna get way too bombed, too bombed to talk me way out of some situation or make a break for it if I have to. I figure when I gets clear of the rig I'll hook meself up with a good blast of whatever the hell is in that IV.

Here's a bottle of rubbing alcohol. There's no way of opening these fucken things without puttin meself through some fresh torture. Like the Tylenol, it was vile, opening that. I tucks the bottle of alcohol in under me right armpit and twists at it with me left hand, holding the bottle in place with my shattered ribs. But that's it, I only got the one hand. Such is the state of affairs for our fucken hero. The cap pops off the bottle and alcohol goes spewing onto the shelves spatterin across the therapeutic insoles and foot powders. I look around to see if I'm being looked at, but there's no one about, no security at least. I dumps half the bottle onto my fucked hand. Feeling the blaze, watchin the pus and dried blood bubble and pop and fizz. It occurs to me that I should be screaming. I twists the cap back on the bottle and drops it into the poncho. I cleaned that out too, the pouch where the urn was smashed. I hauled in on the side of the road and carefully emptied the last of the ashes into a Tim Hortons donut bag. Shockin, that is. Picked out the bits and chunks of porcelain. There was more there than I thought too, maybe four ounces, even. Enough to make it all nice and symbolic at least. Cause that's all I got now aint it? If not for Madonna now I'd be fucked off down in the gutter somewhere, supping out of a paper bag with some fucken street trash. That's the honest to God's truth. I'd be on the hustle for good dope and I'd be banging back way too much of it. On purpose. That's how I feels right about now, like I'm good and ready to slip off the edge. But for Madonna, but for laying her ashes down on that beach out west. I've no other reason for holding it together right about now. She always went on about it, this one summer when she was a kid. A kite she was right taken with, loved it, elaborate neon kite with all the solar system printed on it. Her face, it always lit up when she mentioned it. I at least wants to do that one thing, for her, for Johnny. And it's not just the pain I'm in, or the hobbled state of me, that's giving me the gloomy thoughts about checkin out, it's not just that. Of course it's not. But I dont need to get into it all either, the old ghosts, the fucken new ones. But you gets thinkin. No radio in the van and so the miles and miles of droning quiet, and you gets listening to yourself, after a while. Imagine all the shit spewed outta this mouth. Across the years. All the hate and the bitching and moaning. And you tell these stories, these burnt-out stories that gets crazier and cockier and more brutal and more detailed all the time, maybe to give yourself a boost or something. You run off at the mouth, tellin about these feats. And they all ends, all these stories, they all ends off with someone else being a prick or gettin fucked over. Always about how it's someone else's fault or someone gettin what they supposedly deserve. Shit man. And how much of it is true even? After a while? Sure I'm after tellin that many lies I dont know my own self what's true and what's not. Stories, you know, to arm yourself, to look after yourself. But the worst are the lies you tells yourself. You go on about how the likes of Stevie Puddester is innocent, how he was screwed over by the cops, the courts. Wasnt even in the same part of town. He had a witness! Confessed to an armed robbery! Fuck off. I mean, I mighta done some bad shit, right, but I aint never cut no girl's throat and bashed her skull in off a radiator. That's what they found. This girl, about twenty-four, twenty-five. She was heavy into the speedballs, hooking too, of course. They found her in some grungy hotel room way out on Topsail Road. She was fucken destroyed. They needed her dental records. It was that bad. Bled right out, teeth found on the other side of the room. And who done it? Not Stevie Puddester, no way. He wasnt in that part of town. He's innocent. Lawyer fucked him. Cops framed him. His record made him a scapegoat. This is the shit you fills your head up with. Even though your guts turns every time you mentions his name. And then, one glance at him, one look into them evil little dead weasel eyes and it's all right there. And hey, even if he didnt do it, just a glance and you can spot him for the type anyhow, the type that belongs behind bars. But that's not me now is it? That's hardly our John-John, fucken hero. I mean, we might share the blood thing, but we're not the same. I mighta swiped a few cars and shook me nuts around and I mighta lit a few fires and blackened a few eyes, but I done what I done when I had to, not because I ever *wanted* to hurt nobody. Lots of times it was just a case of me all fucked up on something, lookin to kill meself off, kill the old ghosts. That's all. But lotsa times too, lotsa times I could tell about how when things were alright, when I was nice and easy and laid back and not swinging out at the world, not bulling my way through people. Lotsa times things were kinda normal too. I think. Like when me and Madonna took up, moved in together. Johnny Keough, moving in with a real live woman. Tellin her he loved her every time he left the room, giving foot rubs and watchin movies and making coffee and cooking fish stew. Fucken right. Normal. Not wanting something more from around the corner. Yeah there's all that stuff too, but it's hard to talk about, I guess. It's not . . . well what? It's not slick enough I spose, not cool. You dont go on about how much you *loves* some gal, you goes on about how often you were screwing her, how hard. What she will or wont do in the sack. Cause that's what we're supposed to talk about aint it? No one wants to hear what's going on in some jailbird's heart now do they? Fuck. And you gets trapped into thinkin a certain way. Long after the time is come and gone when you shoulda moved on from all that childhood shit. I mean, that time I got let out of Whitbourne after that McGregor cunt filled me in on the true details of my family tree and I laid Pius flat on the kitchen floor and busted his face open? Well, that shoulda been it then. That shoulda been enough. There was my vengeance. That was me, taking it all back. Why wasnt that good enough for me? But it's never good enough. You drag it on and on, lug it with you down through the years until it breaks your fucken back and it's no wonder youre kicked off in jail eating slimy eggs and burnt toast and soggy bacon and gagging on the stink of farts and man-sweat, watchin over your shoulder every day of your goddamn life. No wonder.

* * *

Needs a bit of deodorant too, Johnny, not to forget. Cause you knows it's pretty bad when you cant stand the smell of your own self. If not for the hassle of it all, taking the clothes off and on again, the boots, be nice to strip down somewhere and get a good hot shower or slip into a steaming bath some place. *Or a hot tub, Johnny.* Fuck off. He's lookin for this stuff, Blade or Hatchet it's called, something like that, this deodorant that Madonna used to get for him, that she liked the smell of. He roots through what's there but cant find it. What's all this vegan shit? Everybody waving this *green* flag? I mean, I knows what it is, vegan and all, where these nimrods dont eat meat or cheese or eggs and whatever. Imagine, bacon and eggs and burgers. Hot dogs. But what's it got to do with aftershave and fucken pit-stick? A bit much, if you asks me, crowd saving up plastic bottles and separating their garbage and tryna navigate the roads with little battery-powered cars made outta recycled beer cans. A bit much. And all a bit late anyhow, they says. I opens up one stick of deodorant called Herban Cowboy and man I pretty much almost gags on it and I can feel a sneeze coming on right away so I have to stop breathing to ward it off cause I dont think the ribs could handle it. There's this stamp on the back of the deodorant, one of them red circles with a line down through the middle, and what's crossed out are the words *Animal Cruelty*. Like a slap in the mouth, aint it? No matter which way you turns there's always something or someone waiting to stick it to you, stir all that shit up. Yes I fucken killed Mikey's hens! Alright? Jesus. Or I didnt kill em, not first-hand. But I killed em all the same. Yes it was my doing.

He gets these hens, that summer his leg was in a cast. His father comes home one evening with about ten of these strange hens and gives em to Mikey to make up names for and to look after, rear up, all that. I mean, they're fucken hens for Christ sakes, everybody's got hens. But Mikey had to have these fancy ones. Fucken bizarre, weird-lookin hens with no feathers on their necks. Naked . . . *somethings*, they were called. And of course they were from somewhere over in Europe or Russia too. Fucken ugly things they were. And the rooster, that jeezly rooster, he musta came in at about twenty pounds. You could hear him all over the goddamn harbour in the mornings. No one needed a fucken alarm clock that summer. So Mikey gets these hens, right. One day he's the poor scrap with the broken leg who cant ride his bike on the new pavement, and the next everybody's over there hanging out on his porch and there's folks coming from all up and down the Shore to look at these ugly fucken hens and to buy eggs. Mikey sat around at nothing, scattering a bit of feed once in a while, making money off these big dark speckled eggs that I heard never hardly had no taste off em. Enough to boil your blood. Next thing there's games of ball starting up in Mikey's meadow and Mikey'd be out pitching or whatever, just not able to run. But the big laughs. One evening I looks across the meadow and pretty much every young feller in the harbour musta been there playing ball. As far as meadows goes, even grown men, once the hay was made, came to play ball in Uncle Austin's meadow. Huge and flat. Dandy evening too, nice and warm, enough of a breeze to keep the flies away and overcast enough so the sun wouldnt blind you when you took your turn at bat. Dandy evening. So I goes over anyhow, with me glove and bat, and I steps into the line while Mikey and Billy O'Byrne are picking teams. I'm stood there not ten fucken seconds, swear to Christ, when Uncle Austin comes out onto the back porch and starts bawling me out. Tells me to get the Christ off his land, outta the meadow.

Go home I said! No one bloody well wants you here!

This is *weeks* after Mikey broke his foot now, fucken *weeks*. Everybody gone dead quiet. I stands my ground anyhow. I kinda got me mind made up that if he comes at me I'm gonna take the bat to his face. I couldnt care less how big or how loud he is, he's not so tough he can take a Louisville Slugger in the chops without buckling under. He stands there sipping his evening beer, belching, staring right back at me.

Well b'ys, if young Johnny wants to stay he can stay by himself. You can all go home out of it.

What can you do? Pretty much every young feller in the harbour dying to have a good game of ball, all staring at me, or not lookin at me atall, waiting for me to fuck off so's they can get on with it. Mikey's old man leaning on the porch railing with this self-satisfied grin on his face. What can you do? I turned and left. Maybe I shoved someone outta the way when I was going, but really I sorta put the head down, propped the bat up on me shoulder and walked on.

Next morning it wasnt no cock-a-doodle-do that woke me up, more like the big horrified screeches outta Mikey, big rasping howls from across the meadow. I jumped out of bed and hightailed it across the meadow to see what was the matter. Uncle Austin running towards the henhouse with half his face covered in shaving cream. Mikey bawling. Turns out my Scrapper was after gettin into the henhouse sometime overnight and slaughtering every last one of Mikey's ugly foreign hens. Ate a bunch of eggs too, the dog did. However he got in there, no one could figure out. I'm leaning on the fence gawkin over towards the henhouse, waiting for good old Austin to come out and make his accusations. But he never did. Poor old Scrapper took a good duff in the hole for his part in it all, yelping up across the meadow with bloody feathers dried into his beard and the belly all bloated with eggs. Austin never said a word to me. But the cops showed up that evening, with this youth counsellor from Family Services, askin me all kinds of questions about how Mikey broke his foot and about how I got turned away from the ballgame. How they thinks I opened the door to the henhouse and let the dog in. Pius was some fucken pissed. Likely he was hoping they'd take me away. I told the fuzz what I told Mikey and everyone else, that I was home in bed and never knew nothing. Tanya even said so cause she was up watchin TV when I turned in for the night. They never had nothing on me, no charges laid or nothing. But it stays on your file, that shit, when that Family Services crowd are in on it. Fuckers. Like Reeves had me youth record and brought up animal cruelty when there was never even any charges laid! Just a report, a file. But it hangs around and torments you. Funny how you can go up before the court as an adult and they can help send you down the line by dragging up shit you were *suspected* of doing when you were only a measly youngster.

Scrapper vanished a few days after the Russian Hen Massacre. No surprise. Me, Johnny, like the proper fool, calling out to him in the nighttime. Came across his puffed up, ragged little body amongst the alders in the lower meadow that spring. Blasted full of lead pellets, old rotted rope around his neck. *Someone* after tying him on to a tree so's they could get a good shot at him. Shit. What you dont wanna be thinkin about. Poor Scrapper never knew no better. But I spose I did.

Gives meself a good squirt with some sample cologne that's not too bad, but I cant tell if it's for men or women. There's nothing on the bottle or the package that might give a hint and it dont really tip towards the girls or the boys in the aroma department neither. But it's alright. Masks the stench of the old poncho. I got some wrapping for the hand, a drop of rubbing alcohol, some Tylenol. I settles for a regular Speed Stick, not that stinky hippie shit. Some bandages to cover me knuckles. Not that I bandages every little cut or scratch, I aint a fucken youngster, but the skin is ground right down to the bone, I mean come on, it's awkward when youre driving, making turns and the like. Fucken hurts, you know. What else do I got here? Packet of Fisherman's Friend, the cherry kind, not the dog's arse kind. And a couple of bottles of that Boost shit, meal-replacement drink. Saul's poison. Either that or I'll starve. Wonder how Saul is gettin on out there on the road? Christ, I turned on him, didnt I? Yes you did Johnny. Shit man, I cant even remember what way I was thinkin, back then, even a week or two behind me. How long am I out here anyhow, on the road? Fucken hell. I dont feel the same. I feels, I dont know, less dead. Not as dead. But deader, all the same. It's complicated. You gives yourself a bit of breathing room and . . . that security gal now, she spotted me, she got my number alright. You can always tell. Or I'm being paranoid. No, no, she's lookin at someone else now. No. She gives the little chin nod in my direction. Now she's smiling though. Fuck, she's either really good or she's not on to me atall. What do you do? Blow it all wide open for a few drugstore odds and ends, wind up in a backroom with some west coast cops. Likely the RCMP around these parts too, so you know they'll find your warrants and your record and there'll be no farther west this day, for Johnny, no big scattering of the ashes ceremony, not this lifetime. But youre not *stealing* until you leaves the shop, hey Madonna? Well what then Johnny, go back into the belly of the shop and empty your pockets and hope they dont make no further fuss? Sure, half what's in your pockets is opened anyhow. She's coming towards me now, walking all slow and steady like, so I tries to straighten up as best I can, sweat rollin down me face in buckets. She's upon me, in my path, I tries to step around her but she dont move outta the way. I staggers a bit tryna keep from bumping into her and ends up twisting the broken toes and I cant help but cry out a little and next she's reaching out for me and I can smell the lotion she must use for her hands, this deep floral smell like spiced roses or something. And I knows she's there in a uniform and I'm the bad guy and she's supposed to be a fucker to me and that's the way it works, but I cant help but let meself ease towards her so that her two arms comes up to me chest to steady me, to keep me from tumbling on top of her. Christ man, what I wouldnt give to disappear into a woman's bedroom for a week or two. A nice-smelling woman.

Are you alright sir?

Wha . . . ?

You are not well sir . . .

I was . . . an accident . . . moose . . .

Do you need to get to a hospital sir? Should I call an ambulance?

She's shouting it all at me too, like I must look like it takes an extra effort to get through to me. There's mirrors behind her, on the shelves, next to the women's foundation and eyeliner and lipstick and all that glop. I catches a look at some twisted version of my face, both cheeks bruised yellow and green and all scraped up, dirty stitches over me eye with blue fuzzies stuck all over em, one eyebrow twice the size of the other, front teeth gone, lip busted in the corner and the jaw . . . my jaw is . . . fucked. And that's only what you can see in the mirror, that's just my face. And here's this gal in a uniform holding me up and tryna steady me, people stopped and gawkin down the aisle at us. Her uniform is softer than it looks, thin and soft. I have no idea if she's twenty years old or fifty-fucken-seven. I have no clue. But she's a soft-smelling gal in a uniform and I'll stay here leant against her for as long as she bloody well lets me.

Do you need an ambulance sir? Do you need to go to the hospital?

N-n-no . . . I needed . . .

You needed some supplies?

She says this part right quiet though, lookin up at me with this fiery . . . this real stabbing kinda . . . lookin right through me, aint she? Doing her goddamn job. Sees right through me. Cause I doubt I've done meself proud to conceal what I'm up to. Christ Johnny, you cant stagger into a drugstore in the middle of some arse-bang town out this way and do first aid on yourself and fill your pockets and not expect folks to be smart enough to suspect what youre all about? Look at yourself. Filthy. It's like you dont *want* to make it to the west coast. Like you dont want to pull this off.

I stares right back into her lovely green or grey or blue eyes and I feels like letting her see me. I dont look at her eyebrows or the bridge of her nose, I looks right into her eyes. She looks at me some more, not at me, mind, not like at the state of my face or the clothes I got on, this gal, she looks right into me fucken brain, right back into my eyes, into my, like . . . what's it called . . .

Lets get you outside for some fresh air sonny. How does that sound?

I nods again and she doesnt quite smile but slowly spins alongside me and hooks her arm into mine and we walks down the aisle towards the store exit like easy lovers out for a stroll. Except she's in full security uniform and I'm filthy bleeding and infected and cant barely walk and half me face is mashed over the wrong way. Other than that, lovers, us.

She pushes the exit door open and then it's that flashing orange light and the long slow moan of the security buzzer going off. Fuck shit piss. It's the deodorant, I betcha. Betcha there's a security sticker inside, up underneath the cap. This is me good and shafted now, cause if she didnt know before, well she cant be this fucken stunned. Can she? I tenses up, braced for the inevitable, but she turns, all casual, to someone over near the cash and waves it off like it's some glitch, same old problem they've been having off and on all year.

Then we're outside, me and this security guard.

She leans me against the cold brick of the building, steps back and takes me in. I dont know what she sees, but she stands there staring at me for the longest time. A thick, gooey green wire pokes through her flesh and springs out of the side of her cheek, below her eye socket. It sorta jiggles and fizzes and drips a greasy black liquid onto her stark white collar. She doesnt pay it any mind so I dont bother to mention it. She stands and stares, finally lets out a big sigh and starts rooting through her coat.

I can list off everything that's in your pockets right now . . .

I . . .

But considering what those items are, and the shape youre in, I'm going to cut you some slack. If you caught me on a normal day, which this is not since my son got convicted of trafficking pills and my daughter hasnt been home in a week . . . well normally I wouldnt hesitate to detain you and call the police and have you charged. Okay? Because that's my job, sonny. But something tells me . . . something tells me that having you *arrested* is by far the lesser evil than letting you carry on to whatever fate is awaiting you out here.

She lights up a cigarette, a menthol, takes a few hard draws, and then places it between me lips. I lets it smoulder there without drawing on it while she pops a stick of gum in her mouth. I cant meet her eye no more, not like I could inside the shop. Wanna say thank you, but it sounds so lame. All that comes out of me is:

One of your wires is poking out of your face . . .

She sorta snorts at me and starts walking back to the store entrance. Her hand on the door handle, she growls back at me:

You have five minutes to disappear, sonny.

Three minutes left to disappear and I'm almost struck down in the parking lot by some coolio in a black Toyota. Yakking into his phone. He jams on the brakes and then gestures at me to get a move on and I wishes with all that's in me that I wasnt so demolished right about now cause I'd haul him outta that rig so fast . . . But the truth is I *am* this way right now. Truth is I wandered out into the road without even lookin. The truth is, according to that cyborg back there, the truth is that there's a lesser evil fate . . . no, gettin arrested is . . . wait now . . . the truth is that she thinks I'm headed for some sort of reckoning, some sort of meltdown. *Well?* Well what? Of course youre not Johnny! Come on man, fuck. I mean you just set yourself up with everything you needs to survive. Meal-replacement shit and deodorant. Throw that twenty-five bucks into the tank and see how far the van takes you. Walk the rest of it. Walk it. What's the difference? It cant be *that* much further can it? After coming all this ways? Another day of travelling. One day. I can make that. Do that with my fucken eyes closed. Shit man, love to close the eyes for a while. Maybe I could find some place to hide away with the van for a few hours before I hits the road, pull off into the woods, somewhere handy. That'll do me. I'll be right as rain then, whatever that means.

The squawk of a crow from somewhere up above, Johnny lookin around the sky for it. It does this huge swooping nosedive at me like it's coming in to finish me off, make away with me eyes and shit. I stands me ground, cause it's just a fucken crow. I watches it lunge and swirl and glide above the parking lot, then it drops all of a sudden and sets down right on the roof of the Dodge Caravan. My Caravan. I stops in me tracks. I mean, I aint going around being all superstitious and shit, but it's kinda strange I think. Of all the cars in the lot. And he hadda go and do this nosedive at me first before he went and perched on the van. Like he wanted me to know that he knew it was my rig? It's like I'm in that movie, that one where the crow shows buddy where to find boots and stuff. What was that called? Some fella was shot while they were making the movie. I takes another step towards the van and the crow starts in cawing and squawking, even does this fluttering kinda hokey dance. I stops moving towards the van. The crow stops squawking. I got Madonna's ashes in me pocket. All's in the rig belonging to me is the IV bag with the mystery dope. I can get more dope. If I really wants to. I got half a dozen Tylenol in my gut, more in me pocket. They're hardly killing the pain but they're taking the edge off, keeping the fever down.

I takes a left, out towards the highway. I dont look back at the van. I dont hear the crow no more. I keeps walking, best I can on the broken toes, but walking. The pavement gives over to gravel, I'm on the curb crossing into the parking lot of a travel agency, lotsa distance between me and that rig. When I'm pretty much in the clear of the lot I does a scan of the streets around it. Opposite the pharmacy there's a woman with two small girls making their way into a hair salon. That arsehole in the black Toyota, he peels out onto the road and almost runs down some maniac out for a jog. Dog-walker scooping his dog's shit into a bag. There's about half a dozen cars parked along the roadside. Aint none of em looks like the fuzz. Nobody lookin like they're watchin the van. Still, I cant go back to it. Maybe I'm slipping, gettin a bit paranoid where I'm feeling, you know, a bit off, what with half the bones in me body broken. But no, it's my gut, a gut feeling. Or maybe it's me being superstitious after all. I dont know. Maybe it's on account of that stupid crow. But I gotta jump ship. It served its purpose, done what I needed it to do for way longer than I expected. I got lucky with it. And there's been too much blind luck these past few days. It dont sit well with me. Cause luck runs out, just when youre gettin comfortable, letting your guard down, when youre kicking back on Easy Street, then *bang*, it all splatters back in your face, tenfold. Fellas like Johnny? Lucky? Fucken hell.

The Caravan looks kinda sad and lonesome in the parking lot with the sky all overcast and the late-morning shadows creeping up the windshield. I almost feels sorry for it. Maybe if I wait and watch for a couple of hours? Or just dart over and grab the IV bag? Ahhh fuck it. Fuck it Johnny.

I pops another few useless pills and sorta scuffs along, scuffing along, shivering, tryna get some of that wrapping to stay on my hand. Foolish twat I am, forgot to rob some goddamn tape. I leans in a general westward direction and yanks the hood of the poncho up around me face to mop some of the sweat off.

14

Well I never expected to win neither bloody scholarship or nothing like that any time soon, but I cant believe I was so stunned to walk away from that jeezly van on account of some fucken crow dancing and squawking. I *am* that stunned though. It was a roof over me head at the very least. Coulda drove it till it broke down and then curled up in the back to wait this shit out. Of course it's fucken raining, hammering down out of the heavens. Of course that's the way it goes, Johnny. You cant imagine such a thing as blue sky, sunshine. What it feels like to be dry and warm. I stops and peels the last of the filthy ragged wrapping off me hand cause where it's fallin off anyhow, soaked and heavy and flappin about and it takes too much energy to keep it in place. The hand is a flame-broiled pus-ridden pulsating mess underneath. Not even gonna attempt to make a fist out of it.

All bad enough, the concentration it takes to stay on me feet now, one foot in front of the other. The left leg, the muscle above the knee, the big one, that dont feel like it's gonna last much longer cause where I'm having to make up for how useless the other leg is, the toes busted open like that. Maybe the night before last I tried to get the boot off but it dont wanna budge. Every time I sets the foot down it feels like there's gonna be this squishy pop from inside and toes and toenails and foot guts are gonna come spewing up the side of me leg. And the pain of that, how that *feels* . . . Sometimes when I forgets and steps on it the wrong way or scuffs it in the shoulder of the road or something, sometimes the pain is so fucken epic that I have to give the jaw a little tap, or I might poke meself good and hard in the ribcage, just to move the pain to some other part of the body, so I'll live through the next ten seconds.

How we takes it all for granted. You dont think about breathing until you breaks your goddamn ribs. Same thing with walkin, the foot is gone and fucked and I never thought about how useful it was before now, or how useless I am without it. My fucken foot. Or you hardly thinks about all the ways you can use your mouth until you loses the use of it. I wouldnt even be able to eat pussy right about now. Truth. But dont get me wrong, I mean I'd try. I'd give it a good fucken go.

Found a rusted piece of iron pipe on the side of the road a ways back and I used that as a cane for a while, but it got to be too heavy. I dont even wanna think about that, not being able to lift a bit of pipe. But for the most part anyhow the pain is after easing off this past hour or two, or the brain is moving the pain onto a different shelf or something, so I can kinda have a look at it from some other side of me head without really . . . I dont know what I'm sayin.

Gone is the money, the twenty-five dollars. Gas station in Princeton. Pack of cigarettes that fell to pieces in the poncho within the first ten minutes of the rain. Forgot they were there. Good pack too, du Maurier kings. I tries to keep smoking, you know. I tries to keep at it. But I aint never really taken to em. I might take a little smokin binge here and there, or have a few when I'm out on the go with the lads or something, but then I'll forget all about cigarettes altogether for a while, maybe weeks. Then it's right exciting, you know, to go and get a fresh pack or to find an old pack. Anyhow, the fancy du Mauriers are gone now, destroyed by the wet. Lucky I wrapped Madonna's ashes in a plastic bag, stuffed the donut bag down in it. Bottle of aspirin I bought too, long gone. Jug of milk, long gone, spilled half of it tryna *run* towards a swanky SUV I thought was after stopping for me but was only some fucker pulled over to take pictures of the mountains. The Crowsnest Highway, that's what I'm on. There's whatcha-call-it for ya. You know, when something is a coincidence or puts you in mind of something else? I dont know what it's called, one of them words you use when youre tryna sound smart I spose.

Saw a sign yesterday morning with the Sasquatch on it too. A joke sign for Sasquatch Crossing with the word *Believe!* stencilled on a separate rectangular piece under the image. Bigfoot, you know. And I tell ya, stinking and moaning down a cold twisting mountain road in the fog and rain in the middle of the night with the woods dead murky and sinister all around you, strangling in on you like that . . . Well it's not hard to believe then is it? It's not hard to piss your fucken pants to be honest, at the sound of a branch snapping out there in the dark. Fucken Sasquatch. Come on you bastard. To the death. To the death. But I walks on, you know. There's nothing to be said, nothing to be done. Not like I can hide or outrun him or nothing. I been hacking up blood now for the past couple of days so it's like I'm leaving a trail anyhow. Yeah, the right ear too. Up where the jaw seems to be most swollen, I dont know, me eardrum popped when I got into the mountains and now there's this itchy trickle inside there, drippin down inside me throat. Dont know if that's even possible, but the hearing comes and goes, or it muffles over, and ever since the eardrum popped there's been blood I've been hacking up. So I dont know, I dont know. Least of my concerns now. Let the fucken Bigfoot come and nab me up, drag me off into his lair and rip me limb from limb. Or maybe it's a female, a girl Bigfoot that's stalkin me. Club me over the head with her big fist, toss me over her shoulder and I wakes up in some filthy cave deep in the woods. Keep me in there for years, making babies, little hairy Johnny monsters. Away we goes.

I needs the strength, that's the main thing. Keep moving Johnny. And there's no one, not a fucken soul comes down this road after dark. Two, three nights in a row I pretty much staggered all the way into the first light of day, dying to sit down, lie down. But the effort to get back up out of it, no mistake. And you dont even notice the cars passing by in the daytime then. Youre so delighted to've made it through the bitter night and finally be able to see what's around you. You remembers that youre sposed to be gettin some place and that you should be sticking the thumb out but then realizes there's been streams of vehicles for maybe hours and youve done nothing to make it known that youre tryna get somewhere.

Drooling. Cant stop that either. Where me teeth dont fit together no more and it's just easier, more comfortable, less fucken horrifying, to let my mouth slack open. Long stringy goops of it all down me chin and slicked onto me neck, blending in with the rain. Salty stench of saliva. Bottom lip, I can grab that and pinch it and twist it but it's numb dead meat. I dont know b'ys and girls. I do not know.

I hooks a ride at the bottom of a long sloping hill sometime in the evening. Couple of old fellas who looks like brothers, coming from duck hunting. There's a sleepy-lookin terrier dog tied on in the back of the pickup, little wiry black-and-white thing. The feller on the passenger side who gets out to help me up into the truck, he dont look too pleased that they're stopped atall. He's got one of those chins, pointed and strict, self-righteous. Thin pinched lips, jowls all wrinkled from clenching his jaw. But he's gentle enough with me I suppose. I slides into the middle of the long bench seat, flanked on either side.

Larry the driver and Glenn the stuffy passenger. They asks me the usual questions, how far I'm going and where I'm from and all that, but when I tries to answer I finds I cant talk, cant make the tongue go where it's sposed to go, cant make the mouth do the little tricks it needs to do to ahhh . . . make words. All that comes out is this slurried mumble. I can feel the two of em exchanging glances at one another. Glenn pipes up then:

Youre a hell of a mess son, a hell of a mess.

I lays me head back against the seat and dozes off for a little and I wonders if they can smell me but prolly not cause it aint like either one of them is too fond of a bar of soap neither. Fuck it anyhow. I snaps to at some point to find Glenn is pressing a wad of tissue under me chin to collect the drool pouring out of me open mouth.

. . . a hell of a mess this one is Lawrence, hell of a mess . . .

Closing in on dark when I comes round again, literally squat in the middle of a halfways heated argument about beagles, whether or not you should ever let em in the house or even rub em down or do any of the stuff you does with normal dogs. But they both seems to be arguing to the same end. Larry says it's a surefire way to lose your dog, if you gets em used to people, cause then they'll take off when you brings em in the woods and they'll go with anyone. Stuffy Glenn says no, it's because you softens the dog too much, that they're not as keen on the cold weather once they knows the comfort of the indoors, that they need only know one purpose, that their sole luxury should be when they're let out to hunt. Either way, I feels bad for the poor old scrap in the back of the truck cause I knows right where he's going when he gets home.

The rain is stopped and it's pretty much full dark when the truck pulls over to the exit for Chilliwack. I tries to mumble the word Vancouver, but I knows I sounds like a burnt-out fucken retard. Larry, the driver, keeps sayin over and over that he wished he could understand, wished he could understand. I spies an old pen on the dashboard as I slips down onto the road. I grabs that and writes the word out on the back of my nasty hand and shows it to the driver. He squints at the scrawl and gives Glenn a look. Glenn, who's standin out on the road next to me now, tryna help me over to the shoulder, he nods on down the road:

Bout an hour and a half's drive thataway son. Think you'll make it?

I tries to nod, but the eardrum thing, well the balance is kinda shot from not being on me feet. Glenn reaches out to steady me. He pulls a bright-orange handkerchief out of his coat and places it to my forehead. I couldnt care less where it's been, whose nose it picked or whose hole it wiped. It's so fucken nice, the cold of the cloth, his hand on my forehead. The handkerchief comes away from me head stained black with sweat. He lays the handkerchief gently across me shoulder and leaves it there. Next the old codger snaps something in front of my face and I catches the flash of a folded twenty-dollar bill that he slips into the pocket of the poncho. He winks, then puts his finger to his lips and nods back towards Larry.

I wanna smile and I hopes I looks like I'm smiling, but I highly fucken doubt it.

Hell of a mess you are son. Hell of a mess indeed.

Blue-green glow of the civilized world on the night horizon. Streetlights. Traffic lights. This must be the promised land. The east is the beast and the west is the rest. Vancouver. I've been scalped, I think. Doused in acid. There's a blurry aura of heat waves radiating from me hands and cheekbones. Any second now I'll burst into flames. Thirsty. Tongue like rotted clapboard. Here's a bench, a bus stop. Johnny misjudging the edge of the bench as he's tryna sit, tumbling into the corner of the shelter. There's no pain. The bus shelter ceiling a busy mess of black marker scrawls and scratches, hasty drawings of squirting cocks and cartoon tits, weed plants, lazy affirmations and slapdash messages from a bygone hour.

Tony '94

Lisa loves Ribbons

J.R. wuz here

Redemption is overrated.

John 15:23

For a good time call your mama

Johnny being hoisted slowly, delicately to his feet. Silky perfume. Shampoo. Smoky sweet flesh. Firm hands on his shoulders, easing him to the sitting position. Grey Volkswagen idling tenderly on the curb outside the bus shelter. Bottle of water. Straw slipped into the gap where his teeth used to be. The water erupting in Johnny's stomach, spurting back up his throat and fuming out his mouth, hot and acidic and yellow. Cold hand on his forehead. Stranger than kindness. No, that's not right.

Youre burning up lover. Youre in bad shape . . .

Johnny's better arm clasping around the woman's slender thigh, pulling her close, resting his head against her stomach. Her fingers running through his hair. Each sob sends new lightning bolts of pain up through his broken torso, rattling his battered skull.

I'm sorry girl. I'm fucken sorry . . .

Shhhh . . . it's okay . . . shhh . . .

No way of knowing if she understands, if the words in his head are anything more than useless grunts of garbled slop by the time they move past his tongue. He tells her he's sorry, again and again.

For the teapot.

Lowest ever I sunk. No excuse. If I could take it back, get back to that morning. Youd be standin here now, in my fucken arms. Or youd be out there, arms open to the world, your heart beating, lungs, blood pumpin through your veins, smiling at people, turning heads, living. Alive. Youd be alive if I hadnt . . . if I didnt . . . I never loved . . . and I wanna come with you . . . I never . . . the look in your eye . . . my shirt soaked with . . . I wanted to feel . . . I wanted it to be . . . I'm sorry girl . . . I'm sorry . . .

Shhh . . . it's okay . . . tell me where it is youre headed . . .

I wanna come with you . . . I wanna come with you . . .

Telephone booth, Shiner's voice cackling through the receiver.

I cant make words.

Squash the earpiece hard against me forehead.

Sorry . . . sorry for the mess Shine, at your pad. I was grieving . . .

Hello??? Hello??? Who's there???

Do us a favour Shiner, tell Tanya I'm good, met a nice girl, went to the beach . . .

Is that you Johnny Keough? Cock*sucker*. See if I gets my fucken hands on you . . .

And thanks man, for sorting me out . . . on the inside. I thought it was . . . I thought . . .

Hello??? Hello??? Who's there?

Cold concrete steps overlookin a frenzied intersection. Manic cars, shuffling bodies. Horns and roars, bicycles. Johnny feeling a sudden burst of energy, like if he hadda get up to walk somewhere he could manage it.

The feeling passes.

Rusted chain-link fence across the way, ten or a dozen old vagabonds sat wrapped in blankets and garbage bags, cardboard boxes.

A grubby and matted little black-and-white dog growling over a greasy KFC box.

Bottles clinking.

Toothless junkie feller with arms outspread, shouting at a cop:

You's a civil servant man! That means you work for me! You work for . . .

Cops cut him short, twist his arm up behind his back and spin him around, slap him over the bonnet of the cruiser.

Folks scurrying past, nobody paying the scene much mind.

Bowl of soup, maybe chicken, maybe turkey. Half an inch of yellow grease lapping off the rim of the Styrofoam bowl. Johnny gags at the thick steamy announcement of it in his cupped hands. But it's not unwanted, the soup. Fucken mass starvation, man. He gawps at the useless spoon, imagines the ordeal of scooping it into the murk of the bowl, loading it up, steadying his hand for the three or four seconds between the bowl and his crusty, blistered lips. Workin the piping spoonful through the wider opening on the left side of his jaw.

Not gonna happen.

A straw lands in his lap, sheathed in white paper. A passing phantom snarls his name, maybe, *Drink up Johnny*. Vaguely feminine voice. *How could a woman know your name?* Johnny staring at the straw.

Commotion, jovial camaraderie all about him.

A quick gritty gust of wind steals the straw from his lap.

The soup stops steaming.

Knuckles on his right hand black and scabbed, oozing cloudy yellow pus.

The soup, a chunky oily puddle on the concrete before him.

Close to three dollars in small, small change gathered in the bottom of the bowl.

A dog lapping at Johnny's dirty rag of a sock. His big toe poking out, the nail purple and bloody. The left foot bootless too, wrapped in some sort of renegade cast made from oily strips of blue plaid shirt.

A lit cigarette poked into his mouth.

Johnny, afraid to breathe.

Man with a beard, beads, braids in the beard, tattered grey blanket with a slit cut through for his head to fit, he's tapping Johnny on the shoulder. Takes Johnny ten, fifteen seconds to raise his chin, focus his eyes on the man. Curdling puddle of blood on the concrete between Johnny's feet.

Johnny is pulled to a standing position.

He's being carried by this man, his dead foot dragging behind in the grit at the edge of the sidewalk.

I even got us some fresh works Johnny, come on, straighten up little bro, *straighten up for the grand finale . . .*

Johnny wants to say, wants to ask *How do you know my name?*

Nothing forthcoming from his throat but a low snarly mumble.

Is that you Shiner?

Shit little brother, youre in rough shape, sick as a goddamn dog, sweating like that. You'll be feeling good soon. This is some black shit, Mississippi Mud they call it. Aint seen this shit in years, round these parts. Make you feel all nice and cozy, *learn you not to fuck with what's not yours . . .*

Shiner wait, hear me out man, I wasnt thinkin clear . . . I was . . .

Keep an eye out for the fuzz bro, that's all you gotta do . . .

Blackened bottom of a tin can, the edges folded inward. Modest pinch of grainy brown powder down there. Johnny holding the can steady, steady. Bottle stopper half filled with water, tipped gently, gently over the brown powder.

Steady Johnny. Steady Johnny.

Shit little brother, we need a light. You got a light under that thing?

Johnny watches the man's arms disappear beneath the poncho, yellow claws snaking through the pockets of Pius's old suit coat, the inside pocket, the crinkle of plastic. Something stirs way back in Johnny's skull, nagging glint of memory, something important, like purpose.

The hands come out of Johnny's coat with a white Bic lighter and a folded plastic bag. The bearded man stands before Johnny, opening the bag. Pulls a faded Tim Hortons donut bag from within the plastic one.

What the fuck you got in here bro? Fuck is this shit?

Dont, dont, dont . . .

Fine curling cloud of grey dust shaken from the bag.

That's my girl . . . that's my girl . . . I did it . . . I did it . . .

A sprinkle of ash from the paper bag falls into the can, into the mixture of brown mud water. The lighter's thin green flame beneath the can, the mixture bubbling, frothing.

Shit Johnny man, that's your name, yeah, Johnny? Youre gonna be alright. Youre gonna make it. The good guys always make it. Should be feelin cozy and warm pretty soon brother, cozy and warm.

Where's the beach? Where's the beach?

Johnny feels like he's screamin it, the effort it takes to string it together in his head.

There is no answer.

* * *

Smutty ragged strip of orange bandana wrapped about Johnny's exposed bicep. Angry worms popping up beneath the flesh of his arms. Distant bite of the needle, the pull and the plunge, the cold, cold burn. Johnny lets his head fall heavily to the left, watches the wind lick at the corner of the donut bag, flipping it over, the last of the contents spilling out, swirling and dancing towards that dazzling brilliance at the mouth of the alleyway.

Ah no, Johnny man. Come on little bro. Where you going Johnny? C'mon Johnny, watcha doing?

Voices.

Easy, abandoned laughter.

Faint squelch of seagulls.

Heaving surf.

Tender breeze.

Barefooted blond girl dashing along the shoreline, coaxing a kite into the air.

Scrappy black-and-white mutt rushing at a wary flock of gulls sunning on the sand.

Sand.

Scoop a handful and feel it stream between your fingers, lustrous and forgiving.

Shimmering golden sand.

Hey Johnny! I got one! I got one! Come on!

To the far left a sandy-haired boy of eleven or twelve leans over the railing of a bridge, fighting to land a monstrous sea trout.

Yawning, broad river curving to the ocean.

Another boy, in orange shorts, bobbing along in a new rubber dinghy, feet trailing the warm foamy waters, hands tucked idly behind his head, sunglasses, basking in the lazy midday sun.

Little dog yapping, leaping, bounding along in the sand.

Solitary crow perched on a mooring post.

The girl runs past again, the kite launched now, high up in the sky.

Johnny shields his eyes from the sun to see the kite glowing neon pink, a map of all the solar system gleaming across the face of it.

The girl turns towards him, running backwards along the beach, her steely blue eyes glinting beneath the summer skies.

She smiles at me.

Hey Johnny! You made it!

ACKNOWLEDGEMENTS

Alright, special thanks to my infinitely inspiring son Percy, love of my life, and to his lovely mama Sherry-Lynn White. Much love and gratitude to the brilliant and beautiful Shauna MacDonald, for plucking me out of the crowd and shining up my tarry old heart—xxx. To my dearly departed uncle Ron Hynes, who read an early draft of this book and suggested I burn it. Lily Hynes. Connie Corkum-Hynes. Lois Hynes. Gary and Dolores Hynes. Blair Harvey. Lois Brown. Alison Gzowski. Ruth Lawrence. Aislinn Hunter. Patricia Isaac. Nicole Kane. Jenny Rocket (and Audrey and Bob and Jackie and Jason). Sherrie Rose. Sheila Sullivan. Des Walsh. Mary Walsh.

Carolyn Forde, my tireless agent at Westwood Creative Artists. Jennifer Lambert, my awesome editor at HarperCollins. Iris Tupholme. Noelle Zitzer. Stephanie Nuñez. My manager Perry Zimel and all the gang over at OAZ.

Staff and residents of Her Majesty's Penitentiary (2008–12). Angela Asher. Amy Bedford. Terry-Jean Bedford. Erin Breen. Jonathan Bronfman. Karen Bruce. Amanda Brugel. Tassie and Amy Cameron. Alan Collins. Kiezauna Gallimore. Eliane Gagnon. Maria Doyle-Kennedy. Kieran

Kennedy. Megan Follows. Risa Braman-Garcia. Rene Garcia. Alexandra Gonzalez. Hallie Gyles. Taylor Hickson. Amy House. Kate Kawaja. Ivy Mairi. Robert Joy. Henry Krieger. Adriana Maggs. Alex Malolos. Greg Malone and White. Eamon McGrath. Melanie Oates. Lori Oberding. Cyril and Vera O'Keefe. Marnie Parsons. Colleen Power. Gerry Rogers. Suzanne Sicchia. Gavin Simms. Christian Sparkes. Lisa Rose Snow. Alison Rideout. Tracey Waddleton. Todd Wall. Sabrina Whyatt. Christopher Richardson. Running the Goat Books and Broadsides. Killick Press. Pedlar Press. The Resource Centre for the Arts. MusicNL. Newfoundland and Labrador Arts Council. Canada Council for the Arts. City of St. John's. The Canadian Film Centre. NIFCO. Take the Shot Productions. Pope Productions. CBC Radio.